HIS MOTHER'S SON

Cai Emmons

HARCOURT, INC.
New York   San Diego   London

www.HarcourtBooks.com

*This novel is entirely a work of fiction. The names, characters, and incidents
portrayed in it are the work of the author's imagination. Any resemblance to actual
persons, living or dead; events; or localities is entirely coincidental.*

Library of Congress Cataloging-in-Publication Data
Emmons, Cai.
His mother's son/Cai Emmons.—1st ed.
p.   cm.
ISBN 0-15-100734-9
1. Violence in children—Fiction. 2. Brothers and sisters—Fiction.
3. Mothers and sons—Fiction. 4. Women physicians—Fiction.
5. Boys—Fiction. I. Title.
PS3605.M57 H57 2002
813'.6—dc21   2002002990

Text set in Goudy
Designed by Cathy Riggs

Printed in the United States of America

First edition
A C E G I K J H F D B

To my mother,
Judith Reed Emmons

HIS
MOTHER'S
SON

PROLOGUE

She and Varney used to go to the 7-Eleven alone for candy and soda. They were young when they started going—she was eight and Varney was four—but no one tried to stop them. The 7-Eleven was only five blocks away, but getting there required crossing two busy streets. She was responsible; she had always been responsible—responsible from birth. "Responsible is your middle name," her mother, Beth, used to say. *Cadence Responsible Miller*, she would say to herself. She knew that was not her real middle name, which was Eloine, which meant "worthy."

Cadence Responsible Miller took her younger brother, Varney, to the store, turning from Via Valencia onto Camino Real where the speedy cars spanked the pedestrians with their wind. Varney's tiny hand in hers was wiggly and hot, always hot. She used to worry, live and active as it was (like a snake or a mouse without hair), that it would squirm away and Varney would tumble into the traffic. She held his money for him, and he kept asking after it. "Do you have my quarter? Do you have my quarter?" Such a worrywart. He had a talent for finding money. He'd find it on the sidewalk, in the gutter, on the beach. "Someday I'm going to have a mountain of money," he said. At the beach he sculpted a giant mound decorated with found coins and called it his "money hill."

He used his quarters for the challenging candies—Fire-balls, Sour Gummis, Red Hots—things that made her salivate so heavily she feared she would vomit. But Varney could devour a whole pack of Red Hots before he got home. Still, he took forever to choose, scouring the candy aisle, up and back, up and back, narrowing the choices as if one day he might really branch out (which he never ever did).

Sometimes he'd prolong the choosing by going out back to pee. She made him go alone, to learn independence as she had. She watched him through the store's glass as he disappeared around the side of the building, giant key ring in hand, looking miniature and almost motorized.

One day when she was ten and he was six, he took longer than usual in the bathroom. She was thinking of going to check on him, when he returned with colossal eyes.

"There's something gross outside," he whispered.

She laughed at him, a bit scared of the way his mind made things up, saw things that weren't there. That day he'd lost interest in candy. "You have to see, Cady." He tugged her arm.

Curious, she followed him out back. Lying in the dirt under a hedge of oleander was a person—man or woman, she couldn't tell—heavily bundled in a brown canvas coat and brown pants, almost camouflaged in the brown dirt and the brown branches. Everything brown except for the hair, which was black and so shiny it looked wet.

"Who is it?" said Varney.

"How should I know?" she said. "Let's go."

The body looked heavy and still as a rock, the kind of still-ness of a thing that has always been there.

"Is it dead?" he asked.

She shrugged.

"What if it's dead?"

"So?" she said. She didn't care. She wanted to leave. The stillness wasn't normal.

"It isn't a person," Varney said. "It's only a body, right?"

"Let's go."

"I didn't kill him," Varney said.

"Of course you didn't. No one said you did."

"I promise I didn't."

What a strange boy. She started walking so Varney would follow, but he had to run to catch up. "You can't tell anyone, you have to promise," she said. "Double promise."

At home they double promised, merging pinpricks of their blood.

"I promise I didn't," Varney kept saying over and over despite her shushing, squeezing his eyes shut so tightly, the skin around them looked wormy with folds.

But she was the one who awoke from nightmares for weeks afterward, her eyes filled with pictures of an all-brown body writhing back to life.

ONE

When Jana returns to the curtained cubicle, she finds eighty-three-year-old Mr. Cianetti has moved off the examining table and is sitting on a low metal stool. His frail crossed legs have hiked up the johnny so his genitals are visible, snuggled in the crack of his groin like resting mice, but he seems not to notice. His steady dark eyes follow her for a moment as she lays down his chart, then his face implodes in a grin which furrows the loose flesh of his cheeks and reduces his lips to mere lines but still comes out looking impish.

Jana loves her old patients. Ambitions all played out, they sit before her, ink still, mysterious with memory, removed from the dirty march of time. Some of these people are the ages her parents would be, though she rarely thinks of this, rarely allows herself to think of this.

"Your parents must be proud," he says.

She leaves his chart on the counter, takes a seat on the other stool, and rolls up beside him. "I'd like to admit you overnight, Mr. Cianetti. So we can do some more tests and get a better idea of what is going on. I want you to see a neurologist. His name is Ren Scofield and I've already talked to him about you."

"Of course." He squints at her. "You can tell me I'm dying."

"It's not a question of dying," she says, though of course it is and he knows it. He probably won't die today or tomorrow, or even next month, but at his age his prognosis is not good even if his brain tumor is operable.

She would prefer to have this discussion when she had time for it, instead of at a moment when she is pressed to leave to get her son, Evan, but one can't always choose these things, and she would also prefer to be the one to talk to Mr. Cianetti rather than leaving it until the next shift when Gaffney and Ettinger come on. They're both good docs, but they can be abrupt with the older patients, often imparting just enough information to inflame the patient's anxiety and exacerbate the physical complaints.

"I'm not afraid of death," Mr. Cianetti says. "When you're my age it has a certain appeal."

She listens to the aftermath of his words to see if he means it, to see if the words don't regroup in the silence to mean the exact opposite. Sometimes, out of the silence, more words and feelings will materialize. He recrosses his legs, reaches up to his earlobe, and strokes it with a single finger.

Their silence is a small bubble in a hurricane of ER sound— a wailing child, frantic footsteps, the squeak of rolling carts and gurneys. And there's another subtler set of sounds embedded here, which only she can hear: the sounds of full-blown illness, not measurable in decibels, or detectable by the human ear, but easily amplified by the mind. The surge of adrenaline, the synaptic havoc of a brain in distress, a heart beating furiously to maintain itself. He glances around the cubicle and she sees his nearly lashless lids have moistened. She touches his loosely fisted hand. Lightly. Briefly. The skin is mushroom soft, and through it she can feel his entire circulatory system.

The ding at the nurses' station indicates another patient has arrived. She hates that sound interrupting every conversation of import, goading her to the next patient, as if what they do here is merely a mechanical transaction. The six other doctors in her ER group, all men, respond with good humor to the sound (more patients, more profits) and at least once a month one of them takes her aside. "You don't have to solve all their problems, Jana, just their medical ones," Ron Gaffney is fond of saying. Or the group's director, gentle fifty-eight-year-old Bill McElroy says: "You were born in the wrong generation. In the old days it would have been fine to work at your pace." But they say these things gently and they keep her on because patients write letters of thanks to her, because the hospital administration wants them to have a woman on staff, and because she does her job quietly and well, taking on extra shifts whenever anyone asks.

"This isn't a death knell, Mr. Cianetti. I only want you to know it could be serious."

"Just tell me what to do, General." He grins. It amuses her to hear him call her "General," which is just what her husband, Cooper, often calls her. She didn't like the term at first, but she's come to accept it—just because she's a general does not make her a dictator, and it's true that she takes charge easily and gets things done.

"You're a good girl," Mr. Cianetti says, as if he's her teacher or her father, his tone implying that she has yet to see much of life. Hearing his words, she wishes he were her grandfather and she was the clear-eyed, naive girl he thinks she is.

"Do you have family?" she asks.

"No. No family. They're all dead."

She touches his hand again and ignores another dinging outside. "We know you have a brain tumor, Mr. Cianetti. The CT scan told us that. But we have to find out what kind you have and whether it's operable."

Slowly, she explains the plan for admitting him. She delivers the words simply, in the soothing way that makes patients old and not-so-old later recall her as a special doctor, trustworthy and fully present. He listens agreeably, squinting through his headache pain yet unwilling to belabor it, but when the nurse, Sue Dennison, comes to wheel him off, he looks at Jana with a panicked realization she will not be accompanying him. He keeps his dark, watery eyes on her with an expression of speechless betrayal as he is wheeled away.

THE ROADS ARE SLICK with a cold rain. Late to get Evan, she chides herself for taking too much time getting Mr. Cianetti settled. Evan is in an after-school program called Little Creations, which he began in this, his first-grade year. Though it is reputed to be one of the best programs in town, it was not Jana's first choice but a last minute arrangement necessitated by Evan's baby-sitter Mrs. Stubbs's sudden decision to "retire." Approaching sixty, Mrs. Stubbs claimed that Evan's energy was getting to be too much for her. She had been sitting for him since he was eight months old, so parting with her has not been easy for Evan or Jana.

A great urgency scrolls through her in these twilight moments when she transforms herself from doctor to mother. She feels a drive strong as a migratory compass. She cannot reach Evan fast enough, cannot believe they've been apart for so long.

Little Creations is located near the hospital—six minutes without traffic—but even so, today she'll be late. She drives too fast. She always drives too fast, maneuvering her Honda Accord deftly through city traffic, trying to outwit and outdrive the other cars as if they are all participants in some Olympic event. Behind the shatterproof tinted windows her demons can prance freely, and she easily outdistances even the surly young SUV drivers.

The water on Bellingham Bay is pimply with rain and the islands, usually visible, are shrouded in fog. The roads seem slimier than usual and she slows. The driver of a red Ford Explorer behind her, a youngish-looking man from what she can see in the dusk, leans on his horn, then he swerves into the right lane. When he's overtaken her, he cuts in front and slams on his brakes, forcing Jana to jam hers so hard that she comes to a full stop and misses ramming him by only a few inches. She sees him checking his rearview mirror, gloating, pleased he's "gotten" her, before he takes off at top speed, weaving from lane to lane.

A symphony of rage rumbles throughout her car. Rage in the pistons and rage in the carburetor, rage in the wipers slapping rain from her vision. Rage slithers through her irises and her flared nostrils. It bongos in her eardrums and travels down her jawbone to rattle her teeth. Rage is awake and alive, loose with possibility. The driver of the red car has long since disappeared, but the fury he has left in his wake has a kind of afterlife. She knows the right thing to do when rage hits—stop everything, shut down. The rage wears itself out and slinks away. But when she is driving, this strategy is impossible; though she tries to keep rage away from the accelerator, it settles there, too, and as she wrangles with it, the Honda leaps along faster than she means it to go.

When she reaches the parking lot of the school that houses Little Creations, she sits in her car for a minute or two, trying to calm herself. Thinking of Evan again, she hurries inside.

The school gymnasium, which is home to Little Creations, initially appears to be empty. Its shellacked floors gleam. Its tables are strewn with art-project materials—paper, brushes, paint, glue, glitter. Sandy, exceptionally tall and dark with the small round face of a ten-year-old, though she is probably at least twenty-five, is tossing paper scraps into a plastic-lined barrel and testing the finished art for dryness with a tapping finger. Evan is nowhere in view.

"Hey," says Sandy, noticing Jana, then glancing pointedly at her watch. It is 6:13, thirteen minutes past closing.

"I know I'm late," Jana says. "I'm so sorry."

"Evan's over there." Sandy nods to a corner of the gymnasium where Evan crouches under a table, his head shielded under the canopy of his arms.

"He's had a bad day," Sandy whispers. "Come on out, Evan. Your mom's here."

Evan doesn't move. Sometimes, at home, Jana craves for Evan to learn such stillness, but now, under the circumstances, it's not something she can appreciate. Sandy approaches the table, which is strewn with forgotten oddments of clothing. Jana follows.

"Evan, it's time to go home," Jana says, her voice sounding tremulous as windblown tinsel.

"I'm not going," he says.

"Of course you are," Jana says. "And we're already late. Daddy will be waiting for us. Please come out."

"No." The word, like a small superball, echoes off the gymnasium's high ceiling.

"There was a little incident," Sandy says. "I think he feels bad about it."

"Incident?"

"He'll tell you."

"I will not," Evan says. "I won't tell her."

Sandy crouches. "Come on, buddy. You have to come out sometime. You can't sleep here."

Evan retreats further under the table and clutches its metal supports. Jana sighs instead of swearing. If it weren't for the endlessly patient Sandy beside her, she would scramble under the table and drag Evan out. This manipulation of his is not acceptable, a fact that seems to make no impression on Sandy.

"Come on, Evan." Sandy calls him like a dog. "Come on."

"I can't come out. My mom will kill me."

Jana flushes; Sandy has no knowledge of Jana that would cast doubt on Evan's contention.

"Of course she won't kill you. You won't be too hard on him, will you?" Sandy addresses Jana in the same singsong she uses with Evan.

"You know I won't, Evan. So come out now and we'll talk."

"Make her promise, Sandy," Evan says. "Make my mom promise she won't do anything bad to me."

Under Sandy's assessing gaze, Jana tries to make light of this, tries to make her voice sound high and agreeable. "Of course I won't, Evan."

"Pinky swear?"

"Pinky swear."

Slowly Evan unballs himself. He crawls on all fours through the table's forest of metal legs, finally emerging from under the shadows and lifting his face. For a moment he looks not like Evan but like Varney, Jana's brother, and love and anger boil together in her so she wants to cry out, fall to her knees, and draw his petal-soft cheek to hers.

One thing Jana has always been sure of is that Evan looks nothing like Varney. Evan has Cooper's round-faced rosy-cheeked look. Her brother Varney's face was always more like her own, long and pale, framed by thick straight hair, and congenitally serious, even when smiling. But watching Evan now as he emerges from under the table, she feels as if an eerie genetic about-face has taken place. Evan has begun to look more like her side of the family, his face narrowing, his curly blond hair straightening and darkening so in certain lights it looks brown. The only unaltered trait he retains from Cooper is his dimples, which give him a charm he can display or withdraw according to his needs. Right now the dimples are out of service, sealed up under slack moping cheeks. He folds his arms, adult-style, jamming his fists into his armpits.

"What did you do?" Jana asks.

Evan devotes his eyes to the floor.

"Tell her what happened," Sandy prompts (*As if it happened to him,* Jana thinks, as if Evan himself had no role at all in provoking it).

"It was Jason's fault. He punched me first. Right here." He feints a punch at his belly, replete with a gasping sound effect.

"And?" says Jana. "What did you do to Jason?"

Evan looks at Sandy. He is the picture of sweetness with his eyes flared wide, like his dimples, to garner sympathy.

Sandy nods. "Go on, honey. You have to tell her."

"I wanted his ball."

"Yes, and—?" Jana says.

"I didn't bite hard."

A hit or a punch is certainly a disdained violation, but biting stands in a category by itself. Primal. Bestial. Rabid dogs bite, sharks bite, mountain lions bite when pushed, but human beings, *Homo sapiens,* are not a biting species, not once they can speak.

Jana latches her hand firmly on Evan's upper arm. "Look at me, Evan. Where did you bite him?"

Evan points to his forearm.

"Did it break the skin?"

Evan shakes his head quickly, beginning to cry.

"Don't worry, Mrs. Johansen. He's not a biter. I've never known him to be a biter."

Jana doesn't look at Sandy. "He bit, didn't he? We're going home. Get your backpack." She turns to Sandy. "Do you have the number of this boy Jason? So Evan can apologize."

Sandy hesitates. "It's not necessary. He can do it tomorrow."

"I think now is better," Jana says.

"Plus, I'm not really allowed to give out numbers."

Jana heads for the door, Evan scrambling in her wake, Sandy trailing behind.

"It was good you spoke up, Evan, honey," Sandy says. "You told the truth. That's good."

Jana stops walking and turns to Sandy. "I'll handle this, thank you. We can sort out if there's any *good* here."

"But—"

"But what?" Jana says, hating herself, her flare-up, hating the bad-parent label she is sure must be forming in Sandy's brain, but knowing, too, that she cannot let these things stop her, that things must be done in the way she knows they should be done, because if she backs down (as her own mother so often did, as she herself often does, too) all bets are off.

"Nothing." Sandy sighs. "I mean, just don't be too hard on him."

It's dark out and still raining, fat drops that burst cold on Jana's neck. In the back of the car Evan sobs quietly, pressing his face against the window. If she watches him too long, she'll weep herself. She fights the part of her that wants to ply him with kisses and toys and sweets, ignoring what has transpired, sealing the bad deed in. But bad deeds don't remain sealed; they live tenaciously, dormant for months, or even years, until they begin to grow like mold on forgotten bits of food, giving birth to new bad deeds. Her parents, educated people, should have known better, should have seen moments like these as teaching ones.

Though with Evan, much as she tries to teach, he seems to

take nothing away. He passes through her lectures and punish-
ments as if comatose or deaf, emerging without memory, without wisdom, then, so quickly it seems, he's there again, not
committing the same violation maybe, but one so like it it seems
he has no power to generalize at all.

She drives fast, she drives loud, music pounding from the
radio to drown out the other sound, the constant reedy natter
that grows and recedes and grows again. Slush on the wind-
shield, heat on her neck, sound pounding, always pounding,
light, then loud in her ears. Water worming down the wind-
shield, mind reciting the weight of elements, cataloging the
order of bones. Sound pounding.

From clear down the street she sees her mother-in-law
Seretha's car, parked in their driveway beside Cooper's pickup.
She cuts the ignition and listens hard as the motor spins off.
There is the omnipresent pounding (low, but loud), and a mu-
sical fourth up from that there's Evan's whimpering, and, yes, if
she's gauging it right, and she's pretty sure she is, an augmented
fourth up from the whimpering is the shrill screech of her rage.
Thirds and fifths are pleasing intervals, Varney used to instruct
her, but augmented fourths, diminished fifths, or tritones are
unresolved intervals that sound demonic, depress people, send
them into madness. Knowing this she is somewhat immune,
but not entirely. Two years ago she replaced the microwave because its beeping made a diminished fifth with the low but au-
dible hum of the refrigerator.

"Aren't we going in?" Evan says, interrupting his sobs after
they've been sitting in the parked car for a good two minutes.

"Yes, we're going in. And when we get in, you may not
speak to Daddy or to Gramma. I want you to go straight to your
room. I will bring you some dinner in there."

"What are you going to do to me?"

Afraid to turn, she watches him through the rearview mirror. His large, achingly beautiful eyes, the gray green of certain beach stones, prey on her so easily. Outside she raises an umbrella for them both, but he dashes ahead, the tails of his red rain jacket flapping like a toreador's taunt. He runs up the three wooden steps of their remodeled two-story Craftsman house, so when she—staggering behind with Evan's lunch box and backpack, her own bag, the umbrella—arrives in the kitchen, he is already sitting on Cooper's lap, regaling Cooper with the story of how he was punched.

Cooper, rosy, cheerful, winks at Jana. "Home from the wars?"

"Evan," Jana says, ignoring Seretha; ignoring the smell of sautéing onions (promise of dinner on the way); ignoring the way Evan has nestled his head at the smooth roots of Cooper's neck; ignoring how Cooper himself has cleaned up and changed from his work clothes; ignoring that the table is beautifully set, candles even; ignoring the fact that she has come home to a sweet scene, "I told you to go to your room."

"Daddy," Evan pleads.

"Do what the general says." Cooper ruffles Evan's hair. Evan clings to Cooper's chest.

"Oh my heavens," Seretha says. "Whatever he's done, it can't be that bad. Nothing Gramma can't handle."

"Mom," Cooper says, admonishing with raised eyebrows.

Jana has not moved beyond the doorway. She has not looked at Seretha. She has not set down her things or taken off her jacket. "Evan, go."

Evan clings.

"Whatever happened to forgiveness in this family?" Seretha says.

"He happens to have bitten someone," Jana says, still not looking at her mother-in-law.

"But he punched me first."

"All kids bite sometimes, Jana," Cooper says. "I'm sure I bit, didn't I, Mom?"

"I'm sure you did."

"Dogs bite. Panthers bite. Snakes bite. People do not bite," Jana says.

"Maybe first-grade people do?" Cooper suggests.

Jana closes her eyes. "Cooper, *please*."

Pressing her lids tight, she wills him not to do this. She does not want to invoke aloud, in front of Seretha and Evan, the Puke Pact, made between her and Cooper when they had only known each other for five months, were not married, and had just discovered she was pregnant. They were living in Portland at the time, where Jana was finishing her residency, and they had traveled to Seattle to see an old friend of Cooper's. On the way back they stopped at a diner for eggs and hash browns. The hash browns were fantastic, crusty and not too greasy and filled with soft fragrant onions, but as soon as she ate them, she went to the ladies and up they came, completely undigested. Back at the table, sipping water, James Taylor singing "Fire and Rain" on the jukebox, she and Cooper made their deal. If she went ahead and had this baby—the baby that Cooper, at nearly forty, so desperately wanted—she, Jana, would need to be the disciplinarian, *she* would need to be the final arbiter. Cooper was startled; he had not thought past booties and bottles. Discipline was years away, wasn't it? She had to assure him—Cooper who wouldn't lay a finger on anyone—that she didn't believe in spanking. She simply believed in standing firm.

"Go, bud," Cooper says. "Do what Mama says."

Evan falls from Cooper like a limp squid, then, staring at the floor, drags himself toward his bedroom. Spider, their pure black cat, slinks up to Evan like a co-conspirator. Evan lunges at Spider, lifting the cat by the upper torso so the rest of his body dangles, long and awkward and temporarily paralyzed, down to Evan's knees. Burying his face in Spider's neck fur, he imbibes comfort.

His room is the envy of any child. Cooper has created an aesthetic tour de force: a four-tiered wooden construction with brightly painted abstract designs and inlaid mosaic tiles that functions as bed and play structure, a potent reminder of his father's love should Evan ever doubt it. The rest of the room is equally colorful. Cupboards across two walls overflow with Lego bricks, blocks, cars, puppets, stuffed animals of every imaginable species, art supplies, and every inch of wall space displays Evan's artwork or bright poster art selected by Jana. Recently Jana has begun to wonder if the room might be too colorful, too stimulating, too disorganized. Optical receptors are hypersensitive, and what comes through them can affect the brain powerfully. She vows to do some simplifying here soon.

Even throws himself on the lowest level of his bed, hurling Spider as he falls. He lies on his side, back to Jana, fingernail picking at an adhesive glow-in-the-dark star. His six-year-old body is small and wiry like Varney's was, its muscles hard as a man's. But when he is close to sleep, he softens. And in the last few months, he has begun to thicken. Varney never thickened like this.

She crouches by the bed. "I'm sorry I got so mad, honey, but you know biting is bad, don't you?"

He nods.

"Why did you bite, then? What made you bite?"

He shrugs.

"You had the mean bug?"

"Yeah, I had the mean bug."

"What did the mean bug feel like?"

He breathes so heavily she thinks he's asleep. She lies down beside him, putting her hand on the rise of his jacketed pelvis. "Silver," he says suddenly. "With pointed claws like a lobster."

Now she wishes she hadn't said anything. The mean bug, who has been in their family vocabulary for a couple of years now, is too easy an out. Maybe this time something else was at play.

"If it's a bug, then you can crush it, can't you? Or you can tell it to go away."

He nods.

She lies there tasting her familiar cocktail of adoration and remorse, wishing she could spend the remainder of the night exactly where she is. After a few minutes she extricates herself and rises, touching his shoulder briefly, probing the way you test the temperature of water you might enter.

"I'll get you something to eat," she says and hurries out.

TWO

Varney said when someone slighted him, his brain turned white. A hot color, he said, that could eat you up like light with its power.

He first told her this at the beach, skipping stones in an unforgiving surf. They'd aim at the crest of the wave just before it broke. Sometimes, when they got it just right, the stone skimmed triumphantly along the wave's crest; other times it caught a rut, upended, its sharp side slicing the water, slowing it so the wave's explosion sucked the stone into soupy foam. Varney was eight or nine at the time; Cady twelve or thirteen.

"White hot," he said.

"Does it feel hot?" she said.

"It just *acts* hot."

Blue was the thinking color, green the eating color, red the moving color, but with white, the color holding all colors, he told her, anything might happen.

FROM THE BATHROOM Jana hears the sounds of dinner preparation weaving around Cooper's and Seretha's colluding voices, Cooper's deep and furry, rising from the inimitable stillness of his body, and Seretha's only slightly higher. Both sound serious.

Seretha is talking about Jana no doubt, asking yet again why her daughter-in-law is so lacking in sympathy, why again and again she mistreats that boy, mistrusts him, deprives him of love. Seretha's version of love—which she has practiced now for over forty years with Cooper—is a kind of indulgence-for-servitude, as though giving in to each small wish of Cooper's will earn his lifelong indebtedness. Now Cooper is incapable of denying any of his mother's wishes, and many nights he goes to bed worrying he has wronged her.

A couple of months after Jana and Cooper met, they drove from Portland to Bellingham, and Seretha made dinner for them.

"She's afraid of you," Cooper confessed as they got out of the car and approached the small ranch house. Jana was startled to see, standing in the front doorway, an Amazonian woman, broad-boned and at least six feet tall, a woman who looked incapable of fear.

"This is my mother, Seretha Johansen," Cooper said. "This is Jana Thomas." Seretha's impassive gaze had the slow scouring quality of a searchlight and it made Jana, at five two, feel tiny. Seretha served them meat loaf and green beans but did not set a place for herself.

"Won't you be eating with us?" Jana asked.

"I'm not hungry," Seretha said.

It did not take Jana long to see that, despite the fair coloring Seretha held in common with Cooper, and the unflawed skin so remarkable for a woman in her late fifties, she did not share Cooper's talent for happiness. Her talent was for being imposing. She was a master of abstemious smiles, deliberate pauses during the intervals she had commanded for speaking. She rarely laughed (except with Cooper) and never seemed to let down her guard. Throughout that first meal, torso angled to

Cooper, she watched him eat. "Tell her about the time you went skydiving. . . . Tell her about the shark," she said, as if her son needed shoring up with stories to prove his bravery.

Halfway through the meal she began glancing at Jana. "I work in a hospital, you know. I'm a nurse. I don't know why anyone would want to be a doctor."

Jana looked helplessly at Cooper, who smiled hard first at his mother and then at Jana, as if his smile alone held enough persuasive power to unite the two women.

"Does she know I'm one of *them?*" Jana asked Cooper later when he was driving her home.

He hesitated and sighed. "She knows. She's afraid you're too smart for me. She thinks she has to protect me, you know." His eyes bore down on the road ahead of him. "Maybe she does."

She loved Cooper for being honest. It was these small moments, not the grand gestures, that attached her to him. He had come to the ER with a finger lacerated by a table saw. Jana was still training, her days made of twelve-hour shifts, brief stints at home for sleep, and then more work, interrupted by occasional meals usually at hours when no one else was eating. A champion of evenness, she was neither happy nor unhappy, merely grateful to have found a life, of sorts, and to be left alone. She repaired Cooper's finger as she would have anyone's, checking for nerve damage, suturing carefully, scarcely noticing the man beyond the digit. She saw only that he was large, blond, and mild-mannered, his round, freckled, cherry-cheeked face sporting dimples that made him look youthful. She had developed a curious way of looking through her young male patients. The fishermen, the college students, the sports enthusiasts, they all appeared similar to her. On the rare occasions when one of them asked her out, she usually demurred. She knew how the scenario would go. She was good on the first dates—a chipper discussion about her work and a chaste good-night kiss—but after that something always happened. She felt herself becoming slippery. In conversations she deflected questions, throwing them back at her suitor. Eventually her evasiveness became too difficult and the man would leave her alone.

But Cooper didn't give up. And though he was persistent, he didn't seem bent on cracking her, either. In the ER that afternoon he was calm and unusually good-natured, given his close call.

"You almost lost a finger," she told him.

"I definitely owe you," he said. "You name it." He was primed to laugh. She heard it bubbling out of him as he was leaving and chatting briefly with the triage nurse. It surprised her to hear him on the phone the next night.

"Dr. Thomas?" he said.

"Yes."

"This is Cooper Johansen. You sewed my finger yesterday. Just calling to tell you my finger is doing just fine. It's sending you its regards."

"That's good," said Jana, startled. She'd never had a patient reach her at home, and it felt odd to be called upon to be professional when she was reclining in bed, drinking hot milk, already in her nightgown. "You've been taking your antibiotics?"

"Yes, sir."

"Good."

Awkward silence followed. She tried to think of something else to say.

He chuckled quietly. "I'm not very good at this," he said.

"Is there a problem?" she asked, suddenly alarmed.

"No, no. I just wanted to tell you I think you're a good doctor. My finger agrees. We think you're very kind." He laughed and his laugh acted on her like warm water. She liked his goofiness.

Still, she refused to go out with him. Relationships—their promises, their probings, the primacy they placed on revelation—made her bridle. She was content to be calm, opaque, and manless. But Cooper kept calling, every other week or so. Not hounding her, but reminding her of his presence. He was new to Portland and not very happy there. He had moved from Bellingham because he thought there would be plenty of work, but he wasn't well-connected yet. The one friend he had known there had recently moved to Seattle, and Cooper found himself with too much empty time. He left messages for Jana with small observations—reporting on the phases of the moon or the quality of Portland coffee, or asking her where he might purchase durable rain gear. One message queried her on what she thought of men who wore mismatched socks. More and more often she found herself calling back, even when the messages didn't demand it. She always concluded those conversations amused and unsettled. He seemed to want to go out with her, but he never actually asked. His reticence was creating in her desire. Eventually they made a date to go hiking one afternoon in the Columbia Gorge. When they were rained out, he took her for coffee at Armonk's Café. Armonk's was closed, so they went to the Foggy Foggy Dew, where there was a line out the door. Finally they decided to go back to his apartment on the second floor of a large Victorian house. It was not fancy, but the abode of a domesticated man who knew how to make a place his own. They drank strong French roast coffee with thick cream and ate berry-laden scones he'd made himself. She felt calm and unpressured in his presence, less obsessional, even after he'd kissed her.

"Yoo-hoo," Cooper calls. "Soup's up."

Jana wishes there were some way to avoid going out there. She washes her face one more time, knowing Seretha won't leave until she comes out. She can't stay in the bathroom all night—she promised she would bring Evan food, though he hasn't made a sound and is probably asleep—but if she goes out to the kitchen, she is absolutely *not* going to rehash the biting incident. It is between her and Cooper and Evan. Period.

She runs a final blast of cool water over the insides of her wrists, pats them dry and ejects herself from the bathroom, infused with the determination to be, at once, civil and cool, not to inflame old arguments but to take command of the evening (it is, after all, her house) and to communicate to Seretha—directly or indirectly, however she can—that she and Cooper would prefer to be alone after work, to unwind just the three of them as most families do on weekday evenings. It's fine for Seretha to come when she's expected, but these spontaneous drop-ins at the end of a long workday, when everyone, including Evan, is exhausted, are simply too draining. Cooper agrees and has told Seretha, but that does not mean that Seretha hasn't conveniently "forgotten" and needs a strong reminder.

The kitchen table is laid for four and Cooper and Seretha have already begun to eat their chicken stew. Cooper has made a dark green salad and warmed a loaf of multigrain bread, which lies on a breadboard, moist and fragrant, waiting to be sliced. At some point, long before meeting Jana, Cooper learned to be a good cook, with an eye for fresh ingredients and a perfect feel for seasoning.

"Sorry," says Cooper. "We weren't sure you'd join us."

She touches his shoulder on her way to the sink for water. The less said the better. Seretha rises from the table, her bowl of stew and plate of salad still full. She pats Cooper's forearm.

"I'll be going now. I can see she don't want me around."

Jana pushes her belly against the sink. Seretha sometimes

dumbs down her language pointedly in Jana's presence. A some-of-us-are-just-plain-folks appeal.

"You've hardly eaten anything," Cooper says. "You don't like it?"

"I know when I'm not wanted."

Jana turns to Seretha and forces a smile. "Eat with us please, Seretha."

Seretha blinks down at Jana, and Jana stands still, knowing this is the punishment she must endure for her accumulation of sins—the sins she has committed, the sins she doesn't know she's committed, the sins she will commit. She has the feeling Seretha sees everything about her—especially her shameful lurching from severity to lenience.

"No, I've made up my mind," Seretha says. "Honey, you punish him however you want. That's your affair. But I'm going to pick him up this weekend, right Cooper? Cooper and I discussed it. I'm gonna take him out and buy him a little something. He deserves a little fun." She stands still, as if listening to the pronouncement of a third party. "Everyone deserves a little fun," she says grimly.

It's all been decided; what can Jana say? Evan will return from their junket with a toy of his choosing—usually a gun, or a sword, or some revolting, shoot-'em-up computer game that Jana will, after a short time, confiscate and hide, making Evan wail and protest for a day or two or as long as his memory lasts. Then he will get distracted and the item will be forgotten.

"Let her," Cooper says to Jana. "A couple of hours."

"This boy's life is about me, too," says Seretha.

HUNGRY, BUT TOO WIRED to eat, Jana stands in the doorway of Evan's bedroom with a bowl of soup and a plate of buttered bread for him. As she expected, he has fallen asleep, not on the bed where she left him, but on the floor, surrounded by LEGO pieces, a large black Bat Mobile, several Hot Wheels of various colors, a small motor that has become separated from his K'nex robot. He lies on his back, fully clothed (including his red rain jacket), mouth open, hands fisted, looking like a felled soldier. The sight of him sleeping never fails to bring her up short, to make her feel at once hopeful and despairing.

What a surprise it was to give birth to a boy. Throughout the pregnancy she was sure she was carrying a girl, as sure as she had ever felt about anything. She whispered to an in utero creature she imagined as a tiny version of herself—wiry, dark, high-strung, shy. "Don't tell me; I know," she told the ultra-sound technician when she was asked if she wanted to know the baby's sex. In that delirious moment when the pushing and the pain finally stopped and Cooper's pronouncement, "It's a boy!" came rising up from between her legs, she did not believe it, thought she heard it wrong. "You're joking," she said. "No, it's really a boy," Cooper insisted. And then when she cradled the slippery creature she had unleashed on the world, she could not keep herself from checking his organ repeatedly and mar-veling at just how wrong she had been. A deeply odd thing, she kept thinking, for my body to have produced this body.

Boy he was from the outset, all wire and wriggle, motion and thrust. His energy ricocheted through the entire house; it had speed and volume, and it left toys and clothes and dirt in its wake. At nine months he walked. At a year and a half he climbed a ten-foot ladder. Before he was three he swam the length of the health club pool. Even now, at six, he learns about the world by roaring through it, by alternately poking or flogging things he wants to investigate, including, sometimes, other children. And only three weeks ago, just after first grade began, he had two tantrums, crying like she hadn't seen since he was two, arms and legs churning like turbines, grabbing everything in sight. Having no idea what to do, she became his straitjacket. Under the restraint of her body, his body heaved. One hour, two hours, they stayed that way until his torment subsided. He slept. Then she slept.

Slowed by a sudden wash of love, she lays the soup bowl temporarily on his dresser. She kneels over him and takes off his shoes, listening to his snoring, light as a whisper. She admires the milky skin (Seretha's bequest), which is so difficult to appreciate when he's on the go. Jana has always soaked in her knowledge of him through touch. He converses erratically, brief odd exchanges that tantalize her, no more, but when he's sick or tired and he retreats to her lap, she learns so much more about him, inchoate things about how it feels to be a live wire in the world, how it feels to live as a continually streaking bolt of lightning.

Shoveling her arm beneath him, she lifts his forty-odd pounds to the bed, pushing the sleeping cat out of the way. An arrowhead clunks to the floor from his unfisting hand. She removes his jacket and covers him. A night in clothes won't hurt him, and though it's doubtful he would awaken if she removed them, why risk it?

The room's chaos will have to wait until daylight for straightening. She clears a path to the door, switches off the overhead light, flicks on the dinosaur night-light. A burnishing amber glow recasts room and boy in a different light, a light which might, if she imagines hard enough, transform her boy biter into a prince. She pauses for a moment, gripped by hope. A slight shift of her head and she sees a face on the floor. It's Bobo the Clown, staring up at her from where it lies deflated, its flattened plastic mouth leering as if a frown has been superimposed on its smile.

When she finally mounts the stairs to bed (after forty minutes devoted to straightening the living room in trivial ways that no one, including she, will see) she is sure that Cooper will already be asleep. They have not spoken since Seretha left. Cooper did the dishes and went upstairs. It is always this way on Seretha nights, each silently reckoning what they cannot change, pondering what it means to have Seretha planted immovably at the center of their marriage.

She disrobes in the bathroom and, clad in her soft, tattered yellow nightgown, creeps in the dark around to her side of the bed and climbs in as efficiently and quietly as she can.

"You make too much of it." Cooper's voice, stitched tight and low, cuts through the dark.

"You're awake?"

A long silence follows. She hopes he is not learning to use silence as Seretha does, as a conversational tool.

"You're mad?" she ventures.

"He's a kid. He'll outgrow it."

"Possibly. But we don't know do we?" Why do people (including herself) pretend to know what they can never know and speak with a kind of bravado in the face of ignorance? So many doctors she has known have delivered uncertain prognoses as if they were incontrovertible, offering reassurance at the expense of truth.

She feels Seretha's specter lying between her and Cooper and wishes she could get back what was once a foolproof way of dispelling that specter, a way of shifting her view of things as you would with a pocket hologram. Whatever it was, it isn't working now.

"He was punched. He had to stand up for himself," says Cooper.

She stifles a moan and sits up. "What if he *doesn't* outgrow it? What if he grows up biting and punching his way through life and one day it's too late and we see that we never tried to control him and it's our fault? And..."

Cooper has sat up now, too, and he holds her face with one hand, urges her toward him with the other hand on her back. "What's our fault? Nothing's our fault. You worry too much, Jana. Have a little faith, won't you. Things turn out. I don't know any grown men—or women—who bite. Mom says I bit as a kid, but have I ever bitten you? Look at you and me—we turned out okay, didn't we?"

She hates this, how all they can do is guess.

He shakes her lightly. "Calm down, General. Relax, okay?"

She nods, still rigid, still tremulous, and she stays tense as Cooper makes love to her with more gentleness and repairing vigor than usual, which still does not make her nerves settle. But afterward, when Cooper has drifted off, the sound gradually recedes enough that she can recite in her mind the periodic table—hydrogen, helium, lithium, beryllium...nobelium, mendelevium, fermium, einsteinium, californium...—backward and forward, and hear the tick of her own thinking, running her tongue along the sharp tips of her incisors, thinking about teeth and their evolutionary purposes, listening to the neighbors' dog barking at a raccoon whose teeth are more deadly than his, until, at 2 A.M. or thereabouts, she finally yields to sleep.

THREE

When Varney was thirteen he bought a rifle to shoot rat-tlesnakes. He'd been saving his allowance for months and "bor-rowed" the rest from his mother's purse. He got the gun from some Mexicans in San Clemente who sold guns illegally. They lived in a pink apartment complex with paper-thin walls.

"Nice men," Varney told Cady. "They're old and they like to smoke pipes."

Varney smoked with them on their apartment balcony be-fore buying his gun.

After school, on the hot days of spring and summer and well into the fall, he hiked in the hills. There were trails, but mostly he bushwhacked—through low grasses and scraggly weeds, a treeless expanse that was essentially a desert, though it would take days and days of walking before you reached the wind-sculpted sand that looked the way people thought a desert *should* look.

He had to look hard for the snakes. It wasn't that they hid; they lay baking in the sun, boldly daring their predators, but even so, with their speckled honeycomb markings they could not be easily spotted. They were enviable—soporific and happy, coiled around themselves, skin-to-their-own-skin, solipsistic. So still you had to watch you didn't step on them. Smart, snakes were, but all their wit was silenced by the sun. The sun was so bright, it stole everything if you didn't watch it—your eyesight, your water, your sense.

Everything was bright—the strip of cobalt sky, the band of dry brown scrub, the wedge of ocean itself. Nothing moved but your mind. And what a kaleidoscope your mind was, churning out pattern after pattern, color after color. You wondered if snake minds did that, too. And then, after looking at the snakes and thinking about their minds, you saw that cross-eyed look of theirs, the meanness oozing through them.

With the first bullet the rattlers would rear up and writhe, their faces flattened, their suddenly animated bodies seeming like heads glued to hips with nothing in between, their rattles giving off a hollow hiss. After a few more bullets they were dead enough for you to pick up and put in your backpack and bring home to slice lengthwise. You removed the meat (offered it in gratitude to the Mexicans) and dried the skin, which you'd learned to do from a book.

All those skins in your closet, gathered with your silent stepping and your vigilance—they would protect you when nothing else did.

FOUR

She awakens at three-thirty in the morning and lies still, listening to the silence, which is not silence. Rain taps the roof. Twitches ripple through Cooper's body, rustling the bedclothes. Somewhere—the upstairs bathroom?—a loosely closed faucet releases an occasional drop.

There is more than a full hour remaining before she usually gets up, enough time to return to sleep, but right now it's out of the question. She isn't a good sleeper, hasn't been since college. Occasionally she uses pharmaceuticals—benzodiazepines like Valium or Xanax—but mostly she has become adept at functioning while sleep deprived. Now, after two months on the night shift, she's still adjusting to a daytime schedule: at work by seven, off by five or five-thirty, sometimes six. She had a brief period as a good sleeper when she was a teenager. She used to lie in bed in the morning, dozing and waking several times before she committed to getting up. She would try, with closed eyes, to guess the time by listening to the density of the passing traffic, then she would open her eyes a crack to see if the light confirmed her guess. Sometimes she could revisit a delicious dream, stretching out pleasure like a large lollipop. But such mornings are long gone; now a hardcore insomniac, she is grateful to take whatever little slices of sleep she gets and has given up aspirations of getting more. If she awakens early, she spends more time doing what she must—reattach to this life of hers, with this husband, this boy, this job, all of which in the predawn darkness have a rather arbitrary cast.

Last night she dreamed she was wandering through a labyrinth of teeth as large as stalactites. Another fugue of twitches rattles through Cooper's arm and shoulder. She remembers being annoyed at him yesterday, and now the memory shames her. He puts up with so much—her obsessions, her shrouded memories, her need to run. He goes on being devoted to her, to Evan, to their family life, and all the while keeps his mother afloat, too. She places a finger on Cooper's moist forehead, vows to be kinder to Seretha and to him, and rises.

In her ritual pass by Evan's room she sees he has sloughed his clothes during the night, and now he lies stark naked and uncovered, his clothes heaped on the floor. Since he was a tiny baby he has hated clothes, peeling them off at the first chance, as if they pained and constricted him. So unlike Jana herself, who loves to pull heavy garments around her—loves the protection, like armor, of their weightiness.

Spider sleeps curved around Evan's shoulder, dark and quiet as a shadow. Burnished by the amber glow of his dinosaur nightlight, Evan's placid face looks so perfect, so smooth, so still, and so odd in its coloration that it appears almost masklike. It is as if during the night his body has been invaded and colonized by someone else who is now simply pretending to sleep like Evan. She has looked at him so many times asleep, in just this position, and never before thought he looked odd or unnaturally colored, so she cannot help thinking that first grade, only three weeks begun, has done this to him. In three weeks he has been claimed and altered by the larger world, by teachers and childcare workers and hordes of unfamiliar children. But that seems preposterous, too. He's had a year at kindergarten already, so it's not as if he hasn't been around other children and adults. Still, this morning, post-biting, he does look different.

It's a few hours from sunrise, a clear, nearly fogless predawn, when Jana heads out on her morning run in shorts despite the cold. After running an hour she'll have worked up a sweat. Her footsteps clomp loud in the hush of dark. The wind has not risen yet, the bay lies calm, and the tremulous, lonely lights of fishing boats dot the water. A light burns in neighbor Carolyn Janklow's bedroom. Jana hurries past, hoping not to rouse Carolyn's two high-strung golden retrievers that never stop barking once they get started, or Carolyn herself, another high-strung mammal.

When Jana and Cooper first moved into the neighborhood, Carolyn was unusually friendly. She stopped by with flowers and fancy hors d'oeuvre plates and information about recycling services. It frightened Jana to think she might have to ward off this woman's good intentions, but Carolyn was quick to size up Jana's lack of neighborliness, and the visits soon stopped. Still, Jana feels guilty each time she sees the woman; last year Carolyn's youngest child went off to college, and three months after that her husband left her.

Jana heads, as usual, down the hill to the waterfront, running in the center of untrafficked residential streets, scooting to the side for the rare passing car. Most of her route to the water is lit by streetlights, though there remain a few places where she must briefly traverse a dark alley or an unlit stretch of grass. A boat horn wails in the distance. A few streets away a car swishes by. A crescent moon slips close to the horizon, holding fast to its silver white light. Cooper used to try to dissuade her from these flights through the dark, but she ignored his concerns, telling him he was a worrywart.

She runs as if dancing with the air, a tango of hips and legs, her fingers all the while sifting the air for portents of the upcoming day—what kinds of emergencies it will deliver; whether, at the end, home will be a sanctuary. Like the captain of a fishing vessel, she reads the winds and tides, taking warnings from lights and buoys, giving wide berth to the other fishermen's nets. As she runs, her mind occasionally goes blank, thought giving way to simple awareness of the meeting of skin and air, tongue and teeth, sole and asphalt, rock and bay, all the places where one thing abuts another, and their differences resound.

Today her mind is not blank. She has a memory of eating, of biting hard, of the urge to chew. When she was in medical school with neither the time nor the inclination to eat much, she used to be stricken sometimes with a desire for sinewy steak. She understood it then as an urge toward iron, or protein, or B vitamins, something her diet wasn't providing in sufficient quantity. But it was more than nutrition she wanted. She wanted engagement of her teeth; she wanted to rip flesh from bone. When she got the steak—always with bone if she could find it—she cooked it rare and shunned utensils. She took the uncut slab in her fingers, raised it to her mouth, and sniffed before biting. The bloody body smell sent up a surge of saliva, making her mouth ready. And when she finally bit, she did so violently, the way she and Varney once impersonated cavemen. The eyeteeth separated meat from bone; the molars pulverized; juices spilled through the troughs of her mouth. Once every few months she devoured meat this way.

She can't remember farther back than that. Did she ever bite people? Did she ever bite Varney? But her memory won't relinquish these answers, and she can't get it to cough up any further details. Her mind travels now to Mr. Cianetti, to the way his eyes seemed to suck at her as Sue Dennison wheeled him away.

She runs for an hour and a quarter—until her T-shirt is sweat soaked, all her muscles twitch, and oxygen has vitalized her extremities. Later she stands on the front stoop, dressed for the day in simple black clothes, lidded coffee mug in hand. Evan and Cooper are still sleeping, and the town is still dark, though light has begun to creep in from the east, between the mountains, looking for the islands, beginning to arrange them in their usual order, with various blue and gray and green hues graduated like a chromatography strip. She sucks in a long draught of cool air to propel herself onward.

She arrives at the hospital before her shift begins, with just enough time to pay a quick visit to Mr. Cianetti. She is not professionally bound to pay such a visit, and the other docs in her group tease her for doing such things, but she ignores them. Mr. Cianetti is dozing when she enters. His blinds have not been pulled, and though it is still dark out, lights from the parking lot illuminate the room. She admires the web of blue-green veins at his temples, showcasing the body's work. She considers his skin, the beauty in its complexity of folds. It seems to mirror something else in nature, but she can't quite get to what. A beehive, maybe, or some kind of lichen. She has been standing there only a few seconds when he opens his eyes and recognizes her instantly.

"Hey, Doctor. This isn't your beat, is it?"

"A friendly visit," she says. "How do you feel?"

"Pretty good. The way they've been testing me, I think they're getting ready to send me into space."

"No doubt."

"Care to dance?"

She laughs.

"Better take me while I'm good. They might operate on me tomorrow. I might not be much of a dancer after that."

"Really? Dr. Scofield said he'll operate?" She had checked his chart before she came in and surgery was not mentioned.

"Not for sure."

She nods. It would be an unusual choice to operate on a man of his age. Radiation is the safer, more conventional treatment. "I shouldn't make you talk. You need to sleep."

"Sit down. I got all day to sleep. It's all I do in here. Other than being the human pincushion."

She pulls a chair from the corner. Slowly he eases himself higher on his mattress. She cranks up his bed, helps him adjust the pillows. When he is settled, he stares at her, breathing deeply as if resuming sleep. "You remind me of someone I knew during the war. Tiny woman like you. A nurse. Beautiful. Very caring."

"Thank you. You were injured?"

"Not me. A buddy of mine."

Jana nods, marveling that this man seems so settled here, so much in control. So often the hospital environment overwhelms the elderly patients.

"You reach a certain age and everyone reminds you of someone else," he says.

"Gene pools, I think," she says. "There are only so many."

"That's the scientist in you speaking. I would say no two spirits are identical."

"So you were in World War II?"

He nods.

"Tell me about it."

"You don't want to know."

"I do," she says.

"You don't have work to do?" he says.

She looks at her watch. "I have some time."

"I was a bombardier. Forty-second Airborne. Bombed people dead from the air. Don't even have any idea what they looked like. Ants, you know, like stepping on ants. Nothing good to be said about it. Almost sixty years later and I still feel bad. I hear people glamorizing that war, and I don't know what they're talking about." His voice fades.

A bit of silence passes. Jana floats.

"If you shake hands with someone, look 'em in the eye, you can't kill that person. They're your brother. But from a plane, from a car speeding by with no touch, no eye contact, killing's easy. Later, of course, you fill in the details and feel like shit, if you'll pardon me."

Jana reaches out to his IV-bruised arm. She strokes it lightly. He grins and she sees he is weeping.

"Do you know what it means for a geezer like me to have a young pretty thing like you go out of your way?"

She laughs. "I'm not so young."

"To me you're a baby." He smiles and closes his eyes. "I'm a guy who can grow a tumor in my head. Miracle, right?"

Ren Scofield stands in the doorway. He is a quiet man who emerged from elite East Coast schools with a passion for the egalitarian practice of medicine. But his body, with its erect patrician bearing, its Roman nose, its way of dignifying the pronunciation of as and os, exudes disdain. And his singular focus on the brain seems to have nullified his awareness of the rest of the body, except as some unclean bearer of symptoms.

Jana rises. She and Dr. Scofield nod, smile, exchange collegial good mornings. She imagines he finds this visit of hers as odd as her colleagues would.

"You're looking chipper this morning, Mr. Cianetti," Scofield says. "And the sun isn't even up yet."

"I've got a special visitor."

"So I see."

"He's got more energy than I do," Jana says. Scofield doesn't react. "I should be going," she says, realizing that Scofield, coming from a discipline contemptuous of emergency medicine, will not be interested in her further observations. As she steps toward the door, Mr. Cianetti's eyes wither, a frank emotional moment that reminds her suddenly of Evan.

"I'll be back," she says. She withdraws to the hallway, taking with her the imprinted pleas from Mr. Cianetti's eyes.

Downstairs, in ER, John Ettinger is on duty. He is called Ettinger instead of John for reasons Jana can't explain, perhaps because his manner does not inspire intimacy. He is Napoleon-short and stingy with words and smiles, though she thinks, from having observed him with patients, that his core is fundamentally kind.

Today he is uncharacteristically happy to see Jana. For the past forty-five minutes he's been trying to coax a fifteen-year-old girl with abdominal pain to let him perform a pelvic exam. He doubts appendicitis, suspects an ectopic pregnancy, but is awaiting lab results.

He leads Jana to the examining cubicle where the girl lies on her side, knees drawn up in a loose fetal position. She does not look up as Jana and Ettinger enter.

"Miss Spettle, this is Dr. Thomas. She would like to examine you."

The girl twists her head to look at them, keeping the rest of her body still. Her face is very round, youthfully smooth, and alarmingly pale. Her cap of thorny hair—black at the roots, blond halfway down the shaft, a deliberate and not unattractive melding of light and dark—shoots from her head in all directions like quills. Displayed across her full upper lip are three tiny silver rings and one gold stud. She eyes Jana with an impassive look, which Jana reads as pure terror.

"We're fine thanks, Ettinger. I'll take it from here."

"What did you say your name was?" she asks when Ettinger is gone.

"You can call me Edie."

Jana scrubs her hands at the metal sink. The thrash of water precludes conversation, but Jana can feel the girl's probing eyes.

"Is your mom or dad here, Edie?"

"I came with my boyfriend."

Jana, hands dried, sits by Edie's gurney. "I think I saw him in the waiting room. A big good-looking guy in a black T-shirt?"

"How did you know?"

"He just looks like he might belong with you."

"He's freaked. He hates hospitals."

"I bet he's not as freaked as you are."

"I'm not freaked. Well, maybe a little. By the way, I would sit up but it hurts like hell."

Jana nods. "Try to relax."

"What're you gonna do to me?"

"Hopefully figure out what's causing this pain. Have you ever had a pelvic exam?"

"Yeah." Edie pauses, hedging. "Well, no, not exactly. I forget."

"Well, it won't hurt you nearly as much as this pain of yours."

"Are you a real doctor?" Edie asks.

"Yes," Jana says. "Why?"

"I don't know. You just seem kind of—like a regular person, I guess."

Jana laughs. "I'm pretty regular," she says thinking how, for the moment, she *is* regular, entirely regular, and there is something almost miraculous in that, how a terrified teenager with severe abdominal pain needs her and normalizes her, a normalcy she has usually deemed impossible. She feels, for the moment, charged and fully alive. If later something shatters her beyond the hospital confines, she'll be able to come back tomorrow and be restored to vitality again by an Edie or a Mr. Cianetti.

She is reminded of a toy she had as a child, a little dog composed of a series of small wooden tubes strung together on a cord. Normally the dog stood at attention, but when she pushed the bottom of his stand, the cord's tension was loosened and his entire body collapsed at the joints so his limbs lay on the stand in a disordered heap like a pile of useless sticks. When she released the button, he hopped to attention again.

A few hours later, when Jana is in the doctor's lounge taking a moment for chart dictation, she thinks again of Evan. She wonders if he woke with a memory of yesterday's wrongdoing, or, as usual, with exuberance and a blank slate of a conscience. She has a sudden yen to see him and draw his dewy skin to hers.

As if summoned by thoughts of Evan, her next patient is a bellowing two-and-a-half-year-old boy who, according to his mother (an outwardly calm but clearly anguished Latino woman who speaks only rudimentary English), has something stuck in his nose. It's not clear why the triage nurse hasn't directed the patient to the urgent care clinic, but Jana decides to treat him, anyway. After getting two nurses to hold the child still, Jana identifies the foreign body and is able to suction it with ease. What emerges is a red plastic bead the size of a small marble, which looks far too large to fit in a nose, especially the nose of a two-year-old. As soon as it pops out, the mother disgorges tears and grateful moans. "*Gracias. Muchas gracias.*" She hugs Jana spontaneously, pressing her pillowy body against Jana's sinewy one. Jana hugs back. She tells the woman to make sure to get the boy a favor at the nurses' station, but the woman doesn't understand, so Jana gets him one herself, a fist-sized transparent superball with a beetle at its center, something Evan would definitely prize. Watching them leave, she feels wistful for a moment, desirous of doing more for them than the simple removal of a bead.

One by one she works through the patients, and each moves into the middle of her mind, centering her, commanding her full attention. It's after noon when she notices a drenched EMT driver ducking into the restroom, and looking out past the portico, she sees the weather has turned nasty—pelting rain, drops thick as slugs, blurring into a solid mantle of gray. She glances at her watch. Evan has already eaten lunch, the cafeteria lunch he begged her to let him buy. She tries to picture him carrying his loaded tray—pizza, perhaps, milk, a cookie, something that passes for salad—to a table of other kids, all boys probably. She tries to envision him making the series of choices required—who to sit with, what to say. What do first graders talk about over lunch? Is it all *butt-face* and *doo-doo head*, or is there more meaningful dialogue? Evan is capable of interesting observations, but usually they are randomly offered, not in the context of what anyone would call conversation. She has not seen him in social situations very often. Except for his morning kindergarten class, he has either been with Mrs. Stubbs or with her and Cooper. He has not had many play dates; he has not demanded them. It seems impossible to her that now he's out there all day, functioning as a free agent, without her or Mrs. Stubbs. The thought fills her with fear and yearning and with the need to scoop him back up into the protection of her arms and belly.

She remembers so clearly what he was like as an infant, a seemingly boneless little creature. The days after his birth bled inconspicuously into nights, the three of them lying together in half-light. She remembers the sucking, all three of them sucking, though how can that really have been? She remembers lifting Evan's floppy body and feeling boneless herself. She took her cue from the baby, sleeping when he did, drinking water as he fed. She was hugely sleepy but alert. The smell of things—her milk, her sweat, his poop—all of it had the same elemental sweetness, all of it streaming from the same place.

In those days and nights, time was defined by the intricate partnership of sleeping and waking and eating between her and Evan. It was as if they'd been wired together like fractured bones to heal together as one unit. Cooper was nearby and helpful, of course, but incidental. She remembers the baby's fuzzy gaze, the way he scrutinized her, learning her, uncomprehending as a foreigner but still taking comfort from her arms, her breast, his little hand finding her soft places, kneading them. She began to feel hope again. She began to feel it was possible to begin again, to tuck away her past experience as wisdom instead of doom, guidance instead of guilt.

What she tried to overlook were the parts of Evan that were already formed, the curious wrinkles criss-crossing his fingers as if he had once dug deep trenches, pushed wheel barrows, pounded nails year after year. How could such new flesh bear so many imprints? Were these signs of past lives, or indications of what was to come? Had her own mother, Beth, noticed these things? Had she, too, felt immensity and ripeness in her heart and known that anything was possible?

When, then, did the worry kick in? Like human development, its pace was slow. But sometimes it would seem to leap forward inexplicably. On a playground when Evan was two, a slightly older child would not play with him and Evan sobbed inconsolably for an hour. He began, at three, to sob when anyone raised a voice to him. "I don't like you," he wailed when a supermarket checkout clerk chided him for disturbing the candy rack.

She tried to imagine a future for someone who could not endure a raised voice or a cross-eyed look. She saw gradually that her child was a slightly odd child, a child whose energy rose and plummeted, whose feelings were easily bruised, whose mind, unprompted, turned strange corners.

There were sudden outbursts of rage. He punished his stuffed animals, hurling them against the wall, attempting to flush them down the toilet, slicing them open raggedly with his blunt toy scissors. "I'm operating on them to remove their bad," he said.

And slowly, over six years, her worry has festered and grown. She knows better than to compare, but she cannot help comparing. Now, today, she asks herself: Is this biting a turning point? Is this *the* turning point?

By the time she has removed all the glass shards and completed the final suture on the foot laceration of a twenty-five-year-old female, she knows she has to get to Evan. She needs Evan by her side, or within easy reach. She cannot have him in that child-care center until six, with his teeth, like unregistered weapons, so available to him.

Nearly an hour has passed since the end of the school day, which means that he has been at Little Creations for forty minutes or so, subtracting twenty for transportation. She's picturing awful things—a free-for-all of kids hanging from basketball hoops, hurling lunch boxes, pinching each other with the intent of drawing blood.

"Something's come up," she says to Ron Gaffney, who came on when she did. "Cover me for forty-five minutes and I'll owe you big-time. Will you?"

Ron is amused. He tortures her a moment, watching her without saying a word, mischief lurking around his mouth. He is forty-one, a rock climber, one of the maverick doctors who chose the ER specialty for its flexible hours. He and Jana see a lot of one another and have always been friendly. He's a good doctor, but congenitally late by five or ten minutes. She has covered for him innumerable times, and they both know he owes her.

"Going out for a quickie? Really, Thomas, I thought better of you." He smirks, punches her upper arm the way middle school boys do.

Playing along, she winks. "I'd never do anything you wouldn't do." She stands as straight as she can, investing all of her sixty-two inches with power.

"Hell yes, go," he says. "But I'll collect; I promise. You're on the clock starting"—he looks at his wristwatch—"*now*. Four-oh-seven."

She drives faster than usual—praying no officer of the law is lurking near her route—and arrives at the center in four and a half minutes. Concealing herself, she peers around the gymnasium door to observe the scene for a moment. There are probably thirty kids in the space, and their shrill voices travel up to the high ceiling and ricochet back down, creating a carnival of sound. One side of the gym is set with tables for quiet activities, crafts and reading; the other side is devoted to gross muscle exertion, ball games and tag. She spots Evan on the gym's active side, where he tosses a rust red playground ball amid a group of four or five boys. "Here!" they all yell. "Over here!" Evan sidesteps over the lacquered floor wearing a jubilant smile. How natural he looks among the other boys, as if he really *belongs*. No outward marking or behavior identifies him as different.

She sees two staff members presiding over a small group of girls at one of the craft tables. There's Yvonne, a fifty-plus bleached-blond with a smoky voice, and George, a bearded soft-spoken outdoorsy man wearing a flannel shirt and soft moccasins. She met them both when she enrolled Evan, and they seemed nice enough if you could make such a judgment in one meeting. George notices her and nods with odd formality. He looks over at Yvonne as if to summon her. Their exchange of looks seems like a well-oiled system—within seconds Yvonne approaches Jana.

"Evan's mom, right?"

Jana nods. "I've come to get him early."

Yvonne stands next to Jana, a few inches too close. Her neck sparkles with flecks of glitter. "Let's go over to the sign-out table so I can hear myself think."

"Is it always this loud?" Jana asks.

"You get used to it."

At the table Yvonne forages through a pile of paperwork. She hands Jana the checkout clipboard. "Sandy told me about yesterday. Evan hiding and all."

"I don't have time to talk now," Jana says, taking a step back.

"Look," says Yvonne confidentially. "I know parents like their children to be perfect and all, but—"

"I'm not one of those parents, but I *would* like my child not to bite. Where is he, anyway? We need to go." She angles her body away from Yvonne. "Which kid did he bite?"

"Jason, the one holding the ball over there with Evan. See, today they're pals."

Jana is too far away to identify any lingering bite marks on the boy's body. "Is he okay?"

"Oh yeah, fine."

Jana is grateful for the din, which fills the silence between her and Yvonne, who perches on the table, legs swinging, looking ready to initiate a difficult chat with her aggressively informal style. "You don't want to scare Evan, do you? You just want him to be happy, right?"

"I told you I have to go," Jana says, deliberately cool. She has lost sight of Evan and frowns into the sea of children.

"Well, let's talk when you have time. You know how parenting is—always fine-tuning." Yvonne grins to show her goodwill. Her teeth are unnaturally white. She looks anything but congenial.

Adrenaline surges in Jana's blood, squeezes her heart.

"Excuse me, I've got to get back to them," Yvonne says. "Don't forget to sign him out." She trots off, her sneakered feet springy.

Jana wants to summon Yvonne back and interrogate her about just what credentials she has that give her the right to dispense parenting advice, but she'll be late if she doesn't leave this second; she's late already. *Protoplasm*, Jana thinks. *We're all just protoplasm.* It's the detachment mantra she uses to help her let things go, but it only sometimes works. She initials the sign-out sheet and rounds up Evan, who shrieks with delight at seeing her. He coils his arms around her waist and won't let go for close to thirty seconds.

"I *dove* you, Mommy."

Jana looks around the gym to see if Yvonne is noticing, but Yvonne's attention is fixed on a group of girls. Does it always work this way? Jana wonders—the boys run wild and the adults gravitate to the girls, such good, serious, mature little creatures, all neat pinkness, all cooperative, all using their social skills and their fine motor muscles so productively.

"I love you too, honey. Let's go. I've got to get back to work."

"Where am I going?"

"With me. To work."

Back at the hospital she takes him to the bathroom and then puts him in the waiting room, near the toy box. They're mostly toys that won't interest him—puzzles and picture books and educational shape-matching games of sturdy plastic—but he is so immersed in gawking at the other people, he hasn't noticed yet. A man in a white chef's uniform holds up a heavily bandaged hand like Lady Liberty's torch. A raggy-haired youth lies on the floor with his hand over his eyes. A woman with two young children tries to suppress a hacking cough. In the corner, on a blaring TV screen, a talk-show host slaps his knee in laughter.

"I wanna come in with you," Evan says.

"You can't, honey. I'm sorry. You'll be fine here. There's lots for you to do. I'll come and check on you as often as I can."

"Do your work fast, okay?"

She laughs, thinking about all the others on the ER staff that would like to say the same to her. "It doesn't quite work like that."

"Try, okay?"

She nods and touches his silky bangs. "I love you, Evan. Be a good boy."

She hesitates, watching the way Evan's eyes peruse the toys. Would she call him happy? He's happy if he has a truck, an ice-cream cone, a pair of skates, a day at the beach. All that talk of happiness, whether Varney was or wasn't happy, drove her to distraction. Happiness was beside the point. It was overrated. Was Varney happy? No more or less than she. Half the world wasn't happy, but that didn't mean they lost control.

Still, she can't resist asking, "Are you happy, Evan honey?"

"Cool truck," he says. He holds up a tiny dump truck with moveable parts.

"Yeah," says Jana. "Cool truck."

ONCE CADY'S FAMILY took a trip to Tijuana. Their father, Walter, wanted something there; she doesn't remember what—a special kind of beer or tequila, a prescription drug, perhaps. Their mother, Beth, wanted vanilla and an embroidered shawl. "Cheap," they kept saying. "It's so cheap."

The streets of Tijuana were, on a Saturday, thick with people out shopping, strolling, drinking coffee and beer in sidewalk cafés, yelling to one another across the streets. Taxis and cars drove recklessly, overrunning the curbs, blaring their horns, disregarding red lights.

Scared, Cady clung to Varney's hand, wishing she didn't have to be responsible for him. At six he was dazzled by everything: the sidewalk carts selling Mexican flags, sugar skulls, sombreros, and colorful dolls; the fortune-teller with the donkey; the juggler in cowboy boots. Walter and Beth ambled slowly ahead of them, looking back occasionally, but still, with Varney wandering here and there, she had trouble keeping up. Varney wanted to watch a pair of young boys flipping knives into the dirt. They were Varney's age, no older, and deft with the pocketknives, which they tossed forcefully, nearly always making their targeted circle. By the time she and Varney looked up from the game, Walter and Beth were out of sight, folded into the pageantry. She dragged Varney away, having to pull with all her might against his fixation. Hand in hand, Cady ahead, Varney tripping behind, their small bodies wove fast through the densely packed crowd. She remembers now the smells—cooking sausage, sweet rolls, exhaust, coffee, body odor—all knitted together, laced no longer with excitement but with strangeness.

Through an opening between torsos, she spotted Beth's pale blue cotton pants, her white sweater. She had stopped to examine some embroidered shirts and dresses. Cady dashed to her side, Varney in tow.

"Oh," Beth said, looking startled. "Walter went looking for you." She patted their heads and took their hands, and they all walked slowly along in a row, Cady and Varney at the edges, bumping into things, seeing oddness, Beth safely in the middle.

Beth bought them sugar skulls, trying to jolly them. Her eyes moved in a constant fluttering search for Walter. "Now Daddy's the one that is lost," Beth said, trying to make light of it. "We have to wait here." And Cady felt for a minute as if Beth was her child and she, Cady, was doing the protecting.

They waited and watched. They sucked the color and personality out of their skulls. Walter finally appeared, fuming, declaring Cady and Varney lost. When Beth pointed the children out and Cady explained how Varney had strayed, Walter flew into a rage, pivoting so fast his Hawaiian shirt flew up with the gust of his turn, showing his flabby, hairy belly. He vanished again into the crowd.

A long fifteen or twenty minutes passed in which Beth looked desolate. She spoke not a word of Spanish. She hated to drive. Finally, Walter returned again. This time he had a long leather dog leash, which he looped around Varney's chest, restraining his upper arms. Varney did not protest. He stood stiller than a reptile, face to the ground, eyes closed. Then they set out again as a family, Varney skittering, obedient, responding quickly to Walter's tugs. He moved, Cady suddenly thought, exactly like a tiny toy dog, his eyes alternately enamored and sad, his lower arms only partly under his control so they reminded her of the jerky limbs of a marionette.

There was no denying that Varney was scared of Walter. Walter was a barrel-chested man with a body so unlike his son's it made you question the ways of biology, how the son could inherit so little of the father's flesh and bones. Walter was full of bluster, always trying to sell something. At work it was insurance. At home it was opinions, theories, schemes. He had been a quarterback in high school, and he thought Varney should be an athlete, too. Not a football player—Varney was too scrawny for that—but why not surfing? When Varney was in middle school, Walter signed them up for surfing lessons together. Varney had no interest in surfing. The surfers were suave blond boys—if not natively blond, they bleached their hair until it was nearly white and dry as kindling—and they were popular with the girls. He felt silly coming down to the beach with his middle-aged dad, who was decked out in long turquoise surf shorts, his chest padded with flesh that sometimes resembled breasts, the only grown-up in a class full of middle school boys. Walter dwarfed his surfboard and couldn't catch a wave. Time after time the ocean upended his board and dumped him from his quavering crouch into the foam. He always laughed and tried again while the other boys tittered and called him Walrus.

Varney got up pretty well but didn't enjoy it. Paddling back out over the swells made him seasick. Belly down on the board, arms digging water fast, his ribs bruised and his upper arms ached. When Moe, the instructor, gathered them all in the sand—"Good work, dudes; now listen up"—Varney stood apart while his father stayed with the rest of the group. Later, at home, his father would talk about the boys as if they were his pals.

Sometimes Walter invited his colleagues home, and he boasted shamelessly. He'd pull Varney into his armpit and say. "My son and I are surfers. We surf together, don't we, son?" Not *Varney*, always *son*, as if he'd forgotten Varney's name or was ashamed of it. "My son is going to be a *scientist*. He's the brainy type." Walter would roll his eyes and tap the side of his head, proud, but pretending he wasn't. And, remarkably, Varney would stay there in his father's armpit, holding up his surprised eyes until his forehead ached. When Walter was done talking about Varney, he would go on to tell his colleagues about the nonexistent house he owned in the south of France, or Hawaii, or Colorado, or wherever he happened to be fixated at the time.

Cady found her father ridiculous (and he, sensing that, avoided her), but Varney feared him. You could see it in the fact that Varney tolerated the surfing lessons, the bluster, the falsehoods. He looked so small and sad, huddled there under his father's armpit, afraid to tell his father to go to hell.

At report card time Varney brought home his undistinguished grades and agonized about how to approach Walter. But, in fact, Walter never really reacted to the grades. If the report card was bad, Walter pitched it aside, ignored it, perhaps rewrote it in his mind. He was a man with a brainy son, a son who was going to be a scientist, a prizewinner. What he never saw was how, at night, Varney punched his pillow into submission.

Jana wants to go back to Little Creations and demonstrate to Yvonne and Sandy and George that Evan is *not* afraid of her. Evan has *never* been afraid of her—well, maybe for a moment or two, but not all the time like Varney was scared of Walter. Evan will never be scared of anything the way Varney was.

At the supermarket on their way home, Jana paws through heads of red lettuce, looking for one without slimy leaves, but it's late in the day and late in the season and all the good ones are gone. The mister goes on, startling her, leaving cool, beaded water on the back of her hand.

"Can we get this?" Evan asks, holding up a six-pack of something in bright blue foil wrapping.

"What is it?" She tosses the least slimy of the lettuce heads into her cart.

"It's new," he says, as if this is all she needs to know. "It's got lots of vitamins."

"I'm sorry, but I forgot your name." Someone is touching Jana's shoulder. She turns to see a woman she vaguely recognizes, a woman of Jana's height with smooth black hair cut bluntly below the jawline and a face whose most prominent feature is a pair of sensual and mobile red lips.

"From the school," the woman says. "I'm Robin Feingold. I have a boy, Max, who's in the same class with your boy."

"Oh yes . . . have we met?" Jana asks, feeling forgetful, a step behind things.

"Actually, we haven't met officially. I saw you at the beginning of the school year and I thought, *There's a woman I'll get to know.* But I haven't seen you since. This is your boy?"

"Yes. Evan. Oh, I'm sorry. I'm Jana Thomas." Jana smiles a little, grips her cart, nodding, beginning to back away. She should have known better than to shop now, at the end of a workday, with everyone else. But Robin is settling in.

"How's it been going?" Robin says. She rolls her eyes a little. The gesture intrigues Jana. A little window into something—passion? Neurosis?

"All right, I guess," says Jana.

Robin frowns and rubs her lips together. "Not for us. Max won't sit still. He won't keep his hands to himself. He gets up and parades around while the teacher is talking. I don't know what the heck to do. I can't *make* him sit still when I'm not even *there*." She shakes her head. "I mean, he is a boy and everyone says boys are so active and all, but—I don't know. I've never *been* one. Hey, would you like to get the boys together sometime?"

Jana looks down at Evan. He has put the foil-wrapped six-pack into the cart along with a pack of ice-cream bars and some Oreos. "All these go back, buddy. Would you like to get together with Max sometime? This is Max's mother."

Evan nods. "Yay, Maxie-Waxie."

"Hello, Evan," Robin says.

"Say hello," Jana prompts.

"Hello fellow," Evan says.

Robin torques her lips in amusement. "You and I should get together, too. Do you work?"

Jana nods.

"Mommy!" Evan calls in his thin falsetto.

"What do you do?"

"Mommy!"

"Evan, I'm talking. Say *excuse me* if you need to say something. I'm a physician in ER."

"Excuse me! Excuse me! Excuse me!" sings Evan. "I'm ready to go."

"You need to put these things back, Evan," Jana says. She shakes her head. "I'm so sorry," she says to Robin.

"I knew you'd be smart," Robin says. "You have the wariness of a smart person. I used to work, too, but I quit a few years ago, not too long after Max was born. I was an assistant DA, but I couldn't take it. Too much fighting. Too many know-it-alls ready to draw blood. When I go back, I've got to find something else to do."

With a triumphant flourish Evan drops two crackling bags of miniature Snickers into the shopping cart.

"Uh-uh," Jana admonishes, "I told you all of these have to go back."

"We need 'em for Halloween." He climbs on the cart. "Roll me, Mom," he cries as if confident his mother belongs only to him.

"Hey," says Robin. "You've got your hands full. I'll call you, okay?" She touches Jana's shoulder again as she rolls off.

Jana feels locked for a moment between Evan's high-pitched demands and the feeling she's been blindsided by an offer of friendship. She's tempted by Robin Feingold, the rolling eyes, the assumption of connectedness. Marriage to a man is one thing—a relationship born of difference—but friendship with a woman is born of communality. It probes too much, it respects no boundaries, it robs a person of privacy. Still, Jana feels a pitch of excitement at the thought of seeing Robin and Max. Distracted, she allows Evan to keep the Snickers.

That night Evan crawls into bed with Jana and Cooper, claiming he can't sleep.

"Why, honey?" Jana asks. It's just before eleven and she and Cooper have just retired. Evan's body spews heat like a small geyser.

"Because if I go to sleep I might forget stuff. I might forget what I'm thinking or my name. Or I might forget you and Daddy and my toys."

Cooper winks over the top of Evan's head. "But you'll remember in the morning, won't you? It'll all come back."

"But what if I don't? I might not."

"You always have before. If you don't, we'll call up the memory doctor, won't we, Mommy? I bet Mommy knows lots of good memory doctors. And we'll get the memory doctor to bring it all back."

Evan thinks for a minute. "Okay," he says in a small chastened voice, and in less than a minute he is asleep.

Cooper reaches over to touch Jana's cheek. "I guess that's it for tonight," he whispers, rueful but resigned. "Sleep well."

"You, too," she says, and soon she hears the enviable duet of Cooper's and Evan's breathing.

Drawn to the heat of Evan's body, she works hard to hold herself back from touching him. She is swamped in memory and counting differences as if they were rosary beads.

FIVE

Caaaa-dy!" Varney used to call in the middle of the night, his voice rasped with fear. "C-Cady, I can't sleep."

He stood beside her bed, naked sometimes, or wearing only a frayed Batman T-shirt, his five- or six- or seven-year-old body tiny and smooth but, from certain angles, showing already the arcs and fissures of manhood. A thin strip of gauzy pink light from her Cinderella night-light danced around his perimeter, running up one side of him and down the other, eerie and holy, coming from a dream.

"Go tell Mom," she said.

He shook his head. "I don't want to." No explanation needed; she knew. How could a fearful person alleviate some-one else's fear?

She looked at him without solutions, too tired to talk, sleep like a third party begging her back.

"Can I get in b-bed with you?"

His eyes, at that age, were still huge in relation to the rest of him, as if his body's primary activity was seeing. His ears, by contrast, were tiny organs, almost vestigial.

"Please, Cady, Cady, Cady, Cady. Cady-did. Cady DO. Cady-did. P-pleeeeese."

She nodded her assent, and sleep took her again so quickly

that his parting of the covers, his squirming underneath, the heat of his tiny overfired limbs, was almost a dream.

That was after the time she had heard him crying in bed. Varney was three then, and she was seven. She had gone to her parents' room. It was the middle of the night. Everything was quiet except for the distant freeway hum and the pillow-muffled sound of Varney's crying.

"Mommy, Varney is crying," she whispered.

Her mother's eyes were open, but she wasn't moving. Cady wondered if people, like horses, sometimes slept with their eyes open.

"Varney's crying," she said again.

The bed was high and she was short. In the dim light her parents' sheets and limbs made a curious country. She stared across shifting mountain ranges—a shoulder, a hip, a hand, and one knee, surely her father's, making a high volcanic peak. A low groan seemed to come from under the bed, no, from her father, and her father's body heaved up (she shrank from its shadow and its sound and the shame that she was there) and shifted from back to side, thrusting a long arm forward, down across her mother's belly.

Cady crouched. She knew her father would not want her there. She knew her mother did not want her there, either. Her parents made a world of their own sometimes—at night and in the evenings—when they did not want to be interrupted, when they seemed to forget they had children. It wasn't that they went out. They still acted like parents—"Feed your fish." "Brush your teeth." "Go to bed."—but she knew things were different. It was something only she and Varney could feel—a quiet erasure, a moment when, in their very own home, she and Varney were cast out for a while, orphans for an evening. Her parents had gone off to their own country again, the country

they'd lived in for the many years they'd known each other before Cady and Varney were born. (They had met in high
school, but Cady was not born until they were thirty-eight.)

Cady, at seven or eight, knew about her parents' private
country and sometimes tried to imagine it. Perhaps it was like
Oregon, where her parents had grown up, thick with trees, wet
and green all the time. "I miss trees," her mother often sighed.
"I miss *moisture*." Cady had never been out of California. She
thought the Northwest must be a beautiful place, filled with
flowers and the feeling of heaven. "Your aunt Helen still lives
there," Cady's mother said. "Oregon heaven." Helen had
drowned when she was seventeen. Cady's mother was eighteen
when it happened, but more than twenty-five years later she
still thought about it a lot, like some fresh stinging grief.

"Mom?" Cady whispered from her crouch, when everything was quiet again, trying not to look at the splattering of
her father's thick hand across her mother's belly. "Varney."

"I know, honey. Now go to bed," her mother said without
moving.

Cady crawled back to the hallway on all fours. Varney was
still crying. She crept down to his room and stuck her hand
through the slats of his crib, where, at three, he still liked to
sleep. He had tented his blanket and crimped his body into a
ball under the canopy. She trailed her forefingers down the
bare skin of his arm.

"Go to sleep, Varney," she whispered.

In his sleep Varney often scratched himself, nails furrowing
his arms with red welts, which sometimes bled. If she happened
to be awake herself, she shook him and told him to stop, but
usually they both slept through his scratching and awoke to see
his limbs scraped, the sheets bloody. In the morning she would
help him find a long-sleeved shirt.

"It's hot for a turtleneck," their mother said. She was slow to awaken, and moving around the kitchen, she would stop suddenly as if she forgot where she was, what day it was, what she was doing. Watching her, Cady sometimes wondered if she forgot even more. Did she recall the functions of objects—the frying pan whose handle she held, the spatula she was about to deploy? Did she recall her own name?

"I like being hot," Varney said.

But Cady knew how he hated to be hot, how he kicked the covers off in the middle of the night.

Their mother never saw the sheets. Cady knew by then how to deal with blood. Before she left for school—her parents long since gone to their respective jobs—she stripped the bed, rinsed the stains in cold water, remade the bed with clean sheets, laundered the old ones. "Varney peed," she would tell her mother later.

ONE NIGHT IN BED she felt it coming. She couldn't say why she felt it coming on that particular night after all those years of sleeping next to him, but she remembers lying there in the dark on her back, wide awake, feeling Varney staring at her. Twelve, he was then.

Mostly he went to sleep right away, pulling his knees up to his chest, the covers over his head, but that night he lay uncovered from the waist up, staring through the dark. And when he said, "Can I?" they both knew what he meant, and she nodded without knowing why. They owed each other things. Their lives weren't like other people's lives. The things they couldn't get elsewhere they had to get from each other.

"Go ahead," she whispered, and he reached over and stroked her breasts while she lay still, looking straight up, rigid at first but gradually relaxing, knowing she was not supposed to be doing this but sure that Varney needed this and maybe she did, too. Sixteen years old and no one else was touching her. Varney did it gently. She trusted him. He stayed on his side of the bed always and reached across the six or eight inches or so between them, and first he used only one or two fingers and he stroked the breast closest to him—"Um," he said—the place where it connected to her side and then all around it, moving slowly to the center, the soft part of her nipple and then the tip, which hardened and straightened under his touch, like an animal with a separate life.

For two years it was always the same, the way he circled her whole breast, arriving last at her nipple. The only thing that changed was that he started to touch both of her breasts, reaching farther across her to get to the right one. And then, when he had touched first one and then the other, he moved back to his side of the bed and reached down to touch himself. She lay still, listening to his quick movements rustling the sheets, to his tiny gasp, followed by wiping with the washcloth which he rinsed first thing in the morning. Each night it was that way. Until he touched her, she could not sleep.

SIX

Jana folds laundry. So many pairs of Evan's grass-stained jeans, threadbare at the knees. The underpants, because he is a lean-hipped boy, look scarcely bigger than diapers. And the endless T-shirts. How did Evan accumulate so many T-shirts, all proclaiming allegiances to zoos or museums or beaches or sports teams? It's silly to feel moved by clothing, but she *is* moved by the smallness of these garments and the vulnerability of the body they fit.

"Mumma!" Evan, who has been playing marbles quietly on the floor, leaps onto the couch.

"Yes, honey?"

"I have a present for you." He opens his fist to reveal a turquoise gum ball dotted with grains of sand. Its blue color has bled into Evan's sweaty hand. "I saved it for you. It's a jawbreaker."

"Oh, Evan, thank you. But you can have it."

"It makes you happy."

"But I *am* happy already."

"Then why do you look like that?"

"Like what?"

"Fish face." He puckers his mouth. "Funny eyes." He crosses his eyes. "Leo looks like that sometimes."

Done with the laundry, she touches her cheek, tapping for what he sees, worried for the thoughts that she might be oozing, unwittingly, through her pores. "Come and help me set the table," she says. "Who's Leo?"

Evan pops the gum ball into his mouth. "Leo is the one with the bad ideas like watching bugs die. He hits the other kids until they do what he wants them to do. Sometimes he bites. He's a nudnik," says Evan, reveling in the Yiddish word whose meaning neither he nor Jana is sure of.

She hands him spoons, and he makes them dance to the table along every horizontal surface. "Really?" she says. "What a terrible boy. Doesn't Miss Tencil do something to stop him?"

"She wants to hit him."

"But she doesn't, does she?"

Evan sails the spoons across the gap between countertop and table. "She wants to though. Her eyes get all mean and yellowish. Animal eyes." He slaps the spoons together so they make a tinny gong.

"But she doesn't hit him." Jana has stopped folding napkins and stands over Evan.

"She puts him in the corner, and Leo cries because he wants to be with his friends again. He didn't mean to do bad things."

"You don't have to play with Leo. You don't have to do what he says."

"I *do* have to play with Leo. Leo is my friend."

"Leo could get you into trouble."

"Leo is a good boy when he isn't doing bad things." Evan's attention turns to the sound of the opening door latch. He tosses the spoons to the center of the table and runs to greet Cooper.

———

WHEN JANA CALLS to request an immediate conference, Rita Tencil resists. "We have conferences scheduled in a few weeks, Mrs. Johansen," she tells Jana. "I'll know Evan better by then, and whatever we discuss will be more meaningful." On the phone Miss Tencil seems more brittle than she seemed in person, her voice slow and graveled with exhaustion.

"Evan has spoken to me about some things that need more immediate attention," Jana says.

"Why don't we discuss them now?"

Jana glances around the doctors' lounge. It is predominantly cream-colored, decidedly sterile. A second-year resident sleeps in the corner, snoring loudly. Down the hall, the bell at the nurses' station rings. Another patient. No one knows Jana's in here.

"I'm at work now," Jana says. "I really don't have time."

"I'm at work, too," says Rita Tencil. It seems an odd comment given that work is where Jana called her, waiting until the official school day was over so Miss Tencil wouldn't be distracted by students.

Jana weighs her options. "It's about this boy named Leo."

"Leo."

"Yes. Evan says Leo is a ringleader of sorts. He says that Leo hits and bites the other children to get them to do what he wants. And, well—its sounds to me as if there should be some intervention with this boy."

"I'm sorry, but who is Leo?"

Jana hesitates. "In Evan's class. A boy Evan apparently plays with a lot."

"There is no Leo in my class."

Someone knocks on the closed door. Jana does not get up. There is no second knock. "Maybe I heard the name wrong. Maybe it was another boy." A better mother, Jana thinks, would know all the boys.

"Well, let's see—we have twelve boys altogether. There's Joshua, Ian, Gregory, Walter, Benjamin, Matthew, Max, Alexander—"

"Any *L* names?"

Rita Tencil hesitates and clears her throat.

Jana tries to mute the tone in her head that makes a diminished seventh with the snoring resident. She's aware of letting too much time go by. "Well, I don't want to get stuck on the name," she says. "Apparently there is one child that plays with Evan a lot and is encouraging him to do bad things, some kid that hits and bites. Evan says you have put him in the corner repeatedly."

Now the long silence starts with Rita Tencil. Jana hears a shifting of papers and wonders if her question raises confidentiality issues.

"I think you should talk to Evan again. There is no such child. I've put Evan himself in the corner a few times—he has a tendency to get *overexuberant,* shall we say—but there's no other child that fits your description."

Jana cannot get off the phone quickly enough. She can barely hear Rita Tencil for the swelling note.

IT IS SATURDAY MORNING of a weekend off. Pale sunlight, a little at least, seeps through the curtains and makes the day seem promising. A little while ago she tried to get up, but Cooper, who she thought was sleeping, pulled her back, touched her to wetness, and pushed inside her. Now he rocks there slowly, intent on prolonging the pleasure. He makes a sound, part hum, part moan, and she feels him urging her to enjoyment. She tries, truly she tries, with all her well-schooled will she tries to do her part, stay in the moment, relish at the

very least the love and the body connection if not the sex itself. How hard he has worked over the years at teaching her to
embrace her animal instincts. It began with taking her to the
beach and making her close her eyes, feel the wind, sift the
sand, and, tongue out, taste the trace of salt in the air. He'd
hold tasting marathons where he would fix tidbits of the most
succulent meats, the sweetest fruits, the tangiest cheeses, and
teach her to savor them with her nose and lips and tongue and
palate and teeth all working at once, wringing out flavors she
had never noticed before in her food-as-nourishment style of
eating. And he would force her to receive foot massages and
back massages and head massages, all the while urging her to
slowness, to reveling in the here and now. And then the sex, of
course, which she has truly delighted in, but this morning she
has trouble staying with it. It helps her to watch him. She takes
pleasure in the degree to which he takes pleasure, feeling his
rise to climax radiate vicariously through her body and nearly
bringing her to climax. Often, though, her mind can't be
quieted, and despite his efforts, she must fight her instinct to
move on to something more productive.

Today, as Cooper comes, she is somewhat aroused, but even
so, she feels the surreptitious creep of memory and responsibility. Later she will go on her monthly trek to her PO box;
Seretha will be here soon to take Evan on his junket; as always,
there's the weekend challenge of keeping Evan occupied; and
today there's Leo to ponder, too.

Cooper works hard on her until she covers his hands.
"It's not going to happen," she says. "Listen." Downstairs Evan
rattles around, talking to himself, or to Spider.

"You sure?" Cooper says.

"I'm okay." She smiles wanly, acknowledging failure.

"Your call," Cooper says, rising suddenly and heading to the bathroom so her eyeline is filled for a moment with his bare buttocks, in which she reads her rebuff.

When she comes downstairs, she finds Cooper and Evan, dressed alike in tattered white T-shirts and jeans, eating pancakes drowned in butter and syrup. On weekdays Jana doesn't let Evan eat sugar for breakfast. The simple sugars—glucose, sucrose, fructose—jack him up, ruin his concentration, then make him sleepy.

"Would you like to have Leo over this afternoon?" she asks him, watching his pale face closely.

Evan fills his mouth with pancake and shakes his head.

"Who's Leo?" Cooper asks.

Evan zooms a neon green Hot Wheels car around the perimeter of his plate, chewing quickly with his mouth wide open.

"Tell him who Leo is."

Evan shrugs.

"Leo is a school friend," prompts Jana. "Right?"

Evan nods.

"I'd like to meet him," Cooper says.

"I'm going out with Gramma," Evan says.

"You could invite Leo afterward."

"Then I'm going to wanna play with what Gramma gets me."

Jana sighs and drinks her coffee, trying to focus herself. It is not necessarily a bad thing to have an imaginary friend, although she was under the impression they were usually the province of children younger than Evan. Varney never had one, at least as far as she knew.

She sips in silence, wondering how an imaginary friend would register on a PET scan. What a complex organ the brain is with its peculiar reticular formations, its hemispheres and glandular secretions, its dutiful corpus callosum, its file cabinets of facts, its dreams and imaginings, its guilts and obsessions and fears, its puffed-up parts and its mea-culpa-for-living ones. She remembers so well how Varney used to say, "I'm not afraid of anything outside—I'm scared in my brain." She knows what he meant. If it weren't for her own brain, with its relentless overblown imaginings, there would be nothing to fear. With brains like hers and Varney's in his bloodlines, isn't it logical that Evan's brain, too, would churn out the fantastical? And is there anything inherently wrong with that? Joan of Arc, a victim of tinnitus, claimed to have heard voices.

For a while during medical school, Jana considered becoming a neurologist. She envisioned herself becoming knowledgeable about every facet of the brain. But she also saw how the brain inevitably outwitted its investigators. A no-admittance organ, it would not submit to being measured and mapped and quantified like the other organs. The brain was always in charge but at the same time unable to conceive of itself.

Usually on Saturday mornings Cooper watches Evan while Jana does errands. It is the one time of the week when Jana does not worry about Evan. The more Evan can be around Cooper, the better. Cooper will teach him to be a kind man, a respectful man, a tranquil man. A man who can control himself. And if Evan is lucky, he will learn something about Cooper's talent for happiness.

Today, however, is the junket with Seretha. Evan and Seretha will go off together in pursuit of "fun." These junkets entail a drive, often to a mall; a luncheon, usually at some fast-food restaurant; and the purchase of the all-important toy (almost always a toy of the kind Jana hates). Innumerable times Jana has explained to Seretha that weapons of any kind are not allowed in her household, but Seretha does not listen, or does not hear, or forgets, or chooses to forget.

Thinking of these things, Jana realizes it's best if she leaves right away. She shouldn't be here when Seretha comes. Seretha will ask Cooper or Evan about the punishment he received for biting, and when she learns there wasn't one, she will gloat, feeling she is having an influence and casting a close-lipped squint-eyed smile at Jana.

Seretha radiates, with her large commanding body, a kind of moral authority that Jana feels lacking in. Perhaps it is only a matter of consistency. As hard as Jana tries not to be, she is inconsistent with Evan, emphasizing limits one moment, love the next, punishing hard for one violation, letting the next one go, a vacillation Seretha sees so clearly.

Jana kisses Evan. "Be a good boy. You know the rules. No, that's enough syrup. I love you, honey—don't ever forget that."

To Cooper she says, "I have to stop by the hospital briefly, but you'll be here when they get back?" She brushes his lips, feeling in them a slight preoccupation.

"I'll be here," he says. "Ain't goin' nowhere. Mitch is coming over. The Sidwell people want more detailed numbers and drawings, so he's going to help me out."

She shakes her head, sharing his disgust with this company that has been toying with him for so long, not saying for sure whether he has the job designing all the cabinetry for a new enclosed mall in the upscale Fairhaven district. She wonders if the other two carpenters who are bidding—carpenters who have become so sought after they've got multiple employees—are being asked for more numbers, too. She doubts it somehow. She thinks Cooper is being asked because Cooper is so obliging.

SHE HASN'T HAD a letter for a long time (five months? six?), but still, like clockwork, every four weeks she goes to check. She drives to a town twenty miles south of Bellingham, where she sits in the post office parking lot and watches strangers come and go, most of them rushing, arms laden with parcels and mail, or bending into the small hands of children. All so enviably normal looking, oblivious to a slight, dark-haired woman waiting in a car.

Once she gets out she is businesslike, heading speedily to the bank of post boxes inside, opening box 435, drawing out one long slim envelope addressed to Cadence Miller, the person Jana was before she fled north, changed her name, became a doctor.

A funny girl, Cady Miller was. Shy. Intense. A bit of a loner.

Back in the car Jana regards the letter, postmarked five weeks earlier. It is addressed in a hand she doesn't recognize as Varney's, and there is no return address. Who might it be that has addressed Varney's letter for him? Fingering it, she tries, as always, to picture him, though she knows that what she imagines is bound to be wrong. After sixteen years she has no idea how he would look. He turned thirty-one in August, which certainly makes him a full-grown man. But how he has aged, she hasn't a clue. She often looks at her male patients with an eye to guessing how Varney looks. Is he still as lean as he was at fifteen, still as surprised looking? He had always been one of those people with a look of perpetual surprise. Would his luminous, white-white skin have reddened and dulled? Would his hair still be as dark and slippery as it had been? Would that same cluster of light freckles still bridge his nose?

She stuffs the letter into her purse, refusing to let herself linger on these questions. She'll open the letters sometime, but not now. Now it's enough to get them, to know he's still alive and thinking of her.

SEVEN

Of course, it wasn't always love she felt for Varney. It's only time and memory that have polished it that way. There was rage, too. She was older than Varney, with all the trappings of power four years brought her, but what she didn't have was friends. There was nothing overtly wrong with her. She was a good-looking girl, enviably lean, a bit on the short side, with pale skin, and hair the variegated brown of lightly roasted coffee beans, but her looks were out of place in that warm climate, the golden state that prized sunny, bronze-limbed, honey-haired girls. Cady looked as if her ancestors had known stormy weather and hardship, and many generations later, the marks of that hardship had not entirely worn off. She was shy, a little too intense. She had a secretive look long before she had secrets.

Once, in early high school, she found herself with a friend, a new girl named Brianna, who some afternoons would come by to see Cady on her way home from gymnastics class. Brianna was a perky freckled girl with long sandy hair, which she kept fastened in a knot with colorful barrettes. When Brianna arrived at the Millers' house, Cady brought out Cokes, which she and Brianna drank in the shade of the umbrellaed table on the patio. Varney didn't sit with them, but he paraded by, pretending to have business that took him into the house and back out again with irritating frequency, or he stationed himself on the patio wall, playing the Casio keyboard he'd found in a dumpster. It had a few sticky keys, but Varney didn't care. With an uncanny ear for pitch and melody, he had taught himself to play. When Brianna was there, he would play his most impressive songs over and over, lusting for her attention, making a fool of himself until Cady told him to get lost.

Brianna stretched out on the lounge chair. Her legs, skinny and coltish from a distance, were muscular up close. Sweat curled the errant wisps around her hairline. She unfastened her barrette, sighing, always sighing with the unfastening, so her loose hair fell gratefully down over the chair back. She wasn't interested in Cady's collection of glass and porcelain figurines; Cady could feel the disinterest in Brianna's sighing. But Cady wasn't sure what else to show Brianna. The tiny tea set painted with Chinese characters? "We could watch TV?" Cady suggested, but at that hour nothing good was on.

"Mind if I take a shower?" Brianna always said after a while, as if she needed *something* to alleviate her boredom.

One day after a month of afternoon visits, Brianna stepped out of the shower to find Varney in the bathroom staring at her without apparent shame. Brianna dove for her towel and shrieked. "What's *wrong* with you? Get out of here." He turned slowly and dragged himself to the door.

Brianna never came back to the Millers' house. Cady went to Brianna's house once or twice but didn't feel welcome. Brianna had by now found a group of friends that didn't include Cady. Once, in the cafeteria, Cady sat near Brianna, wondering if they might be friends again. "He just stood there gawking. She knew and she didn't do *anything*," Cady heard Brianna tell her new friends in a loud voice clearly intended to be overheard. "They're *weirdos*."

After that, Cady hated Varney. He would ruin her life, she was sure of it. Rage jolted through her like a suddenly inflating parachute. It filled her up and gave her ideas. She wanted to poke Varney with pins, burn him all over with cigarettes so he'd be permanently maimed. *Punk, pervert, asshole.* She made him wait on her, bring her Cokes and strings of red licorice. At night she banished him to the floor. He coiled up his body, covered his face with his hands.

"Hit me. Hit me as hard as you want," he said. "No, really. Hit me." Every night for close to a week he said this.

"Okay," she finally said.

She flew at him with her fists. She pounded his back. She pulled his hair. She bit (yes, she now remembers, she *bit*) into the flesh of his shoulder, leaving marks that turned red, then purple. She remembers the pleasure of releasing the hardness inside her. She remembers the power. She knew it was flesh she was pounding, but with his face hidden, it did not seem like Varney. What she does not remember is sound, the sound of her palms and fists landing on clothing and flesh. The sound of his sobs. Her rage, the sucking silence of a storm's eye, deafened her to everything.

And then suddenly her skin recognized kindred skin. Or was it the tremors of his crying that stopped her? She pulled him from the floor and, arms circling his scant girth, she tried to unball him. Now she was the one who was sobbing. Inconsolable.

FROM THE END of the street, she sees Cooper's truck is gone, a fact that does not surprise her. What does surprise her is seeing Evan and Seretha sitting on the front stoop under Seretha's wide baby blue umbrella. Seretha's shoulders are hunched unhappily; Evan aims a bow and arrow into the grass. If Jana could backtrack, she would, but Seretha has already seen her.

"Hey!" Jana says as brightly as she can as she approaches under the canopy of Seretha's dark gaze.

"Look, Mom. Look what Gramma got me."

Evan lets his arrow go and it zips past her, landing silently in the muddy lawn and sending him into hearty laughter. Can he really be oblivious to her hatred of such toys, or does he merely feel protected in Seretha's presence?

"We've been here an hour," Seretha announces.

"Isn't it cool, Mom?"

Jana frowns. "Cooper is supposed to be here."

"Well, he isn't."

Seretha rises slowly, shuddering with the cold or the freight of her feeling. In one hand she holds two shopping bags, in the other a flat Tupperware container. Jana offers to relieve her of something, but the offer goes unacknowledged. Jana unlocks the door, and, dripping, they traipse into the dark kitchen, shedding jackets and umbrellas and bags and purses onto the catch-all kitchen table, an impressive carved oak piece that Cooper stripped and refinished. Evan relinquishes his jacket but clings to the bow, restringing another arrow.

"No!" Jana says sharply, then feels Seretha's look. "That's an outdoor toy."

"I'm going out." He races back through the front door without his jacket, and Jana, enervated by Seretha's annoyance, decides not to call him back.

"He might be in his shop," Jana suggests, flipping on lights and turning her attention to Cooper's absence.

"We looked there. Besides, his truck isn't here," Seretha points out. "I have something to give him."

Jana does not say, "Leave it here and I will give it to him," because she knows Seretha would accurately read that as an attempt to get rid of her. "I'm going to check in the shop, anyway," Jana says.

"Do what you want. I'll wait here."

Jana looks for the woodshop key on its hook by the back door but finds it missing. She considers the possibility that Cooper might be out there, hiding from Seretha. But where would his truck be? And hiding from Seretha is *her* behavior, not his.

Outside, the drizzling rain is soft; its drops bounce off her forearm and travel upward, resistant to the pull of gravity. She shouldn't be so hard on Seretha, who did a noble job bringing up Cooper alone, working as a nurse. And she and Seretha have had some good times. Not many, but a few. The most notable was the time they painted the kitchen together. It was Seretha's idea that they do it, and it took them all day. Seretha, who never wears trousers, appeared at the door in a pair of overalls, hair concealed under a bandana. She got right to work, first taping the woodwork, then covering the large spaces with a roller, and following that with expert brushwork. She was a meticulous worker with astonishing stamina. She hardly spoke but her silence was a comfortable one. Jana felt, for the first time ever, as if they were colleagues with a similar goal. They painted all day, from eight in the morning until dinnertime, listening to country music on the radio, taking only a brief lunch break, and when they were done, Seretha, who rarely drank, celebrated with a beer and got wonderfully silly telling stories about the superstitious rituals performed by the fisherman friends of her husband before they went out to sea. When things get tense now with Seretha, Jana tries to remind herself of that day. But there is something about Seretha's stern intelligence, her watchfulness, that brings out the worst in Jana. Cooper once joked that the two women were alike, but Jana found that neither true nor funny.

Cooper's woodshop is a converted garage equipped with all manner of tools. In some arenas Cooper is a slob—he leaves his clothes where he sheds them, routinely discards his wet towels in a heap on the bathroom floor, leaves a wake of dirty pans when he cooks—but in his woodshop he is fastidious. Two walls are devoted to hanging tools, carefully ordered on hooks, according to size and purpose. The third wall is lined with shelves for sandpaper, gloves, rope, wire, things that can't easily be hung. The fourth wall is the sliding garage door. At the center of the space is a long rectangular table, where he does most of his work. If you do the kind of carpentry work Cooper does, it's a pleasant place, Jana thinks, with warm tungsten lights, a portable radio, a coffeemaker, and enough windows to let in the sun when the sun is shining. Cooper takes pride in the place. Tools are never left out. Surfaces are always wiped clean of sawdust. And it is the only part of the house where Evan is forbidden to enter without permission.

The side door, where Jana enters now, is unlocked. The place feels inhabited. The light is on. A few sheets of mechanical drawings are spread on the table, along with a T square, a pencil, two mugs (Mitch must have come), each with a remaining inch or more of coffee. But there's no question that Cooper and Mitch are not here. She can see the entire room from where she stands, and it is definitely empty. It's odd for Cooper to leave things out like this, to not lock up.

She sees Evan running around the corner of the house toting bow and arrow.

"Hey!" she calls from the doorway. "Come in here, buddy."

He stops a few feet from her. His face is stippled with rain. "I'm not allowed in there. Only if Daddy says so."

She nods, struck by his law-abiding nature and unreasonably pleased by it. She wants to draw him close to her, hug him, ask him about Leo, but he is already edging away. She also wants to warn him she will be taking the bow and arrow when Seretha leaves, but it occurs to her that if she tells him this while Seretha is still here, Evan might report to Seretha and Seretha will intervene. Better to hold off.

"What?" he says, stopped by some noise she was barely aware of making. She is startled by the responsiveness in him, a hypervigilance she has thought of as her province alone.

"Nothing. Have you had lunch?"

"Are you going to take away my bow and arrow?" he says, his voice flat, the beloved bow clenched against his cheek just where his dimple would normally be.

She looks at him. "What do *you* think?"

"Gramma says it's a Native American study toy. It's *educational*."

She nods, watching him closely, still wondering about Leo. "We'll talk about it later. Come in—you're soaking."

"But if I come in, do I have to stop playing?" He doesn't move and stares skyward as if fixated on the pinnacle of an ascending thought or targeting a celestial body he hopes to shoot.

"A few more minutes out here," she says. "But you must come in when I call you, okay?"

This she insists on. Varney never came when he was called. He ignored their parents' commands as if he hadn't heard, or as if responsible to a higher authority he was under no obligation to explain. *They never made him.*

"Okay?" she says, her voice rising, along with a low hum, cued by Evan's silent resistance, and even by the noiseless pulse of the rain.

"Okay, okay."

She heads inside, hoping Seretha has made her way to the TV, which is usually where she ends up. Jana keeps her head down—a don't-interrupt-me habit formed long ago—and only looks up when she hears a strange scuttling. Seretha is sitting just where Jana left her, but retreating to the back of her chair and wearing a forced smile. She opens her Tupperware container.

"Would you like to try one of these Moon Dreams I made for Cooper? They're his favorite." She shoves the open Tupperware toward Jana.

Jana eyes the chocolate squares—then her unzipped purse on the other side of the table. "What are they?" she says, riveted by the small white triangle of Varney's envelope sprouting from the purse. The sound comes from a cold ball of nausea in her stomach. She swallows hard against its pounding.

"Chocolate brownies with marshmallows, peanuts, M&M's, and those little white chocolate morsels he likes so much."

"Oh," Jana says, eyes still stuck on the triangle of envelope.

"You've never made them for him?" Seretha says.

Jana shakes her head.

"I'm surprised. You'll have to start. Well, I'm having one." Seretha reaches in and selects a Moon Dream. She sniffs it and bites, eyes closed. A contented sigh, the sound of a slowly deflating tire, escapes from her. The loose skin under her eyes twitches.

"Help yourself. Unless you're watching your weight, that is."

Jana moves around to the side of the table with the Tupperware and the purse. She reaches for the purse first, shouldering it as nonchalantly as she can. Could she have left it unzipped, just as Cooper left his woodshop unlocked?

Seretha smiles in a way that Jana has trouble reading—two parts guilt, two parts chocolate contentment. Even if she was snooping—which clearly she was—what could she have learned? Beyond the name that is. And a name on its own means nothing. A name like Cadence Miller could belong to anyone.

Jana reaches for a Moon Dream because Seretha wants her to, but as soon as she has it in her hand, she realizes her mistake. A wave of nausea mounts.

"Excuse me," she says. By the time she reaches the bathroom, the wave of nausea has passed, but the sound pounds out its beat louder than ever. The Moon Dream oozes from her fist.

She throws the wad of chocolate into the toilet bowl where it thuds and splashes up water. She flushes and scours her face and hands.

JANA HAS SEEN Cooper drunk on occasion—high and happy, not stinking and lurching—but never in the middle of the day. Jana and Evan and Seretha have been playing cards on the living-room carpet for almost an hour—Go Fish, Slapjack, Crazy Eights—Evan sitting cross-legged, the bow stowed under one knee, Seretha sitting amid the folds of her brown wool skirt so she rises from the carpet like a stranded monument when Cooper stumbles through the door and stands in the lit kitchen blinking at them, oblivious to the raindrops swarming off his bright blue jacket and making rivulets on the floor.

"Hey, guys."

Jana drops her cards and goes to him quickly, seeing his unsteadiness, hearing the words lumber off his slowed and thickened tongue. She tugs him out of view. "Where *were* you?" she whispers.

"Is someone asleep? Why are we whispering?"

"I don't think Evan should see you drunk."

Cooper speaks slowly, loudly; his eyes aren't focusing on Jana. "I don't think Evan has to be ashamed of his dad. Anyway, I'm not drunk."

"Cooper. What *happened?*"

"I may not be a doctor or anything, but I'm pretty handy with a hammer."

She winces.

"Maybe my son can go and tell those Sidwell assholes how handy I am with a hammer."

"You didn't get the job?"

"Did I say that?"

Jana pulls Cooper's jacket off and watches him move into the living room, his body disassembling and reassembling with every step. It frightens her to see him this way, his gaze so unfocused, his control unnotched.

Seretha has moved from the floor and is scratching in her purse for something. Evan hurls his cards into the air so they flutter to the carpet.

"Hey, big boy," Cooper says, bending down to lift Evan, who leaps like a chimp into place at Cooper's waist. "You and Gramma have fun?"

"I made you some Moon Dreams," Seretha says.

"Look what she got me!" Evan points to the bow and arrow on the carpet.

"Cool." Cooper picks up one of the arrows and, face lifted to the ceiling, tries to balance it on his nose, where it teeters for a minute, then spirals to the floor. Evan hoots.

"Would anyone like coffee?" Jana says.

No one seems to hear her, so she sets about making the coffee anyway. So much depends on Cooper, she thinks, the man among them. Cooper is the caretaker. Before Cooper no one had ever protected her. There was the roof her parents gave her, a place to sleep, but under that roof no one but Varney truly paid attention to her.

She sets three mugs of coffee on the table. She would bring it to the living room, but Cooper is testing his strength there, throwing Evan almost to the ceiling and catching him as he used to when Evan was a tiny baby. Why do men do that with babies? To prepare them for danger? To prove their reliability as fathers? Is there some death wish involved? It scared Jana when Evan was little, but it scares her even more now. Seretha laughs. Evan laughs. Cooper laughs. Jana looks away. There are certain emergencies she is powerless to avert.

"Coffee's ready," she announces.

Cooper is putting Evan down and in doing so he spots Evan's bow. "This bow is cool. Show me how it works."

"Come on, Dad. It's an outdoor toy."

Evan, as he leads his father outside, glances at Jana with the defiant look of a boy changing alliances. Jana observes the rush of their energy, the boil of their blood, their eagerness to push outside, grabbing as they go two Moon Dreams each, the boy in both of them released and condoned.

The only ugly fight she and Cooper have ever had was about guns. Cooper's father was a fisherman and a hunter. He was a man who owned guns, who used guns, who cherished and understood them. Shortly after Jana became pregnant, she found a gun in Cooper's bedside table. It was small and silver with a black handle, not the fiercest-looking of weapons, but the sight of it paralyzed her. She could feel the perilous bite of adrenaline filling her blood. For a moment she lost her voice, and when she found it again, she was yelling. "I'm protecting you and the baby," Cooper told her calmly. But her fierceness eroded him. "I'm not a criminal," he finally shouted back at her. And it was true—he was the gentlest person she knew, and this hunk of metal wouldn't change that. Guns weren't the point, or they were only a small part of the point. Still, she couldn't stand the sight of it—the fatuous way it lay in Cooper's palm and the way he drew one finger down its ridged barrel, the same finger he had used to stroke her face. She couldn't stand the claim this gun, an inheritance from his father, had on him. Cooper expected things from this gun, it seemed to her. Tired from her explosion, she tried to explain to him how the caustic look of the metal invaded her psyche, how she shrank from it as she would from lead or asbestos, how it threatened to poison their unborn child. Maybe it had nothing to do with anything, as Cooper said, but still she begged him to get rid of it, to get it out of their house at the very least. And reluctantly, holding back a smidgen of his sweetness, he promised.

Jana and Seretha stand at the living-room window, watching Evan and Cooper shoot the bow and arrow in the backyard. It's a small yard with a slight slope to it, a single gnarled apple tree, and a high hedge for privacy. Since the summer no one but Evan has spent much time out there, and it has turned muddy and forlorn, out of keeping with the comfortable, well-tended interior of the house. Cooper has tacked the rain-bedraggled paper target to the trunk of the apple tree. He lets Evan show him how to string the bow, but again and again— intention or drunkenness, Jana can't tell—he botches the arrow's release, and it sails into the mud behind the apple tree, prompting uproarious laughter from Evan. "No, Dad!" he corrects Cooper. "Not like *that!*" It would be touching—boy instructing clumsy dad—but for the fact that the dad is drunk and the object of the lesson is shooting.

Jana and Seretha don't speak. Jana cannot tell if their silence bears only its usual weight or if there is more in it today. Is Seretha pondering how Jana came by a letter addressed to Cadence Miller? Or is she thinking of what might have motivated her son to arrive home drunk at three on a Saturday afternoon? Jana can only speculate, as she knows she won't be privy to Seretha's thoughts.

"Well, I guess I'll be going," Seretha says.

"Thanks for the Moon Beams."

"Dreams."

"Moon Dreams."

"You may not appreciate them, but the boys do."

Jana nods. "Yes, they do." She wonders if she will think of Evan as a boy long after he has passed into manhood.

Jana brings Seretha her umbrella and coat. Seretha ties a

navy kerchief over her thinning hair. She dyes it a dark red, but with each washing the underlying gray pushes to the surface, changing it to the color of rusty nails. As Jana helps Seretha with her coat, it occurs to her that she should try to think of Seretha the way she thinks of her patients. She is immune to her patients' oddities, their orneriness, their criticisms. She is able to stay composed and appreciative with them, or at least put up a show of being appreciative.

"I'm fine," Seretha says. "You don't need to walk me to the car." At the bottom of the front steps, she stops. "Trust him. Don't take away his manhood. He'll get the job."

Jana nods, expecting Seretha will move along to her car, but she doesn't. She lingers, thinking of something, trying to get it into words. From Jana's top-step perspective, Seretha looks diminished and bent.

"You know that Cooper and I haven't always lived on Easy Street. You have to excuse him sometimes."

"Oh, yes," says Jana. "I do." How many times has Seretha said these exact words, how she and Cooper have been the victims of her husband's early demise. She wonders if Seretha believes that each time she says this, Jana is hearing it for the first time.

"Some people, if they knew what it was like to be alone in the world, to have only yourself to rely on, they'd be different, wouldn't they?" says Seretha.

"Yes," Jana says. "They would."

She hears the *pock* of the arrow releasing in the backyard, the spray of laughter from Cooper and Evan as it lands. "Bingo!" Cooper calls.

"Maybe you know about things like that, maybe you don't. How would I know? You never talk." Seretha pauses as if waiting for Jana to divulge things right now.

Jana shrugs.

Seretha lays her broad bony hand on the wrought iron rail as if she intends to remount the steps and come back inside. "I know you lost your parents," Seretha concedes. "Cooper has told me many times how he wishes he'd met your parents before their car accident. It was very sad, I'm sure. But you were grown up by then."

"Nineteen."

"Not like Cooper, you see, who was only five. Younger than Evan is now. Now *that's* a tragedy." She nods at the ground like a professor who has just drawn a very important distinction and, before continuing, wants to allow time for it to be fully appreciated.

"Yes, it is," Jana says.

"Too young to know his father. Too young to understand anything like death. At least you were on your own. At least you knew your parents..."

"Yes," Jana keeps saying, bringing out her best sympathetic smile.

COOPER FALLS ASLEEP on Evan's bed while he's supposed to be reading. Jana hears his snoring from the kitchen and goes in to find them both snuggled on the bottom tier, Evan in his underpants, Cooper fully clothed but for his shoes. The book, *The Billy Goats Gruff,* lies open on Cooper's chest, taking measure of the rise and fall of his breathing. A copse of beard hairs sway and shiver under the torrent of his outgoing breath. Evan sleeps on his side, the crown of his head pressed against the sidewall of Cooper's chest. Cooper's hand rests on Evan's jutting pelvic bone.

She tugs the bow and arrow out from under Evan's shoulder. He sleeps on. She takes them into the kitchen and wastes no time cracking them in half and stuffing them into the trash. The arrow is wooden and it cracks easily, but the bow is a sturdy plastic and requires more effort. *I told you I would,* she will tell Evan the next morning. *It's what I always do. You should expect it by now.*

She goes to bed alone, missing the comfort of Cooper's body, though tonight Cooper's presence might not have brought comfort. Still, she wants it, wants the forgetfulness of sex. It is a good proud history, their sex. She will always be grateful for the release Cooper showed her the first time they'd been able to get free of Seretha's watchful eye. Seretha had always been there, it seemed, invited or not, saying one more thing and then again one more thing until all their time was used up and Jana was late for work or bed or wherever. But the time came— oh, how scared Jana was, almost thirty and nothing in her past she could call desire, no liquid insides, no drive toward someone else's skin, only a feeling of needing to keep others from touching her. Then with Cooper something changed. Something in his tranquil body, his gentleness, the beard and the smile that crinkled his face, his apparent purity or simplicity, so that suddenly she was drawn to this laborer, this man who worked with his hands, and for days it seemed, while she was suturing wounds, reading EKGs, examining lesions, writing prescriptions, she could think of nothing but the woody smell of his skin and the way he glanced at her tentatively, askingly, out of the corner of his eye, so when that first time, still terrified, she let him unbutton her shirt—a blue one, she remembers, with a small Betadine stain, as she had come to him from work—and he cupped her breasts and used his thumbs to play with her nipples, and later buried his bearded face exultantly in her moisture, she trusted him and knew he would teach her things she did not know.

At three or four or five in the morning Cooper crawls into bed beside her. She awakens from a light sleep, stays still, fully present for once. "I'm sorry," he whispers. "We got pissed at those Sidwell jerks, and we got on a roll. We thought we might sack the whole thing. I'm an asshole. I'm sorry." He moves up behind her, slipping his hand between her legs, rubbing her to wetness before sliding inside and, breath rasping in her ear, pumping slowly, deep, so in her drowsiness she pictures him pushing way up past her cervix, her stomach, her lungs, straight to her sleeping heart.

On the cusp of sleep a memory fills her—of the excursions she and Cooper used to take when he still had his fishing boat. They would motor out past Lummi Island into the fish-rich Strait of San Juan de Fuca. She would hold a line to be game, but mostly she watched him. His body balanced as perfectly as a gyroscope as he hopped around the boat, setting up lines, reeling in fish, removing them from hooks, starting and stopping the motor to get a better angle on things. The son of a fisherman, he took fishing seriously, almost reverently, even though he only did it for sport. He would hold his face up into the wind, sniffing, then gaze hard at the water, his body a highly sensitized instrument, a weather vane, a servant of the elements.

Around them, just water. A few passing boats. The islands floating in the distance, purple or blue, seemingly uninhabited, like mirages you could stick your hand through. A briny, fishy salty smell oscillating around them. The sound of the water slapping the sides of the boat. The gulls screeching in their perennial search for food. Sometimes it brought to mind the harbor where her mother's shop had been. But how tame that harbor was compared to this experience of being cut loose from land. Here they were alone and at the mercy of wind and weather and currents. It was peaceful here—but ominously so.

They didn't talk much. Cooper was filled up with messages from the sea, with sensing peregrinations of fish, and she thought conversation would interfere. She envied his ability to lay his mental preoccupations aside and occupy the physical world so completely. She supposed that was what happened to her in ER, but it was a skill she wished she could take outside the hospital.

One day the motor broke down and they drifted without power under a glowering sky. Cooper went to work tinkering, tightening and loosening screws, checking gas and oil, verifying all the important connections. After a time—half an hour? forty-five minutes?—when he seemed to be having no luck and a light drizzle was thickening to rain, he stopped his tinkering. Overheated, he sloughed his windbreaker and put his hands on his bait-streaked thighs. He looked up at clouds moving pell-mell overhead, and he squinted as if he could see portents on the other side of them. His silence scared her. "My dad died out here," he said. "Never even had a chance to get his nets." Cooper went back to work. He never started the inboard motor that day, and he had to attach a small outboard. They motored ashore in a drenching, unfriendly rain.

From Cooper she understands how her mind has been warped. Everywhere she goes, she sees disease; she sees the shapes and colors and rhythms of the human body in distress. The pulsing wind makes her think of gasping lungs. In the fibrillating rain she hears the damaged human heart. The smoke-spewing lumber mills downtown suggest projectile vomiting. She has been trained in the lexicon of pathology, and it permeates her vision. The jaundiced skies. The inflamed sunsets. The tumorous seas. She has no other way of seeing and thinking. She has chosen biology, though still she chafes against it.

EIGHT

Jana and Evan walk into a house smelling lusciously of tomato, oregano, basil, garlic, and melting cheese. A lasagna bakes in the oven. Cuban music, dancing music, fills the whole house. Cooper hurries to the living room to turn it down.

"I got it. I got it. I got it." He spins her around in one of those dance moves she never learned to do. As well as she can, she follows, laughing, misstepping. Evan hops around them. She is trying to absorb it all—Cooper's new job, his ebullience, the fact that he's shaved his beard.

"Daddy, you look *weird*."

He does look weird, she thinks. His chin is white, his upper lip chafed red and swollen. The gentle woodsman in him is gone. He looks thinner without the beard, more angular and determined. But his dimples are still there. And yes, she's happy for him. Of course, she can love him with or without facial hair; still, if she'd been asked, she wouldn't have recommended the shaving.

"*Totally* weird," says Evan. "You look like a drowned rat."

"A rich rat, no doubt," he says. "Your daddy's in Fat City."

"What's Fat City?"

"Easy Street."

"What's Easy Street?"

He bends over to Evan and whispers loudly in his ear. "Moola, my boy. Money."

"Goodie! Can you buy me a remote-control car?"

"Whatever you want, because I am now Daddy Big Bucks," he says, ignoring Jana's look. She doesn't like to talk about money, especially around Evan. She doesn't want to foster too great an interest in it.

Cooper sits at the head of the table and serves dinner with fanfare, a red polka-dot bow tie clipped to his navy blue T-shirt. "What can I help you to, Dr. Thomas? And you, Mr. Johansen?" he asks, preparing to dish out food. He has laid out fancy silverware and the special linen napkins they rarely use. He has put Evan's milk in a champagne flute. He leans across the table to Jana with his wine-filled glass held high.

"To the beginning of a new era."

She raises her glass. "I guess I can quit my job, then," she says.

He pretends to panic; they both know she won't quit, she who takes on extra shifts, she who can't bear the formlessness of unbooked hours.

Jana and Evan eat, but Cooper sits for a while, admiring them, admiring the meal, admiring, Jana thinks, the life he has created.

"See, I'm not so passive after all."

She looks at him. *Passive?* She supposes he has been a bit passive (if he hadn't been passive, he wouldn't have been un-married until close to age forty), but she has not thought of him that way.

"What's *passive?*" Evan asks, watching his father closely, a strand of hair, still sinuous with curl, rappelling down his forehead.

"Sitting back and doing nothing," Cooper says. "Waiting for things to happen."

Jana has thought of him as gentle and patient, not passive. "Am I passive?" asks Evan.

"Heck no," Cooper says. He laughs, his cheeks curving up to roundness again, bringing on the soft look of him she loves.

"You were fine the way you were, you know," Jana says.

Cooper squints. "You don't want me to have the Sidwell job?"

Is this what she thinks deep down? Does she not wish him the success this highly visible job could bring? His squint and stillness, as he awaits her response, is almost ophidian, the look of a rattler or a cobra gauging whether it is most advisable to attack or to retreat. Even Evan, quietly watching his dad, seems to sense the altered atmosphere.

"I didn't say that," she says carefully. "I just meant there was nothing wrong with you then. You're fine now, too."

"You preferred me as a wimp, though." He's smiling at her and she cannot read him. The grammar of his lips is different. Once framed by hair, they now move alone, free and stark. She shakes her head.

He nods. "I think you liked me better then."

AT SNOQUOLICUM HARBOR the wind has come in like a rowdy guest. It lashes the yachts so they rock uneasily in their slips, their stays chiming against the masts. Bits of litter eddy across the asphalt paths. Out on the bay, whitecaps are visible now where the wind has spooned up the blue water and revealed a dark underbelly.

Cooper, Jana, and Evan are well bundled in thick fleece and wool. Jana wears dark glasses to shield her eyes from wind and glare ("Mommy, the movie star," Cooper jokes), but Cooper and Evan prefer to squint. Evan rides his bike. Once a month or so they come down here to the harbor together, even in winter, when only the fishermen are out. They come down here for the exhilaration, to see the water up close, to smell the salt and fish, to see how far the wind will carry their spit. They come down here to see the memorial to the fishermen lost at sea and to point to Cooper's father's name inscribed there: AUGUSTUS JOHANSEN, 1932–1963.

Evan balances on his bike seat, his toes touching the ground precariously. He closes his eyes and uses his finger to trace the engraved letters. "I bet a shark ate him," he says.

"Maybe," Cooper says. "No one knows."

Jana follows the voyage of Cooper's eyes as they stray from the monument and rove over the bay, along the spit of mainland, to Lummi Island, then off into the distance to Orcas Island and beyond. Eyes still searching, despite what the mind knows—that certain questions have no answers.

"Or a whale," says Evan. "A great white. They're the ones that eat people. Right, Dad?"

But Cooper doesn't hear, his mind still dredging Bellingham Bay, the Strait of San Juan de Fuca.

"I thought it was great white *sharks*," says Jana.

"I asked *Dad*." Evan scowls at her.

She walks ahead of them, wind whipping her ears, competing with her ears' own noises. "Shall we say a prayer for Granddaddy?" Cooper says behind her.

Evan rarely asks about Jana's mother and father, though he knows that they're dead. Once, about a year ago, she told him they were cremated after their car accident, and for the next three nights, he dreamed he was on fire. To her relief, he hasn't mentioned them since.

After walking twenty yards or so, she turns. Evan and Cooper have headed off on another branch of the path, Evan riding his bike, Cooper jogging along beside. They both are filled with inordinate amounts of energy today, Evan because he is meeting his schoolmate Max, who will come here with his mother, Robin, and Cooper because he is still so pleased to have gotten the Sidwell job. He is certain that the tide of his fate is changing. He has said things in his glee of the past few days that have told her more than she's ever known about him, about the depth of his feeling of ill-fatedness and inadequacy. When they met, they told each other their union would change their lives, and it has, but not in ways they'd imagined. They've found comfort in one another, but Jana's fears have not been dispelled, and Cooper's confidence has not been boosted. Perhaps, with this job, he will find the confidence and good luck she hasn't provided. She understands an unarticulated truth: They have given up on each other in little ways, silently. They have made do with being let down.

She thinks of Cooper's new job, of what it means for them both. His mandate is to build all the cabinetry and woodwork in the conversion of an old industrial building into commercial space in the upscale shopping district of Fairhaven. It is a job that will get Cooper noticed, and its success could bring lots more business. She really is happy for him, but worried, too. Already the job is changing him. He drives himself all day, thrashes at night. The tranquility that drew her, that quieted her, too, has been interrupted.

She watches Cooper and Evan negotiate the curve, laughing at something. Evan lifts one hand from the handlebars and raises it for a wobbly high five. From a distance they still hold a reassuring resemblance to one another with their round cheeks and fair hair. She watches them shrink as they cross to the other side of the jetty to examine the commercial fishing boats, the heavily rigged purse seiners that, in contrast to the yachts, look as if they've been around for centuries. Nets, their phosphorescent green glowing and winking even under the sun, are laid to dry, fathom upon fathom. Fishermen scroll through the mesh, looking for holes to repair.

She sees in the distance the man she fell in love with: a quiet man who watches more than he participates, who seems unaffected by the world's fickleness. Up close it's hard to see that man anymore. *It's good for Evan and Cooper to be together,* she thinks. Still, the farther into the distance they recede, the more insubstantial she feels. She is protected by the minutia of domestic life and the clamor of child rearing, and when her boys stray from her, as now, she feels at once empty and exposed, on the edge of some precipice.

Her eyes, dried by the wind, click with her blinking. In the distance the land masses, so easily differentiated at dawn and dusk, have bled together as they always do at the sun's zenith. Sometimes seeing the landscape change as it does so regularly in the course of a single day makes her think perhaps there really are a bunch of wrangling gods out there—ocean gods and island gods and gods of rain and sun—and the fracas of the weather is, just as ancient civilizations believed, an expression of their conflict. She wishes she had never agreed to this rendezvous with Robin. She has mostly managed to steer clear of complicated relations with women (most of the few play dates Evan has had were arranged and facilitated by Mrs. Stubbs, so Jana has not had extensive contact with other mothers), but something about Robin is inviting. She feels coaxed by a kind of defiant empathy she has found in Robin, a sense that Robin wants to build an alliance among skeptics. But it occurs to her that just because Robin rolls her eyes in a certain way does not necessarily mean she is a skeptic. And even if she is a skeptic, it doesn't mean she might not be a prober, one of those women who confesses secret crushes, eating binges, masturbating practices, and wants you to do the same.

She leaves the walkway by the boat slips, cutting across a stretch of green grass that leads to the bay's edge. The noise crops up now, a quiet throbbing just a halftone below the wind. As if summoned, Robin strides across the lawn, trailing Max, who is also on a bike, as planned. A red balloon, tied to his handlebars and punched by the wind, strains against its tether.

Robin mouths something—a greeting?—as she approaches, but the words dissolve in the wind. A short person solidly fixed to the earth with resolute, muscular legs, she is dressed in layer after layer of color—a purple and red scarf, a red hat, a bright blue fleece vest, tight red jeans, a hip-length black corduroy jacket. Her expressive lips are covered with the same bright red color she wore when Jana first met her.

Jana isn't quite sure what to make of Robin's colorful attire, her outsize greeting (the hug, the kiss on the cheek). She isn't sure what conversation should follow—she is out of practice with these things; she was never *in* practice—so instead she makes much of summoning Evan and Cooper, raising both arms high over her head.

"Mom. Mom, show her," says Max.

Robin holds up a wrapped kite. She shrugs. "We brought it just in case."

In case of what? Jana wonders. *In case the kids don't get along? In case conversation fails them all?* The boys greet each other with hoots. They straddle their bikes. "Fadata, fadata, fadata," they say, lobbing the greeting back and forth.

"What you say?" Cooper asks them, codgering up his face.

"It's something they're reading in school," Robin says. "Or something being read to them. That's as much as I know." She shrugs. "You know—six-year-old secrets."

Max is a stocky, black-haired boy with lips almost as thick and red as his mother's. And like his mother, he exudes a feisty good nature. When Cooper and Robin and Max have been

introduced, the boys swerve off on their bikes, Cooper loping behind. Behind him, the two women saunter into a sudden bubble
of fishiness brought in by a gust of wind. Robin makes what is
quickly becoming to Jana a trademark face with her labile lips re-
coiling and her eyebrows falling to half-mast. But while her face
is reacting to the fishy smells, her mouth motors on.

"See the thing with Max is—," she says.

Jana wonders if she's missed something because of the
sound in her head, sustained as it is, making an augmented second with the haggling wind.

"Al, my husband—who is gone all the time; that's why he's
not here now—he says Max is fine; he's just strutting his stuff.
You know, learning to be the proverbial rooster, the kingpin,
the alpha male—but Miss Tencil, poor sweet Miss Tencil, I
know she is going out of her mind. She won't say so, but I'm absolutely positive she wants to chain him to a desk or sedate him.
She's good about it—you know, so soft-spoken and understanding—but I know deep down she thinks he's a lunatic. And then
I go in there with my big mouth and do I help things? I can't
keep my mouth shut and Rita Tencil thinks not only is the son
a maniac, but the mother is, too. Sorry, I know I'm going on.
Now you also think I'm a maniac. Which I certainly may be."

Jana laughs.

Robin looks pleased. "God, I love you already. Where have
you been all my life? I'm amazed we've never met before.
Bellingham being the booming metropolis it is. How long did
you say you'd been here?"

"Six years," Jana says. "Since I finished my residency in
Portland. Cooper has lived here most of his life."

"We've only been here two years. Newcomers still, I guess. I
like it, I think, though the hippie and outdoorsy quotients are a
bit high for me. And I could do without those Georgia Pacific

smells. Some days it smells like a goddamn cat box. Everything here is odoriferous—a word I never used until I moved here. Have you ever noticed that? Everything smells—the fish, the lumber mill, the saltwater. Anyway, it's nice to be around people who're thinking about more than what peak they're going to climb next. I might be wrong about you, but I get the sense that's not your major concern. I'm from New York; we don't think about those things in New York. The only thing we climb is the stairs to our apartments. I'm sorry, I'm talking too much—the only quality I have that equipped me to be an attorney."

A cloud has moved in over the sun. Across the park the boys are bicycling at top speed, standing on their pedals, leaning into the wind. Cooper has stopped jogging behind them. Jana isn't sure whether she wants the boys back here or not. There's something exhilarating about Robin's candid rush of words, her irreverence. But she wonders if, lurking in the future, there isn't too much expected of Jana herself?

"So I have to admit I admire you for working," Robin says. "I tried working again when Max was a year or so, but I guess I'm just too lazy to be a mom and a worker both. Too much hurrying here and there. But I'm sure you're good at it—you've got that lean, hungry-woman look. You can probably hurry without letting it get to you. Me, all I really wanna do is sit around and talk about my anxieties and laugh."

She does a hip-stirring dance move and belts out a line of "Girls Just Wanna Have Fun." Jana smiles. So far she has hardly said a word. Maybe she won't have to say much. Her system settles, and as if her metabolism is conducting the weather, the cloud passes on.

The boys return with sticks. "Where did they find sticks around here?" she asks Cooper, who has now joined them, too.

"You know about stick magic, don't you?" Robin says. "Where

there's a boy, a stick magically appears. Al and I are always want-ing to get Max outside, you know. I mean, that's why we moved up here to the Northwest, to be all wholesome and outdoorsy. So as soon as you get the boy outside, you get the rocks and the sticks, the hurling and poking and swatting, and it's pretty much all-out war. Wholesome? I'll say." She shakes her head.

Jana laughs. She feels a distinct pleasure in hearing Robin speak her mind. Not that Jana could be that way, or would want to be, but she likes thinking how it would feel to look at things head-on as Robin does.

The boys have dropped their bikes and begun to fence with their sticks.

"Cooper," Jana says, aware of the tremor in her own voice. She smiles at Robin. "We kind of have a rule about sticks. Well, about weapons—you know?"

"Oh, that. I just think that boys and men have been *stick-ing* each other since cavemen days, and it isn't going to change. Who am I to interfere with history like that? But if it makes you feel uncomfortable, let's stop them."

Sticks confiscated, the boys spit downwind; the sluglike wads splat heavily onto the pavement, and the boys laugh each time. Max is a robust boy with an energy that seems more reg-ular than Evan's, which has a tendency to come and go in manic spurts, but mostly Max and Evan seem like twins in the way they take to each activity with matched eagerness and mis-chievous intensity. The grown-ups watch, shrugging, exchang-ing hopeless smiles that seem to conclude: At least disgusting isn't dangerous.

The boys move out ahead. When they are thirty or forty feet away, the swashbuckling wind obscures their thin voices, but even without the benefit of sound, Jana can tell the tide has turned between them. She sees how Evan's eyes shrink, his face pinches, his entire body spirals to a sharp point. Max's face, too, is undergoing changes, but with its full cheeks and lush lips it does not look like a likely conduit of evil. She sees these things, but she has missed what went before. Who slighted whom? And how?

"Did you see what happened?" she asks Cooper and Robin. They look back at her blank-faced. It is always like this—she is always the first to notice. Every nerve in her body keeps a vigil and knows the moment a conflict erupts. She follows its movement, knows its habits through and through—how conflict can grow in a sudden bold conflagration; other times it is stealthy, wily, slow-growing

Jana jogs ahead to the kids.

"That's cheating!" Evan is yelling. "You're a cheater!" He lunges at Max, prepared to wallop.

Max, Evan, and Jana take off at the same moment, as if snared by the same burst of adrenaline. Max in the lead, followed by Evan, followed by Jana. The boys are young and sprint fast, but Jana is an experienced runner and overtakes Evan easily, capturing one of his shoulders, then both, and pressing him to stillness.

"No," she says. "Stop now. Right now."

Evan hunches over, bringing his crossed arms over his face, splaying his hands over his ears.

"Do you understand me?" she demands. "You're going to stop right *now*. Do you understand? You may *not* hit other kids."

Evan crouches lower and lower, trying to slip from her grasp, so now she holds him only by the elbow and he tugs hard. Max has doubled back. Jana feels him hovering nearby but cannot see him. All she sees is Evan's contorted body in the throes of its anger and hers, all of it limned by gray and accompanied by the rush of the wind.

"Do you understand?" All the unanswerable questions wail through her jawbone.

"Ow! Ow! You're hurting me."

"What the heck is happening?" Cooper says, coming up next to her, a shadow moving in. "Geez, Jana, let him go."

But she does not let go until Cooper moves in himself and draws Evan away by unpeeling the grip of her hand, finger by finger like stale fruit rind. She stands apart from the others blinking, breathing heavily, her cerebrospinal fluids sloshing. Gradually her vision expands again to include more than Evan. She has made a fool of herself.

"What *happened?*" Cooper says again. "Evan? Jana?"

"They fought," she says. "They were fighting." She could say this over and over and no one would understand the world she spies in a small speck of rage.

A shudder passes through Cooper. It's something no one else but she can see. It reveals itself in a flickering of his lids, a lip lifted slightly. Petit, petit mal.

"I missed it completely," Robin says. "I guess I was spacing." She mugs, urging levity. "But they're over it now."

Jana looks at the boys, who have fallen to the grass and are rolling back and forth, bumping into each other and roaring with laughter, willing forgetfulness. Evan forgets everything, easily oblivious, but she remembers it all. Tabulating, calculating, refiguring, keeping perfect track.

Now, as she watches the boys frolic, remorse parades in. She mustn't be so hard on Evan—he's still a little boy; a normal, high-energy boy. She should not be riding him so much, or raising her voice so readily. If there were no other adults present now, she would fall to her knees and pull him toward her, silently begging forgiveness.

———

THEY'RE BACK at the house. Cooper has gone to the Sidwell building to take measurements. Jana and Robin drink milky Chai tea in the kitchen while the boys play upstairs in Evan's room. Jana hadn't meant to prolong the visit this way, but there seemed to be no natural way to conclude things, and so they are all here. Robin has admired the house—its fine cabinetry and skylights, its picture windows with views of the bay. Jana tells the saga of Cooper remodeling what was once a wreck of a house, room by room. "Yes, it is beautiful," she concedes, but she feels impervious.

"You hear that?" Robin says.

Jana listens. From the bedroom come whoops, simulated car crash noises, the sounds that so easily become white noise in the life of the mother of a son.

"You ever tried to make that sound?" Robin asks. "That vroom-vroom sound? It's impossible. My glottal equipment won't do it. Vr—vr—See, it gets stuck. I can't get the right implosion. I'm sure it's hardwired in boys."

Robin closes her eyes and, holding her tea mug with two hands, sniffs deeply of its fragrance. Her lipstick has faded so the natural color of her mouth, a deep dark pink, has asserted itself; it occurs to Jana that Robin's lips, the place where she talks and tastes and kisses, are central to her personality.

Rain has begun to drum the roof. The wind smears it over the windows so the outside blurs.

"I guess a full day of sun was too much to ask for this time of year," Robin says. "I have to confess, I'm no sun worshiper, but every once in a while I miss *light*."

Jana nods. "You get used to the rain, I think."

"But how long does it take?"

"Some people I work with use UV lamps. They say it helps."

"Yeah, I survive. It's not like I'm a stranger to weather.

There's pretty hefty weather back in New York. Where're you from?"

"Oh, around. Everywhere, you know. The Midwest mostly."

"Yeah, I know those childhoods. New school every year. Nowhere to call home. But where were you *born?*"

"Ohio," Jana blurts. She isn't sure why, when to Cooper she has always said Illinois, but hearing the word *Ohio*, she thinks it sounds like a balanced place, with those *o*s on each end.

"That explains your calm. See, I was born in New York, where everyone's crazy and hyper to begin with. I think it sinks into a person—stuff about the place you were born. Whether you stay there or not."

They are silent as they drink their tea and listen to the rain pounding the roof. It's falling at a rate faster than Jana likes. She likes languorous rain, not this urgent soaking variety, which feels too insistent and proximate, as if it is trying to enter her skin. She thinks of Ohio, industrial and flat, and tries to imagine what personality traits it would impart to a person.

"I would go crazy in ER," says Robin. "I honestly don't think I could handle it. All that pandemonium and blood. You've obviously got the temperament for it. You're tougher than I am and a lot calmer. I'm sure I would take it home with me and worry about everyone and never let Max or Al leave the house. I would just feel that everyone was so frangible."

Jana frowns. "'Frangible?'"

"Oh, sorry. You know, breakable. Stop me when I do that. I hate being that way. Do you know, I became an attorney for the stupidest reason. People said I was good with words, and I do love words, but it turns out being a lawyer has nothing to do with words. Oh, of course on the surface it does, obviously, but the words are just a cover. If you took the words away, attorneys would just do what they'd probably feel more comfortable doing, anyway—they'd duke it out with sticks. So now, instead of being an attorney myself, I'm probably raising one, god forbid. Hah. So how do you deal with the ER thing?"

"Mostly I leave it at work," Jana says. "I've gotten good at compartmentalizing."

It helps that her own body has always been so strong. Except for her ears, her body has come through for her. The worrisome *frangible* parts—if that is the word—are more hidden.

"I feel guilty. What am I doing staying at home when all I've got is one kid?"

"Oh, don't feel guilty," Jana says. "That's the perfect place to be. I would quit in a minute if we didn't need the income."

And if idleness didn't drive her crazy. The four months after Evan was born, she did not work—she was home with Evan all the time and nearly lost her mind. She remembers taking long walks, Evan, in his black skullcap, bundled to her like a little barnacle, humoring her with grunts while she talked. She told him everything, all about Varney and her parents and California. He was only a baby and didn't understand a thing, but she knew there would come a time when he *would* understand and she would have to stop talking. Now she could never remain home day after day in a silent house with only herself and Evan.

Robin keeps talking, and Jana nods her on absently with no idea what she's confirming.

"If I go back to work, I think I'll find something else to do— something more humane. Every once in a while I think about practicing law again. Al talks sometimes about wanting to go to California. Can you imagine? California has got to be crime central. I mean criminals are downright *original* with their crimes down there. I wonder what it is about that state that makes it a magnet for mass murderers and drive-by shooters and rapists and god knows what all. Probably all the sun and smog and promise of riches. It gets to people, I think. It's not normal."

Abruptly Jana gets up and empties the dregs of her tea into

the sink. She tunes in on the extreme quiet coming from Evan's room.

"Evan?" she calls, going to the kitchen door. No answer. Upstairs she pushes open the door to Evan's room. The room is a pigpen, but a quiet empty one. She checks the master bedroom, the den, both bathrooms. All empty.

"I can't find them," she announces to Robin.

Robin smirks. "I bet they're hiding." She sighs. "I suppose we should find them, but it's been so nice *without* them for a while. This is the first real adult conversation I've had in *ages*." She rises and takes her mug to the sink.

"Outside?" Robin suggests. "Would they go outside in rain like this?"

"They could be in Cooper's shop. They're not supposed to be, but who knows."

The shop key is missing. The two women run through the rain, taking shelter under the woodshop's eaves. They peer through the windows; the inside, unlit, is too dark to see. But they hear something, Spider meowing loudly, clearly unhappy.

Jana pushes open the door and flicks on the light. The boys, standing at the worktable in the center of the room, turn quickly, their faces bearing twin expressions of alarm. Max is holding Spider firmly down on the table; Evan grips one of Jana's pink plastic Lady Bic razors. Several used razors lie strewn across the table.

Most of the hair on Spider's back and sides has been shorn. The skin beneath is thin and gray, and in certain places, tufts of black hair remain where the shaving was slowgoing. The new shape of the cat's body makes him almost sinister-looking, long and lean and hairless in the middle, with fur remaining on his head and legs and tail, like some punk poodle.

Everyone is silent except for Spider, who, sensing help is at hand, meows louder than ever. Jana breathes deeply. She notices a few wisps of blood striping Spider's belly. But the sight of Spider, odd as he is, is nothing compared to the sound of him. His usually reedy meow has become a full-throated wail that gutters at the back of his throat and then breaks into the air as protest. It is worse than the wail of research rabbits Jana used to hear in medical school. Jana's own sound immediately kicks up in duet, borrowing Spider's volume and intonation and the forfeit to despair.

"Evan Sibley Johansen," Jana manages to say out of the cacophony in her head.

Evan lowers his razor. His hand is docile, but his eyes are not. Max releases his hold on Spider, who leaps from the table and races to the door, scratching fiercely against it. Evan and Max remain welded in place, shifting their gazes from Jana to Robin and back.

Jana hears a sound behind her, a sound she doesn't recognize, blending with her own sounds. She turns to find Robin, mouth wide, eyes crinkled, chin lifted, giving in to manic laughter. She shakes her head back and forth, and her laughter grows and disperses around the room. *It's not funny*, Jana thinks. *This is not funny*. Though she understands Robin's laughter is borne of nervousness. Robin wipes at her tearing eyes.

"It's terrible," Robin says. "Boys, this is a terrible, terrible thing you've done, and I don't find it funny, even if I am laughing."

The boys snicker. Spider still scratches the door.

"Oh dear," Robin says, and, trying to contain more laughter, she splutters, her mouth parted so Jana can see the gleam of spittle on her teeth, a muscular tongue, two big gold fillings, and, way at the back of Robin's mouth, Jana can almost see the epiglottis and tonsils, quivering uncontrollably.

The sound of the insurgent laughter detaches from Robin herself and assumes a globular shape. Airborne, it rises.

Jana lifts Spider and cradles him, tries to console him—
"*Poor baby, it's okay*"—all the while watching Robin.

"Well," says Robin later in the kitchen after they have spoken sternly to the boys about violating Spider. "They say that
adolescence, at least, is a piece of cake with boys."

NINE

When Varney was eleven he was picked up by the police. He called from the station and Cady answered. He chirped into the phone, as if someone was poking him and causing him to hop around.

"I'm at the police station. I was on the beach with my Casio and they got me."

Beth stood at the kitchen sink, belly against the porcelain, hand on the faucet handle, poised to turn it on. Sometimes, when the phone rang, she looked as if her life was about to end, as if the news on the other end was going to be unbearable, even though all the calls seemed so harmless, like the neighbor Helen Bissell calling to borrow an egg.

"What did you do?" Cady asked Varney. "You must have been doing something bad."

"I was just there playing some riffs." Commotion rose in the background—voices, a roar. "Put Mom on. Or just tell her to come get me."

"What's that noise?" Cady said.

"A bunch of crazy people."

Beth wanted Cady to drive even though Cady didn't have her license yet—or her learner's permit. She had, however, taken driver's ed. "You know the basics," Beth said.

Cady drove because she didn't want to argue, and because she thought it might be dangerous to let Beth drive. Cady was used to rallying when her mother needed help—fixing lunch for Varney, running letters to the mailbox a few streets away, taking a phone call from a creditor. She wasn't nervous. Beth put a butter rum Life Saver in her mouth and leaned her seat back. She closed her eyes and hummed something very low using thirds and fifths, the happy intervals. Cady heard the Life Saver rattling against Beth's teeth. She was glad Beth wasn't asking questions about Varney, because what did Cady know? Cady shifted her eyes from left to right and to the rearview mirror as she'd learned to do in driver's ed, making sure not to let her gaze linger on the oncoming traffic, cars that seemed bigger and faster than hers. She tried to get the Big Picture. And she kept her hands at ten and two. Once parked, she took her mother's hand and they walked the block and a half slowly. Cady thought this was how it would be when her mother was old, the two of them plodding along the sidewalk arm in arm, her mother smelling cheesy-stale in the way old people did.

Varney, wrapped in a huge olive blanket, sat on a bench in a room full of dozing drunks. He looked like a child king with his small surprised head emerging from the cone-shaped enclosure of wool. The cops had found him naked on the beach. Someone from a nearby house had called in. Varney hadn't known where his clothes were, and the cops couldn't find them. They took away his keyboard.

The two cops on duty drank coffee and reclined far back in their chairs, so it didn't look as if they were working. One of them, a solid man with flat black hair, which looked like cloth more than hair, stood up and asked Beth to sign some papers. He said they wouldn't press charges due to Varney's age. He gave Varney a silver thermal blanket and directed him to the bathroom, where he could trade it with the wool one. When

Varney came out the blanket's glinting silver made him look even more regal. The cop smiled as if Varney were his own son.

"Better keep your clothes on, bud. Keep a little mystery going. Girls like it better that way."

"Can I have my keyboard back?" Varney said.

"Oh, yeah, sure. Sal, get the kid's keyboard, will you?"

Another man, un-uniformed, appeared from the back with Varney's keyboard. He looked too old to be a police officer. "It's broken," he said, pressing one of the missing notes.

"It's always been broken," Varney said.

"Let's hear you play something," said the officer with flat hair. "That thing you were playing on the beach."

Keyboard back in his possession, Varney huddled under his shimmery blanket and played a slow mournful rendition of "Stairway to Heaven." Beth closed her eyes, hummed along quietly.

"Not bad," said the flat-haired officer when Varney was finished.

"Not bad at all," the other office echoed.

"Is that enough?" Varney asked, hands still poised on the keys.

"Yeah, sure. Go on home."

On the way home Varney sat in the front seat beside Cady. "I thought I was dead meat," he said.

"So did I," Cady said.

They both cackled, pressing their laughter past the point when it naturally would have subsided. The silver blanket fell off Varney's shoulders, fluttering into his lap. He gave Cady driving instructions, coming to life as if nothing had happened.

"You're sure this won't happen again?" Beth said from the backseat. It was part statement, part question, part plea.

"No, Mom," Varney said, his voice suddenly small. "I promise."

TEN

Jana and Evan walk hand in hand along the sidewalk, heading to the Costume Arcade in the mall, where they'll buy Evan's Halloween costume. Jana arranged for her colleague Glenn Fishman to cover for her and she left work early so she could pick up Evan when there was still a bit of light to the day. Evan's hand in hers is hot and alive, raising in Jana inchoate feeling. The sky is orange and the clouds gathering at Mount Baker's summit are a deep cobalt blue.

"How about you're a poor person and you're going to die soon because you don't have any food. And I'm a flying magician. And I fly by and I see you don't have food and I feel sorry for you, so I send out my magic horses, which are yellow, and they can fly, too, and they fly through space to a special planet very, very, very far away, so far away it takes three years to get there, but they have to go there because it's the only place that has food. And some aliens give them a special food that tastes like cheese pizza and grapes and ice cream, and it makes people live forever."

"Okay," Jana says. The *how-about* game is one of their staples. Jana always plays the weak one, the one who is starving, dying, being tortured. Evan is always the rescuer.

Evan's hands pull at the air. "I've got the food."

"It looks sticky and icky."

"It is. How about you almost choke on it." He lifts his hands to her mouth and mimes feeding her.

"Okay."

"But then you get to the magic part and you like it. And you get strong and you live forever."

She laughs and pretends to eat, chokes, then lifts her spine and puffs up her chest in a pose of superhuman strength.

"Okay, now be regular," Evan says as they pass through the doorway into the mall.

Often trips to the mall feel dangerous. The press of traffic in the parking lot; the panorama of merchandise; the people seeming aggressive and acquisitive, even here in small-town Bellingham. Evan's eyes devour the mall, seduced by its promises. She remembers how, as a baby, his eyes were unnaturally large. She felt she could see the world entering him through those eyes, coming to possess him. She still sees it now, the way his eyes open to the gleaming hyperactive world of television. When she is close to him and the angle of the light is right, she feels she sees miniaturized people populating his eyes, as if they've leaped directly from the screen, through his eyes, to his psyche.

Varney was like that. He saw everything, too, his pupils blooming like wide tropical flowers. He could watch two people talking across the street and report later about their small gestures and the emotion those gestures carried. "One of those guys was angry," he might tell her. "The other was sorry." Perceptions she herself could never have begun to see.

Evan doesn't see people like Varney did. Evan sees objects; he is transfixed by neon and flash, by the come-hither of shiny color, by Game Boys and Sega stations and crackling video images. Such glorious movement and enticing brevity; like blown bubbles, like spun sugar, they won't let themselves be captured.

"Look!" Evan says, stopping to stare at a window display of burbling lava lamps. "I need one of those."

"You don't *need* it, Evan," she tells him.

She wants to blindfold him, remove the rods and cones from his retinas, and create a boxed, conditioned B. F. Skinner boy. But if he is to exist in this world, he will see most of the things she wishes him not to see, and so she charts a course of moderation—a little TV, some superhero toys, occasional fast food, a nod to the culture without all-out submission.

"Do aliens wear underpants?" Evan asks.

She laughs and considers. She loves the cool, fluid, gut-soothing taste of laughter. She thinks of Robin and wonders if she might already have learned something from her. "I suppose some do and some don't. Like people, really. What do you think?"

"I don't think they need to. I think they're like animals. Animals would not wear underpants." He nods decisively, extends his arm straight out to the side and spins several times. Jana intercedes to stop him just before he collides with a woman pushing a stroller.

"Alice is wrong," he says.

"Who's Alice?"

"She says aliens have to wear underpants because they fly so fast."

In the shop, they look at every costume. There are clowns and monkeys, lions and pumpkins, magicians and wizards, as well as every recent Disney character. He tugs her sleeve. He wants to look at the scary costumes—vampires, Grim Reapers, skeletons. She has already decided to let him be what he wants to be. She is quiet when he examines the cowboy costume with its smart holster and two silver handguns, the Ninja costume with its tunic and knee-length sword. He wanders farther, fingering the fabric of the robes like a fine tailor until she loses him in the maze of racks and shelves. When she finds him again, he is fondling the shiny plastic of a Darth Vader mask. "This is what I want to be," he says.

He stares at the costume for a long time before he will put it on. Then, robed and masked, he stands before the full-length mirror. The huge mask enlarges his head and dwarfs his body so he is unrecognizable—the embodiment of meanness. He evaluates his reflected self. She expects him to make a sound, but he doesn't. The image stills him, impresses him. She and Varney never had transforming costumes like this. They never shopped for costumes with their mother. In the final hour, just before they departed for trick-or-treating, they jury-rigged something—a bandana tied partway over the eye to simulate a pirate; dirt-smudged cheeks and a stick with a bundle at the end for a hobo. Not elaborate and never transforming.

Evan takes the mask off suddenly.

"Did you scare yourself?" she asks him.

"No," he says. He blinks rapidly. "I want it," he says. He shoves the costume at her and wanders away, and after she's paid, she follows his laugh and finds him in front of the mirror again, wearing a Marilyn Monroe wig.

At home he hides the costume at the back of his closet. "It might scare Leo," he says. He lugs a box of blocks into the closet to make a barrier, then he reinforces it with a stack of board games, some of his heaviest books, his box of Lincoln Logs. She stands in the doorway watching. He is so busy, he has forgotten about her, so when he turns on one of his trips out of the closet and sees her, her presence startles him. His pale face dims. "Don't look at me," he yells in dismay, in fright, as if she herself is now Darth Vader.

From the kitchen she hears him resuming his work. She unpacks his yellow backpack and finds a strange smell rising from its bottom. His lunch box is full, not one bite eaten. The tuna sandwich, the Tupperware of fruit salad, the carrot, the milk, the two Oreos—all remain snuggled in the places she packed them. But the smell does not come from the lunch box. It comes from underneath the lunch box. Her fingers touch something inert, and she knows instinctively that there is something dead down there.

Peeling back the sides of the backpack as far as its seams and zippers will allow, she sees what it is—a dead mouse, a tiny nearly spherical gray thing with a bare pink tail. She lays several thicknesses of paper towel on the table and pulls the mouse slowly out of the pack by its tail, bringing it to a landing on the table. She has never minded rodents—Varney often had rats she held; it was snakes she disliked—but this mouse here is different. She tries to tell herself plausible stories. She feels Evan glancing at her as he travels from bedroom to living room with an armload of toys, mostly cars, balanced on the Candyland box. He turns from her, settles on the living-room floor, out of her sight line, and begins his *vroom-vrooming*.

"Evan?" she says, moving to the doorframe to watch him (always these days watching him from one doorway or another, the thread of her consciousness like a lasso).

He doesn't hear her (or doesn't respond; it's hard to tell). This deafness, willed or not, scares her because, despite not being a talker herself, she believes talking brings relief. It may not solve things, but it soothes. At the very least, talking is like treading water; nothing bad can happen while people talk. If she had kept Varney talking, things might have turned out differently.

"What's the rat doing here?" She has no idea why she used the word *rat* when she knows it's a mouse.

"Vroom," he says. "Vroom-vrooooom. It's not a rat, it's a mouse."

"Yes, mouse. How did a dead mouse get in your backpack?"

"I don't know. Someone must have put it there."

"Leo?" Knowing as soon as she utters Leo's name that she is violating boundaries.

He shrugs. "Spider caught him and I tried to rescue him, but I think he died."

"He died," she says. She keeps watching as he drives his cars in ever more frantic arcs, up over the arms of the sofa. What is it she wants to know? What would bring satisfaction or relief? His fears, his bravado, his tenderness—they are all terrible fodder. It is as if she holds some bizarre daisy, the petals of which she keeps plucking—*He will; he won't*—to find answers to the unknowable.

His eyes skate by hers, locking for just a second in the midst of transit. "Don't look at me like that," he says.

He hurls himself facedown on the floor, so hard she worries for his nose. "You don't like me anymore," he wails, and those are the last words she hears from him for the next two hours because he is possessed, kicking and screaming and flailing.

What prompted this seems disconnected from the life they are in. They were happy just an hour ago, walking along the sidewalk in the orange light, hand in hand. They were happy sorting through all those different costumes. They were conversing back and forth—statement, response, statement, response—just as adults do. She does remember looking at him just now somewhat more intently than usual, but that seems like such a small violation. Yet small things, she knows, should not be overlooked. Size is always relative—a small piece of cheese, a small galaxy, a small problem.

The small F Varney got on Mr. Phillips's math test. That's what he'd talked about the night before the day the world changed.

"I g-g-got them all right," Varney told her on the phone, the stutter he'd had as a young child returning. "B-but he couldn't read what I wrote. He said I had shitty p-p-penmanship. Okay, I d-do, I agreed, but he w-won't go over it with me." He pulled away from the receiver for a moment. "He hates me, Cady."

"I'm sure he likes you."

"No, I swear, he hates me. He's paid to like me, but he never gives me a break."

She had had Mr. Phillips for math, too, four years earlier. Everyone liked Mr. Phillips. Mr. Phillips liked everyone.

"You asked to go over it with him and he said no?"

"I d-didn't ask him. Because—God, Cady, he gave me the evilest look when he gave me my test back. It's a look you never want to see. I'm the only one he looks at that way. '*Pure laziness,*' he said. I hate his *guts*, Cady." Varney moved into and away from the phone so his voice was loud one minute and almost inaudible the next.

"Calm down, Varney. You can straighten this out, but you have to calm down first."

"It's not the F, Cady. It's the *look*. Like he wanted to get rid of me."

It made no sense to worry so much about a look. He had to know this. It was such a small, meaningless thing.

"Looks can't hurt, Varney. You *know* that."

But Varney knew better.

Now Jana knows better, too. So she pays attention to details—the small headache a patient complains of, a slight rise in white cell count, a trace of sadness around the eyes. She tries at once to forget and remember.

First she lets Evan cry. He beats his fists on the carpet, then rolls over and kicks everything in sight. Cars careen around the living room. She stays in the kitchen, listening but out of sight, thinking he is putting on a show for her. Cooper should be coming home soon. She can't bring herself to move the mouse. Spider, poor shorn Spider, has smelled it and leaped onto the table, where he now paws the dead thing as if he might bring it back to life. He quickly loses interest and slinks away, as if ashamed, as if the mouse's lack of vitality is a commentary on his hairlessness. And, indeed, without hair, Spider does not look like a fit competitor. Jana pulls dinner ingredients from the cupboard and fridge but can only stare at them against the din of Evan's tantrum. After a while she cannot endure his misery; principles dissolve in the face of this enormity of grief.

She goes to him, where he writhes in the center of the room on his belly; his cheeks and forehead have gone red from carpet burn and the exercise of crying; his fine hair is soaked with sweat. She touches his back tentatively, but he is too squarely at the center of his fury to feel it. She crouches, then kneels, steadying herself and pulling him to her, grasping his arms to keep them from hitting her. She stretches her legs out and puts them over his, gradually working her own body around his in a straitjacketing hug. Now that his limbs are restrained, he yells in full voice and the word *fortissimo*, a Varney word, streaks through her brain. He is surprisingly powerful for his six years. She feels his face, hot and slick against hers, and his wailing enters her body. An hour goes by, the two of them entwined on the living-room carpet, her lower back aching, her ears filled with sound—his, hers, who knows.

Then he is quiet. She holds her breath, feeling an end in sight, and loosens her grip a little. It turns out to be only a refueling however; suddenly he howls again, louder and more shrill this time, his limbs exerting a steady force against her own thin arms.

She closes her eyes, feeling the cold foreboding of one who loves, one who is inextricably bound to another's fate. Binding love. These are the words that are on her mind when she opens her eyes and sees Seretha standing in the kitchen watching them. She has not removed her coat or her paisley head scarf. She says nothing, but her eyes are speaking reassurance. After a moment, Seretha turns and goes out the door with so little fanfare that Jana cannot say later if she was there or not.

Cooper comes home around seven. The sight of Cooper. She wants to leap up; she wants to cry out; she wants to laugh. All she can do is sit limply with Evan's sleeping body and eke out a wilted smile. She has been on the floor with Evan for almost two hours. Evan only whimpers now. His limbs have gone quiet and heavy. He seems to be falling asleep. Even the sound in her head has receded to a low rumble.

"There's a mouse on the table," Cooper says softly.

LATER, WHEN THEY'VE put Evan down, eaten a quick dinner of omelets and bread, and dragged themselves to bed, she tries to explain. "I think Darth Vader scared him," she says. "Or I did."

"Don't be silly," Cooper says, lifting her nightgown, finding her breasts, putting his mouth to her nipple. He has the Sidwell job and nothing bad can happen.

"I was scared for him," she says. "We need Mrs. Stubbs. This wouldn't be happening if we still had Mrs. Stubbs."

"Don't be scared," he says, brushing his lower lip slowly across her chest. "All kids have tantrums. It's nothing you did. He just had to have a tantrum."

That's what everyone told her. "It's nothing you did," they said. But how would they know? They didn't know of the F on Varney's math test; they didn't know about Mr. Phillips's dirty look. They didn't know that she had failed to keep him on the phone, that he hung up abruptly, still agitated, still stuttering, and that she, in the middle of her frivolous college life up in Oregon, never called him back.

She would have kept him on the line if she'd thought she could make him feel better, but she knew you couldn't get rid of someone else's sadness. She knew this because she had tried hard with her mother, Beth. Beth had a gift shop in Dana Point, where she sold whale knickknacks to tourists. The shop's windows looked out onto a sparkling harbor filled with boats, a harbor so idyllically situated and crisply cared for, like an ad with false promises of things that could never really be. They were pleasure boats for sportfishing or cruising the coast, made of Plexiglas and expensive wood, and painted ocean shades of blue and green and white, with accents of wood and chrome. Most were rarely used; they sat in their slips collecting salt and seagull droppings until someone thought to hose them down.

Cady and Varney liked to walk the docks and look at the boats and imagine they owned one. Beth, fearful of water, especially ocean water, made them wear puffy orange life vests, but as soon as they were out of her sight, they ditched the vests, leaving them on a railing, to be recovered before Beth saw them again.

While Cady and Varney were out exploring, Cady never stopped thinking about their mother back in the shop. If there were patrons in the shop, Beth would wander around rearranging things—a paperweight here, a mug there, bringing the things she liked into better focus. She would be wearing the lacquered smile Cady hated for its faraway feeling, the feeling that there were other places to be that were far better than this one. If she started conversations, they meandered and died. If there were no customers in the shop, Beth would sit at the desk, with bills and purchase orders in front of her, but she rarely looked at her papers; instead she stared out the window, past the boats with shiny keels and the diving pelicans and the gently pulsing water, and she would think of her sister, Helen, missing Helen, rewriting the family history so Helen wouldn't have to drown.

Thinking of this made Cady so sad. "We have to bring her something, Varney."

And Varney, with a sharp eye for treasures, was usually the one to find it. A pretty feather, or a shell, or a nickel to buy a candy stick. Their mother liked candy to raise her spirits. When they delivered the treasure, Cady watched her mother's eyes and saw, no matter how special their gift, no matter how much love they declared, their mother's eyes only brightened for a moment before reverting to their still gray, faraway dullness, like stones beyond reach of the polishing sea.

REN SCOFIELD CALLS Jana to talk about a patient. Does she remember the eighty-three-year-old brain tumor a few weeks ago? Of course she remembers. As memories go, hers is sharp, but even if it weren't sharp, she wouldn't forget the pleading eyes of Mr. Cianetti. His body crumbling like the shell of a beached crustacean, his consciousness thrumming on as acutely as ever. It always seems like such an injustice for the mind and body to fall so far out of sync.

Mr. Cianetti, Ren Scofield reports, has not done well with radiation. The tumor has shrunk only a little, while his strength has declined significantly, and now he has been rehospitalized. Scofield apologizes for involving her, but Mr. Cianetti has spoken of her repeatedly and Scofield thought Jana should know. Of course she should know, she tells Scofield. Of course she's happy to drop by.

Consciousness, a restless butterfly, drifts lightly over Mr. Cianetti. Since she last saw him, he has lost weight. His cheeks have sunken and his skull's shape is visible, a preview of his postmortem appearance. He lies on his back, eyes closed, nose pointing ceilingward like an alpine peak, the rest of his features part of the steep ascent. His breathing crackles with the kind of unpredictability of a package being unwrapped. Not far from his bed, a young woman sleeps, mouth open, head fallen sideways onto the cushioned chair. She wears four or five skirts of varying lengths, one layered over the next. On top she wears an olive-drab sweatshirt with its neckline cut and unhemmed, sleeves similarly cut to three-quarter length. *His granddaughter,* she thinks, then remembers he has no family members living.

Jana watches the two sleepers, loathe to interrupt. Their sleeping is a shared sacred rite. But in sleep the girl senses Jana's presence, and within a minute or so she awakens, gathering her dispersed consciousness like humidity coalescing into a cloud.

"I'm Dr. Thomas," Jana says in a low voice so as not to awaken Mr. Cianetti. "You are—?"

The woman doesn't answer.

"What's your name?"

"Regine. He's my granddad."

Jana nods. "It's nice you came."

The girl yawns and stands. She wears hiking boots beneath her skirts. Her hair, a dark brown and matted into thick, sausagelike clumps, shifts around her shoulders, moving with the same insouciance as her skirts.

"It wasn't nice of me. My dad made me come." She speaks in a full voice, oblivious to her grandfather. "I don't know what the hell I'm supposed to do here. He can't even remember my name."

The girl yawns again. She has dark circles under her eyes, and she is so thin that the joints of her fingers stand out, making her fingers look gnarled.

"Is he your mom or dad's dad?"

"My dad's."

"Where is your dad?" Jana whispers.

"He's where he always is. Where everyone in the world is. In the Bay Area, making money hand over fist in computers. Like he doesn't have enough already."

"He couldn't get away?"

"He *wouldn't* get away."

"I think perhaps you should get him here. Your grandfather isn't doing very well."

"Dad doesn't give a shit."

"Of course he does. Otherwise he wouldn't have sent you."

The girl laughs and shakes her head. She looks directly at Jana. Her eyes are very large and very dark, and their direct gaze is both dazzling and frightening.

"No, *really*," she says. "He doesn't give a shit." She laughs again as if Jana doesn't get it.

Jana breaks off eye contact and goes to Mr. Cianetti's side. She checks his IV line to occupy her hands. Regine wanders to the window, where the parking lot lights bleed orange over everything. Jana wonders how long the girl has been here and how, with this attitude, her father could have forced her to come.

The girl sits on the windowsill and stares at Jana. She seems engaged now, ready to talk. "I can't totally blame my dad. I probably wouldn't have anything to do with my dad, either, if he did to me what his dad did to him."

"Like what?"

"Hit him. Send him to bed without any dinner. Sometimes they'd be driving in the car and Granddad would make Dad get out, and he'd just leave him there. Dad would have to walk home. Sometimes he had no idea where he was. When my dad and mom got divorced, my granddad said he'd never forgive my father. That was when they stopped seeing each other finally."

Jana nods to keep her talking. "Is your dad an only child?"

"He has a sister. She got out ages ago. I only saw her once. She told me she grew up in a toxic household and there wasn't any hope of changing it."

"Do you think that?"

The girl shrugs. "Who knows?"

"Where do you live?"

"Portland. I went there for college. Now I'm a *dropout*." She says the word with deep relish. "Dad said he'd give me some cash if I came up here, so—"

Mr. Cianetti snorts, wrinkles his nose, continues sleeping. Jana wonders if he did the things Regine says he did. She wishes he would wake up and set the record straight. She stares at his fingers, which are more delicate than those of his grand-daughter.

"What did your grandfather do for a living?"

"He fixed vacuum cleaners."

An American tale, Jana thinks. The son of the modest manual laborer becomes a wealthy computer mogul, then the child of the mogul becomes a dropout. The American Dream achieved and rejected.

It's almost six. Cooper is picking up Evan today, but Jana needs to get moving, anyway; she has charts to dictate and she promised she would be home for dinner no later than seven.

"Death is pretty final, you know," Jana says.

"Duh," says the girl.

Jana tries to ignore the tone. "Now's the last chance for your dad to say good-bye."

"I told you—he's not interested in good-byes. That's why *I'm* here. Tootle-oo, Grandpa. I report back. Yeah, it's happening; he's checking out. Close that chapter."

Jana says nothing and focuses instead on Mr. Cianetti's er-
ratic breathing, trying to estimate how long he'll hold on. He
opens his eyes as if he feels her query. It takes him a moment to
get oriented, then his sluggish muscles move to a grin, the same
impish one he first showed her.

"The party can begin," he rasps.

Regine comes to the other side of the bed. "Hey, Granddad." Regine looks over at Jana. "Now you can ask him if he
and my dad hate each other."

"What's that?" Mr. Cianetti says.

"I don't need to ask," Jana says.

SHE AND COOPER MEET just before five in the parking lot
of Evan's school. Cooper, still irrepressibly exuberant, has
washed his face, splashed on aftershave, changed from jeans to
khakis. He hops out of his truck, eager as a new lover, hungry
and courtly at the same time. He bounds to her Honda, pulls
her out, and kisses her voraciously, sexually, right there in the
parking lot.

In Rita Tencil's classroom, they sit at a low table on plastic,
child-sized chairs, which seems at first like a joke—putting a
sizable man like Cooper on toy-sized furniture so his knees rise
in front of him like khaki-clad posts. Jana decides it must be a
deliberate attempt to encourage the parents to experience the
point of view of the first grader. Amid the children, Rita Tencil has seemed at ease, but now, holding Evan's folder, her eyes
arcing between them, she seems uncomfortable, formal, slightly
officious, as if she conducts these parent conferences only because of contractual obligation.

"I know you're worried about things, Mrs. Johansen, and,
well—Evan is real rambunctious," Rita begins slowly after

they've introduced themselves. "But rambunctiousness, especially in a bright boy like Evan, can turn into a very positive quality later in life. I think we just have a lot of *boy* on our hands." She smiles nervously at Cooper.

The sound in Jana's head, which was low and legato, now turns staccato. What is *boy*? What is beyond *boy*? Jana remembers all the tendentious professionals making declarations about the state of Varney's mind. One thought he was borderline. Another said he was bipolar. Incipient schizophrenia, declared another. She never believed any of them.

Cooper moves his hand onto Jana's knee, where it splays like a lopsided starfish. Rita rifles through Evan's papers, producing examples of his writing (rudimentary at best), his artwork (elaborate, mazelike, pointed), and his adding-and-subtracting exercises (unchanged since Jana herself was in school). His reading skills are coming along, she reports. She raves about his fine motor muscles. "Exceptional," she says, "especially for a boy." As if boys are doltish, compromised people for whom exceptions must be made.

"And of course he is devoted to his bugs. You must see his collection."

Rita fetches an egg carton from a shelf by the window and opens it to reveal a carefully sorted collection of shriveled bug carcasses.

"He's *obsessed* with finding bugs. In fact, all the other children have started to call Evan when they've found a bug. Evan comes and gets it for his collection. It's very sweet. Apparently he has ways of killing the bugs that keep them mostly intact."

"Wow," Cooper says.

Jana stares at the pile of tiny exoskeletons, translucent, brittle, light as eyelashes. She thinks of Evan and his honed bug-killing skill. The only kid.

"One of the wonderful things about teaching," says Rita Tencil, "is seeing how different kids are. They all have their own passions."

"How exactly does he—?" Jana begins. She catches Rita Tencil's eyes, wanting her questions to be intuited so she won't have to say them aloud.

Rita Tencil closes the egg carton. "The bug collection is helping Evan learn to work with the other children. Frankly, he's a bit of a loner, and this collection teaches him coopera- tion. He's learning to respect the other children's wishes and not be so easily offended by them. So if we lose a bug or two in the process—" She trails off and looks pleadingly at Cooper.

Jana doesn't mean to scare Rita Tencil. In the past Cooper has said to her, "Sometimes you don't smile enough, honey. It turns people off. You seem so severe. When you do smile, you light up everything." She knows he is right, she should smile, but what if she does and the point is lost and the consequences of losing the point turn out to be dire and irrevocable? Because the point—should she shout this out?—is that *no one knows*. No one knows if the murderer is made during a long slow tra- jectory with an accretion of slights, an escalation of meanness, a gradual toughening of the soul, or if instead there is simply one sudden moment of unchecked rage.

No one knows. She, the one closest to Varney, the only one in a real position to know, she herself has no idea. Cruelty to animals, they said, was a sure sign. But nothing is so simple. Their cat used to bring home birds and mice he'd caught and maimed but not yet killed, animals with fight still in them, though doomed eventually to die. The cat loved taunting these half-dead creatures, slapping them with a paw, gloating over their entrapment. Varney routinely freed the animals, took them outside, and with a stick or a hammer or whatever else was at hand, he put them out of their misery. Was killing like that, killing borne of compassion, the same as any other?

Jana fingers the list in her pocket—questions for Rita Tencil. Have there been any biting incidents? Any tantrums? Is he a candidate for Ritalin? For therapy? For a neurological workup? What is the correlation between imaginary friends and later trouble in life? Is he *different* from the other children? But now she sees that Rita Tencil will think her list is extreme. Rita Tencil is no scientist. She is not thinking neurologically. "You worry too much," Cooper always says to her.

"I just learned that you're a doctor," Rita Tencil says suddenly. "That's very exciting."

Jana smiles, accustomed to such comments, to their strange blend of pandering and sneering, to a way people have of making you into a stranger, an oddity, someone not like them.

"Maybe someday you could come in and talk to the children?" Rita Tencil says.

"Maybe," Jana says vaguely, thinking of how she both yearns to see and dreads seeing Evan in a classful of kids.

"All these questions," Jana says. She takes out her list, scans it—*tantrums, Ritalin, biting . . .*

"Yes?" says Rita.

"What about Leo?" she finally says.

"His imaginary friend? It's true that imaginary friends are seen more commonly in younger children, but I wouldn't make too much of it if I were you, Dr. Johansen." She gives Cooper a quick glance, a quick smile, both offering sympathy and culling support before turning back to Jana. "Is it possible you—being a doctor and all, and no doubt having high expectations—put too much pressure on Evan to perform, so he escapes into fantasy? This is just an idea. He's coming along fine, really. My advice is just love him to death, and we'll get the kinks worked out."

"I agree," Cooper says. "Love him to death."

Rita Tencil stands. She's done with this conference. Another couple waits in the corridor. Cooper stands, too. Jana remains seated, lost in a maze of genomes and testosterone, of threat-assessment and Ritalin, of what it means exactly to love someone to death.

"It's time to go," Rita Tencil says. She guides them to the door. "You have a lovely son," she says. "What does he plan to be for Halloween?"

Cooper, already out the door, doesn't hear, and Jana lets the question drift away.

"Right," Rita says as if she has gleaned an answer, anyway.

Jana looks at Rita Tencil's flat, round, professionally cheerful face, a public face that must hide, under its powdered pores, its own stash of worries. Rita Tencil has no solutions; she doesn't even worry about Evan. Cooper doesn't worry. Mrs. Stubbs worried once, but she is not around to worry anymore. Only she, Jana, worries for Evan. Everyone else has particles of information, puzzle pieces; she is the only one who knows it all, or almost all. She is the only one who has held him through tantrums, felt the dislocation of brain and heart, the random firing of synapses and hormones.

She should have told Cooper about Varney when she had the chance long ago, when they met or when she got pregnant. If she'd told him back then, he would be standing by her now, her companion in worry.

Of course she has imagined telling him. She has thought of words. *My brother is a murderer* (a pianist, a jokester, a skipper-of-stones). Or: *He is a person who has murdered* (and loved his sister and failed math tests and tried to surf). She has imagined the conversation beginning as a dialogue but quickly becoming her monologue—an out-loud, solo debate about the perennial questions. She has imagined the end of her words, the silence that would follow, like the long tail of a shooting star. She has imagined the reckoning of muscles under Cooper's cheeks that would steal his dimples and curdle his sweetness. She knows how she would regret the words as soon as they were out there. They would misrepresent so much. And words, once spoken, cannot be erased. It takes years to forget them.

Year upon year her secrets have gone unsaid, and now there is a chasm between her and Cooper, and if she speaks of these things, she and Cooper will each be relegated to opposite sides of the gorge. He will fear her influence, her deep hidden parts, her tainted heritage. He will leave her, perhaps, or worse, leave Evan.

Driving home alone through the dark (Cooper has gone for Evan), streetlights strobing the car, she sees the lights of small fishing vessels making their way across the bay and back into the harbor. She feels the enormity of her error, the enormity of her solitary burden.

ELEVEN

Once, Jana had faith in knowledge. The density of elements, all the body's bones. In medical school her classmates liked to study with her. She was their walking resource. She memorized *Gray's Anatomy,* reveled in the minutia of cell biology. She couldn't get enough of facts. They were friends; they were solutions; they were nourishment and armor. She would be the woman who knew things, the woman who wouldn't be ambushed.

But the facts, it turns out, are no defense against the sound in her head, with its blitzkrieg, its thunder, its cracking, its rasp, its howl. Facts do nothing to eradicate the sound or lower its volume. She cannot, with facts, control her out-of-whack cochlea. She has a name for it—tinnitus—but she learned long ago that a name, a diagnosis, sometimes supplies only the illusion of control, a stand-in for understanding, really no control at all. Yes, you have *malignant melanoma,* but we cannot cure you. Yes, you have *autoimmune disease* but there are, as yet, no treatments. Yes, you are a *Homo sapien* and certainly you will die.

Tinnitus is the perception of sound where no sound is present . . . the noise can be intermittent or constant, with single or multiple tones; it can be subtle or at a life-shattering level.

In all the knowledge and research about tinnitus, almost

nothing is known for sure. Everything is conjecture. She wants reasons, but no one has reasons.

Some people report that their tinnitus began immediately follow-ing a single exposure to intense noise, like that from an air bag de-ployment or a gunshot blast.

Some people is not good enough. So she has given up on facts, though she still spins theories of her own, fashioned from tidbits of her accumulated knowledge. She wasn't there when it happened, but she has certainly imagined and reimagined it all: the light beginning to bleed up over the humps of the brown hills, gigantic and unmoving like drugged elephant seals; the bacon slabs Beth, their mother, chose so uncharacteristically that morning to cook, which eventually shriveled and black-ened and sent up smoke like bulletins that the neighbor Helen Bissell eventually smelled (as if Beth, choosing bacon, sensed her own fate). She has imagined the soft padding squish of Beth's and Walter's bare feet on the cool kitchen tiles, the hum of the freeway, muffling everything, then the shots—one, two, then a third and a fourth—deafening but so brief that the sound could scarcely be registered beyond something startling that might have been, in the waking day, a car backfiring, a plate shattering, a temporary stutter of the heart.

And then later: the gleaming linoleum of the long locker-lined corridor, the dry dusty heat of the Santa Anas blowing nerviness over the students like some spell, the smells of Comet and pepperoni churning from the cafeteria, the very same classroom in which she took Algebra I herself and the very same teacher, beloved and blond, an aging surfer, adored by most students but disliked by a few for the way he favored some while ignoring others and then handed out marks accordingly. Who could blame a boy like Varney? Small for his age and bright, but not a performer. An outsider. The other boy, the

dead one, Andy Carnack, was quiet and brainy and destined
for Stanford or Harvard, a boy who might have been hated if
he'd stood out more, but as it was he was purely a background
boy (like Varney) who went unnoticed until his premature demise, and then all people could think to say was how smart he
was. "*Andy, oh yeah, he was a real brain.*" As if nothing else mattered about him except his head. Varney had nothing against
Andy, but he was there on that day in the wrong place.

In Oregon that morning she had sat in a class where they
plodded through a discussion of Hegel's *Philosophy of Right*, and
halfway through the hour her heart quickened. She laid her
hand on her chest and felt its fluttering against her palm. She
looked behind her, saw nothing. A trickle of sweat wormed
from her armpit over her ribs. The sound of a breaking wave
drowned her professor. Looking at the student beside her, she
saw her fear reflected in his eyes.

At lunch she sat in the campus watering hole with her
roommate, Kristen, and a boy named Blake who was interested
in her. She'd forgotten the fear by then. She ate a thick ham
sandwich and drank Oregon pale ale with the rest of them,
knowing, but not caring, that it would make her sleepy in her
afternoon psych class. She watched Blake's lips cleave to the
rim of his glass as he drank. They laughed about a kid who,
protesting a grade, had peed on the steps of the administration
building. Everything was funny, especially the thought of some
kid using his penis to change things. In the darkness under the
table, Blake's knee pressed against hers. She wondered what
move he would make next. There was air inside her, filling her
chest and her heart, making her lighter and prettier than usual.
Her hand seemed to float as it reached for a pretzel.

Occasionally they glanced at the TV mounted above the
bar. A college football game was on with the sound muted, so

the players, tumbling over one another in silence, seemed immune to injury. A newscast interrupted, still with no sound. She saw shots of a school, close-ups of kids crying. Blake shook his head with contempt. "California."

"What?" she said. She stared at the monitor. She saw yellow police tape fluttering. She saw a house, a familiar house, her parents' house. She saw Helen Bissell talking to an interviewer, wiping tears. She saw Renee Sanchez, her old guidance counselor, hugging two girls.

"You didn't hear?" Blake said. He had said this before, she was sure. Hadn't he said this before? *You didn't hear? You didn't hear?* Hearing was seeing, and seeing was smelling, and smelling was touching. There were no edges to things. There was no sound when there should have been sound. She laid her ham sandwich on the table, and its meat and cheese spilled out.

"You didn't hear? About the kid in California who blew away his parents and one of his teachers this morning? How can you stand living in a place like that?"

Like a fish in a tank. Swimming around, looking out with fish eyes. No longer human. No longer a speaking creature. One eye looks one way, the other eye looks somewhere else.

"Hey, you okay? You don't know those people, do you?"

You blink. You blink again. You are a fish. Blinking is what fish do. No more expression than that. Fish are cold. They have brief lives.

"Fifteen-year-old suspect Varney Miller was taken into custody this morning," says the TV.

Around the table the nonfish draw back with the shock of their new knowledge. They stop their human speech. Something happens in the air between you and them. There is a lifting. A hardening. Like a scab forming, making ready to separate. Like a chunk of land sundered from its continent, left to float alone. You are broken from them. You blink again. Fish don't speak. Words are nowhere. One of your minds thinks: *Look at the face of the boy in the handcuffs. So what if we share the same last name? Can't you see I have nothing to do with him?* Your other mind creeps behind the police tape and pokes around in blood.

Nonsense piles up around you—pretzel pieces and spilled beer and salt as big as glass chips. The sound that will be yours for life flourishes, and the double life takes seed. You can do one thing and think another. You are a fish and a person. You are coed and scum. Everything and nothing. Never again Cady Miller. You reach for a pretzel. You laugh.

"No way," you say.

TWELVE

I t's almost time to get dressed," Jana tells Evan. It is four forty-five on Halloween evening, and Evan has not yet brought out his costume—it is still in its bag at the back of the closet, blockaded by toys.

Evan's eyes dart around the kitchen where Jana is heating the chili Cooper made.

"I can't be Darth Vader, because you won't let me carry a sword."

"Darth Vader doesn't carry a sword does he?"

"He has a light saber. You won't let me carry a light saber, either, so I want to be a pig."

He tosses a Beanie Babies lobster from palm to palm, evading her eyes. He wears underpants and a T-shirt with a picture of a caped Batman unfurling across his chest. Is Leo involved in this sudden change of heart, or is this a play for a sword?

"How would you be a pig?" she probes, thinking of the hour, the impossibility of creating a pig in the first place.

He shrugs. She stirs the chili. "I'd be pink," he says.

"Would we paint you pink or cover you in pink fabric?"

He shrugs again. Then, palming the lobster he looks up at her, his eyes unexpectedly guileless, his cheeks pouching as if he is rolling a thick thought around in them. "What're you gonna be?" he says.

"A witch."

"The same witch you were last year?"

"Maybe a slightly different witch."

"Leo is going to be a pig."

They cut a construction-paper tail, which they roll to curliness around a pencil. Clumsy with the scissors, Evan brings all the musculature of his upper body to the task, hunching within inches of the paper, tongue clutched between his teeth, fine hair sliding forward and tasseling off his forehead. His concentration surprises her, pleases her, after a long raucous Saturday in which, waiting for trick-or-treating, he could think of nothing to do. Cooper was working—as usual these days—on the Sidwell job and unavailable for shooting hoops. Whenever Jana let down her guard, Evan sneaked to the TV, scuttled in close to the screen, and his appearance took on the the guilty facial nomenclature of an addict. When she turned the TV off and brought him Legos, puzzles, cars, he looked dumbfounded, as if he'd forgotten what to do with them. He kept wandering forlornly to the window where dark, surprisingly geometric clouds striped the horizon and threatened rain.

"It's not supposed to rain on Halloween," he moaned, his body flopping from chair to couch to rug, his fingers prodding Spider, who lay curved in unresponsive sleep like a wheel of pale cheese. She talked herself out of fretting, but it frightened her to see him like this, without resources, his mood vulnerable to the vagaries of weather.

She wishes Cooper would come home. She is adrift with him gone, especially on weekends. She and Evan are not enough to fill the house, and her efforts at parenting are strangely random without Cooper. She feels a pressure to play with Evan, but when she presents herself, he often acts silly, rolling cars off his head, calling her a nudnik or a doo-doo-puss, stretching his upper lip so it touches his nostrils, and she takes these behaviors as signs he wants her to go away. Now she would especially like Cooper here. He is the wizard of homemade creations. She doesn't have a ragbag, or a sewing machine, and the few art supplies she has are insufficient for creating a costume that will withstand the rigors of trick-or-treating.

"How is Leo doing his costume?" she wants to ask, but the details of Leo's tastes, his methods of doing things, his responsibilities for bad-boy acts, are elusive and must, she senses, stay mysterious. Leo is a vaporous creature of the id. He's the bubble you want to hold but which pops before you get to it, the drop of mercury that slides from your grasp, a creature risen from the liminal space where mind and body meet, gaseous and shape-changing. Leo is like an organ slipped out of position, a hernia of Evan's mind, which as he grows older will resume its proper place. (She thinks; she hopes.) If she asks too much about Leo she might do Leo harm. And a harmed Leo could become a harmed Evan. She would love to know what Leo looks like, where he sleeps, and when he likes to visit, but she will not ask; she will wait for Evan's brief enigmatic revelations.

At five fifteen the doorbell rings with the first trick-or-treaters, who turn out to be Cooper and Mitch, Cooper's old friend and now partner on the Sidwell job.

"Trick or treat!" they say in unison, and then they freeze, their arms extended in gnarled tree positions, their faces rippled and scrunched as old bark.

"Daddy!" yells Evan. "You can't have candy, because you don't have a costume."

"This *is* my costume, buddy," Cooper says. "This old face and body of mine."

"That's not a costume," Evan says, giggling.

Cooper and Mitch step inside. They are happy, ready to

create a party wherever they go. Mitch places a six-pack of Corona on the kitchen table. He's a short, wiry man in his late forties, with darting eyes and a quiet, accommodating disposition. He and Cooper have been friends and sometime coworkers for years.

"Okay," Cooper says, "you don't like our costumes? We'll get better ones, right Mitch? Let's go. Time to get dressed, Darth Vader."

"He's changed his mind," Jana says, catching Cooper's eye. "He's going to be a pig instead. Here is his tail." She holds out the pink coiled construction-paper tail—which suddenly seems puny—and winks at Cooper.

"Cool," Cooper says. "A pig."

"Yeah, neat," says Mitch.

"I saw you wink, Mom," says Evan. "It's not funny."

"Of course it's not funny," Jana says.

"You winked. I saw you wink at Daddy."

"I winked because pigs are nice," Jana says. "It's going to be a good costume, and Daddy is going to help you with it."

"It's a stupid costume." Evan grabs the pink tail and shreds it to confetti, then runs to his bedroom and slams the door.

Cooper gives Mitch a "Happy Halloween" look. Mitch, who has no family of his own, smiles wanly. Cooper reaches for a beer, uncaps it, and takes a swig. "Help yourself," he tells Mitch, who shrugs and takes one, too.

The wails coming from Evan's bedroom are gradually climbing the scale, bringing to the forefront other sounds—the drip of the kitchen faucet, the hum of the electric clock—sounds which were, a moment ago, merely white noise. The intervals are changing so quickly she can't identify them. Is this a tantrum cry, one of those episodes of possession where Evan will be inconsolable for hours to come? She steadies herself with palms on the table, eyes closed. "Cooper, do something. Please."

Cooper sips his beer, chuckles quietly. "Here goes nothing." He heads to Evan's room, opening the door and leaving it open so Evan's cries shoot out like freed demons.

Jana remembers the heating chili and hurries to the stove. The doorbell rings. "Mitch, could you get it? The candy's by the front door."

The chili has stuck to the bottom of the pot and begun to burn. She turns off the heat. She hears Mitch telling the trick-or-treaters, "Don't take it all!" She has no control over what is happening. She has never liked Halloween. She has never liked any of the holidays—Thanksgiving, Christmas, Easter—when exhilarating things were supposed to happen but never did.

She stands on the staircase landing, where she can see into Evan's room. Cooper has disappeared into the closet, and she hears him moving things. Evan sobs quietly under his quilt. It seems as if these two people are only distantly related to her, as if she is dead and watching descendants of hers she cannot touch. Is this the way Varney felt, dead already?

Cooper emerges from Evan's closet, wearing the Darth Vader mask, the robe slung across his shoulder. He perches on the edge of the bed, rapping the frame.

"Trick or treat. Knock knock? Are you home?"

Evan goes silent, then slowly lifts his quilt. Seeing Darth Vader he retreats again.

"Daddy?" he whispers. "Daddy is that you?"

"It's me," Cooper says. "I thought I could be Darth Vader since you want to be a pig."

"That's *my* costume. *I'm* going to be Darth Vader."

Cooper feigns tears. "Oh no. What am I gonna be, then? I wanted to be Darth Vader."

Evan throws back the quilt and sits up, his face pale and whittled with compassion. He leans into his father's face. Jana jumps back, out of view.

"Maybe we could get you a Darth Vader costume, too," Evan says.

"Could we?" Cooper begs.

"I'll ask Mommy. Mommy knows where to get it."

She hears the sorrow warbling through Evan's tiny tender heart, the same sorrow he had felt a minute ago for himself. Isn't it just like Varney? The suddenly shifting heart, the brain like a seismometer, sensing everything, reacting to everything. But how can sensitivity like that be bad?

She turns and heads back down to the kitchen, where they will come looking for her.

"Naw," she hears Cooper say. "I guess I'll be a fish."

It seems impossible that she will remain intact through the long slow march to Evan's adulthood. She sets the table and serves up bowls of chili, hoping no one will taste the burn. Mitch is still tending to the endless stream of trick-or-treaters.

Evan and Cooper and Mitch come to the table in costumes, Evan as Darth Vader, replete with concealing mask. Cooper has made him a light saber from a paper-towel roll with a small flashlight fixed inside it, solidly mummified in gray duct tape. Cooper has put himself together as a fish, with a cap that features a fish head swimming out of the front of it, fins and tail behind; one of Evan's bright blue Superman capes—its color suggesting aquatic scenes—is pinned to his shoulders. Mitch is suited in Batman regalia, a tiny black cape (from when Evan was four and went nowhere without a cape) and a Lycra hood that fits him like a skullcap. Jana has put on her usual Halloween garb of black skirt and black hat.

Levity reigns again. They eat chili and no one notices it's burned. The grown-ups drink beer. "Swish." Evan passes his light saber over the chili. "You're all poisoned."

The moon, a few days shy of full, trots in and out of the clouds, cobbling the sidewalk with shadows, which deepen one moment, fade the next. The rain has held off and the air is warm, almost balmy. Evan walks between Jana and Cooper, testing the reach of his tiny light.

"Hey," he says, aiming the light overhead. "My light isn't working anymore!"

"It's working. It just isn't strong enough to reach the stars is all," Cooper says before breaking into song. "The worms crawl in, the worms crawl out. A nice big juicy one up your snout."

"Up *your* snout, Daddy," Evan screeches. "I don't have a snout. So ha-ha worms. And anyways, worms are scared of Darth Vader. And *I'm* Darth Vader." He leaps ahead of them and swivels into a Zorro-style crouch.

"Trick or treat!" he yells.

"Treat, treat, treat, treat," chants Cooper.

"Treat, treat, treat, treat," echoes Mitch.

"I don't like this old light saber," Evan says. "It's falling apart. I want a different one."

"I don't think we have a different one," Cooper says.

"I wanna go back and find something else."

Cooper looks askance at Jana.

"Okay," she says, "but hurry. It's getting late."

Mitch and Jana wait on the street while Cooper unlocks the door for Evan. "Go to it, buddy," Cooper says. Evan sprints inside. A minute later he comes back empty-handed. "I'm ready," he says.

"Where's your light saber?"

"I don't need one."

They move on, the grown-ups shrugging. They go first to Carolyn Janklow's house, arriving as a group on her porch and arranging themselves awkwardly, Evan in front.

"Trick or treat," he says, his quiet soprano more muffled than usual by the mask and a sudden bout of timidity.

"Let's see, who do we have here?" Carolyn asks. She is

dressed up herself, ostensibly as Marilyn, or some other blond bombshell, in a formfitting pink spandex dress and a blond wig, possibly the very same one Evan tried on in the store. Proprietary and overeager, she bends to Evan.

"Darth Vader," Cooper says, filling in.

"Well, Darth Vader, hello there. Aren't you looking scary tonight."

Evan says nothing.

"Does Darth Vader like candy?" Carolyn says.

Evan nods vigorously. "He does."

Carolyn winks at Jana and Jana prays Evan doesn't notice. Evan lifts his mask and takes a handful of mini Hershey's bars. Jana is just about to warn him not to be greedy when Carolyn urges him to take more.

"These are for Leo," Evan tells Carolyn.

Jana feels like an interloper with her parental impulses and her halfhearted witch costume.

Evan comes away cackling, his bag filling with candy, his mind filling with Halloween lore, with the miracle of being able to approach people for candy and receive it—no questions asked. Small groups of nylon-clad trick-or-treaters swarm through the shadowy streets. Shrieks and giggles stab the night, flashlights jerk, plastic pumpkin candy receptacles swing wildly. As far as Jana can see, most of them are not freighted with adults.

At the fifth house Evan, brave and giddy and sick of his chaperones, begs to go by himself. The grown-ups wait in the street and watch as he heads up the walkway and mounts the long cement staircase, glancing back once to make sure they're not joining him.

"I remember I used to fill an entire pillowcase with candy," Mitch says.

"You bet," says Cooper, though Jana knows for a fact that Cooper was not allowed to trick-or-treat after a poisoned-candy scare in his town. He was taken instead to boring Halloween parties, accompanied by his mother.

A yelp jolts her. At the top of the staircase a couple of indeterminate age retreats into their house. The door slams. The porch light goes off. Evan is left standing alone in the dark. Cooper, more oriented than Jana, races up the walkway, taking the steps two at a time.

"What the *hell*?" she hears Cooper say. "Get down there."

They descend the unlit walkway, emerging into the sidewalk's dim and largely unrevealing light. Evan is crying, but oddly without commitment. He stands a few feet away from them, mask removed, his gaze wedded to the sidewalk.

Cooper holds up a steel barbecue skewer. "His light saber."

Jana's limbs are weightless. The sound growls in, voracious, multitoned. Cooper's face is bland as a pancake. Doesn't he see it—how people shrank from their son, slammed the door on him? Their son is a *real* spook with the power, even the *wish*, to scare strangers. Doesn't Cooper see?

She cannot ask such questions with the sound roaring as it is, making even thinking a task. They're all simply standing there in the weird watery light without doing anything, statues for passing trick-or-treaters to gaze at, defined by this moment, by the aftermath of something no one quite understands. Evan is paralyzed by his crying, Jana by her sound, Mitch by being an outsider. Cooper—she doesn't know what paralyzes him, but something clearly does.

And how can they stay so paralyzed when there is so much to do? For starters, they must apologize to that poor, terrorized couple who will now have visions of violent, skewer-wielding children on their porch. Someone needs to say something to

them; someone must beg their forgiveness. Then there's the
larger problem of Evan, Evan who is crying and no doubt feels
sorry for himself. Evan who has been carrying a concealed
skewer under his robe and threatening to use it.

But it seems as if years pass through them on that sidewalk,
an eternity of fully lived seconds in which nothing upon nothing is done and the habit of passivity compounds itself.

Mitch is waving. "I think I'll be going," he says.

Before Jana can summon herself to acknowledge his departure, he's been sucked into darkness, Batman cape and all.

"*Do* something," Jana says to Cooper, fighting her clattering head.

"Me? Why me? Aren't *you* the disciplinarian in this family?" Cooper is not easily riled, but now his hairless lips look
sinewy with tension. Evan stops crying to listen. He snatches a
look at Jana.

"Jana?"

"I want him to apologize." Her voice is raised, probably too
loud, but with the noise, it's impossible to calibrate and she has
to hear herself. "Evan, you're going back up there to apologize."

Cooper snorts. A frightening hardness has come over him.
She shoots him an admonishing look, and in the moment their
eyes lock, she has a feeling, stronger than ever before, that
Cooper—fair, dimpled, amiable Cooper—is not of her tribe,
not like Varney was, dark and quick and brooding. She's had
this feeling before but only as an amusing observation (how
good it was they weren't alike), but now, seeing his irritation
with this supposed brouhaha she's making, she feels a growing
rage at him and his glib, uncomprehending tribe.

Evan begins crying again; it's one of his fake cries, deliberate as the sound of typing.

"Go on," she says.

She nudges him from behind, but he doesn't budge. When she pushes harder, he feigns falling forward but catches himself and very slowly begins to move.

"I want you to go back up there and tell those people you didn't mean to scare them."

"It's Halloween; you're *supposed* to scare people."

"Not with skewers you're not."

"You don't have to yell at me."

"Don't I?" She knows she's yelling, but it can't be helped.

Snuffling, whimpering, he baby-steps ahead of her. "It was Leo's fault."

"Just keep moving."

Consequences, she thinks, as the sound natters away and she feels, for a minute, as if Varney is right there with them. *You needed consequences.*

Cooper watches in contentious silence as she and Evan make their way back up the darkened walkway to the front steps. On the porch Jana waits for her eyes to acclimate then finds the doorbell. It chimes eight notes. No one comes. No downstairs lights are on.

"What're you going to tell them?" Jana says.

"That I'm sorry?"

"*Are* you sorry?"

"Yeah," he says without conviction.

His unmasked head looks tiny poking up out of the black gown. What is he responsible for at a mere six years?

"What exactly did you say to them, anyway?" she asks.

"I forget."

"You forget."

His voice is very small. "I said if they didn't bring candy I'd kill them."

She blinks, goes cold. Swimming above him, through murky

water, she is a cold-blooded creature incapable of speech. One eye looks one way, the other eye looks somewhere else. The porch shimmies. *Give me the child at seven and I will give you the man.* It's all there, some experts say, waiting to emerge. An imp, of as-yet-undisclosed character, is taking refuge in Evan's spleen right now until, at age fifteen or twenty or more, it will leap forth in a formidable act of assertion. Mute, she steadies herself on the porch railing. Evan's head shrinks and expands by the second.

The house seems dead. They wait and wait.

"Give it up," Cooper calls.

She contemplates ringing again but guesses the couple has gone to bed.

"We're going home," she announces.

That is what they do: they walk home, the moon swimming through the clouds, the skewer swinging on Cooper's belt, the sound in her head an unprecedented clatter, Leo and Varney weaving spectral dances around them.

THIRTEEN

She was picked up at the airport by Bill Hanneman, a friend and colleague of her father's. He had called her up in Oregon, leaving message after message until she called back. Though she hardly knew Bill Hanneman—she had only met him once or twice at her father's insurance company picnics—his voice stood out as a bright beacon of the familiar among the rash of harried messages left by the police and the media. She sat silently as he drove his Lincoln Continental with one hand and told her how much he would miss her father, what a good man Walter had been, how fortunate she was to have had him for a dad. He spoke loudly, as if he were giving a speech, pressing his voice louder whenever it threatened to break. "Your mom, too," Bill Hanneman said, "we'll miss her, too."

He did not mention Varney and neither did she. Like her father, Bill Hanneman was a big man. He had a receding hairline and small features clustered together at the center of his face, giving him a worried look.

It suddenly occurred to Cady to ask where she was being taken. "Back to our place," Bill said. "Judy's making us a nice meal."

"Take me home," Cady said.

"Home? You mean—"

"To my parents' house."

The car slowed. "Oh, you know, hon, I don't think that's a good idea. It's too fresh, you know? It's not gonna look too good there. I was by there this morning—and well, it just doesn't look too good. Forensics guys were there, you know, and the coroner's people and all sorts of photographers and journalists."

"Are they still there?"

"They finished up."

"Am I allowed to go there?"

"Technically, I guess so, but—"

"Take me home, please."

Bill Hanneman went quiet. He didn't say another word for the remainder of the drive. He pulled up in front of Cady's house, the house she had lived in all her life until she went to college. Like most of the other nearby houses it was single level, white stucco, with a red-tiled roof. Not large, but adequate for four. It had an interior open-air courtyard with shelves of succulents and cacti. On the tiny front lawn was a magnolia tree shaped like a giant lollipop and a row of gardenia bushes that bloomed year-round.

"Can I come in with you?" Bill Hanneman said.

Cady shook her head. Was Bill Hanneman crying? How could Mr. Hanneman be crying when she was not crying herself?

"It doesn't seem right, letting you go in there alone. I don't even know if it's legal."

"I'll be fine, Mr. Hanneman."

Simultaneously they spotted the uniformed guard (not a policeman) smoking at the end of the gardenia bushes.

"I'll talk to him," Mr. Hanneman said.

Cady watched from the car as Mr. Hanneman talked to the guard and gave him some money. The guard went and sat in his black car on the other side of the street.

"He says you're okay," Mr. Hanneman said when he came back to Cady. He frowned and glanced around as if people were hiding in the bushes eavesdropping. "But call me later, all right?"

Cady nodded. He unloaded her luggage and drove off, telling her he would phone her instead. For a long time after he left, Cady stood under the magnolia tree, looking at the house, trying to identify what was different, if anything. But everything looked the same. Piles of dead magnolia leaves clicked against each other at her feet. The scent of the gardenias tongued the air around her. A mourning dove stood on the driveway, cooing as if to comfort her.

She pushed open the gate to the courtyard. The slanting light of late afternoon sliced the courtyard into equal parts of sun and shade. She blinked hard. The pots of succulents and cacti lay smashed across the courtyard's salmon-tiled floor, a jumble of dirt and broken pottery and sinewy celadon stalks. Some of the cactus thorns had been stripped from their stalks and laid in a neat row, like sharpened fingernails, along a windowsill.

She dropped her suitcase, fumbled for her key, made herself go inside. She walked from room to room. It had been raining in Eugene when she left, and she was still wearing her blue waterproof jacket, which whined against itself as she moved. In the living room jagged triangles had been sliced from the wall-to-wall carpeting. The drapes were shredded into fine strips, which trembled with the wind of her passing. One of the cabinet doors in the kitchen hung from a single hinge and listed into the center of the room, threatening to fall. The smashed glass of the bathroom mirror bore the shape of a mangled spiderweb. The toilet bowl was filled to the brim with blood-stained Kleenex. On the sheets in all three bedrooms were fingertip smears of rust-colored blood. In her bedroom nothing was broken, but everything—her high school dresses, her collection of glass figurines and tiny tea sets, her complete collection of Judy Blume books, her pyramid of stuffed animals—had been handled and put back differently. She wondered who had moved these things: her mother, Varney, the police?

Everything she saw, she forgot; she looked back at each thing again and again until she was sure she would remember. The sound of her own breathing roared around her like the respiration of a scuba diver, and she had to concentrate hard to keep it going. In-out. In-out. She had never realized how fragile breathing could be.

When the phone rang she was standing in the den adjacent to the kitchen. The kitchen was roped off with yellow plastic tape, and the phone hunkered on the other side. She wouldn't have answered, anyway. She listened to Bill Hanneman leaving a message on the answering machine, asking if she was okay, urging her to call.

Something stopped her meandering—on the stove top lay an unwashed iron skillet crusted with blackened remnants of food. A membrane of soot had trawled across the ceiling, leaving ghostly flourishes. Her mother had been cooking in this kitchen the morning before. Her mother probably died while thinking about breakfast, perhaps calculating the days she was taking off her husband's life by feeding him bacon. Cady realized that this house must now be hers.

It could have been an hour she stood there, thinking these things. It could have been minutes. She only moved when she saw the guard looking in at her through the kitchen window.

That night she never went to bed. Bill Hanneman called two more times. Cady reached over the yellow tape and turned down the answering machine. For a while she lay on top of her bed and tried to imagine herself back in high school. But she couldn't; high school was another planet. She discovered black Varney hairs on her pillow. She tried to picture Varney now, detained in a tiny cell somewhere. He probably wasn't sleeping, either. Was he thinking about her? She kept thinking other people would call, but no one did.

The guard came to the door and asked to use the bathroom. He looked younger than she had first thought, maybe thirty. He said his name was Roberto. Later, around 4 A.M., when she went outside and sat under the magnolia, the guard came over and said she could get in his car, so she did. She was grateful he didn't try to talk. She dozed against the seat back until the sun came up.

At dawn more journalists and news crews arrived with their swollen curiosity, their antic cameras. She blinked at them through the darkened glass of Roberto's car. She had nothing to say to them, just as she had had nothing to say to the journalists who besieged her in Eugene, or the ones who circled her as she got off the plane. She had nothing to say to anyone. She watched them scrambling in front of one another, and it seemed preposterous that they were doing this to get at *her*, a nobody, a less than a nobody. Roberto intervened. He told the journalists to go away, that Cady Miller didn't want to talk. But they didn't go away.

Followed by news crews with lenses nearly the size of telescopes and a hail of shouted questions, she fled from Roberto's car to the cool darkness of the garage, where she crouched under her father's workbench and stared at the idle cars—her father's black Jeep and her mother's white Ford sedan, cars she used to beg to use in high school to drive anywhere—the mall, the beach, to school. Now they were hers.

The size of her loneliness was unspeakable. It coated her

like a tight bramble-studded sheath, and it stretched out for miles in all directions.

THE VISITING ROOM in the juvenile section of the Orange County jail smelled like cleaning solvent. She and Varney were separated by thick distorting glass. Looking through its wavy lines nauseated her. He kept his head down so all she could see was his crown, where the hair was matted and looped. There was a small patch of bare scalp, pale as unsalted butter.

He wouldn't pick up the phone through which they might speak. The only thing that connected them was the stool whose steel beam traversed the partition and supported them both like a cranky static seesaw, a twisted reminder of childhood. She tried to get him to look at her—waving, tapping the glass—but he wouldn't. Only when the warning bell sounded did he finally raise the phone. "Oh, Varney," was all she could say for at least a minute. And then, "Are you all right?" And then, "What happened? Please tell me. Please."

She knew he heard her—he'd lifted his head and she could see how his eyes registered her words—but he would not say anything, would not explain himself. She wasn't asking him stupid questions like the journalists had been yelling at her—questions that had no answers at all like: "Why did he do this?" As if the idea of irrationality or impulsivity escaped them. As if there were some single coherent reason he'd done what he'd done. All she wanted was a catalog of the events—first this, then this, then this—but he gave her nothing, and after a while she got mad, not as much about what he'd done as his refusal to talk about it.

After two or three visits with him stonewalling her, she couldn't stop herself. "Fuck you, Varney!" she yelled into the small black holes of the phone's receiver. The other visitors looked at her and scowled, and Varney turned his head from his hugged knees, staring with eyes stretched unnaturally wide. Big as his eyes appeared, they had lost their surprised look. He seemed mild and wise. After maybe a full minute, he shook his head and looked away.

The second night she was in California, she went next door to the Bissells'. Helen Bissell came to the door before Cady had even knocked. She was a kind, maternal, German-born woman with a thick neck and thick legs and long thin-ning hair. Sputtering, she threw herself into Cady. The top button of her flowered housedress dug into Cady's chest. Cady hardly knew this woman beyond borrowed sugar and conversa-tions about skunks. She waited for Helen Bissell's medley of emotions to run its course.

"You know what happened?" asked Cady.

"Of course I do, and I simply cannot believe it. I heard the shots and found your poor parents. I was the one who called the police. I am so, so sorry, honeykins."

Cady felt the bristly sheath around her again, the noise and fragility of her own breathing. It made her calm to think of this armor she had. Helen Bissell led her into the house, past her two gawking little girls, and Cady felt like an invalid— untouchable, odd, released from normal responsibilities.

"Why did your brother kill those people?" asked five-year-old Beate Bissell.

Cady blinked.

"I think that's mean," Beate said.

Helen Bissell baked incessantly and left plates of cookies and cakes outside the guest room where Cady stayed. Beate played with her dolls in the hallway, waiting for Cady to emerge. When Cady came out, Beate followed her, watching with wary interest as if Cady were some sort of unpredictable zoo animal only recently brought into captivity.

After a few days Cady moved from the Bissells' to the Sleep E-Z Inn, for privacy and to be closer to Varney. The "inn" was a no-frills place off the Santa Ana freeway. Her room smelled of stale smoke. It had miniblinds caked with hardened dust, a shower that ran hot and cold at will, and burn stains in the orange carpet. She noticed these things, but it never occurred to her to complain or request another room.

Traffic sped by without letup at all times of the day and night, a reminder to Cady how life went on. She wanted for everything to stop. She wanted everyone to notice how much can go wrong when you stop paying attention. She had a suitcase of clothes and a suitcase of books. When she was not in court or visiting with Varney or sitting in a café with Bill Hanneman, being pursued by journalists, she sat near the window with a book in her lap, open but unread, and she stared out at the cars with a sogginess throughout her body, amazed that others found the energy to drive, the interest in going places, the pride to keep their cars so clean. If death had come to her, she wouldn't have resisted. If desire had been possible, she would have desired death.

An odd assortment of people contacted her to offer their support. Odd because Cady hardly knew them. First, there was Bill Hanneman, who continued to call. No matter where she was, he tracked her down—at the Bissells', at the Sleep E-Z Inn. When Varney had court appearances, which Cady always attended, Bill Hanneman was always there to chaperone her. "I promised your dad I'd take care of you kids if anything happened to him." He had no children of his own and had no idea how to talk to her, so instead he held forth, usually about legal matters, such as the ineptitude of Varney's court-appointed lawyer. Cady could not get herself to care about these things—wasn't Varney doomed no matter what happened? When Bill Hanneman held forth, her mind meandered, leapfrogging around for a safe subject on which to rest. He had chronically bad breath. On herself she noticed an odd-smelling sweat. When they sat next to each other in court, he sometimes patted her knee in a fatherly way. She thought of how soapy clean her mother used to smell—almost babyish, as if life had not yet tainted her chemistry.

One night Cady dreamed she and her mother were swimming underwater, dodging moray eels and stinging octopi, pressed to arrive somewhere on time. Throughout, her mother was humming. Cady awoke in tears, and a memory came to her of the time she and her mother had gone to the mall together for bras and underpants and ended up buying Beth a gold silk tunic flecked with black threads and a black silk skirt to match. The skirt was short and displayed Beth's lean and inexplicably muscular legs. Cady wanted the mother she saw reflected in the store's mirror—a confident, sexy woman who would surely be a good guide. Beth wore the outfit out of the store, and she and Cady were giddy with expectation that men would descend and find Beth irresistible. But nothing out of the ordinary happened, and no one seemed to notice them, and her mother never wore the outfit again.

So many people hovered around, wanting access to Cady. They came to the hearing and corralled her in the lobby, or they called her at her hotel. Parents of people she'd been to school with; friends of her parents; the two women, Gloria and Ann, who had worked in her mother's shop; Renee Sanchez, her old guidance counselor. Renee Sanchez was an outgoing person who Cady had always liked. In Cady's freshman year Renee used to see Cady in the halls and say, "Are you all right, honey?" with sincere concern twitching around her eyes and mouth. But now she stood in front of Cady in the courthouse lobby with a smile so white and big and inspecific, it made Cady feel hopeless for everyone. They would all sink, all of them, she was certain.

It was odd how confidently people presented themselves, as if they were sure Cady needed them. They walked into her life without her consent. People who knew her a little acted as if they knew her well. It dawned slowly on Cady that some people felt there was currency in knowing her.

In court Cady tried to focus on the words of the judge and the attorneys, but the words tumbled away. There were so many court appearances and no trial had begun, only the endless legal haggling over how to proceed. Was Varney a child or an adult? Was he sane or insane? She was his sister, his closest surviving relative, the one who should be his advocate, but she felt no power to change things. They brought Varney in wearing hand-cuffs, and though he sat only two rows in front of her, it seemed as if he was thousands of miles away, on some Pacific island. He tilted his head to his lap, so she could see the sharp vertebrae that formed his neck. She could see the side of one cheek, slackened to a new shape as if he'd been drugged. She couldn't keep her eyes off him. She couldn't stop trying to get his atten-tion, but he never turned toward her. Sometimes he lifted his head to look at the judge or his attorney, but mostly he stared into his own lap. His hair was still matted, his mouth remained open, round as a surprised eye. A muttered yes or no was all they could get from him. "I bet you miss your parents," Bill Hanne-man said to her. She nodded. Her parents were gone and she mourned them, but it was Varney she yearned for deeply.

While she looked at Varney, others looked at her. Like Byron Johnson, Varney's arresting officer. She had spent some time looking at Byron Johnson, too. According to the papers, Officer Johnson had found Varney on the beach in San Clemente. The ocean was flat. Varney was skipping stones. When Officer Johnson told Varney to come, he came without resistance. Cady didn't disbelieve this necessarily, but she wanted to hear it from Varney.

Byron Johnson was cool and smooth as a Greek statue, with jutting hips and skin the color of creamy, slightly yellow coffee. His face never moved but remained set in a look of permanent contradiction. One day Officer Johnson stopped near where Cady was sitting, and he whispered to her, "Tough break." He shook his head. After that he would try to catch her eye and nod to her in court. Eventually he took to sitting with her and Bill Hanneman.

She tried not to look at the other people in the gallery, but sometimes she couldn't help it. The families of Andy Carnack and Mr. Phillips were always there, and when they sat in the adjacent row, her heart ticked like a Geiger counter. Andy Carnack's mother was a thin dark-haired woman who never stopped crying. Sometimes her sobs filled the courtroom. Her husband told the papers, "You have to understand Andy was all we had. Our lives are over."

Mr. Phillips's parents were retired; his wife was young and athletic-looking. They all had tight, small mouths and hard-set, sun-damaged faces. Sometimes all the members of both families stood in a circle in the courthouse lobby as if they were conducting a ceremony, as if, in their bereavement, the courthouse belonged to them. When they sat in court—they, like Cady, came to all the hearings—they watched Varney as closely as she did. Their looks were sadistic, scary, she thought. What were they there for but to exact blood? They wanted Varney tried as a sane, fully responsible adult. They wanted him put to death.

They wanted him to burn in hell. They told the papers this. Bill Hanneman told her not to read the papers, but she couldn't help it. She read about her parents and Varney—and herself—as if they were strangers. It was all other people's ideas of who they were. People described them as a normal family, but they made other claims about Varney that seemed to challenge normalcy. They said Varney had been an unhappy child, sensitive, introverted, troubled. None of what they said seemed entirely wrong, but none of it was right, either.

Varney had been full of fun, too. He always laughed a lot. He was sensitive, yes, and easily hurt, but he wasn't unhappy. She had a photograph of him laughing. It used to hang on her bulletin board, but now she carried it in her wallet.

"Talk to me," she begged into the jail's visiting-room phone. Varney stared back at her through the thick glass. Who knew how that glass was distorting him, how he really looked, what he saw? If she could just lay her hands on his skin, she was sure he would talk.

She targeted one of the nicer-looking journalists from an Orange County paper, a man who, from the beginning, had seemed less predatory. He didn't leap in her face as some of the other journalists did. He had kind eyes and puffy skin that dimpled under his eyes and near his ears. She felt a bit sorry for him. She asked him to go for coffee. In a small bodega a block from the courthouse, she said to him: "You have to set the record straight. Varney was not unhappy. He laughed all the time. He had a good life. He was kind to me and to my parents and to animals. Certain things bothered him, that's all." She pulled out the photo.

It was a slightly blurry black-and-white photo that showed Varney with his head thrown back in laughter, his mouth wide open, his eyes squinting. She remembered the moment, the *hawing* sound of his laughter and the pleasure it gave her, though she couldn't remember what had been so funny.

The journalist, Marc Andrews, took the photo from her and nodded slowly. "May I keep it for a few days?" She nodded and thanked him.

MURDERER FOUND HUMOR IN ODD THINGS read the next morning's headline. The story that followed quoted Cady saying: "A lot of things bothered him." Cady reread the words three times, four times, five times, trying to recall exactly what she had said. Greg Finley, who claimed to be a classmate of Varney's, was also quoted. "The guy had this laugh like a girl's. It was psycho. He was the kind of guy who, like, wouldn't stop laughing if someone had slipped on a banana peel and broke a leg. Okay, first it's funny, but then you see it's not and you get serious. But Varney would laugh for a long time after everyone else knew to stop." The article depicted Varney as a demented character who took pleasure in the macabre.

When Marc Andrews returned the photo to Cady in the courtroom, she refused to look at him or reach out a hand. His kind eyes counted for nothing. A hard embolus of hatred floated through her. She heard the roar of her breathing again. He laid the photo on the handrail beside her and it fluttered to the floor.

FOURTEEN

She falls into a comalike sleep, and the next day, Sunday, she sleeps unusually late, awakening to the murmur of Cooper's and Evan's voices downstairs. The voices bring to mind pictures of furry caterpillars, a whole cadre of them, dense and squiggly and moving left to right. They seem determined, these caterpillars, and on the verge of something. Evan's voice alone has always been suggestive to her of trembling yellow Jell-O, but coupled with Cooper's voice, the caterpillars have replaced the Jell-O. Then, quite suddenly, the memory of the previous night takes shape. She sees a faceless couple retreating quickly into their house. She sees the demonic turn of her own child's face. It wouldn't be so bad if she actually knew the people he had threatened, but her habit of reclusion has kept her from the neighbors. Except for Carolyn Janklow, she has only a nodding acquaintance with the others who live nearby, and she cannot remember precisely who lives in the house Evan terrorized. She lies in bed, listening to the solid stream of conversation and trying to bring back the caterpillars, or even the trembling Jell-O. "Fadata, fadata, fadata," she whispers. "Fadata, fadata, fadata."

Robed and still unreasonably sleepy, she wanders downstairs. Cooper and Evan sit at the kitchen table, eating toasted bagels and chatting. The morning paper lies open beside Cooper's place. Evan's plate is strewn with bright orange Butterfinger candy wrappers. As he listens to Cooper, he plays Bonk the Hippos, a game that "tests reflexes" by asking you to whack hippos on the head with tiny hammers activated by your thumbs.

"The other girl is in a coma," Cooper is saying. "You know what a coma is? It's like a sleep you can't wake up from. Like Sleeping Beauty."

"I wanna see," says Evan, stopping his game to lean over the paper. "Where's the dead one?"

Jana stands behind Cooper, looking over his shoulder to the headline that reads: HALLOWEEN HORROR. "What's going on?"

"There was a murder last night. Only a few blocks away. Two college girls were attacked. One is dead, and the other is in a coma."

"You're telling *Evan* about this?" Jana says. "He doesn't need to hear this."

"I do, too. I saw it first. I read *Hall-o-ween* right there." He points to the headline.

"He's going to hear about it, Jana. It happened four blocks from us."

"She got shot, right, Dad?" says Evan, proud of his knowledge, knowledge his own mother doesn't yet have. "Right *here*." He punches his belly, doubles over, and comes up grinning. "Ow."

"They've taken a Lummi into custody," Cooper says.

"What's a Lummi?"

"A Native American from the Lummi tribe."

"Native Americans are good at killing," Evan says, showing off yet more of his store of knowledge. "We learned about them. They kill fish and buffalo and—"

"Not people, though," Cooper says.

"Stop. Stop right now." Jana covers her ears. Evan turns and stares at her, his eyes blazing with interest.

"Jana. Jana. Jana," says Cooper. He shakes his head and closes the paper.

She removes her fingers from her ears, which whir with the loud white noise of her own blood flow. At the counter she gets herself coffee, strong and black.

Every so often it happens again—an act of violence occurs (a school shooting, an assassination attempt, a parent killing a child) that captures the public's attention. People react with disbelief as if what has happened is a startling human aberration, as if men and women had *not* been inflicting violence upon one another for millennia. They debate again about what it means to be human and put forth the tired notion that human beings are fundamentally beasts. They suggest the equally worn idea that modern life has reached such a frantic pitch that it has caused an epidemic of craziness and violence. Each time there is an outcry—a plea for more police, or less-easy access to guns, or stronger families, or better schools, or more mental health facilities. There are dire predictions that the world is coming to an end. The pundits puff themselves up, strut and pontificate, peddling their black-and-white view of things, their unidimensional solutions.

And each time what dismays Jana most is that no one has a memory. It is as if John Wilkes Booth and Charles Manson and John Hinkley and Varney Miller and myriad others have never visited this world. People's memories do what they do with childbirth—they repress the nastiness. A pact is made and everyone signs on. *Forget this, and if you happen to remember, for God's sake, don't tell.* A collective willed amnesia.

And each time when one of these violent events has occurred and the newspapers have been splattered with pictures of the detritus of human rage, and Jana is asking herself where all these people were and why their memories have shrunk to the size of dust motes, she feels both relief and disbelief and even spasms of indignation that the events that have shaped her life mean nothing to anyone else anymore. She holes up, shrouds herself in work, and holds her breath, waiting for something—for discovery, for change (in herself? in the world?). For thunder or silence. For a prophet or an apocalypse. Something. *Something*. But then amnesia has its way of swallowing her, too, and now it is hard to recall how each time in the past she has simply resumed breathing again.

"What happened to the body, Dad?"

Cooper's voice is low, controlled, but Jana can hear the anger rumbling through it. "Mommy doesn't want us talking about this."

"Go to the living room, Evan," Jana says, her back turned to both of them.

"Go, son," says Cooper.

Evan, sensing the seriousness of the occasion gets up without resistance and goes to the living-room doorway, where he hovers.

"All the way," Cooper orders.

Evan vanishes around the doorframe. Cooper's whisper cracks loud. "What're you trying to do to him? This is *life*. You can't protect him from *life*."

"It's not *life*. It's *death* and there's no need to rub it in."

"You think *not* talking about murder and violence is going to make them go away? You're overprotecting him. You've got to talk to him about this stuff and teach him how to look at it."

She looks out at the firm gray day. Her vision blurs. His voice pummels her back.

"I'm telling you, you scare me sometimes the way you lock yourself off in your little cocoon. You can do it to yourself, but I'm not going to let you do it to him. My mom tried that with me, and it's taken me close to forty years to recover."

A seagull comes to an abrupt landing in the middle of the street. He twists his head quickly this way and that, turning it in ways it seems it shouldn't turn.

"Okay, *you* do it," she says. "*You* decide how many guns he should have and how much murder he should have for breakfast. Because I can't make these decisions anymore, and someday that skewer of his is going to end up in someone's *gut.*"

The air swooshes out of her. Her voice withers into stillness. The phone rings, perforating the silence. Cooper lips the rim of his coffee mug without drinking.

"Isn't it freaky," says Robin's voice into the phone machine. She seems to invade the house, bold as a vagabond, pillaging all the untouched shrines, filling the crevices with sound. "I need to talk to you, Jana. I want to know what you're going to tell Evan. Stuff like this isn't supposed to happen in towns like this. This town is supposed to be *safe.* That's why we moved here, isn't it?"

"I want Max. I want Max," Evan chants from the living room.

"How long are you going to let her go on?" asks Cooper.

"You're free to answer," Jana says, the chill of her voice matching Cooper's.

Wide awake now, she glances at him. His mouth is drawn to one side as if he is reining in further words. His face is splotched with patches of red and white. She has not touched him this morning, and now she won't.

"Evan, where are you?" she says.

He steps out from behind the doorframe, smiling, cocksure, confident that his own gleeful spirit will get him out of trouble and cure whatever is ailing his parents as well. "I want Max. Can we have Max over? I wanna show him my Halloween candy."

"I want you to get dressed *right now*. We're going out."

"Mom, you know what? You can't *eat* murder."

"Right *now*," she says.

"What about Max?"

OUTSIDE THE AIR is clammy. The street is empty of traffic. Though it's nearly nine-thirty most of the curtains are still drawn, making the houses look tight and refusing.

The house in question is four houses down. On the sidewalk near the steps up to it lies a smashed pumpkin, the one that last night spread its artistically plotted grin onto the street from a high pillar. In a neighborhood of beautifully kept houses, this is one of the most elegant, a large Victorian restored with perfect authenticity. Jana has admired the house from a distance, but approaching it unnerves her. Evan stoops to examine the pumpkin innards, sticking his finger through what was once a grin. In his crouch he seems small and forlorn. He looks up at the house, back to the smashed pumpkin, up at Jana. "Do I have to? I already said I was sorry."

"You have to say it again. When you said it before, they couldn't hear you."

"Will you come with me?"

"I'll come to the door with you, but I'm not going to say anything. It's up to you to do the talking."

They mount the stairs at a glacial pace, Evan shambling in front, a drooping, joyless body, like some mollusk cast from its shell, living on without its usual support. At the top of the long flight of stairs, they look out over the rooftops of the houses across the street to the petulant gray waters of the bay.

"Go ahead," Jana prompts, pushing him forward. "I'll ring the doorbell for you."

A fit-looking woman in her sixties comes to the door, clad in belted khaki trousers and a pale blue fleece. Her gray-brown hair is neatly, almost mannishly cropped, but despite her good grooming, she looks frayed. She holds the door only partway open, as if threatening to close it at any moment. Though Evan stands in front of the woman, she looks over Evan's head to Jana.

"Yes?"

"My son has something to say to you," Jana says.

Evan looks at Jana. His face clouds as if he might cry.

"Go ahead," Jana prompts. "Say what you have to say."

Evan stares at the ground. "I'm sorry," he whispers.

"What?" the woman asks. "Speak up; I can't hear you."

"I'm sorry," he says, his voice no louder.

"I still can't hear you," the woman says.

"You have to talk louder, Evan."

"I'm sorry!" This time Evan nearly shouts.

The woman's mouth tightens. "I take it this is the child from last night?" she asks Jana. "The one who almost gave my husband heart failure?"

"Yes," Jana says. "We're so, so sorry."

"I should hope so. We almost called the police, you know. Where in the world does a child learn to do that kind of thing? I know you'll tell me it's TV or some such thing, but—Are you his mother?"

Jana hesitates, then nods. Of course she's his mother, who else would she be? Evan has sidled around behind her legs. She hears her own deep breathing and Evan's. She hears a gravelly click in the woman's respiration. The woman has opened the door wider in her ire, so Jana can see the slats of the back of a Mission-style rocker and the limp legs of someone rocking.

"You can imagine how we felt waking up to this morning's

papers. That boy of yours needs help." The woman is working herself into a controlled tizzy. Her spine is straighter than ever, her voice quietly bristling as she looks down at Evan. "Didn't anyone ever tell you you need to look at a person when you talk to them?"

"Thank you for listening to his apology," Jana says. Like an impaired learner, she intones the words slowly with spaces between. "I'm taking him home now," she says.

She finds Evan's hand, walks with deliberation, step by step down the flight, down, endlessly down, into some abyss only she can see. She no longer sees the vista before her—the smashed pumpkin, the recoiled neighborhood, the inky bay beyond—she is aware only of Evan's cold bony hand, the quiet tinyness of him, his quelled bravado, and her own urge to defend him at all costs in this world where the best intentions go awry and there's nothing you can count on, even yourself.

"I hate that lady," Evan says.

"No, you don't," Jana half whispers, half croaks.

"You're a good girl. I don't have to worry about you," her mother used to say.

But what did her mother know? She was *not* a good girl. She lied to her mother. She went to the beach when she said she was going to the library. She lied to her friends, too—or the people that passed for friends—about how she'd been to Hawaii, how she'd seen Mel Gibson there. At the swimming pool she once took a bathing suit that didn't belong to her. It was only by chance that it was never revealed and circumstances shone the light on someone else.

Forces lined up. Chips fell. Chance reigned. But if circumstances had been different—and it wasn't all that hard to paint them differently—she knows she could have been there looking down that barrel just as easily as Varney.

FIFTEEN

At home, as soon as they close the front door, she kneels, clutches Evan, stamps him all over with kisses. She feels the relief of her love, the way it blots out everything. Evan relaxes into her shoulder for one glorious soothing moment before wriggling free.

Cooper is gone, but the house is full of him; it thrums with his haste and his anger. He has left his crumb-strewn breakfast dishes on the table, a pile of muddy clothes in the bathroom. He has even left a light on in his workshop. Everywhere there is too much fierceness, too much friction. She can't get the neighbor woman's caustic face out of her head. Normally she would run it off, but she can't leave Evan unsupervised. She paces from room to room, checking for dust, picking up toys, until she finally settles into dishwashing, keeping an eye on Evan. He has fallen into himself, lying on his side in the living room, driving a Hot Wheels car repeatedly across the same stretch of carpet, a behavior that has, in the past, concerned her for its resemblance to autism. Back and forth, back and forth he does this, Varney-like in his self-containment, his *vroom* a quiet drone, which she borrows now for her ears' own repetitions. What can he be thinking of? The murder? The punitive neighbor? Maybe the woman is right; maybe they should consult someone to find out if these sudden lurches inward are normal or if they bespeak incipient disturbance. Perhaps not autism, but bipolarity. She has never had much use for psychiatrists. In medical school she did a psychiatry rotation, and it did not seem as if the patients improved much under psychiatric care. Except for the pharmacology, the treatments seemed speculative and unscientific.

She scrubs hard at truculent jam and burns her zealous fingers with scalding water. "Are you okay, Evan?" she asks after a while.

"Vroom, t-t-t-t, vroom, t-t-t-t."

"Evan?"

Is it active refusal or does he really not hear? She can't say. The phone rings, and this time it's Seretha.

"Are you there? Cooper, honey, pick up...Hell-o-o. It's me...I assume you've read the papers. I just hope you're okay....Are you there?...Well, I'll be seeing you soon."

Evan sits up. "Why didn't you answer, Mom? It was Gramma."

"Would you like to have Max over?" she says.

"Max, Max, Max."

Jana, receiver at her ear, sits at the round oak table in the kitchen and uses her fingernail to scrape at black dirt sunk deep into the table's grain.

"We need to huddle," Robin is saying on the other end of the line. "Like primitive people would gather around a fireplace to shore each other up in threatening times. Droughts, battles. Maybe we need to do some crazy collective dance. Put our Halloween costumes back on again and go wild. How *was* your Halloween by the way?"

Evan, not yet a master of furtiveness, tiptoes by her, heading for the den to sneak a few cartoons while she's on the phone. She lets him go, trying to adopt Cooper's attitude (A *few cartoons, what the heck difference does it make?*).

"Halloween is a story," Jana says slowly, knowing that by saying this she is opening a door through which she will eventually be coaxed.

"Well—do tell," Robin says.

But it's all too new—the story itself, the idea of telling it.

"Go on. I won't laugh."

"Laugh? I don't think laughing is the issue. In person I'll tell you." She's accustomed to lying, but not to the nip of shame she feels when lying to Robin. She thinks how in each of these exchanges with Robin there are small promises, tiny links, the start, she supposes, of friendship.

Not hearing cartoon sounds but instead a reporter's voice, she gets up.

"So maybe an hour or so, is that good?" Robin says.

On the screen a wobbly camera pans over a bloody sweatshirt, then along a patch of dirt to a log strewn with trousers, underwear, socks. The camera pulls back to reveal yellow police tape and a reporter standing in a grove of evergreens. Evan stares at the screen, transfixed.

"Evan, turn that off right now."

Evan continues staring.

"I've got to go," Jana says. She disconnects the phone. She places her body in front of the screen, douses the TV. With the remote control Evan turns it on again, snorting with laughter. Once more Jana kills it. She lunges for the remote control, and when Evan holds it out of her reach, giggling, taunting, riddled with high humor, she sees her hand, palm flat, inflamed with feeling, sailing through the breezeless air and landing with a dull *thwack* on Evan's cheek.

Silenced for a second, he begins to titter, but his titter soon turns to sobbing, and he runs from the den up to his bedroom, where he slams the door. The pitch of his weeping rises.

Jana stares hard at the nineteen-inch TV, which rests inside a large wooden cabinet on rollers. A compartment below holds the VCR. The cabinet is Cooper's workmanship, beautiful, but large and heavy, and though it's designed for moving, they never move it. She unplugs the TV, disconnects the cable. Now nothing can enter the house unbidden. Standing behind the cabinet, she pushes. The rollers squeak into motion, making a diminished fifth—a mournful interval—with Evan's wails. The cabinet crashes into the doorframe. She backs it up, tries again. It *eerks* its way through the doorway, almost getting stuck.

She pushes it slowly down the hallway. Inch by inch she goes, running ahead to steer, behind to push, accomplishing with the brute force of her will what would normally be a two-person job. When she reaches the back mudroom, the doorbell rings. *Seretha,* she thinks. She creeps back to the belly of the house. Through the side kitchen window, she glimpses Max and Robin on the front steps, frowning, curious, concerned. Jana shrinks. The doorbell sounds again. Evan's wails crescendo. Jana plasters herself against the kitchen wall where she can't be seen from outside. She waits for the ringing of the doorbell to subside. After a minute or two the ringing stops and she hears Max's and Robin's footsteps plodding back down the front stairs, their chatty voices fading.

Evan's wailing is a wall, a permanent fixture, a Life Condition for them both.

With effort she guides the TV cabinet through the back door, where three impassable concrete steps await her. She searches the shop for something from which she might fashion a ramp. She finds two ten-foot boards, which, unwieldy as they are, will have to suffice. She lays them side by side and struggles to lift the bulky cabinet over the lip created between them and the step. The rig slides precariously down the boards and clunks onto the driveway, making a worrisome noise but resulting in no apparent damage. She pushes it over the last few feet of driveway and through the wide garage door. Finally, it's in there; the TV and its cabinet are smack in the middle of Cooper's woodshop, out of Evan's easy view.

At last she stops moving. Only then does she look at her palm, see the swirl of its unnatural color, the crosshatch of its lines, the browned calluses, the too-much life.

Inside, Evan is no longer crying, but his face is swollen and he pouts into his pillow. With a Snickers she coaxes him to sit up. He takes the chocolate and eats it voraciously so it leaves a wide brown path across his cheeks and lips and teeth. She does not try to clean him; she laces her hands, hating her knowledge of them, and brings him another Snickers when he requests it. "I'm sorry," she whispers. "Evan, honey, I'm so sorry. I love you. You know that, don't you?" She carries him downstairs, relieved to see that neither of his cheeks is redder than the other. She builds a fire. They hold their bare feet and hands straight out so the flame glows through their flesh. They play Slapjack. Evan's high spirits inch back. They are safe and warm. Tales of murder cannot separate them when they're here within reach of one another.

Cooper returns, looking as if he bears news of import. His jacket collar circles his neck stiffly. He wears only one glove, and he picks at its fingertips. "It's going to be okay," he says quietly, looking in at them.

"Of course it is," she says. She notices the prominent tendons in his neck, the eyes missing their usual luster. "You were working?"

He nods.

"It's going okay?" she says.

He nods again and shies away from her gaze. He usually

gives her details: the special woods he was thinking of using, the changing minds of his customers, his ideas about a new design.

"I've got 'em all, Mom. You weren't paying attention." Evan holds up a wad of slippery cards, almost the whole deck.

"So you do."

"Mom's a slow slapper," Evan tells Cooper.

"Is she?"

Jana blinks, strokes her palm. "You shouldn't work so much," she says. "You'll tire yourself out."

"I'll decide how much I work," he says quietly. He sits on the green carpet with them, holding a beer, crossing his legs awkwardly. (*He's trying*, she tells herself.) He hasn't removed his green jacket and cold from it leaches into the air.

"Hey, Ev," he says. "Why does the burglar cross the road, roll in the mud, and cross back to the other side of the road?"

"To go pee-pee!" Evan says, tittering.

"No, silly. Because he's a dirty double-crosser. Hey, did Mom call?"

Jana nods. "I didn't pick up."

The game is falling apart. Evan has spread the cards around the carpet, and he is slapping all the face cards. Distracted, Cooper stands up and moves to the fire, rubbing his hands together.

"Are you home for good?" she asks.

He stabs the logs with the poker, moving them to new positions. "I've got to go out again," he says.

"Can I come with you?" Evan asks.

"Maybe. We'll see."

"We can go see where that girl was killed," Evan says.

"I'd rather he didn't go out right now," Jana says.

"Mo-om."

Cooper frowns. "I wouldn't take him there. What do you take me for?"

He stalks into the den. She holds her breath, waiting. The flecked green carpet fibers march across her sight line.

"What the fuck happened to the TV?"

"Uh-oh, Daddy said a bad word."

Jana rises.

"Wait, Mommy, we're not finished."

She looks at Evan but cannot get words out. She is floating, already removed to another world, already sure her own death is imminent. It is best for her to die now, before she ruins Evan or does something equally dire. But she must tell Cooper to be kind to Evan. Quit the Sidwell job if necessary, but remember to be kind.

"I moved the TV to the garage."

Cooper, standing in the space where the TV once stood, looks at her blankly, all his warmth depleted. "You did *what?*"

She is scared of him and doesn't dare repeat herself.

"Why are you doing this to me?" he says.

"It's about Evan, not you. I don't want him watching programs about murder, and I'm trying to reduce the retinal stimulation in his life."

A smile toys with Cooper's dimples. His chuckle loosens her. His head rocks slowly from shoulder to shoulder. "I *know* you're kidding. *Reduce his retinal stimulation?* Tell me you're kidding."

She says nothing. Their eyes duel, making her scared again. She looks for bravery. "I'm *not* kidding, Cooper. There are studies—" His expression sheds all traces of humor, and the look that remains is opaque as obsidian. "Forget it," she says.

"Sometimes I think my mom is right. You're too educated for your own damn good."

Something isn't right with him. His normally gentle brown eyes have become glazed and they seem to be shrinking inside his head. "Come here," she says. "Sit down. What's wrong?"

"What's next? No beer? No chocolate? You want me to be one of your experimental subjects like Evan is? See what you can make me into? You earn the big bucks. I'm willing to cut you some slack. But this—uh-uh—"

"Cooper, why are you like this?" she pleads. "Just be—"

"Be what?" he snaps.

"I don't know. Nice, I guess. Like you usually are." She hears her own lameness. You can't command niceness. You can't assume influence. Everyone moves on an uninterruptible trajectory.

A car passes, pumping rap from its open windows, and the sound enters Jana and takes hold of her heart's rhythm. Cooper wanders to the window and looks out, thwacking the empty beer bottle against his flat palm. The rap has disappeared into the distance but it has left its insistence behind. Her heart beats so loudly she is afraid it will summon Evan.

Thwack, goes Cooper's beer bottle.

Kerthump, goes her heart.

Cooper turns to her and leans back against the windowsill. He speaks to her in a low, formal voice, and she has the eerie feeling his brown eyes have turned blue.

"Why do you want to make my son into some prissy kid who doesn't know the first thing about TV shows or *anything*? Do you think that's *helping* him?"

Later she will wonder how long it was that they remained in those positions, her entire world controlled by the *thwack* of his beer bottle, the *kerthump* of her heart, her fear. It will have seemed like hours, but it is only minutes.

"Don't get crazy on me, Jana. Please."

"I'm not crazy," she whispers. "The world is so bad."

He sighs. She takes his hand. He lets it be taken. She leads him outside to his workshop. The TV stands there like some giant moose, lost and baffled, not sure how it got there.

"You see?" she says. "You can watch out here whenever you want."

Cooper sighs again. "Sure. It'll be fine." He puts his arm around her back and squeezes her upper arm. "Yeah. We'll do the whole shebang here—reinstall the cable, et cetera. I just hope this is going to work out for you, because I'm not going to do it again next week in some other place."

"Work out for *Evan* you mean. Not me. *Evan*."

"Whatever. I watched a ton of TV when I was a kid, and I turned out fine. Well, true—I'm only a carpenter. But I'm a darn good one. But if you say it's not good, it must not be good. You would know—you're the doctor."

"Oh, Cooper, don't do this, please."

"Do what?"

"You know, give in like this."

"You don't want me to resist. You don't want me to give in."

"I want you to quit Sidwell. It's putting too much pressure on you, and we don't need the money."

"Okay, I'll quit. Just as I get the biggest job of my entire life, I'll quit and be the househusband so my wife can wear the pants in the family."

"That's not what I'm saying. I only—it was right in our *house*. In front of us anytime we pushed the button. All that death. All that meanness—I couldn't—you know how Evan is, how *fascinated* he is by electronics and TV and—I'm think-ing of getting his testosterone level checked—that skewer thing last night—they almost called the *police*—"

He watches her losing her words, hyperventilating. He does

not move to her. He does not take her in his arms. "Listen to yourself," he says.

"What?"

He shrugs. "Whatever. You do whatever you need to do. Right now I need to stay right here and watch some football, maybe boost my testosterone a little."

WHEN JANA TURNS in she hopes Cooper is asleep, but he's not. They lie awake without touching. Jana moves the side of her hand to the side of his. They lie inert, exchanging warmth, taking measure of the degree and severity and cellular depth of their disagreement.

"Is Sidwell going okay?" she asks.

"Sidwell is fine."

"And Mitch?"

"Mitch is fine. Why do you care about Sidwell?"

She has no answer.

"Do I ask you about the ER?"

"There's nothing to ask," she says. "The ER is fine."

YOU FEEL THE gangrenous creep of rage. There must be something to do, but what? What turns rage back once it has moved in? Love does not turn back rage. You've known love and it didn't fix anything.

Wouldn't it be such freedom to let rage take hold?

SIXTEEN

One day, after a month or so had passed, Varney spoke to Cady. He clutched the visiting-room phone and the words leaked out of him in a slow drone. Start to finish he told her what he had done. He remembered such small things—how the cooking bacon smelled; how oil hopped off the pan with sharp pops; how their mother whispered "Varney, Varney, Varney," before her eyes, engorged with imminent death, rolled up; how his finger on the trigger felt stiff as an old man's; how their father hurried out to the kitchen with his shirt unbuttoned, exposing a triangle of sad gray chest hair; how he shouted, "*Jesus.*" How dirt had collected in a deep wrinkle of Mr. Phillips's neck and looked like a string of tiny ants marching to his ear; how Andy Carnack said, "Give me a break," in a disgusted, dismissive way as if he were acting in some movie, and though he didn't move, he looked across the room as if he could will himself elsewhere; how after pulling the trigger—*click-click-click*, a sound which unfurled before Varney's eyes pictures of chrome hubcaps spinning madly—after which, each time, he closed his eyes and found his inner lids slicked a bright purple. He remembered the looks they all gave him before he started to run in a mad tear to the beach—looks of pity and disgust, the looks you would give to a rabid animal you mistakenly thought you had cornered. And he remembered arriving at the

beach, sweating, trembling, cold, thinking (mistakenly) no one
was behind him—how was it possible no one was in pursuit?—
and wondering how the water could possibly be so calm.

The whole time he spoke he watched Cady, his eyes
trolling her face for signs of judgment. She nodded a bit, but
did not frown, did not smile, did not utter a sound. When he
was done talking, he hung up the phone (though visiting hours
weren't over) and lowered his head. "Varney," she said, shaking
her receiver, trying to revive the dead connection, "Varney, I'm
with you, okay?" She was his sister; judgment was beside the
point. Couldn't he see she wasn't going to criticize him?

Outside the jail it was a war zone. People had gathered with
signs urging the death penalty or action to stop school violence. The sun was white, and dry hot winds wouldn't stop
blowing. Cady squinted at the mob. They swarmed around her
as if she were at the center of it all and could single-handedly
put things to right. They yelled things she couldn't hear but
could surmise. She ducked and ran to the shelter of Bill Hanneman's car. Byron Johnson was there, too. He had taken to
protecting her also, coming to court even when he was off duty
to escort her through the pressing crowd. He leaned into her,
whispering instructions. With his arm linked in hers and Mr.
Hanneman on her other side, she was sandwiched in safety.

But she wasn't safe. The Phillips and the Carnack families
thought she was as guilty, by dint of blood, as Varney himself.
Their eyes, in the courthouse lobby, speared her with contempt. What did they want her to do? Sometimes she imagined
lying in their midst and letting them trample her, squeezing her
flatter and flatter to unconsciousness and death so she wouldn't
have to listen anymore.

Instead, she let herself be ferried through the tempest of
people with opinions (she who had none) and she learned to
float and let the fury ricochet off her. She felt herself becoming

slow and tough. She let others walk and talk for her, the way people use artificial lungs during surgery.

One day she went to the courtroom ladies' room during a break in the proceedings. It was a bleak place with greenish brown walls, dim fluorescent lighting, a cracked mirror, stained toilet bowls, and dripping faucets. As she emerged from her stall, she caught a glimpse of some woman in the mirror who turned out to be herself. As she was absorbing the shock of seeing in herself the same gaunt intensity she saw in Varney, she saw someone else—Mr. Phillips's wife, Maureen. Maureen had bright blond hair and a shiny, sunburned face. Their eyes met in the mirror. Maureen Phillips's unnaturally green eyes seemed to protrude from the rest of her face. Cady stared so hard she lost track of which face was hers. Both of the mirror's faces looked like strangers. Maureen Phillips's eyes moved from the mirror to Cady herself; Cady's eyes moved to Maureen. Cady wanted desperately to look away, but returning the gaze was her only protection. Trapped, she couldn't get to the door without walking past Maureen. Maureen twisted her mouth.

Cady cleared her throat. "I'm sorry I—"

"*You* didn't do it. *He* did." Maureen shook her head in a movement that seemed as unlikely to stop as a pendulum. "You must feel icky, icky, icky," she said.

She took a few steps toward Cady, and Cady felt like running. Maureen reached out and touched Cady's upper arm, only a light pressure, but it seemed to radiate everywhere in Cady's body, as if Maureen had special powers to damn or to heal.

"Every time I think I can't keep going, I look at you and I feel so bad for you." She leaned forward and wrapped Cady in her swimmer's arms with awkward, nearly savage force. The smell of chlorine and floral perfume wafted over Cady.

Maureen whispered. "You probably hate him even more than I do." Abruptly, Maureen let go, turned, and pushed out through the swinging door. Then Cady was alone, surrounded by the din of her own breathing.

SHE STOOD ACROSS the street, ankle deep in ice plant, staring at the house she'd grown up in. The garage door had been spray painted with huge red letters. FUCK YOU, ASSHOLE. Cady thought she had never seen such ugly words. Their letters carved troughs in her brain, and her mind flew to Maureen Phillips. She couldn't believe no one had told her about this painting, or that none of the neighbors had covered it up. It was a huge blight on the entire block. On the other hand, maybe one of the neighbors—she didn't know them well enough to guess which one—had done it. It wasn't here the last time she had come. She'd come by two or three times over the last two months to think about putting the house on the market and to catalog what had to be done, but she hadn't been able to bring herself to go inside again.

Today she was supposed to be meeting a realtor, Betty Flannagan. But maybe Betty had driven by the house, seen the scrawled angry words, and changed her mind.

"It's going to be a hard sell, honey," Betty had said over the phone, sounding tired and dubious. "Now that the house has a history."

Finally Betty had agreed to come by. Cady tried to think about how she would feel with the house sold. She couldn't imagine spending another night in there, obsessively reviewing all the details Varney had described. And everyone told her to sell it—Bill Hanneman and Byron Johnson and the neighbor Mrs. Bissell. It seemed to be something everyone had to say to her—"Sell that house"—even Renee Sanchez, her old guidance counselor, said so.

But if she sold it, where would she belong, with her parents dead and Varney doubtless locked up for life? This stucco dwelling was all that remained of their family life, and it still held drawers full of clothes and kitchen utensils and photo-graphs, not to mention all her own things, like the glass fig-urines. She tried to imagine walking away from all that, and it was the same as picturing herself with a shaved head, light, re-lieved, and full of regret.

Betty Flannagan drove up in a silver Mercedes. She rolled down her window as she parked. "I know. I know. I already heard about it." She was a dervish, with mannishly short hair dyed a bright brick red. She sprang from her car, red miniskirt hiked high, red tennis shoes bounding. With a can of spray paint, she attacked the garage door, squirting white arcs until only the faintest whisper of letters remained. "Asshole your-self," she said as she sprayed. "Someone out there *wants* this place. I'm sure of it." Something had changed in Betty since their earlier phone conversation.

Cady remained in the dirt-strewn courtyard while Betty toured the house. The door was open, and Cady could hear Betty moving from room to room, opening closets and cup-boards and cabinets, turning on faucets, testing sliding doors. She was trying to turn these bloodstained rooms into a com-modity. In Betty's capable hands, it would no longer be the site of a tragic event but a source of dollars and cents.

Cady gazed at the chips of broken pot, the desiccated stalks, the dirt no longer in piles but spread in a wide flat swath across the patio. She should sweep away this blunt reminder of Varney's rampage, but the sight exhausted her. She left the patio and went back out onto the street. She thought of the friends, Kristen and Blake, she had come to know shortly be-fore she left Oregon. Now she had almost forgotten them. It seemed arbitrary that they had become friends in the first place. They had not even tried to contact her since she'd been down here, at least not as far as she knew.

Betty came out to the street snouting her lips and jotting notes on a clipboard.

"Well, you'll want to do some major cleaning and painting. And some deodorizing—there're some pretty ripe smells swirling around in there. And there is repair work to be done. I know a great guy for that. Normally I recommend furnished, but in this case I think it might suggest—well, something unsavory."

It is unsavory, Cady thought.

"As for a price," Betty said, "I'm going to have to go back to the office and plug in a few figures. I'll get back to you."

After Betty Flannagan left, Cady drove down to the harbor. She was driving her mother's white Ford sedan, which seemed too bright, but it was better than driving her father's Jeep, which seemed too big. Bill Hanneman, who had been handling all financial matters, had received an eviction notice from the landlord of the harbor building where her mother's shop was housed. It was up to Cady to make a decision about the inventory.

"Take what you want, hon," Bill Hanneman told her, "and I'll have the rest boxed up. We'll do a bulk sale. I know some interested parties."

It was a brisk day in mid-December. The shops were dressed up for Christmas, with garlands of evergreen and holly and little white lights. The pine scents mingled with the moist salty chill of the air, infusing shoppers and diners with a rush of well-being. Cady wore dark glasses and an oversized navy sweatshirt, the huge hood of which she could draw around her cheeks like blinders. She moved quickly along the path that led to her mother's shop, sidestepping people, avoiding eye contact, wondering if anyone here would know who she was.

Inside the shop a layer of dust had gathered on everything, on the porcelain dolphins, on the whales and manta rays made of ebony and marble, on the outer glass of the ships in bottles. It had worked its way into the fur of the stuffed seals, and it scummed the keys of the cash register. Even the postcards were coated. She ran a finger over the countertop and realized the dust had been there long enough to turn gummy. Removal would require more than a quick swipe of a rag.

Now that she was here, she had no idea what to do. She had never much liked her mother's shop when she was young— there was too little to play with and too much to break—and now she still didn't see anything she wanted to save. Let Bill Hanneman box it all up and get rid of it however he wanted.

Then she thought of her mother, whiling away her daytime hours in the middle of these things, never making much money, never finding happiness, and Cady decided she should keep something, a memento to honor her mother. On the cash register counter was a cassette recorder; beside it, an empty cassette case for a tape called *Whale Songs*. She pushed the PLAY button, and the shop filled with the baleful calls of whales "singing" underwater. The sound froze Cady, and she stared out at the shimmering water, which sent off shafts of blinding light. She thought of what Varney had said: "Mom told me she wanted to die ever since Aunt Helen died. After you left she said that to me at least once a week. So all's I did was help her get what she'd been wanting all along."

The whales sounded so pleading, so lonesome. No wonder Beth had wanted to die, if this was what she listened to all day long. Through the window Cady watched a dive-bombing pelican come up with a mouthful of fish. Two seagulls fought over a morsel on the deck of one of the fishing boats.

Varney wanted to die now, and she did, too. Perhaps their family would die out altogether without sending anyone into the future. They were a family with a predisposition toward early death. Victims to drowning, murder. What did it matter, though? What good had anyone in her family been to the world? They were the kind of family line that should be extinguished.

She fingered the stack of business cards saying THE WHALE SHOP, BETH MILLER, PROPRIETOR. Outside, seagulls swooped from mast to mast. Strains of "O Little Town of Bethlehem" churned from one of the adjacent shops, mingled with the whale's crooning, and rose dolefully around her. She left the shop with nothing but a hand-carved ebony porpoise and a small stack of her mother's business cards.

The peace-and-love talk of Christmas rattled around her, but none of it mattered, because fear was all she heard. It circled around her and inside her—in her neck and belly and breasts. It surged in her nose and roared down her throat. Most of all it laid claim on her ears. Her ears took to borrowing sounds from everywhere and burying them in her body's cavities for later excavation. When the sounds came back to her, they were mangled, frightening, nothing like their original selves. A wave rushing to shore. A train clacking northward. The squeal of an injured rabbit. The pulsing of boom boxes. Their tones and rhythms lodged inside her and found new force. Even sweet sounds—the bleating of crickets, wind in the trees, Christmas carols—took on a satanic timbre. Now the whale songs were in there, too, ripe for mangling.

SEVENTEEN

Everyone in ER has a story, a version of things. And they all want to tell Dr. Jana Thomas. One of the nurses, Jane Rizzo, knows the parents of the dead girl, Alison Granger. Alison's parents were worried about her. She was a college student who didn't attend to her studies. She hung with a fast crowd, drinking, doing drugs. Jane Rizzo shakes her head as she reports this to Jana. "I'm not saying she brought it on herself," says Jane Rizzo. "But—" She shakes her head, turning down to her clipboard.

Ron Gaffney was there when the ambulance arrived. The dead girl was not yet dead. "Not a pretty sight," he says, raising his eyebrows and leaning against the nurses' station counter. "Someone had really worked her over." He pauses, waiting for everyone to lean in, to question him further, and when he feels properly attended to, he begins *his* version of things. He tells of Alison's white sweater, ripped to shreds, so it was only really a pair of scantily connected sleeves. Whatever she'd been wearing on the bottom was completely gone. He catalogs the bruises on the dead girl's thighs, the imprints of teeth on her shoulder, the broken neck of the beer bottle they removed from her vagina, and the three bullet holes in the chest, fired at close range.

"Who does stuff like this?" says Kurt Klug, the male nurse with the New Age softness. "Is it anger? A brain thing? I really, honestly, truly don't get it."

"I don't care why," says Jane Rizzo. "I say just lock him up."

"But you know it won't be that way," says Susan Dennison, who is the senior nurse on the floor and likes to speak last. "It'll be a trial that goes on forever, and people will be coming forward and saying what a sweet, caring guy he was and how he always loved his mother."

"What drives me crazy," says Adare, the unit secretary, "is this idea people have that guys like this can be rehabilitated. I don't buy it. Do you think a guy that's molested and killed a girl can just wake up *normal*? I'm sorry, but I don't think so. Once an animal, always an animal."

Ron Gaffney grins. "Well, everyone, I should tell you right now, it was me. I couldn't help it."

"Don't joke about that, Dr. Gaffney," says Adare.

Jana, writing out test orders, bends her head to her work. The noise comes with the rhythm of surf, in-crash-out, in-crash-out.

"I don't think it's that Lummi they've got in custody," says Kurt. "All he's done before is small burglaries. He's never been violent against *people*. And they say murderers usually know their victims. He didn't know those girls. It's racism, pure and simple. They're holding him and they haven't even charged him—that's not legal, is it? Hey, Dr. Thomas, didn't this thing happen over near where you live?"

Jana looks up, appears dazed. "What's that, Kurt?"

"Didn't this murder happen over in your neighborhood?"

Jana shakes her head. "I wouldn't know."

"You okay, Dr. Thomas? You look really pale."

She seizes the next clipboard and heads down the hall, the noise surging again alongside a wave of nausea.

"You keep being all quiet and weird like this, and we'll think it's *you*, Thomas," calls Ron Gaffney after her. Jana doesn't acknowledge him. Eyes fuzzy, she glances quickly at her clipboard—*thirty-five year-old man with chest pain, high BP, acute tachycardia*. She pauses a moment, swallows back hard, knocks, and enters.

"Hello, Mr. Ruiz, I'm Dr. Thomas."

Mr. Ruiz is a short stocky man with the muscular arms of a weight lifter. He grips the arms of his chair, breathes heavily, eyes beaming fear.

"Tell me how you're feeling, Mr. Ruiz. What happened?"

He is hyperventilating so extremely, he cannot find words. His eyes bug out as if apparitions have appeared, luring him to the underworld.

"It's okay, Mr. Ruiz. Just answer yes or no. I know it's hard, but try to calm down. Chances are, this isn't a heart attack, okay? Either way we'll take care of you, okay? You understand?"

She touches his arm. Her vision clears. The noise recedes. "You have chest pain?"

He nods. Tears have accrued at the corners of his eyes.

"Can you tell me where?"

He thumps the upper left quadrant of his chest. She listens with her stethoscope. His heart is galloping—130 beats per minute. He is an animal threatened, already in flight.

"We're going to get an EKG, Mr. Ruiz, but first I want you to breathe into this bag." She reaches into the bottom drawer of the supply cabinet and brings out a small brown paper bag. "Hold the bag over your mouth and nose and breathe slowly, in and out. All right? I'll be back."

In the hallway the noise returns, trumpeting through her, bringing her to a standstill. She forgets where she's going, looks up the hall, then back down it. Her body runs cold as spring-water, and in a second she, too, is hyperventilating. She struggles for breath, pushes back on a saliva-rich wave of nausea, stumbles toward the doctors' lounge, shoving the door closed behind

her. She stands still a minute, dizzy, disoriented, then goes to
the kitchenette and vomits into the metal sink. Trying to gather
herself, she rests her elbows on the countertop, runs the water,
and tries to clean up with paper towels. She is rinsing her
mouth when Ron finds her.

"I'm fine," she says, before he has said anything.

"Get your body the hell out of here. Adare already called
Bill, and he's on his way in to cover for you."

"I'm fine, really." She draws herself up straight. She has always been fine, always responsible. Cady Responsible Miller. "I
don't need coverage."

"Go be fine at home. You need a driver?"

A hospital van takes her home. She doesn't talk, just sits in
the back with her eyes closed. She steps out of the van into
jaundiced sunshine. The driver takes off before she remembers
to thank him. It is odd being here midday, midweek. She has
never missed a workday in her life. Everyone was so nice about
it—Bill McElroy, the ER group director, coming in on his day
off; Ron arranging a ride home for her—it was almost as if they
wanted her gone. She lugs herself up the front stairs, squinting
against the sun. Inside her body she feels skittish, her head
light and unfocused, but her limbs are too heavy to respond
quickly to anything. She can't be sick. She's never sick. You
learn this when you become a doctor: Your body is above sickness; your mind can always prevail.

It takes a moment to find her key. She drops everything in
the foyer and heads straight to the living-room couch, where
she collapses and closes her eyes. She pictures Mr. Ruiz breathing into his paper bag, waiting for her to come back. She was
fairly certain his "heart attack" was an acute case of hyperventi-
lation, but now she can't be sure. Of course someone must have
taken care of him by now, but the thought of her desertion

bothers her. She is not in the habit of abandoning her patients. Coming through for them is the bulwark of her life; if she can't come through for them, then what good is she? She thinks suddenly of the Lummi in custody and wonders if he's been charged or released and if the other girl, Tara Fenniston, is still in a coma.

The noise has subsided into an eerie early-afternoon quiet. Not a car passes. Not a child shouts. She can't hear foghorns or ferry whistles or garbage trucks or televisions. It's an uneasy, stalking silence. Postapocalyptic. She wants to get up, call work, call Cooper, resume something normal, but nothing *is* normal, and she is glued in lethargy to the couch. Spider pads over her belly and curls up there to sleep. Through the fringe of her lashes she sees in Spider's sparsely fuzzed body a chimerical creature, part rodent, part mollusk, part winged cat.

When Jana awakens, Seretha is sitting with her knitting in the easy chair beside the couch. Jana lies in the shadow of Seretha's body and hears the deft clicking of the needles and the great quantities of breath filling Seretha's lungs.

"You're not feeling good?" says Seretha.

"I'm fine," Jana says, surveying her parts. Her legs lie lifeless across the couch, with no observable blood flow. Her fingers, white and cold as if fresh from outdoors, won't move freely. But mainly her brain seems out of sorts, dull and frightened, skittish and slow, a brain that has misplaced its ability to solve things. There's too much in there, too many tributaries making a bulging river with no egress.

"Don't get up," says Seretha, as if she knows Jana is trying. "I made some minestrone. Let me know when you're hungry."

Jana says nothing. She watches Seretha's forefingers unraveling the dark red yarn, which looks vaguely intestinal. Seretha isn't wearing a hair covering today, so her thinning red-dyed hair resembles tulle, stiff and light-admitting. It's rare to find Seretha as quiet as this. Usually Seretha pelts her with questions, but now she is sitting in a nimbus of mysterious quiet, presiding like a nurse, attentive to nourishment and vital signs. Jana drifts, losing then regaining this strange new view of Seretha. It is as if Seretha has moved in her relations with Jana, from judgment to understanding. Nevertheless, Jana feels exposed. She turns her back to Seretha and pulls the crocheted afghan over herself. She thinks again of Mr. Ruiz. She thinks of the Lummi in custody and wonders if he's talking to anyone. She imagines going to him, comforting him, telling him some of the few things she knows. She thinks of the conversation at work. What an illusion that she belongs there, that she, tainted as she is, belongs anywhere. The life she's put together has always been provisional, doomed to shatter, but for so many years, things with Cooper and Evan seemed to fall into an easy, numbing routine and she forgot her destiny. Now she feels the unraveling. The truth will come out about her, about Evan, about where Evan's perilous path will lead, and possibly hers, too. Perhaps she and Evan should go away somewhere, find some cabin in the wilderness far from civilization and learn to live meagerly, without human contact.

Something gradually dawns on her, and she lifts her head from hibernation under the afghan. "How did you get in?" she asks.

Seretha stops knitting. "Cooper gave me a key. I thought you knew."

Jana shakes her head. "He didn't mention it." She can't catalog this information, her brain malfunctioning as it is. She cannot tell if Cooper's not telling her was intentional or not. She stares at the loose, pale flesh draping Seretha's neck like soft rayon. She imagines how safe Cooper must have felt as a child with a large mother like this who could sit and knit and preside over his illnesses, warding off harm. She and Varney had to fend for themselves in illness, lying for hours alone in an empty house, no one to bring them hot soup, or cold water, or to help them to the bathroom. As for Evan's illnesses, Mrs. Stubbs has seen more of them than Jana has. The thought of Mrs. Stubbs piques her yearning and when she closes her eyes, she imagines the woman's cheerful hand on her back.

She sleeps fitfully, dreaming she's running in bare feet on a pebbly beach in California. Her feet are shredded and bleeding, but the rest of her body is enraptured with the movement, so she keeps going. She ignores her feet until Mrs. Stubbs calls out to her to stop. She looks down and finds her feet are gone. She's awakened by a sound coming from the kitchen. Seretha is not in her chair. Jana listens, hears Seretha opening cabinets.

"Can I get you some soup, dear?"

Seretha stands in the doorway, her smile close-lipped, the smile of a helpful stranger. Jana needs strength. She needs to get up, get moving, go for a run. She nods and forces herself to sit up, despite her terrible languor. As she moves, the fluids in her head ripple noisily. Seretha brings a tray with a bowl of minestrone and saltines. She sets the tray on the coffee table, and Jana leans forward to eat. The soup is hot and satisfying, and Jana takes the first few spoonfuls eagerly. Seretha returns to her chair but does not take up her knitting. She pushes the sleeves of her red sweater up over her fleshy freckled forearms and watches Jana eat.

"Bad about those murders, isn't it?" Seretha says. "Is Evan scared?"

"We try not to talk about it."

"You have to talk about things."

"Some things, yes."

"I hope you don't mind my saying so, but you're too private. It's up to a woman to talk. Get things out and set the example for the man. When everyone clams up, the marriage is over."

Jana lays down her spoon and rubs her temples, trying to ease the low growl. Where does Seretha get the authority to speak of the long-term survival of a marriage, she who knew only a short marriage terminated by the early demise of her spouse?

"You know Cooper's under a lot of pressure these days from that job?" Seretha says.

"Of course."

"I have to believe you're there for him."

"Of course."

"Are you?" Seretha licks her lips. In her dry mouth her tongue moves loudly. "I'm going to be honest. I think you're hiding things."

Jana looks directly at Seretha whose eye sockets are stretched long like overworn socks "What things?"

"You know what things. I see them. I'm just looking out for my son."

"What things?" repeats Jana, jarred from her lethargy.

"Okay." Seretha raises her shoulders and lowers them hard. "Okay, you asked. I happen to know you're paying California property taxes. Don't say no—I saw the bill, several of them, in fact. I haven't told this to Cooper, but I've seen with my eyes, and I'm telling you that *you* ought to tell him. You own some property down there in California, then he oughta know about it. That's his right. If you choose not to tell him, it raises questions. What else might you have going on down there? All right, I said it." Seretha flicks invisible crumbs from her lap.

Jana stands up, jittery. There is no telling now what else Seretha might know. "I have to get Evan."

"I'll get Evan, dear. You're in no shape."

"I'm *fine*," Jana says.

"I'm off," Seretha says. "I'll be back with Evan in two shakes, and then I'll get out."

As soon as Seretha is gone, Jana spins into high gear. She combs through the day's mail and finds, indeed, a bill (unopened, it seems) for the property taxes on the house that she was never able to sell. The unoccupied house is still furnished, and in its garage are two perfectly good cars with expired registrations. A manager oversees the property for a fee. It was an arrangement Jana made initially as a temporary one, but it has slid into permanence. Occasionally she gets a solicitation from a realtor who wants to try to sell the house, but she never responds. Year after year the management and property tax bills arrive in the mail, and year after year Jana pays them, unsure what else to do and loathe, even now, to part with the house, though the thought of it, untouched all these years, is frightening. How is it that Seretha has seen the bills that year after year Cooper has overlooked?

In the bedroom closet Jana locates the garbage bag holding the stash of Varney's unopened letters. The bag is stuffed behind the shoes, behind the hanging dresses and skirts and jackets, in the darkest and most distant corner. She keeps it tied closed and it is still tied closed, just as she left it. She opens it with the care she brings to surgery, her fingers working with quick precision, despite the rattling querulousness in the rest of her body.

One by one she goes through the letters, more than a hundred of them, collected over the years and, except for the early ones, all unopened. As far as she can see, nothing has been touched.

She reties the bag, her mind sailing over the house's hiding places. Her closet seems too obvious now, no longer safe. Downstairs she moves fast, aware that Seretha will be returning soon.

The day has moved into dusk, and the gray-blue sky over the bay is marbled with luminous purple clouds, elegant as the frontispiece of an antique book. She checks the kitchen cupboards, the closet in the mudroom by the back door, but each space seems either too small or too public to be a repository for the letters.

In the living room she looks for spaces behind the stereo cabinet and behind the heavy reference books. But these places also entertain too much traffic. She needs a place that is not obviously private but is rarely visited. The front hall closet is a possibility. Above the hanging coats are two shelves, the lower one junked with hats and scarves and mittens, the upper one home to an electric space heater, a dehumidifier, a few afghans they never use.

Standing on a step stool, she is able to reach up and push the afghans aside (ugly things—one in hideous colors of olive and ocher, the other pink and purple, equally awful, both brought out only rarely to appease Seretha, who made them). Jana runs her palm over the dusty shelf surface and touches something hard. She rises on tiptoe, straining to see. Seretha's car pulls up at the moment when the image is crystallizing, when the certain knowledge, garnered only through a moment's touch, whirls through her. She hears Evan laughing, running up the front steps. She drops the garbage bag, kicks it behind the coats, collapses the step stool, and closes the closet door in time to open the front door for Evan. She will keep Seretha out at all costs.

"Buddy!" she calls to Evan. She kneels on the stoop, letting him leap at her, so he almost knocks her backward with his zeal, and despite the dirge inside her, she laughs. She pulls him against her to feel his cold cheek against her sweaty one. The boy of her blood.

Seretha, dressed in a gray overcoat and a separate woolen

hood that, worn together, give her the shape of a fire hydrant, watches this display from the bottom of the steps. She wears a strange expression of what? Disdain? Jealousy? Jana can't figure it. She is too focused on holding Evan. She'll hold him as long as he wants to be held, because each good moment might be the last.

Evan peels off and heads inside at a run, hooting, leaving Jana in a crouch that makes her feel like a track athlete seconds before a race.

"Well, if you're feeling better." Seretha sighs. "I guess I'll be going."

Her brain, as she watches Seretha pull out, feels split in two: One half is a pixilated blur, old images faded into nonsense, on the verge of disappearing altogether; the other half perceives things almost too clearly, like overcorrected vision in which everything is a bit odd, a bit off. It is as if she is seeing through a medium that is not air. She hears Evan rattling around in the kitchen; she hears a percussive chipping somewhere else. It is no longer clear to her where the sounds are coming from—some external place or her own ailing brain.

She goes inside, locks the door. Evan has dropped his jacket, his backpack, his shoes, and a pile of artwork in the middle of the kitchen. He sits on the countertop, stuffing his pockets with cookies.

"One," she says, reeling a bit from rising too fast, feeling at once nauseated and empty.

"Two, please?" he says.

"Two," she says. "Off the counter. Come on. Off."

Her words sound flat and uncommitted, even to her. Sensing this, Evan stares at her and hops off the counter without further urging. He hovers near her legs, looking up with leviathan eyes. "Are you scared, Mommy?" He pats her thigh.

"No, honey." Her skin and eyes must look different. Her own child senses it. The smell of peril seeps through her pores.

"Is that man in jail?"

"What man?"

"That man who killed the girl."

"Yes, honey, he's in jail. Don't think about that man."

As if you can command your mind not to think. It thinks what it wants to think. It returns, like the most reliable homing pigeon, to the place it is commanded not to go.

"Tommy said they let him go because it's another man that did it. And so now the other man can come and get me. Do you think he can smell my cookies?"

"No, honey. People can't smell cookies through the walls of a house."

"Yes they can. I can." He brings one of the Oreos to his nose and inhales the scent.

"You know, honey, I'm going to let you do something I don't usually let you do. I'm going to let you go out to Daddy's woodshop and watch cartoons. Okay?"

Evan pushes out his lips. "It's okay, Mom. I don't want to."

"Really, why not? I have some things to do."

Without warning Evan races around the kitchen table. "Yee-ha. Car-TOONS!" He gallops through the back door, and she follows, unlocking Cooper's woodshop, flooding the place with light and TV sound, turning on the space heater, and covering Evan with a fleece blanket. Evan, mouth stuffed with Oreos, sinks into Road Runner.

Back inside she gallops through the house, returning the letters to her closet, finding a garbage bag in which to deposit the loathsome object, the very same gun Cooper promised years ago to trash. She should have surmised back then that he wouldn't. She remembers their argument so well—how wedded they each were to their positions, how Cooper took her objections as an indictment of his father, how irrational she had sounded. And she understands now something she did not fully register then— the light veil of withholding that filmed his eyes.

She transfers the gun without touching it to the plastic bag. She can't tell if it's loaded and doesn't want to know. She stares at its inert weight at the bottom of the bag. It seems so odd that he would have stored it in the closet instead of in his woodshop. In an hour or so he will be home. She will show it to him and make him explain. But the sight of it—she can't have it inside. She bundles it and stuffs it behind the dense juniper bushes in front of the house.

"What's that?" Evan's voice prowls up behind her. She shoots to a standing position.

"What're you doing?" Evan says.

"I thought you were watching cartoons."

"I got scared."

"Weeding. I was weeding." She's up on the front stoop now, hustling him inside, thinking, trying to think. The house seems unfamiliar, cold and full of danger. Of course Evan was scared out there in the woodshop.

"Come here," she says to him. She leads him into the living room, where he sees a few of his favorite cars. He swipes one from the floor as they pass. She gathers him onto her lap, hugs him into her shoulder, smelling his soapy hair, the damp mustiness of his green wool sweater. He squirms, submits for a moment, then pushes her away, *vrooming* his car impatiently over the couch back. She draws him tighter, trying to suppress his squirming. His cry of protest she only hears faintly—"No, Mom, *let me go!*"—as she breathes him in, and with the pressure of her arms and fingers she tries to let him know he should cherish this and use the memory of their embrace to soften the hail of misfortune that lies ahead.

He jams his knee against her belly and bursts from her arms, rolling onto the carpet, glaring at her. "I'm sorry," she whispers. Adare is leaving a message, wanting to know how she's feeling and if she'll be in tomorrow. "All hell broke loose after you left. We need you! But if you're sick, we'll manage."

Then Jana is dialing wildly. "Yes," she tells Adare. "I'll be in."

Next she dials Robin. Robin's voice, that delicious, throaty, bubbly, warm-as-bathwater voice.

"What're you—?" Jana chokes but she can't complete the thought. What is it she wants from Robin? Robin is thrilled to hear from her, but busy cooking dinner. *Dinner*, Jana thinks. *Of course, dinner. It's time for dinner. I'm sorry.*

She looks out the picture window—pouchy shapes of black and gray are punctured with white lights; the world is bigger than she ever imagined. How she envies those fishermen down there, alone on their boats, engaged only with winds and currents and tides.

"I'm going to cook dinner," Jana announces to Robin, trying to sound firm. "I'll talk to you later."

She bolts from the phone, pulls out pots, stares at them. In the living room Evan snakes around the carpet, cars in hand, making them talk to each other, making them shoot each other. Outside, the plastic bag is still there behind the bushes. She pulls food from the refrigerator, the freezer. The cheese and pasta and broccoli look like household objects, and she regards them without connecting them to anything one would eat. Was this how her own mother felt, drifting around the kitchen in the morning, preparing food, but so distractedly it seemed she'd forgotten its purpose? The thought of her mother calls up a pulse of longing. She remembers a song her mother used to sing. "My pigeon house I open wide..." Cady never knew what the song was about, but rendered by her mother's voice, quiet and lonely as an echo, it always brought her to tears.

Robin stands at the door with Max, her arms open in a shape that suggests a spacious basket. "You sounded awful. I had to come."

Jana blinks, backs up, thinks of fleeing, regrets her call. It's too late to learn friendship now. But here is Robin, short and throaty, with her array of colors and her stream-of-consciousness talk. She is in the house now, peeling things back. They stand in the dark at the picture window in the dining room, Jana thick with awareness of the difference between her life and Robin's. A while ago, for a fraction of a second, she had thought she could confide in Robin, but how wrongheaded she was. *I found a gun in my house. My brother is incarcerated for murder.* You do not say such things to enlightened people leading charmed lives. It is not just Robin—she cannot confide in anyone. No one would understand how she has gotten where she is. It has been a mistake. She does not belong here in this house in Bellingham, Washington; she should not be tending the seriously ill people who come to her thinking she is knowledgeable and strong. Knowledgeable, perhaps, but not strong. And certainly not good. She is no better than the man Evan says is at large, the man strolling around in the dark wanted for murder. She should have been incarcerated herself alongside Varney. "You're a good girl," her mother used to say to her when Varney got in trouble. But long before Varney went bad, she herself did despicable things. She lied to the other girls; she filched things they had. No, her mother was mistaken. Jana had never been good.

"I think you need to relax," Robin says quietly.

Jana shivers through her sweat. Tears are damned somewhere at the back of her eyes. Robin, hand on Jana's back, guides her to the couch. Upstairs, in Evan's room, the boys are squealing.

"This murder," Robin says. "But what *about* this murder?"

Jana shakes her head. She doesn't know. She truly doesn't know. This recent murder isn't unusual; murders have been happening all along.

Robin gets up to turn on a light, then returns to the couch. They've been sitting in the dark, Jana realizes. "Your dinner?" Jana says. "You were fixing dinner."

"There's no hurry."

If only she could begin again, here in this room with Robin, without history. She could learn the art of confiding, learn to speak of things that matter. With one finger Robin strokes her eyebrow slowly. Her face is suffused with a kind of sympathy that sickens Jana and makes her want to flee. It reminds her of the courthouse days, when she had to sit still and endure endless hours of people watching her, some with hate-filled faces, others' faces rife with pity. The hateful faces she learned to ignore. The pitying, *poor-dear* faces were, in the end, more irritating. Their owners seemed to want something from her; they seemed to be using her to applaud their own lives.

"I need to—" Jana stalls. Cook dinner? Be alone? Go to bed? What does she need?

"Yeah, we need to go, too." Robin, ready to stand, moves forward on the couch. "Hey, look, I'm just going to put this out—if you ever feel like talking, just say so, okay?" She leaps to a standing position, scissoring her legs and falling heavily on her feet like an aging but still vital cheerleader.

"*Fadata, fadata.* By the way, I found out it's a password. Ma-ax, we're go-ing!"

SHE IS IN THE bedroom, putting on her running clothes, when Cooper comes home. He stands in the doorway, his jacket still exuding the scent of chilly rain-soaked air.

"What the heck is happening here?" he says, drawing his bottom lip through his teeth. "It's eight o'clock and Evan's downstairs on the kitchen counter eating handfuls of Wheat Chex. He says you didn't give him any dinner."

She blinks, feeling tiny next to Cooper. Is it past dinnertime?

"You think you're going out *running?*" Cooper stands in front of her as if he intends to block her way. For all his dimpled blondness, he looks to her utterly menacing.

"Where were you?" she says, trying to turn things differently. She zips up her sweatshirt, covering a strip of naked belly.

"I was at work. My mother called just as I was leaving."

Cold, like a sudden injection of sodium pentothal, rushes from Jana's belly to all of her limbs. Cooper shakes his head. She cannot read him. She sits on the bed and concentrates on her breathing so it fills up her ears.

"She told you about the house," she says. *The house means nothing,* she tells herself. *It's only a house.*

"What house?" Cooper says.

At first she thinks he's goading her, but his face, a know-nothing face, shows she is wrong.

"What house?" he says again.

"I thought Seretha told you. I have a house in California." She says this slowly, bringing the house to her mind—its red tile roof, its white stucco exterior, the ivy along the patio wall, the tiny gray-green lizards skittering across the courtyard. She tries to think of the pleasant parts, the comfort she once felt there.

"I've had it forever." I she hears herself saying, as if she has no family of origin. "Before we were married."

"Why didn't you tell me?"

They sit on the bed, four feet from each other, looking down at the floor. She shrugs. "I never got around to it."

"Yeah." He seems to blow out the word. He nods, long and slowly. It is a skeptical nod, a slurred *ooo-kaay* that understands that a truth is only a half-truth and the full truth will be hard to come by. A nod that posits the beginning of something, the staking of turf, the digging-in of feet.

"I thought we were married," he says in a voice so cynical it frightens her. "I thought married people told each other things."

About everything but hidden guns, she thinks, but she won't let herself say this. She can't look at him, not when he's speaking to her with that superior, Seretha-inspired sarcasm.

"What else did she say?" Jana asks, knowing she mustn't assume, mustn't anticipate.

"You tell me. What else *is* there to say?"

"I'm going out running."

"No, you're not."

But she is already up and making for the door, and though he tries to grab her arm, she is too quick. She runs down the stairs and out the front door and is swallowed in darkness by the time he calls out for her. "Jaaaa-naaa! Jaaa-naaa!" Her name recedes behind her, and for a moment he seems to be calling, "*Cady! Cady!*" but she cannot stop to listen closely, and his voice fades, becoming more distant than her old life as she races to the waterfront.

She runs straight down the hill, ignoring her creaking knees, ignoring thoughts of Cooper and Evan foraging dinner for themselves, pushing away questions about what Cooper does and doesn't know, shutting out the images of the bagged gun in the bushes.

After running for more than an hour, Cooper's calls replaying in her ears—*Cady! Jana!*—she returns. The house is dark,

but the light in the woodshop is on. Breathing hard, touching her necklace of sweat, she tries to read the silhouette of
Cooper's head in the window. He is standing, looking down at
something, but beyond that there's little she can tell—what he
is doing and whether he's still angry, she isn't sure. For seven
years she's known Cooper, and never has she seen him angry as
he was tonight. His anger made her angry, too. She had hoped
to run it off, but she hasn't. She had no choice in her secrets.
They were bequeathed to her by other people, and they have
not endangered him, but his secret gun, he has chosen to place
right here in the house, within Evan's easy reach.

She checks behind the bushes—the bag is still there. She
peers inside the bag; the gun is still there, too. Nausea returns.
She who has always been fine (mostly fine) with lizards and
spiders (if not snakes), she who cuts and stitches human flesh,
she whom Ron Gaffney describes as a "doc with teeth," a
woman to whom blood is merely a fluid, she cannot stomach
the sight of a gun. She starts to retch but thinks herself out of
it. She stuffs the gun, bag and all, inside the waistband of her
Lycra running pants, where it makes an irregular bulge. She
glances again at the woodshop. The light is still on, but Cooper
is no longer visible. She takes off again, more furtive now, trying to ignore her body's exhaustion, its thirst. Now that she's
armed, she pictures herself being confronted by someone.
Would she be capable of something heinous? Could this short
jog down to the waterfront become her pivotal moment to give
up, to begin to see people as mere roadblocks, or as inconse-
quential as spiders, or lizards, or plastic Lego people? Could she
fire as Varney did, again and again and again?

Oh, the look of your brain, now, the look of your brain. A
quick brain, to be sure, but a harsh ugly thing, scabbed by the
hundreds of hot mean thoughts that have sizzled over it, setting

down layer upon layer of scars. It is not a pretty thing, this brain of yours, and it has never been a pretty thing. Its ugliness has only been well concealed.

The thought has been coming for a long time. At first it was only little pictures tumbling together and apart like the glass shards at the end of a kaleidoscope. It lacked definition and clarity. But tonight, as you run, the thought appears to you fully formed.

It is not your boy to be feared. He is only a child. He still pees in his bed and believes in Santa Claus and has an imaginary friend. *You* are the one to be feared. It is *you* whose adult mind is wrecked, *you* who wants to slash the tires of the drivers who cut you off, *you* who must stop yourself from cursing the neighbors' dogs, *you* who—

She traverses the wet grass; a strange greenish color emanates from the streetlights. The water seems gentle tonight, slurping quietly over the rocks. She looks for a place where the shoreline is dark, somewhere she can do what she needs to do without the lights making her feel she is taking center stage. She jogs off the path, through brambly branches that catch the fibers of her Lycra pants. Soon she stands balanced on a few rocks by the water's edge. She is not invisible, exactly, but at least she isn't lit. Quickly she does her business, satisfied by the water's decisive gulp as it takes Cooper's father's gun to its bowels.

EIGHTEEN

Sometime during all the legal haggling, Cady began running. She would drive through the maze of concrete, past row upon row of beige stucco houses, one indistinguishable from another, past mini malls and car dealerships and Mexican-restaurant franchises, finally arriving at the beach. Even midmorning, midweek there were always a few people there—retirees, housewives with kids, the unemployed—but she never lingered among the people long enough to be recognized. The sight of the sand and waves and wheeling gulls raised the possibility of escape and sent her flying, down to where tiny seabirds foraged and the expiring waves licked the hard sand. A borderland. The edge of things.

Only down there, with the wind huffing and the surf chafing, could she cleanse her mind of the legalese and the psychobabble that surrounded her. Only down there, unrecognized, unhounded, *moving*, was she a creature who could imagine still living.

She ran for an hour, an hour and a half, two hours, past elegant beachfront homes, around rocky points, over public and not-so-public beaches, stopping briefly sometimes, when she found herself alone, to look out at the water and wonder who she was now and who she could continue to be.

Back at the jail she held her growing anger at bay and begged Varney to explain himself, to say something that would make her understand. Was he sorry? *Not really.* Did he care they were dead? *No.* Was he psychotic? *No, of course not.* Not even for a minute? He stared at her blankly, his face flat. His neck, stringier by the day, looked too weak to support his head. *How would I know?* She could see why some people wanted to crucify him. She wanted to do something to him herself: shake him hard to get a rise out of him, poke him with needles, pour cold water on him, tickle him. But all they had between them was words, words delivered in semipublic over an immovable plastic phone. *You owe me*, she thought. She was the one who came every day to see him. Her life was as unalterably changed as his. He owed her words, at least. But it was as if all the words had gone out of him—they had dried up, gotten buried or frac-tured. Whatever the fate of lost words was, they were gone, along with the feelings he claimed not to have.

When he did speak, he spoke in a monotone. "Sometimes I think about snakes. How happy they are sleeping in the sun. I guess I'm free now. I guess I could do just about anything. I could probably even kill you."

"You don't mean that, Varney," she said. "Say you don't mean that."

He shrugged. "I guess I'm free to die."

She couldn't look at him when he said that. It made her want to scream. It made her feel like dying herself. How was she supposed to stand by him if he couldn't even stand by him-self? How was she supposed to understand him if he gave her so little?

"You should get out of here," he told her, "or I'll bring you down."

That same day he confessed. His case wouldn't go to trial.

He would be sentenced as an adult. Finally convicted (four times life), he was taken to a maximum-security state prison.

Cady went back to Oregon. She changed her name and rented a cottage on the coast. It was winter and raining most of the time. She ate very little. She ran. She took long night walks on the beach, adjusting to the wild sounds her ears produced. She felt no hunger, no cold. She hardly noticed the drama of ocean-sculpted rock and the water's array of blues and greens and blacks. The Oregon coast could have been exchanged with a grassy plain or a bayou and she would hardly have noticed. What she saw was inside her head, where she replayed events, changing pieces of them to come up with different outcomes. In the replays, she gave herself patience and she kept Varney on the phone. She let him talk and yell and explain the details of his disgruntlement with Mr. Phillips. He said hateful things about Mr. Phillips. He used swearwords. His voice was an octave higher than usual, unpleasant to listen to, but still she listened. And listened and listened. She knew this talking was good. *Uh-huh. Uh-huh. I know what you mean.* She could feel Varney's fire working through its fuel, overpowering Mr. Phillips with words, only words. In these replays Varney's agitation always ran its course, and the days thereafter passed for her without incident. She was an ordinary girl, blissfully ordinary. In other replays her parents were on vacation in Hawaii. Varney had no one to talk to (or kill), so he called her in Oregon. They had an ambling, rambling, shoring-up kind of conversation, discussing music and food. Nothing radical. And if he seemed a bit depressed at first, the depression was gone by the end of the conversation. Whatever anger he had had was punctured and unremembered so he got on smoothly with his day.

But in the end she knew this reimagining went nowhere. It was as useless as the speculation in court had been about Varney's state of mind. (Was his mind the mind of an adult or a child, a sane person or an insane one, a person with a disturbed moral compass or no moral compass at all?) It had tired her then and it tired her now. She hated the insubstantiality of it, the vagueness.

Gradually, through rock and wave and sand, fact began to reassert itself. She started to see beauty in stones, in their observable shape, their measurable density, their palpable texture. She found herself drawn to reading about science. She loved what was verifiable. She was like a child who revels in gripping a toy, or chasing a bright color, or tasting ice cream. In the library she looked at the highly magnified color photographs of cells and read about how, time after time, cells behaved predictably, manufacturing nutrients, reproducing, reacting to the stimulus of light or nutrition.

Only in unassailable fact like this could she begin to forget.

NINETEEN

The smell of mold has set in around town. The scent of decay. Great putrid clouds spill from the Georgia Pacific plant and bivouac over the whole city. She thinks of the murderer trying to conceal himself. At this time of year it should be easy to hide, with so much of the day given over to darkness. Even when the sun is up, it is rarely out, and the skies look tarnished.

Jana and Cooper avoid each other. Jana is gone before Cooper wakes up. Cooper does not return home until Jana is in bed. They leave each other notes, politely curt. *Don't forget Evan's leaf project in den. Need milk.*

Reporters camp out in vans at the hospital parking lot. They're waiting for Tara Fenniston to recover, but meanwhile they'll talk to anyone. Jana walks by them with practiced imperviousness.

"Dr. Thomas!" they call out (they know her *name?*). "Can we talk to you? How's Tara Fenniston doing?"

She does not speed up, she does not slow down, she does not change her eye line.

Inside she does her work as well as she ever has, plowing quickly and methodically through the patients: a cardiac arrest, a bleeding ulcer, a detached retina. The only thing on her mind is keeping these fragile bodies alive so they can eventually reenter the fray.

"You got a buzz on today, Thomas," Ron Gaffney compliments her.

Her ears are focused on ducts—the heating ducts, purring like supercats; the pulsing ducts and valves of the body. She reproduces these sounds and transposes them to every key so her head is filled with the tonalities of transport.

News bubbles through the hallways. Tara Fenniston has come out of her coma and has identified a college student as the murderer. He is now being sought. Jana doesn't need to hear the details. Work is enough; *just keep working.*

A hypothermic mountain climber arrives on a stretcher. She sees blond hair, a wide forehead, a red face. It is the body of Mr. Phillips. She excuses herself for a moment and stands in the doctors' lounge, checking her reaction. Of course it is not Mr. Phillips: (*a*) Mr. Phillips is dead, (*b*) if Mr. Phillips were alive, he would be much older than this climber. She returns to his bedside, telling herself it is only a small and short-lived lapse.

When she picks up Evan, he is strangely subdued. "What's on your face?" he says.

She pats her cheeks, her forehead, her nose. She feels nothing there.

"Your face looks fuzzy," he says.

"Maybe I'm growing fur and becoming an animal." It is half wishful thinking.

"I would be a cheetah," Evan says, "because cheetahs run six hundred miles an hour."

He *should* be a cheetah. He should run as fast as possible. He is only a boy who dreams of running fast, being strong, learning to fly.

She hustles him as quickly as she can away from Little Creations, away from the bright probing eyes of George and Yvonne and Sandy. She wants to hug him but feels strangely careful, too conscious of what her hugs may be imparting.

"How was your day?" she asks when they are safely settled in the car.

"Good," he says. He stares out the side window. Dusk has just tipped over into night.

"What did you do?"

"I can't remember." His head shivers as if he is sloughing off a thought. His face looks angular and eerily mature in the car's shadows.

"You were a good boy?"

"You always ask me that."

"Well, were you?"

"I don't know."

"Did something happen?"

"Leo died."

She pulls over to the curb and looks back at him. His lips and forehead are smashed against the window. Traffic tears by, dangerously close. She turns on her hazard lights. "Honey, tell me about it."

He pulls his face back from the window like an octopus unsuctioning. "The man that killed that girl killed Leo, too. He stabbed Leo's stomach. There was blood everywhere."

She tries hard to penetrate the dim light to read Evan's body language more exactly. Is he making an eloquent metaphor for something that has happened to him, or have his fears converged with his gallivanting imagination? Things must be said and done, but she cannot think of what they are. She watches him hopelessly, feeling the tight weave of their blood. An ambulance speeds by, heading toward the hospital. How close and ineffectual she is.

At home Evan goes to his room. He closes his door. She lurks in the hallway, listening. What is he doing in there? Burying Leo? Weeping silently? It may be the first time ever that she has overheard nothing from Evan, only silence, a terrifying blob of it. The silence becomes a howl. A train seems to clack straight through the kitchen. She can't wrap her mind around this event, this death of a person that never had a real life. The death of a hope or an unfulfilled dream. A life imagined but never fully lived. It seems to her akin to awakening from a dream of flying to despair about gravity.

She thinks of Ren Scofield, Mr. Cianetti's neurologist. What would Ren Scofield have to say about Evan's brain, his racing imagination? What would he have said about Varney's? She goes to the phone book and thumbs through it, wondering how Ren Scofield would feel about a call at home, but he's unlisted. All the specialists are unlisted, fancying themselves to be sought after. She'll try to track Scofield down tomorrow. No doubt he'll tell her that a shrink is what Evan really needs. The shrink that evaluated Varney was such a bickering, unpleasant man. She hated the way he sat so primly in front of the judge and delivered his diagnosis, claiming to know the way Varney's mind worked, claiming to know the intricate workings of his synapses and hormones. It was hateful—the presumption of pretending to know what lay inside anyone else's skull. How could you presume to know the brain without at least scanning it first? Neurology is guesswork, too, but at least neurologists admit all that they don't know. Neurology begins in science, what can be seen and measured, but it understands that there are certain things that are ineffable in the human brain and soul, an idea that psychiatrists, in her experience, have always been less willing to acknowledge.

She goes to bed thinking of Leo. He is "dead" now, but what was he when he was "alive"? Did he have a shape, a density, a human likeness? Or was Leo the ineffable feeling of a friend—elusive, shape-changing, vaporous? Was he around all the time, or only at Evan's convenience, like a genie, or Jiminy Cricket, or God, for that matter—one of those helpers you summon when flesh-and-blood helpers have failed you?

She thinks through all the algorithms: Is her son different from her? Possibly, but his imaginary friend, her noises—aren't they both the outpourings of hyperactive brains, brains that cannot stop figuring, and speculating, and *producing*? If he is similar to her and she is similar to Varney, then Evan must be similar to Varney, too. A troika of odd brains.

But who is to say—she, the student of bodily functions, of anatomy, of cells, of DNA, asks this often—that it is not the nature of the whole human race always to harbor oddness and contradiction? Alongside altruism lurks the possibility of rage. Beside the caress festers the possibility of a beating. Can't it be said that in all humans love and hate are bedfellows? And sometimes it only takes a single cockeyed look to unearth the rage.

ADARE PAGES HER, tells her there's an agitated man in the waiting room who *claims* to be her husband. Adare laughs, as if the man's assertion is outrageous. Jana spots the man in question—he wears dusty jeans, a green plaid flannel work shirt, a blue rain jacket. He shifts hyperactively from foot to foot.

"You should keep your cell phone *on*, for god's sake," Cooper tells her as she strides over to him. They've argued over this before. She hates her cell phone, abhors the idea of being always locatable, but she acquiesces to it for Evan's sake. Still, at work she really doesn't need it. He can call the ER line.

"You know I never do at work."

"Well—," he says.

"I only have a second," she says. She looks at him suddenly, and in her diagnostic mode, she sees not her husband but a patient—a middle-aged Caucasian man with bloodshot eyes and tense demeanor.

"I think someone broke into our place," he says. "But I need to know something."

She frowns. A break-in? Since she left this morning?

He pulls her around the corner, away from the handful of people who are waiting.

"Did you happen to—my father's gun was in the hall closet—I know, I know—but now it isn't there anymore—" His forehead ripples. She feels her face fill with blood the way a sponge fills with water. "Damn," he says.

He needs a tranquilizer, a nap. "Sit down," she says.

"You *do* know something, right?"

"You need to relax."

"What did you do with it?" His face is splotchy. "You have to tell me. This isn't a game."

"I need to get back to work."

"I had to keep it—it was my *father's*. And *of course* I didn't tell you. You know you would have freaked."

She starts to leave; he grabs her wrist. "It was valuable to me. It doesn't mean I'm a *murderer*, for god's sake. What did you do with it?"

He bites his consonants hard—separating the syllables: *mur-der-er*—and the sound of it stops your whole organism, taking your breath away, roadblocking your heart, as if an aneurysm is there in your head, waiting to rupture. A man in the waiting room with both hands on his temples stares at you, but you don't care about making a scene. When you look back at your husband, he seems dear to you. He has always been a better person than you, and you still think he is, but his dearness seems endangered.

You think of telling him, of finally letting him in. You

would tell him how a history like yours is always there in your mind, graven in stone, an immovable pyramid entombing so much. Family sins burn in your blood, are written into your prophecy. They make you do things, good and bad. With a history like yours, you are ruled by dread. But as you imagine telling him these things, you see also how his dearness would vanish, his face would crust over.

He says, "I was protecting you, but now I wonder what I was protecting. It's not worth protecting someone you don't even trust. Mom is right."

You hear the phrase *Mom is right,* and you wish it made sense to you, wish you knew a mom, any mom, that is or was right. Your own mom wasn't right, and you aren't, either. Dread disperses and hangs on the air like a thick roux.

You do the only thing you can do. You leave him there hating you, accusing you, mired in his sense of inefficacy in making you confess and beg forgiveness. But why, after all these years, should you begin now? It is too incriminating to defend yourself. You will let yourself be guilty of the present crime and seal the larger one a notch deeper. You return to your post, still breathing, wondering where you came by this will to continue, thinking of the apparatus of breath, of lungs—the inflation and collapse, the alveoli, like tiny buds, performing their magical microscopic exchange. You hear the double doors swing closed behind you, the rubbery professional efficiency of your footsteps on the linoleum.

"You were right; it was a psycho," you tell Adare. "I took care of him." You laugh. The laugh sounds sinister.

You reach for the next clipboard, and in the stretching of your arm you feel your yearning. Were you not at work, you would cry out for Varney, though you are sure that only the most abhorrent of people can love a murderer.

TWENTY

The parking lot at Little Creations is unusually empty. Other than Jana's Honda, there is only Sandy's car, a beat-up orange VW bug parked in the same space as always. Relations with Sandy have been brittle since the biting incident. Jana is careful to be polite, works hard at appearing relaxed, forces her severe facial architecture into shapes that feel like cheerfulness, and is careful to coddle Evan, but still she feels Sandy eyeing her.

Sandy stands alone in the vast, high-walled gymnasium, piling up papers on the art table and packing paint bottles into boxes. So intent is she on this activity that it takes her a moment to see Jana. She stands up straight, sucking authority into the impressive length of her stature. Despite Jana's greater age and her medical degree, she still feels strangely outranked by Sandy's height.

"Hello?" Sandy says, as if she has not a clue why Jana is there. "If you're looking for Evan, he went with his dad."

"Thank you," Jana says, trying to conceal the fact that not only was this not the plan, but it is also decidedly *not* good news. According to papers signed when Evan was enrolled, either parent has the *right* to pick up Evan, but Jana usually *does* pick him up, except when other plans have specifically been made.

"I guess you forgot," Sandy says.

Jana nods and skulks out the door with a quick, "Goodnight," before Sandy can lure her into a convoluted conversation about parenting. In the car Jana does not recognize the smell of herself. Her hand, passing close to her face smells salty, unwashed, barnyardish. She fixes her eyes on the mist creeping stealthily across the parking lot, trying to think herself through the geography of this new world she inhabits. The sound has settled (over the past few days) into a high-pitched wail, rabbit-like—awful, really—but as long as it doesn't vacillate, she is mostly capable of ignoring it. She grips the firm studs of her logic, trying to separate the givens from the possibles. It is a given that Cooper has Evan. At present that is the only known fact. From there the possibilities abound, branching out like hundreds of capillaries. She tries to factor things out. Cooper's rage about the gun, counterbalanced by his fundamental responsibility. Seretha's suspicions.

The fog, lit to an ethereal glow, and moving with distinct speed, has begun to cavort with her logic, pester what little certainty she has. Is this how hallucinations begin? With full awareness that the laws of science have begun to misbehave? Do you lose your knowledge of physics, forget how objects behave in space? Do you happily accept what your senses send you as truth—such as the tiny flying army you now see emerging from the fog, and the parking-lot pebbles levitating like bit players in a cartoon?

She drives home slowly, too slowly, she knows, but she cannot drive faster when it seems as if the street is a fault line with magma pushing up beneath it, on the verge of bubbling through. Honking cars streak past her, but she is beyond caring. As she heads up the hill, she has other pictures—Cooper, Seretha, and Evan on the stoop, armed and ready. She sees Varney behind the picture window, beckoning to her.

She parks in the next block down and approaches on foot. Carolyn Janklow is coming up the street with her excitable golden retrievers straining against their leashes. They want to nose Jana's crotch.

"Down, boys. Down," Carolyn says. "I'm so sorry."

"*Hi,*" Jana says so belatedly and in such a huge voice, that Carolyn looks startled and moves on quickly, half dragging her overeager dogs.

The kitchen light is on, but from the street she sees no one inside, and Cooper's truck is absent. The quiet inside is galactic, the kind of silence she once witnessed in a science-fiction movie when an astronaut became untethered from his space module and floated off without hope of rescue into the vast silence of eternity. She remembers how that image, that sudden shutdown of all sound, stunned the movie audience so they stopped rustling and whispering and munching, as if they suddenly realized they would die alone, far from everything they had ever known, without even one lone representative of the human race to hold their hands and wish them well.

They are gone.

Sixteen years of hyperactivity—of move, run, serve—have brought you right here, to paralysis at this kitchen table in the bitter silence of a Northwest night. Cooper and Evan are gone. They could come back later, but you know they won't; you know that as you know the most elemental things. They will not come back, because they do not really need you. You are only good at servicing strangers, those who will only see as far as your learned bedside manner. Cooper and Evan are with Seretha, who will serve them without restraint.

You hover between the joint gravitational pulls of rage and despair. It is a tug-of-war in which either side can win. Cooper and Evan are right; no one *should* need you. You are a culpable girl, one who has stolen and lied. You have never been able to help the people close to you, the ones you really love.

You find yourself gasping, thinking or dreaming (you can't tell which) of your son's skin. You feel it against yours, warm and moist. It is skin that talks, tells stories of its day. It is skin that is mourning, mourning the death of Leo. And you cannot help.

Now it will not matter what you do. You could choose to make a scene on your mother-in-law's doorstep, but you understand the limitations of that choice, the ease with which the law judges crazed and negligent mothers. You could drown yourself. You could head to the slopes of Mount Baker to wander until claimed by hypothermia. You could vanish to Alaska to get eaten by bears. You are up for grabs. Living and dying seem equally hard, with the people you love so far out of reach.

She drives to Seretha's bungalow on the north side of town, feeling the way she used to feel in medical school when every new disease she learned became a catalyst for the scrutiny of her own body and health. At various times she was convinced she had Crohn's disease, meningitis, Guillain-Barré.

She thinks of her patients, sick and obsessed, most often worried about maladies of the heart and brain. Now, like them, she is sure both these organs are failing. Her brain has lost its powers to distinguish what's real, to predict outcomes, to judge what is important. She can no longer chart the right course of action, or point to the real murderer.

And her heart, her stalwart runner's heart, has always misfired.

She parks near Seretha's bungalow and stares across the quiet street in disbelief. There is no car in Seretha's driveway, not a light on. The blinds are pulled. The place has the battened down look of a house prepared for high winds or pelting rain. Even at the best of times, the beige house, with its dark brown trim, is grimly rectangular. Its yard is empty of trees or shrubs, which makes it appear brave and alone and somehow as if it is holding its breath. Jana imagines all three of them inside, Seretha peeling back the curtains just a hair to peer at Jana through the dark. Jana stares at the undisclosing house long and hard, trying to return to logic, trying to calculate as clearly as possible if her son is, or is not, in there. There are three possibilities: (*a*) They are in there and won't come to the door, (*b*) They are in there and Seretha will come to the door and tell her to leave, and (*c*) They are not in there. The odds of finding them are low, but nevertheless Jana drags herself from the car, crosses the street, and knocks. She hears nothing. She pictures Seretha holding Evan's head to her massive breast, shushing him. Jana is in a losing battle with that woman.

AT HOME SHE LIES on the couch, sucking a chocolate Tootsie Roll Pop from Evan's Halloween stash, reading the note Cooper left on her dresser. *We have gone for a while. Pull it together. Don't get in touch. There is no more to say at this time. C and E.* The lines of blue ink, written with a drying pen, seem to race across the page, skinny and desperate as refugees. Does the brevity and coldness of this note mean they know everything about her? It now feels of so little import. What they know is the fundamental and indisputable fact: The woman they've been living with is dissembling and possibly dangerous.

She does not sleep, but she is used to that. Outside, the sky is jeweled with stars, lit and doused by moving threads of mist. A lovely, delicate, almost holy sight, but she tries not to look at it because her child and his father have fallen from their places with the stunning abruptness of shooting stars. Without them she is nothing.

Her thoughts move as if she is living all the years of her life
at once. Often it seems as if she is a child again, alone, waiting
for something to happen. She thinks of the nights she and Varney fell asleep together, his tiny three- or four-year-old body
only a blip under the covers. She tries to imagine herself as the
mother of those children bedding down together. Wouldn't she
stand at their doorway, admiring them, touched by their intimacy, trying to see and hear more? How could a mother drift as
Beth had? Jana does not think she has ever drifted like that.
She has always been there for Evan, watching, taking notice
(too much notice?). Yes, he does occasionally do terrible things,
frightening things, but his terrible things, are they really so terrible? Hasn't he turned out to be a good boy? .

She is the one with the black withholding soul.

She thinks back and everything confirms this. She remembers how, as a child, she would step on the tails of lizards.
She would watch the lizards scuttle off, leaving their jiggling
tails behind still wired with life. She laughed at this again and
again. A new tail would grow, but that was of no importance to
her. It was the moments of torture she reveled in. It is of no account that patients rave about her. If they knew the true Jana
Thomas, they wouldn't rave; they would flee. She is the woman
who, just last week, slapped her son.

When help was called for, you failed to help. When judgment was called for, you failed to judge. Your fuzzy sympathy
blurred the edges of everything.

She wanders through the house, noticing signs of the
clothing Cooper took for himself and Evan. Evan's space paja-
mas, his robe, his black and red sweatshirts. Cooper has scooped
the top layer of Evan's clothing, the things Jana remembers so
clearly because she folded and put them away just yesterday.

She takes a Butterfinger from the giant plastic hand, Evan's

Halloween loot bag. She chews the bar in three big bites. Its sweetness sticks to the gullies of her molars. She roots around in the bag for more chocolate, more sweet, more charge, but she pulls out instead a crayoned note that reads: *I love Leo.*

She stares at the crayoned line, crude and red like a bludgeoning. *"Leo,"* she says out loud. Leo is dead before she ever knew him, before she got used to the unsettling fact of him. But how long had Leo been around without her knowing? And did he die simply because she had learned of him? She pockets the note. In the bathroom she pees in the dark, then switches on the light and looks in the mirror. Behind the toothpaste smears, she sees the austere armature of her bones. She looks like a woman who fights off friendship, who thinks she knows what she needs, who believes it's enough to know about all the *–ologies* and *–itises*, and the chemical exchanges between cells. But she will never know enough.

She scans the rows of medical texts in the upstairs study she shares with Cooper. If only she knew what Leo had looked like, if he had an appearance at all. Was he woolly and leonine? Was he in the shape of a boy? A big boy or a little one? Fierce or mild? Handsome or strange? Or was he merely a wand of light, a bit of fairy spittle, a blue flame, an ineffable muse circling Evan like a vapor?

She pulls down her old physics text from college and thumbs through it, thinking of all that wasn't known when the book was written. All the new conjectured particles, all the attempts at finding workable supersymmetry and superstring theories. None of that is in here. Even physics is a speculative science, an edifice built in part on unproven hypothesis, just like psychiatry, not nearly as clear and comforting as the repair of suffering bodies. But now she needs conjecture. She needs to know things she cannot put her hands on, things beyond the possibility of healing. She flips through the book, distracted, eyes glazed, wanting to read, but not being able to.

It's 4 A.M. and cold, and her skin has developed a texture like lichen. She'll be grateful to go to work.

Leo, Leo, Leo. The etiology of Leo, who came and went like some weather vane of Evan's deep mind. Evan's companion; Evan's dead companion. Evan's Varney.

THE GENESIS OF LEO? she thinks the next day when her digit is deep in the rectum of a sixty-five-year-old man, feeling for polyps, fingering the tongues and flaps of mopey internal flesh, palpating the mysterious universe in there, cell by cell. *What was Leo's etiology, his genesis; what was Leo in the beginning?*

She withdraws her gloved digit, an inadvertent *fuck-you* finger, and bile floods her body.

TWENTY-ONE

Someone is shaking her, sending messages down her ear canal, knock-knock on the brain, but her body is gooey and won't be aroused no matter what the brain says. It's Kurt Klug, his voice like a cat's, gentle but insistent. "Hey, hon. We need you out there. Sorry, but we need you. Gee, I'm glad I found you. You just disappear into a closet like that . . ."

He lifts her to a sitting position. She lusts for prone. Beneath her the linoleum is cool and hard. The eyes are another matter; you can't force eyes open, not without instruments at least, and Kurt wouldn't do that. She moans softly.

"Are you sick? Are you still sick?"

She shakes her head in denial. Evan fills her mind. She wants him near her with the same urgency she once had about Cooper.

"I wouldn't do this to you," Kurt says. "Honest I wouldn't, but we're swamped out there. A couple of cardios, a pelvic fracture. Some crazy craziness. Seems like the spooks never went to bed."

She's supposed to be good at this, rising to full attention, moving in to address the problems at hand, but today something fails her; her spirit doesn't ignite, and all the usefulness in her feels used up. She opens her eyes, sees that she's in the supply closet but cannot remember coming in here and has no idea how long she has been here.

"I'm coming," she says.

"Stand up. Have some coffee. Shall I get you coffee?"

"I'll be okay."

But he doesn't trust her. Oh, those doe eyes of his; he should have been a woman, with that sweet voice, those soft eyes. He hovers over her, his body curved and loose as a noodle, his red hair like a carefully pressed ruffle. What a good nurse he is. But a minute or two of his care is all she can take. She sighs and stands, and habit carries her quickly out the door. Shaking off Kurt's clucking assistance, she runs a hand through her pony-tail, squeezes her cheeks. At the nurses' station she takes the next chart. *Chop, chop. Business as usual. Ignore the curious looks. Ignore the pity with the growth curve of dandelions that causes mouths to pucker oddly. Ignore the shards of life falling around you like sputtering fireworks.*

BILL MCELROY RISES, shuts the doctors' lounge door, and returns to perch on the edge of the easy chair. She's been sum-moned here. *Drop everything. Come.* And of course she came— Bill is the director of their ER group, a silver-haired avuncular man whose manner is usually characterized by an evenness borne of impregnable nerves and a strong constitution, but today he appears nervous, a state that contrasts sharply with her continuing stupor. He called her in here suddenly, midday, mid-patient, an unprecedented move. The closing of the door has created a vacuum, and now she keeps thinking of the finite amount of air in here, the possibility they'll both expire. She thinks of mentioning this to him, but he's avoiding eye con-tact, so instead she tries to be parsimonious with her breathing. Outside people are walking on tiptoes and speaking in palin-dromes. Bill's eyes now seem like apertures leading directly to his brain.

"You're a wonderful doctor, Jana. You know I think that. You've put in many good hours here and we value you as a group member."

She holds as still as she can to hear if this preamble will go where it seems to be going. He leans toward the couch where she sits. His leaning makes her feel like his daughter. Or his subordinate. They're supposed to be colleagues, but she has never felt that way and doubts she ever will. He's twenty years older than she; he started their ER group and hired her; it would take lifetimes to overcome these inequities. Still, it is true, he has always respected her. She studies the line of dark follicles along his jaw, which seem to stem from deep inside his skull, and tries to imagine him with a beard.

"But something is getting in your way of late." He holds up a hand, palm facing her, policeman-style, though she has made no move to speak. "No, no. I'm not prying. Marriage, whatever; no need to explain. However, you do need to rest."

"I'm not tired," Jana says. She wonders if Adare said something to Bill about Cooper's visit and if it is now common knowledge that she and Cooper are at odds. Her voice is a slow trickle she tries to hasten. "I will speed up," she says. "I promise. I know I take too much time. That abdominal is a real bear. The blood work gave me nothing. I should get back to it."

"No, Glenn is coming in. He'll finish up with the abdominal."

And then she stops talking because their conversation has begun to seem like a tired minuet, something so old and obvious it's not worth doing anymore. Bill McElroy picks at the fraying chenille on the arm of the chair. A plume of soot dances outside. The ghost of the word *hello* drawn a few days ago lingers in the window's condensation.

"You're firing me." Someone else's words purloined for the situation at hand.

"No, no. Take some time off, that's all."

"I don't want to." More words (Evan's words?) swindled.

He straightens, fixes the imploring slant of his eyes. "I'm asking you to take some time off."

"Is it the abdominal?"

"No, of course not. I'm sure that's tricky. It's—" He stands, frowning. "Come here."

Hand on her shoulder, he leads her to a small mirror hung on the wall by the sink. It's hung at her height and, she now realizes, was probably hung for her, the only female ER doc. She's never thought about it before, because it was there when she came, and beyond the occasional quick glance, she rarely uses it.

"Look at yourself," he says.

The mirror holds a world like the opening to Hades, a long serpentine path guarded by shimmying creatures. At the center she stands, gaunt and disheveled, eyes bloodshot and underscored by eggplant circles.

"You see?" Bill says.

She nods. Bill could not possibly see what she sees.

As she is being chaperoned out, she passes Glenn Fishman in the hall. He looks down at his chart without acknowledging her. What a serious man he is. She laughs. "*You are too serious, Glenn Fishman*," she says, or thinks, she's not sure which. She supposes she has looked serious like this before, but not anymore. She's free now, and she'll learn to laugh bigly like Varney and Robin. She'll be equal parts blood and phlegm and bile. *Oh yes, I am an embarrassment.* And she laughs again and hears a weary carousel *um-pa-pa* from one of the curtained cubicles, or maybe from her own spleen.

The staff has gathered, mute, goggle-eyed, at the nurses' station. Adare's birthday cake, leftover from yesterday, half eaten, sits on the table, looking mauled as a career-end prizefighter. "See you," they all mumble. "Feel better." Automatic as prayer.

———

MIDAFTERNOON. A BRAVE new world Bellingham has become. She sees buildings she's never seen before, gilded with western-sky light, ripe as autumn fruit. From her cell phone she calls the school (to confirm what she already suspects). Her son is not there. He never arrived at school today.

Any one of the buildings she passes could be concealing her husband and son and mother-in-law. They could be squatting anywhere, spying. A laughing matter or a crying one, she's not sure which. She drives as if drawn by a supermagnet, to a pistachio-colored, cottage-sized house not far from the hospital. It stands out from the other gray and white houses on the block, for its color and for the general well-being and cheerfulness it exudes.

She struts to the front door, but by the time she arrives there, her confidence has withered. Mrs. Stubbs has already spotted her and opens the door, aproned and beaming, just as you would want her to be. She forces you over the threshold, though you've lost your nerve, or verve, or whatever. You know Evan isn't here. If he were here Mrs. Stubbs wouldn't be crowing like this. But her crowing doesn't last. She downshifts quickly. She sits you down. She feeds you tea and chewy ginger cookies. You bask in the warm aura of her concern, her attention, admiring the fine white hair of her accumulated wisdom, saying nothing much, letting your disheveled body translate for you.

"How's the little guy?" she asks.

You tell her he is a big boy, he loves first grade. You marvel at the speed of his growth—he'll soon be a man.

Now the lies get sticky, blended as they are with truth, and like a child wallowing in sugar, the very sympathy you devoured so eagerly a minute ago gets cloying. And you see that once again you are in front of the impossible. A bad habit, beguiling others with your evident sadness, courting their sympathy, then girding yourself and pulling away just shy of confession. Nevertheless, you're out the door, promising you're okay, promising to stay in touch, wondering what you ever thought Mrs. Stubbs could do for you.

At home the newspaper sits in its slot by the door, uncollected. She leaves it there but can't keep out the headline about the raping, murdering college student still at large. There's another smaller headline about the outrage of the Lummi community.

Inside, the lethargy returns. The house echoes like an empty underground station. The carousel sounds are still there. A calliope and an *um-pa* band. She sits in the kitchen, wrapped in a fleece blanket, bare feet on the windowsill, looking out the bay window, her view onto the world. Spider, still a homely patchwork of skin and fur, comes nosing around looking for a lap on which to leap, but she pushes him away.

Carolyn Janklow's dogs, alone all day, are going crazy, barking as if they've seen the devil. Silvery spears rise from the bay, made from the alchemy of water and light. Is Evan sad without her, or simply oblivious? Is he a less volatile boy under Cooper's care?

Cheesy, eggy smells from Cooper's and Evan's breakfast of the day before still linger in the air, and a few of Evan's Hot Wheels ring his chair and place mat. She doesn't dare move a thing, afraid that restoring things to their places will be like packing things belonging to the dead when you have resigned yourself to their absence. On the other hand, leaving things as they are might make the house seem like a monument to their departure. She decides it will be a mausoleum to them no matter what she does.

She gets up for water, and the opening of the cabinet— some familiar thrust of her arm, or the cabinet's woody smell, or the regular arrangement of the glasses—brings to mind a cramped, accusing look of Cooper's and a feeling he is behind her, ready to block her way. She closes the cupboard quickly, without taking anything, and the glass inside rattles from the disruption. She turns and surveys what she can see of the house from where she stands. Every room, every cupboard, every drawer is bulging, waiting for her to release its array of feelings and memories.

"Where are they?" she demands uselessly of Seretha's phone machine.

She lugs herself up to bed, though daylight still scavenges the neighborhood, looking for things to illuminate. She lies under the covers, fully clothed, shivering, thinking of the embarrassed pitying looks the ER staff gave her as she was leaving, how she was caught in their dark penumbra. Kurt Klug's and Bill McElroy's and Mrs. Stubbs's looks were made by the same arrangement of facial muscles, developed by the species over years and years of responding to the most pitiful humans.

Despite exhaustion, she does not sleep. She stares out the bedroom window. The apple tree is almost bare. One of its few remaining leaves dangles precariously at the extremity of a branch, straining for freedom, or is it rest? At the very least, something different. She's reminded of Varney on the beach. Altered by the wind, he would transform his body like a sculptor. *"I'm a leopard!" "I'm an orangutan!" "I'm a snake!"* he would yell, and he would sprint or lumber or slither accordingly. This wildness didn't fit with the other part of him, the part that was cautious and law-abiding. When she stepped beyond a no-trespassing sign on the beach, he refused to join her. When she confessed to taking a pack of Juicy Fruit gum from the 7-Eleven, he begged her to go back and pay. His chiding became so annoying, she always relented.

She imagines now, as she never has before, Evan and Varney

together, racing down the beach, arms flung wide, faces raised to yell into the wind and feel it's smooth-rough hand on their cheeks.

The garbage bag of letters. Approximately one a month for more than fifteen years. Over one hundred and fifty of them. She has dumped them on the bed, and now they are strewn here and there, wherever they happened to fall. She rifles through them, finds the most recent one, the one addressed in the neat hand with a different return address. The stationery is a porous pale blue, personal not institutional. The postmark's date is six weeks ago.

Wind roars in her ears, snuffing the distant calliope.

Dear Cadence Miller,

I do not know if this letter will find you, but I pray that it does. I am writing to you on behalf of your brother, Varney Miller, who, as you know, has been a California inmate for almost sixteen years. He was transferred recently to the hospice program on the grounds of the state medical facility due to the fact that his HIV infection has progressed, and despite the fact that he has been taking protease inhibitors, the infection has caught up with him. He has a serious lymphoma. We do not expect him to live more than a few months. Here, he is receiving three-tier palliative care.

I am the chaplain of our hospice, and Varney has asked me to seek you out. He understands that you may be angry at him for deeds and events of his past that have affected you, but he has instructed me to tell you that he loves you dearly. He wants to make sure you know that before he passes on.

For my part, I will say that I almost feel I know you, as Varney has shared many stories of your childhood. From his stories you sound like a wonderful person, as Varney is, too. He is very caring and his stories keep us all entertained. I hope you can find the strength and love in your heart to contact your brother before he departs this world. I think you would find him deeply changed.

> Sincerely,
> Chaplain D. J. Michaels
> aka "Chaplain Jack"

The silence at the center of a lake. Faraway on the shore, people live lives that are not discernible at this distance.

The body still. The brain spiraling to the inner coils of silence. So many boys in peril. And you are under the covers, surrounded by the intractability of paper, cut off from the sustaining warm bodies of family and patients.

Sound downstairs cuts through the silence. Not the repetitive sounds your ears usually churn out. This is the sound of a person moving. Of footsteps taking the stairs.

You stare at your husband, standing in the doorway, the husband you thought was gone. His face has become a hologram, one minute Varney, one minute Cooper.

"You're back," you say, not sure which face you're addressing.

"Just to get some things. You're supposed to be at work. Are you sick?"

You shake your head no. "Where's Evan?" you say.

"He's fine."

"But where is he? I called school. He's not at school."

"He's fine."

His hand rests on the doorframe. You can just make out the

scar dating back to the day you met him. The wound you sewed for him is covered over now with a ridge of shiny alabaster skin, as different from the rest of his body as something man-made.

"You can't just take him away," you say. You are thinking of Evan. You are thinking of Varney. You are thinking of everyone you love.

"The hell I can't. When you're going crazy on us."

"Evan needs—"

"What? A mother who's pretending to be someone she isn't? Who the hell is Cadence Miller? And the house in California—"

"How do you know about Cadence Miller?"

"See?"

"Cooper," you say, trying to invoke your history of intimacy. "Things have changed. Just now—My brother—"

"So now you have a *brother*? I thought I was supposed to pity you because your family was dead. Forget it, Dr. Miller, or whoever the hell you are."

He darts to the dresser, opens the bottom drawer, and loads a pile of wool sweaters into his arms. He rushes out, rummages in Evan's bedroom, then heads downstairs and out the front door. The silence he leaves is deeper than before. Everyone, you think, has the power to surprise—the way Cooper has surprised you, the way Varney did, the way you have surprised your colleagues. You would like to sleep or die or vomit, but none of these can you do on command. So you sit, propped by pillows, in a restless stupor, surrounded by letters you don't have the heart to read.

You get up slowly and wander into Evan's room. It is messier than you remember, the floor a mosaic of colorful pieces of things that have no readily identifiable use or origin. If you picked them up, you might know what they were—Lego bricks,

K'nex pieces, Lincoln Logs, perhaps—but spread on the floor, they seem like things you have never seen before, part of a complex equation that has no solution.

You spy in the middle of it all a single plastic-tipped dart. It galvanizes something in you. You pick it up and take careful aim at the target on the wall. You hurl with all your might. The dart ricochets off the ring around the bull's-eye and falls to the floor, its plastic tip broken. You look amid the mayhem for a better dart but fail to find one. Again and again you hurl the broken one. Each time the dart fails to adhere to the target. Snapping the unruly dart in two, you return to your room.

You gather the letters into a pile, the most recent on top. It occurs to you that you might have followed Cooper, keeping the front bumper of your car to the rear bumper of his until you forged a path to your child. But then what? As you contemplate this, you see beneath the letters what you have long ago forgotten, the ebony porpoise you took from your mother's shop and the photo of Varney laughing.

Stroking the smooth curve of the porpoise's back, you stare at the photo. It is almost twenty years old, tattered and fading. But the laugh hasn't changed. He stands on the patio with his head thrown back and his mouth open in a mad cackle. Hibiscus flowers grow on the wall behind his head, with their tongues thrust out in chortling sympathy. A once-happy boy.

Reminded, you rise. Wearily, warily, you rise.

TWENTY-TWO

She hurtles down I-5, out of the Great Northwest, with its straight proud evergreens and impenetrable fogs; Spider, behind her, producing guttural meows as he leaps from seat back to seat back. In Ashland, Oregon, she stops for coffee and gas. She drinks the coffee, standing outside her car, hands white with the cold, her breath making steamy curlicues, while the attendant fills the tank. To the east, brown foothills rise out of the high plain like the ascent to a pyramid.

Fragments of his letters stream through her head, the outpourings of a person she only half knows, a person whose body has grown (and withered), whose language has changed, whose color-morphing brain is different every day.

Doing okay but the food is terrible. The guy in the cell next to me went crazy last week and drank his own pee. Don't worry, I haven't done that yet.

I've lost twenty pounds, but I'm strong as an ox. Hey, Cady-did, is you out there?

Today I've got the gray brain. Flat as a pancake. Dead as a doornail.

This place sucks and everyone in it sucks like I suck.

The coffee is a terrible metallic-tasting brew, but she drinks it, anyway. How long had he been on protease inhibitors?

Years, perhaps. She can't tell yet from the letters. She also hasn't learned (in the letters she's read so far) how he contracted AIDS, though given what she knows of prison life, it's easy to surmise. She hasn't read all the letters or even sorted them. They're in the back of her car now, still in their plastic bag—her brother's life in words.

She pays the attendant without registering his face, without awareness of his really *having* a face, like the mosquito you later realize must have been there only because you've been bitten. Back in her car she drives beyond the speed limit. Her body is a vapor; she is all urge, the way she was in labor, pushing Evan out with every cell. She bargains with any power that may be out there to keep Varney alive and coherent. Death, even when you expect it, is always sudden.

Some people in here are mad about being treated like animals, but if you are an animal, how can you object to being treated like one? I know I'm an animal.

Piss Cat wants to do me and I'm scared, Sis. Piss Cat is big and he is mean and he is gruzzly. HELP! SAVE ME FROM PISS CAT!

They call me The Ferret 'cause I'm little and quick. They think they know me, but they don't know nada. But I'll be their ferret.

The mind travels when the body does. Hers is chasing lives, trying to pin them down. She had a life once without Varney. She was alive for four whole years before Varney was born. Some of that she should remember. But all she remembers is the feeling of living under too-bright lights, as if she was on stage, blinded by spots, which made it hard to see who was looking at her. Even now she can scarcely think what her parents looked like. Her mother was thin and pale and ethereal, her father big in every way, but their faces are mere sketches in her memory, detail faded. There was a sound track of tears, intermingled with song. (*That* she remembers clearly—her mother loved singing.) And there was a lot of TV. Entire days spent tunneling into the grainy screen.

One day Varney simply seemed to appear. A baby with melon eyes that stared out at the world with astonishment. "Like an extraterrestrial," Walter used to say. Cady couldn't stand it when her little brother cried. It was an itchy, sticky little sound that worried her even when he'd stopped. But by the time he was three, they were fast friends.

She is stopped for a fruit check at the California state line. "No," she tells them, "no fresh produce," and she is waved through. Cars and trucks pass by her with the nonchalance of cats, but the sterile green highway-department greeting— WELCOME TO CALIFORNIA—forces her to the side of the road. Since moving to the Northwest, she has only been to California once, for an ER symposium in San Francisco. The entire weekend she was jumpy and sleepless. Now she forces herself back out into the traffic, willing another return.

I THINK ABOUT THEM *every day. I've decided Mr. Phillips and I are from different tribes. That's the only way I can see it. He rubbed me the wrong way from the beginning. (And I rubbed him the wrong way.) The very first day, he pranced into class and told us what a good dancer he was. He turned on a cassette and wiggled his fanny to some tunes and waited for us to laugh. Most people did, but I didn't. He sees that, and he stops by my desk and he says, "What're you so glum about?" I can see in his eyes he already doesn't like me. So I just watch him. Okay, so maybe that was stupid and childish of me, but this guy was a case and he ticked me off. A full-grown grown-up still worried about being cool. He had this black leather vest he wore every day, like a uniform over whatever else he was* wearing. Like he was some biker or something. And sometimes he'd put a streak of blue or green in his surfer-blond hair, like he was saying, "See, I can still hang with the cool crowd." He was trying to be a surfer, and a punker, and a brain all at once, but he actually wasn't any of those things. He was really a pathetic kid still trying to get attention. He had this habit of holding his hands around his face. He'd use two fingers to tap his cheek, and it made a sort of hollow drum sound, and he'd flick his thumb off his nose when he was thinking. And kids who liked him started imitating him, flicking their noses all the time and drumming their cheeks, and Mr. P.—that's what he liked to be called—he just ate it right up. Anything for attention.

That red-faced wife of his, Maureen, used to come into class all the time, bringing him lunch and stuff he'd forgotten. Her boobs were always half rolling out of her tight shirts, so it took you right out of the math mood. I kept thinking: Doesn't she have anything better to do?

I think about Andy Carnack, too. He was a nobody, a real wall person. He hardly had a personality. Everyone raved about his brain, but that's only because he'd had a personality lobotomy. He was as nowhere as I was.

I'm supposed to say I like these guys now that they're dead, but I didn't like them then and I don't like them any more now. Deadness has nothing to do with niceness. Believe me, I won't be any nicer when I'm dead. Just easier to deal with maybe. Easier to dismiss.

But still—and this is what I've been trying to say all along—I'm still sorry. Every day I'm sorry. Every day I'm sorrier than I was the day before. I live in the sorry kingdom 'cause you've got a right to live your life no matter how pathetic it is.

TWENTY-THREE

She stops near Mount Shasta. Symmetrical and alone, with its ragged hat of snow, it has the look of an ancient mountain, home to many gods. Tiny snowflakes have begun to drift, fine as ash, unsure of down. An elderly woman in the rest area's ladies' room, dressed in pink fleece, wants to make conversation. She has a wide face and tight gray curls.

"Looks like we'll have snow for Thanksgiving," she says as she fluffs her curls in the mirror. "I just love snow. Being from Wisconsin I guess I'm just used to it. It makes me feel all comfy. Whereabouts are you from, dear?"

Jana finishes her washing and leaves, pretending not to hear. At the car she digs out a wool sweater and tries to dial home on her cell phone, but it's beyond its working range. The snowflakes have gathered heft and momentum; they're heavy enough now for gravity to claim them. They materialize five or six feet from her eyes and land intact on the sleeve of her navy sweater. (*"Each one different; each one perfect,"* she remembers her second-grade teacher saying.)

She leans against the hood of her car, unmoored, pulled both north and south, her fears floating in and out of prominence like ice floes.

In the phone booth by the restroom, she stomps to keep

warm. She pulls the hastily scrawled hospice number from her pocket. The answering voice is recorded and officious; it instructs her to punch in numbers. When she finally gets a real person on the line, she asks (in a voice so altered it does not seem to be hers) for Varney Miller, and she is sent through a maze of receptionists, voices of people she pictures all seated in a row. "You have to call the inmate line," she is told.

A man outside, wearing tight jeans and a cowboy hat, taps on the Plexiglas. She holds up a finger and dials Seretha. Jana is momentarily speechless when Seretha, the real flesh-and-blood Seretha, answers. Jana tumbles into her question without a hello.

"Are they there?" she says.

Seretha draws breath. "This is Jana, I take it? Cooper and Evan are here, if that's who you mean."

Jana closes her eyes hard against the distraction of snow and cowboys. "Can I talk to Cooper?"

"Hold the line." Seretha puts down the receiver, and Jana hears her moving off into the bowels of her house, calling Cooper's name.

Jana looks at her watch. It's almost dinnertime. She vows not to accuse him. Her breath splashes a growing globular shape on the scratched Plexiglas. She strains to hear conversation, but if it is happening, it is too far away from the phone. She has never been so cold. Her feet feel wet. The extremities of her fingers have turned yellowish. She hears Evan's trilling in the background. How young he sounds, his voice a delicate, meaningless patter. He talks to Seretha, who serves up slow deep yeses and nos that sound a little like belches.

"Hello?" There is softness in Cooper's voice; it could be uncertainty, it could be weariness. Could she hope for sympathy?

"So you're staying with Seretha?" she says.

"Yes." The word is a plateau, a bog. Nothing rises from it. She recognizes his stance so well—how he is waiting to be wooed from his hurt.

"Why did you leave without saying anything?" she says, pitching her voice so he'll know she really wants to know. What she truly wants is something much more global, but she'll settle for small things first.

"Not now," he says to Evan. "Go in the kitchen with Gramma. I'll be there in a minute." He moves somewhere, clears his throat. Even over the phone, wariness hangs between them as a thin rubberized veil. He laughs quietly. "Jana." He pauses. "Jana, you have a house I never knew about, a brother you've never mentioned. Who isn't saying things?"

"I know." She exhales, and the flowering condensation from her breath now blurs her view to the outside. "There are reasons."

"What is that supposed to mean?" He sighs. "The thing is—" He pauses, and she hears the click of his teeth meeting. He sighs again, as if to sweep things clear. "Look, I'm in the middle of making dinner. I can't really talk now."

"I'll call you back," she says.

"I'll call you after Evan's down."

She thinks, working her fingers in piano movements to warm them. "That won't work. I'm on the road and beyond the range of my phone."

"What do you mean 'on the road'? Where?"

"I'm going to see my brother. He's sick, Cooper. *Really* sick."

Cooper waits. She closes her eyes, parks the receiver between shoulder and chin, and rubs her hands together fast.

"Dying sick?" he says.

"Yes."

Something opens, and they seem to stand for a moment on the vestibule of renewed intimacy. "I'm sorry about that. I really am."

"Thank you," she says.

"Hey, I really have to go. Call me tomorrow night, okay?"

"Can I talk to Evan?"

"Tomorrow night."

The dial tone roars like an idling jetliner. Jana lays her forehead against the cold Plexiglas of the booth and stares at the wrinkled skin that bands her knuckles, wondering what Cooper is making for dinner, imagining his spaghetti with a touch of peppery heat, or the cheesy polenta. She thinks of Evan, a creature of the moment, so attentive to the miracles and agonies of the present, so delighted always with Gramma Seretha. What if he's forgotten about his mother? Maybe he hasn't forgotten after only two days, but couldn't he soon forget?

Behind her the tapping comes again. She looks up and finds the man in the cowboy hat has come around to the back of the booth and is scowling at her. She realizes now she should have called Chaplain Jack, the one who wrote her the letter. But she can't make that call now, not with the impatient cowboy trying to oust her.

"Public phones are for *business*," he says as she exits. "You're not supposed to *yak*."

Back on the road the eddying snow makes a continuous tunnel of the road. It forces her to slow down, though she still wants to drive like a hooligan. In the backseat Spider wails. It seems cruel to have brought him—his small shorn body must be cold—but it would have been crueler still to leave him alone in the house untended. Every once in a while Jana raises her own voice to join Spider's lament. It feels good to howl.

Huge trucks barrel past her, so she feels wedges of air pressing against the side of her car. She grips the steering wheel hard, obsessed with the difficulty of keeping the car on the road, feeling as if the trucks are malevolent and trying to force her off, and that she, too, might swerve suddenly, prompted by some sudden uncontrollable urge that has nothing to do with the trucks. The road begins to descend from the mountains. By the time she reaches Redding, the snow has tapered off, night has settled in, and the road traverses vast stretches of unlit, uninhabited land.

She spends a restless night in a motel just off the interstate. The trucks sound as if they're rattling by dangerously near her head. Through the thin motel walls, she hears the movements of a drunken couple in the next room. She lies in bed, stroking Spider hard in an effort to keep him still and quiet. Pets are not allowed in the rooms, but it doesn't seem like the kind of place that will be checking. Spider purrs full tilt, then drifts into sleep. Jana thinks of the various AIDS patients she has treated. They came to the ER in the advanced stages of their disease, with complaints of yeast infections, vomiting, chronic diarrhea, extreme dehydration. Some of them were covered with purple spots from Kaposi's sarcoma. Nearly all of them were cachectic, their muscles so atrophied that their skin had collapsed into the concavities of their skeletal structure. Their cheeks were indented as kettle holes, their legs delicate as kindling. But what she remembers most now is the abstracted look in their eyes, as if they had already glimpsed what it might be like to cross over to the other side.

She drifts into sleep with images of these patients congregating in her head, defiant, bug-eyed, confrontational, as if they were attending an important union meeting. A bright red light flashes on and off. It's the light at the nurses' station indicating a new patient has arrived. She knows she can't keep up with all these patients, but she seems to be the only one on duty. One of the patients, she knows, is her father.

She awakens to full alertness at three-thirty in the morning, and she phones home. The machine yields only two messages, one from Carolyn Janklow, asking if Jana and Cooper will look after her house and dogs while she goes away for the Thanksgiving holiday, and the other from an attorney named Frank Mordecai. The first message is pushed from her consciousness by the second. Is it possible that Cooper is initiating divorce proceedings already? It seems ridiculous, precipitous. She wills herself not to think of this.

COMING TO THE state prison medical facility, where the hospice is located, is like passing through a funnel, gradually paring away the trappings of the outside world. First she turns off the freeway and drives into an unpopulated area, a place without businesses or domiciles, only grassland and livestock and acres of sky. Then, in the middle of nowhere, the institution presents itself, set off on its own like a medieval village, walled and guarded.

Jana watches the sun seep slowly into the parking lot, which is only half full of cars. She feels as if she is a long way from everywhere. Nothing is visible from where she sits but the massive white prison buildings and, beyond them, an expanse of low hills, their color a dead brown. It is a dry and desolate place, appropriate, she supposes, for a prison. She imagines the deserts of Saudi Arabia must emanate this same lonely feeling. You could not live here unless you knew how.

Chaplain Jack is summoned to prison reception. He is a big, quietly charismatic man, somewhat hermaphroditic in appearance, with an unusually large bald head and a two-part nose with a long straight shaft ending in a tip of sculpted roundness. Instead of clerical garments, he wears a polyester polo shirt of pale yellow. His laugh is of the hee-haw variety, and he seems—in appearance, at least—like a man you might

run into on a golf course, a pulled-up-by-the-bootstraps busi-
nessman of middling fortunes rather than a chaplain.

"Cady Miller!" he says, greeting her with a hug as if she is
one of his own family.

"Yes," she says. "But I go by Jana Thomas now."

"Jana it is," he says as if it is the most natural thing in the
world to have a new name. He insists that the prison officials
speed up her background check and promises to return for her
when she's been approved. She waits in a cell-sized waiting
room, on an orange plastic chair with a two-day-old newspaper,
while an officious, grumbling parsnip of a woman, who seems to
resent the entire situation as well as Chaplain Jack himself,
takes Jana's license and Social Security number and runs a
check on them to verify that she has no criminal record or out-
standing warrants. Jana watches the woman through a crack in
the door and tries to hear her conversations on the phone and
with a coworker, but without success. An hour passes, then
two—so much for the "speeded up" check. *Who is this woman
with multiple names?*"she imagines them saying as they dig back
into the past and discover Cadence Eloine Miller.

Just before noon Chaplain Jack reappears. She is signed in
and escorted through a metal detector, and then she is inside
the prison. She notices the chaplain has the lopsided gait of
someone who was once a polio victim. There is something in
this small defect that makes her trust him. He guides her along
a maze of concrete pathways to a small building, which houses
the hospice. The other buildings, he explains, are for sick inmates who, on recovery, will be returned to other correctional
institutions throughout the state.

They sit in Chaplain Jack's office, where he describes to her
(in patient teaching-man tones) the hospice philosophy. She
does not stop him, although she already knows the goal is not

to heal patients but to help them achieve physical and spiritual comfort as they are dying. Chaplain Jack's person and his office show little overt evidence of his faith except for a single row of books on the bottom shelf sporting titles about thanatology. It is only through the soothing effect of his measured speech that she can detect a religious bent in him. She has not known many religious people, and she is surprised by the ease she feels in his presence. Sun soaks the air, illuminating the mesmerizing dance of dust motes. The table is spread with donuts and apple Danishes, small cartons of juice, a dish of grapes, another of chocolate kisses. He urges her to help herself, but she is too distracted to eat. Through the half-open door she sees a few slippered inmates shuffling around the horseshoe area just outside. No one looks like Varney. In bathrobes they do not look like dangerous men, only old and tired ones.

Chaplain Jack watches her with nearly alarming attentiveness. She is not sure what his purpose is in detaining her for so long. His eyes follow hers to a large hunk of enameled volcanic rock. He lifts it.

"Odd, isn't it? It's a holiday gift from one of the guys. He made it in ceramics class. He tells me, 'There's a pearl in here, but it's so tiny I bet you can't find it.' He wouldn't tell me where it was. He says it's a representation of his life. See if you can find the pearl." He tosses the hunk to Jana. It is heavy, and it is smooth in some places, pockmarked and rough in others. Except for its blue and purple enamel, it looks more found than sculpted. She rotates it, looking for the pearl, but if there is one, she can't find it.

"You wouldn't believe the stuff I get around the holidays," says Chaplain Jack. "I have to clear out a whole shelf for it. They crochet, string beads; some write poems. When they get here, if they have energy, they feel free to do things they've

never done before. Some feel so free, they start to get better."
He watches Jana, completely at home with his own silence.
"So you're the shy one in the family and Varney's the talker?"

"I always thought Varney was pretty shy," she says.

"Varney? Shy?" He hee-haws briefly. "Not in here he isn't."
Again he issues laughter as if he has a lot more stored up inside.
"When he's feeling good, he's one of the all-time big talkers.
He and I have had some pretty late nights together." He shakes
his head, privately amused.

Silence drapes them again. Someone in the common area
rasps a few lines of "I Wanna Hold Your Hand." Jana returns
the volcanic lump to the table without having located the
pearl. She is seized with the sudden unnerving notion that
maybe Varney is already dead and Chaplain Jack is trying to
get around to telling her so.

"Varney tells me you're an actress," Chaplain Jack says.

"He said that?"

The chaplain nods. "You're not?"

Jana shakes her head.

Chaplain Jack laughs. "He fooled me. He said you had a
role in some big movie with what's-her-name—you know, Julia
Roberts. I don't follow movies too closely."

Jana laughs because she feels she's expected to. Why would
Varney make this claim; though it's true he had nothing more
real to offer about what she does, and his letters have already
revealed his speculation. "I couldn't act my way out of a bag.
Does he—" She is stuck on Varney's choice, his eerie intuiting
of her charade. "Is there dementia?"

"Heck no. Not yet, anyway."

Distracted, his eyes swerve past Jana's head out into the
hallway. Something he sees or remembers has moved him to
alarm.

"Can I see him now?" she says.

The chaplain's attention returns to the room. "When did you last see your brother?"

The shame has a shape now and words attached to it. Chaplain Jack waits. He waits. And waits.

"Years ago," she says softly.

"You never visited?"

She shakes her head.

"Well, you're here now."

She says nothing.

"Right?" he says.

She nods.

"And that's good. That's the important thing. Right?" He presses her, suddenly insistent, leaning forward so she sees a patch of dark sweat in his armpit. Under his pressure she nods.

"The pearl," he says. "You see? Just the pearl. What did he look like when you last saw him?"

The picture is in her purse, where she has kept it since finding it again. She takes it out and hands it to Chaplain Jack. He studies it for a long time as if he must commit it to memory.

"A great picture," he says after a while. "I like knowing there has been happiness. If you've had happiness, it's easier to locate again. I'm sure you know he doesn't look like this anymore?"

"He was much younger then," she says.

"That's not what I mean. The disease—"

"I know about the disease," she says. "You don't have to tell me."

"You've known people with it?"

She nods. Chaplain Jack rises and moves slowly to the door. "I'll tell him you're here," he says.

She listens to the syncopation of his tread as it fades down the hallway. Her heart runs like a cat's heart, or perhaps a bird's. She hears its effort in her ears. She feels the preposterous stretch of its fibro-elastic webbing. How can she have waited all these years before coming here? She tries to imagine what she and Varney will say to each other, knowing what will be said is certainly beyond planning.

It seems forever that she hovers between Jana and Cady in the uneasy limbo of Chaplain Jack's office, waiting for the next moment to clarify itself. Chaplain Jack's silent reappearance takes her by surprise. He touches her shoulder as he passes by to reseat himself. Back in his chair he smiles ruefully. "He won't see you," he says.

She's confused. "I thought he wanted to see me? Isn't that why you asked me here?"

"Yes to both." He watches her with a look of clinical detachment, a look Jana knows she herself has used after telling a patient of a dire prognosis. He shrugs. "Now he feels differently."

"He won't see me right now today? Or ever?"

"His words were: *I can't see her again.* You have to understand, Jana," he says in a voice he no doubt learned from the pulpit, "he's dying. He's ashamed of his body. He's ashamed of what he's done. There's depression. And he was close to you, so he feels accountable. It's very, very hard."

Outrage and frustration bubble up, though they're not what she *means* to feel. "I just drove fifteen hours to get here. He's my *brother*. He's *dying*. I *have* to see him. I—"

Even as she speaks, she knows it doesn't matter. Varney doesn't want to see her; his desire is what counts. She is making a fool of herself, blubbering like this. She hasn't cried in public for years, and it is a messy, humiliating operation. The back of the throat constricts. Breath and words stall. Cheeks swell with heat. How can they not see one another when they're on the same premises, only a few rooms away?

She wants to be alone, but Chaplain Jack has interposed himself. He has moved behind her chair and rubs her shoulders.

"He might change his mind," Chaplain Jack says. "I hope he does."

"When?"

"That I can't say."

She tries to rally. "But what if he dies before he changes his mind?"

"There's nothing I can do. Nothing *we* can do. I can only put it out to him that you're here and you're available. That's all."

TWENTY-FOUR

For a while she stays in motion, as has always been her habit. She fills the car with gas, buys 7-Eleven crackers, a carton of strawberry yogurt, a six-pack of Coke, reregisters at the same motel right by the thundering freeway (though this time she insists on a room bordering the courtyard), checks her home phone for messages, unpacks, and stows the few pieces of clothing she brought.

On her final trip to the car for Spider's litter box, she stares at the freeway. It cuts a straight, unforgiving line through the brown hills. It reminds her of a fallen curtain rod, its position random and rude, its metallic gray depressing. There is not a person in sight. Even the speeding cars look driverless, brought to life with hard grasping souls of their own. She feels as if this stretch of arid Central California land is a place where people only pass through, stopping for gas and a soft drink, then moving on, west to San Francisco, east to the Sierras, south to Los Angeles, or to the Northwest, from where she came.

It is early afternoon. Back in her room she is engulfed by the stillness, which enters her as sound always has, taking over her entire body as if manufactured from within. She lies on the bed, eats a cracker, sips Coke. Small movements. Something to do, but without real purpose. She imagines Varney is doing the

same. Lying still in bed, taking nourishment in tiny incre-
ments. She falls into a thought that Varney's movements are
hers. As she lies, so lies Varney. When she sips, Varney does,
too. All her life, she realizes, she has been in silent dialogue
with him. *What do you think? What shall I do? Am I doing okay?*
The roar of the distant freeway winds around the perimeter of
the stillness, knotting her in like a tightly tied parcel. Would
he have changed his mind by now? Can she call so soon?

She won't move. If she's still enough, if she can keep the
noises at bay, she can hear Varney's thoughts. Not his actual
thoughts, maybe, but what he *might* be thinking. He might be
trying to picture her, trying to gauge her frame of mind. Perhaps
he is rehearsing words he might speak in a meeting between
them. She pictures him as a child, eyebrows like punctuation
marks, his husky little voice saying, "I'm scared in my brain."

She wishes now that she had become a neurologist. She's
spent too much time with bodies, their pallor, their pustules,
their pain. Now minds, the secrets of their reticular formation,
are all that seem to matter. Her ignorance of minds feels huge
and shameful. Varney's. Evan's. Cooper's. She knows the brain's
anatomy and the basic spurting and pooling of its secretions—
the serotonins, the epinephrines, the norepinephrines, et
cetera—but she is ignorant of the interplay of all its elements,
the subtle dance of volition and reflex. Maybe if she knew the
brain better, she could have outwitted her own cochlea, she
could have helped Varney untangle the colors he saw, she
could have penetrated the miscreant in his amygdala.

She sits in a coffee shop booth, the garbage bag of letters
beside her, out of sight like loot. She sits still, furtive, less like
the criminal's sister than the criminal herself. A plate of bright
yellow scrambled eggs lies in front of her. Coffee and juice. All
untouched. She feels the stillness, especially in her thighs. Her

runner's muscles are loosening, weakened by inertia. She watches a middle-aged woman bringing a bite of cherry pie slowly to her face. The woman is very large; the skin of her cheeks jiggles; the skin of her forearm loops off the bone. Jana can imagine being fat, the protective glue of fatness, the pleasant torpor of it. A smattering of early lunchers gathers. They are driving cars with license plates saying NEVADA, NEW MEXICO, WYOMING. Unlike her, they do not look like the relatives of criminals. They're simply travelers, pausing for sustenance, soon to return to their leisurely search for wondrous things.

She reaches into the bag without looking down, one hand touching the coffee cup; eyes fleet and unsettled as bugs, the only part of her still committed to motion.

No one notices her. Why should anyone notice? She reads. The letter is undated, without salutation; the postmark is five years ago. Across the top it reads, in crooked scrawl: *AIDS*. An arrow points down to a stick figure labeled ME. Below that are two faces, side by side, one a conventional smiley face, the other a smiley face with a down-turned mouth. The sign-off says: *Love me*. More like a command than a sign-off.

"Something wrong with your eggs?" asks the waitress.

"They're fine," Jana says. "Fine."

The waitress, still in the puffy pinkness of prolonged adolescence, hesitates and crimps her mouth briefly. Jana feels the dough of her own face looking back at the waitress. Like the face of a prisoner, expressionless, as a way of clinging to dignity.

Two sides of a coin, I guess. How Piss Cat still scares the bejesus out of me and how he's the best thing in here. When he does me, he's slow and careful. He strokes the skin of my back, then puts his nostrils down onto it and sniffs deep. He smells my hair and strokes that, too. And he moans, his voice low and quiet like a prowling animal lying in wait. And then he whispers my name so only I can hear it. In the way he says it, there is amazement or awe or something like that. Something halfway like worship. I can tell that this ugly, hairy, scary man feels love, and I can't help feeling love for him back. When your eyes are closed and all you're feeling is skin inside and out, and all you're smelling are those human body smells, a little different with everyone but basically the same, too, then you feel like you're just one more animal getting what you can when you can get it and nothing else, not even dying seems to matter much. You breathe deep and you go inside yourself, see the red of the organs, the kernel in you swelling, the blood going haywire. You take what you can get and don't say anything. And I forget then how later I'll see Piss Cat across the cell block, and he'll look huge and tall and thick and heavy as a tank, and with his tattoos and his temper (the worst) I won't be able to imagine him touching me.

Dear Cady,

Today I got transferred from the Youth Authority to the big boys' joint. There are so many things from today my tiny brain will remember for the rest of its life. I didn't say good-bye to anyone, and nobody said good-bye to me. Why should I say good-bye to people I never even talked to, guys like DeSoto, who thinks he's Mr. Tough, Mr. I-Don't-Need-Anybody. Guys like that think I'm just some annoying little mosquito. I suppose you could say Marcus was a sort of friend, but it wouldn't have done him any good for me to tell him good-bye. He'd just get screwed for being sentimental.

*Was I happy to leave? I was glad of a change, I guess.
But if I'd've known what I was coming to—*

*First of all. There I am in this Youth Authority bus—
you know, the kind with bars on the windows. One other
guy was in there with me. He was a black guy with a big
scowl on his face, and every time I looked in his direction,
he looked away. He probably thought I was part of the
Aryan Nation, which of course I am <u>not</u>. So we're there,
zipping down the freeway, and my eyes are bulging with
the colors and the brightness and the speed of it all. It's
like life has erupted around me and I'm not quite reading
it. The whole world is right out there—cars zooming by,
bright red and blue and chrome sparking under the sun,
and the people in those cars are rocking out to tunes I
can't hear. We're high up above the other cars so I can see
everything people around us are doing. I see women putting on makeup looking back and forth from the rearview
mirror to the road. I see a guy picking his nose, a woman
sucking off a driver. All that's going on in the cars. And
beside the road there are malls and movie theaters and
huge parking lots. And I keep thinking how everyone out
there is doing whatever they want. I can't imagine anymore what that would feel like. What would I do if I could
go anywhere?*

*We drive for hours through the flat, then over dry,
brown hills. The sun is shining so hard it makes me tired.
It's a hard, yellow color, too bright. And the more I think
of it, the madder I get that it won't stop shining. Imagine
being mad at the sun—what good does that do anyone?
So then we pull up here, away from everything. There
are these towers, of course, mean as pit bulls. And miles
of steel fencing and barbed wire. I'd heard stories, but*

there's nothing like seeing this thing for yourself. You walk into a place like this, and you feel like the lowliest of the low, like you're covered with slime.

And then inside, all these guys, these grown men, are giving me the hairy eyeball, checking me out, catcalling to me. Their eyes are bullet hard. My mind starts to hurt, turning all blue and achy like it's been in cold water and is shrinking fast. I never in my life prayed before, but I get in my cell, with its gray walls and its stinking shithole, and I fall onto the floor and I pray to God Almighty to get me through.

Your scared-as-shit brother,
Varney

Cady, Cady, Cady,

All the time I try to imagine your life, Cady. Every day I think how I screwed you. I wonder what you do every day. (Do you ever think of me?) When you were a kid you said you wanted to be a doctor, but you're probably waiting tables somewhere; maybe you're a store clerk. I don't think you're a doctor, because, let's face it, low people like us don't get to be doctors. At the very top we're salespeople like Dad was. Woop-de-doo. Plus, with a brother like me you've got a big load; I know that. So maybe you're a nurse or something. I just hope you've got some happiness. Maybe you got the happiness for both of us.

You know what it's like here, Cady. I've told you before. The urine-chemical stink of it. The clattering doors, the rattling keys, the brainless, thick-thighed, thick-bellied, fleshy-handed guards, ready to whack. Yes, sir, No, sir. Might as well be in the army. The worst part is the never-alone loneliness of it. Eyes everywhere, people set to jump if you turn your backside. You've got nothing to yourself, not even your butt hole. Every little thing you got—a cigarette, a pencil—someone else wants, so all the time you watch out, and you learn the zombie face. No blinking. No smiling. No frowning. No nothing.

There is one thing: You've got your mind and you've got your memories. You stare at the painted cement walls and you travel back where you've been. You would not believe the stuff you remember.

When I'm in white brain, I remember stuff I didn't even know I knew. Like Pythagoras. Here I am in the joint and I'm thinking of Pythagoras and I'm wondering how the hell he ever thought up his stuff. That theory of his just came to me like it was there all along. A squared + B squared = C squared. Stuff from biology, too—phenotypes and genotypes. These things just come to me somehow when I'm not even looking for them, and it seems like I know them better now than I ever did back then. Maybe some things need to settle for a while.

There're some things I remember you and I did, but I have no idea if we really did them or if I'm making them up like some cockeyed story machine spewing out pointless memories and trying to pass them off as true to make my lame time on this planet seem worthwhile. Did we really play Pie Passer? *Do you remember being out on the patio with bowls of chocolate pudding? Do you remember how we passed each other bites? "Pie Passer," we'd say, and the other person would open up their mouth so we were passing and eating at the same time. Pretty soon we were practically throwing pudding at each other? Did we really do that? Lamebrain here doesn't know.*

Your brother (still?),
Varney

Mother's Day. My black day. So many guys getting visits and calls from their mommas. Filling themselves sick on I-love-yous and vending machine candy, coming back to their cells with these dreamy grins that make you want to punch their lights out. Piss Cat's mom came. After the visit he wanted to tell me all about her. What a saint she is, how beautiful. I told him I didn't give a damn about his mom, but that didn't stop him.

People in here talk about their moms all the time. Their moms are gods. Sometimes they cry over their moms. These big men crying is something to see. They fight hard against the thing in them that wants to cry. Their faces get all red and twisted and lined like road maps. They bend over like they've been knifed and they don't want anyone to see.

I think about our mom a lot, do you? Lots of guys in here won't talk to me for what I did to Mom. If you hurt your girl, that's supposed to be okay. But your <u>mom</u>, that's another story. But, Cady, what <u>is</u> the real story? See, I'm sorry about Mr. Phillips and about Andy Carnack, but I remember what happened with them. I remember the feeling I had. I remember the tigerish feel of the feeling when Mr. P. tried to shrug me away. I remember my mind being so mad it turned purple and red with the madness. I remember the feeling my brain was going to bust. I remember the linoleum smell of the school when I walked out the side door, still holding my gun, everyone going bananas, but nobody noticing me.

But Mom? Why Mom? I didn't hate Mom. Mostly I was too rattled to notice her. She was easy to miss, wasn't she? Tell me if I'm wrong about this, but to me it feels like she drifted around places, like she never knew where she

wanted to be. She was a bee's breath around our house.
Her voice all low and whispery, like she didn't want to
disturb anything or anybody. That asking look on her face
all the time. But why would I hurt her, Cady? You're the
only one who might know. Why would I do that to my
very own mom? I didn't hate her, Cady, did I? Didn't I
love her? I remember some good things with Mom, do
you? She took us to the Fun Zone once and we did the
paddleboats, remember? We took turns doing the feet,
and some little bird kept dive-bombing us. And finally
Mom held out her hand—it had half a Snickers in it—
and the bird came and landed on her arm and took it
straight out of her hand. And she sang to the bird.
Remember?

Remember her stash of candy? She always had candy
in the pockets of those loose dresses she wore, and she'd
sneak it like we didn't see. She told me once, "The sugar
cheers me up." That day at the Fun Zone she said we
could have as many ice creams as we wanted. And I had
four. You only had one. You never went crazy like I did.

I hope Mom knows I never meant to do what I did.
Dad, either, but especially Mom. I don't mean to make
excuses, but I hope she understands that I got a brain with
chinks in it. More like big holes, really. And thinking
back, I'm pretty sure there was love.

Cady,

I can't figure if you're mad at me or not. I write you,
letter after letter, to the place you said to write, but you
don't write me back anymore. You don't even tell me why.
One day the letters just stop. Fed up, maybe? Or pissed
off? I used to think maybe you had died, but I know you

haven't died. I know because of those magazines you've been sending me. Dead people don't send magazines. I thank you for those magazines. The <u>National Geographic</u> especially. I sink into those pictures of all those far-off places and I forget for a while where I am. I guess those are the two big activities of my life—forgetting and remembering.

So why do I keep writing back to you, my deadbeat sister? Well, don't take this wrong, but who else am I going to write to? You're all I've got. But I know you probably don't even read all these words, and I don't blame you. I write 'cause what else am I going to do in here? If you lie around here and do nothing during lockdown, your head is going to get seriously screwed. When you lie around here looking at the no-color walls day after day, you feel like a zombie. You start to doubt if you're really alive. Maybe you died and this place you've come to is your own personal hell—the hell of no color, no taste, a place where the only thing you ever feel is mad. Time just slides over you like water you'll never grab on to.

The light is low. The scrambled eggs are long gone. A new waitress, older, more curious, has come on. Jana sits at a different table with a different plate of untouched food. Turkey sandwich and minestrone soup, cold by now, small lakes of fat congealed on its surface. "I'm slow," she tells the inquiring waitress twice before wrapping most of the sandwich in a napkin, stuffing it into her purse, and stirring the soup, making as if to eat.

TWENTY-FIVE

It is dark when she leaves the coffee shop, paying more than double for all she didn't eat, shucking the prying looks of the waitress. She crosses the parking lot with her bag of letters. She is all head, no body, dizzy with thought, years worth of Varney images boiling through her head. In a phone booth she places a call to the hospice, but it is after regular hours, and though she knows there must be people on vigil, she can't get through.

Lying on her back on the motel queen, feeling anything but queenly, smelling the stale cigarettes from a prior guest, studying the patterns of the cottage-cheese ceiling, stiff, still, hunger present like the whistle of a train, but too far away to distract her. She remembers sitting in the patio's heat, watching Varney smear chocolate pudding on his face, smoothing it over forehead, cheeks, nose with ritualistic pleasure. Was that Pie Passer? Spider pads over her belly, looking for a comfortable sleeping spot without finding one. His hair is growing in unevenly so he still looks more like an exotic rodent than a cat.

The backs of her thighs are numb and beginning to twitch from inactivity. She thinks of what she could have written back to Varney, what she *should* have written back. About her patients, of course—their traumas, their diseases, their pain. How needed they made her feel. But could she have told him about the looks in her patients' eyes—the aggregated fear, the loneliness, the betrayal—how they made her think of him? Once a man was dropped off at the ER drive-through, a gunshot in his chest, blood pooling on the sidewalk. They brought him in, set to work prepping him for surgery. "No surgery," he moaned over and over. "Let me go. I want to die." *Diiieee, diiieee.* The word got in her head and stayed there, ringing, gonglike. But no one (herself included) paused to listen to the man, to talk of his misery. There was a life at stake, an oath to honor. They stabilized him and sent him off to OR for removal of the bullet and a blood transfusion. To this day she thinks of that man. She visited him two days later on the floor. Medically he was doing well. But his eyes had a glazed, lifeless look as if they'd been replaced by glass. His back was turned to the door, and he looked out the window, immune to the comings and goings of caregivers. Thinking of Varney she never went back.

She rises and steps outside. Night has come at last. A slimy, tangerine light covers the parking lot. Wind carries debris in sudden uplifting gusts; it creaks against the motel windows, clambering to get inside. The traffic pounds on. There is nothing for her out here.

Back inside her room she makes the call because she said she would, yes, but mainly because the lonely sound of the wind has lodged in her head, and because the olive brown of her motel room decor matches the suit of her solitude. Cooper answers on the first ring.

"Yes," he says, as if he knows who it is.

"It's me," she says. The line seems dead for a minute, then she hears him swallow. She feels as if no one else is alive but the two of them. A long dark tunnel between them. "Is Evan down?"

"It's after ten, Jana, of course he's down."

She looks at her watch. Time feels so malleable. "Did he go to school today?"

"What is this—the Inquisition? Trust me, he went to school."

She sighs. "I'm sorry. I just—I went to see my brother to-day—" She loses steam. She pictures Cooper on Seretha's frayed green chenille couch holding a bottle of Corona by its neck.

"Go on," he says.

"He wouldn't see me. My brother, Varney."

"He's dying and he wouldn't see you? Why?"

She opens the curtain and looks out over the motel court-yard. Wind jabs the surface of the pool, sending up nervous darts of reflected light. Cooper's breath weighs heavily against her ear, bringing to mind pictures of her college friends' faces staring at her so hard they turned her into someone else.

"I can handle him being gay, Jana. You're telling me has AIDS, right?"

"Yes, but— My brother's in prison, Cooper. He's dying of AIDS in a prison hospice."

The air seems dead.

"Cooper? Are you there?"

"I'm here."

She needs to see his eyes; she needs so desperately to see his eyes. "Say something, please."

"Slow down. I'm trying to understand. He didn't *just* go to prison. He's *been* in prison?"

"Yes."

"How long?"

"Sixteen years."

She can hear the number settling into Cooper's brain, rewriting the seven years of their joint history, casting every conversation and kiss in a malevolent light.

"What did he do?"

She closes the curtain and sits on the edge of the bed. A

cold numbness climbs up her legs, a neuropathy that feels deep and possibly permanent. "Don't make me say it. Please."

"I am sitting here in my mother's house miles from you. Do you really think I could *make* you?"

He sucks at his beer. Crowding her thoughts are the faces of her college friends. She remembers the way they registered the information, at first quivering with uncertainty and questions, then turning inside out, finally becoming cartoons of faces, feigning friendliness. If only Cooper were here and she could speak while hibernating in his skin.

"I can handle it, Jana. I really can."

This is the time. There will be no other time. "Years ago, when he was fifteen and I was nineteen—sixteen years ago," she begins, her voice a low slow monotone, unraveling from her mouth with the infinitude of galaxies, "he shot our parents, one of his teachers, and another student. You might have heard of it. It was in the news." By the time she completes this sequence of words, she has run out of breath. She waits. The phone is her enemy. It gives her nothing. It was a promise of redemption, but that promise has marched out of reach.

"Uh-huh," he says. He drags on his beer. She recognizes the sound so clearly, his lips nibbling the bottle's rim before sucking.

"That's all you can say?"

"I'm thinking. I honestly don't know what to say. I don't remember anything about this in the news."

Now the deep well of silence regurgitates her fear. She sees her quaking Cady self returning, a spurned, pathetic, untouchable girl with no place to go.

"I've never told this to anyone before," she says. And she fervently wishes she hadn't; it's out there now and there is no way to reel it in. It will travel fast. Soon the whole world will know.

Cooper's breathing is slow as a sleeper's.

"Say something, *please*."

"How many years did it take to tell me this?"

"I guess you're furious?" she says. "I guess I would be."

"I don't know what I am. I don't know what you are, either."

"Yeah." She sighs. *I'm Cady*, she thinks, but it's too much to say. "I miss Evan."

Cooper says nothing. She hears him, rising from the couch, preparing to quit the phone.

"I shouldn't have told you," she said.

"No, you should have told me years ago."

"Things just kept moving on. It was never the right time."

"Yeah," he says.

In the long interval of silence that follows, she feels as close to dead as she's ever felt; she stares at the overhead light fixture without knowing what it is; she is not aware of her limbs occupying space; words are out of reach; she senses a sound pulsing around her, so deep and low it should be beyond the range of human hearing.

"That day I first met you in the ER, while I was waiting to be seen, I watched you talking to an old woman in the waiting room. You were so gentle with her. I'd never seen anyone so interested in an old person. It blew me away, that kindness. Sometimes I think it would be a hell of a lot easier to be your patient than your husband, you know?"

He hangs up after that with only a grunted good-bye, without a plan for talking further, his embedded accusation hanging in the motel's silence like some sinister, burglarizing truth.

THE COLOR OF insomnia is gray. It is cold and granular, nervous and torpid. It holds you in its grip without mercy. It is three in the morning. She feels gravely ungentle. She tries to sense, in her newly quiet body, if Varney is dead. She doesn't think so. Not yet.

She lies down again, desperate for sleep's oblivion, certain it will elude her. She will not think of Cooper. Or Varney. Or Evan. But the exhausted mind is intractable, it makes its own choices. And there is Varney, situated firmly in her frontal lobe. A person who has come to hate the sun's brilliance. He is a three- or four-year-old, crying in his room. She is walking down a long hallway trying to get to him. Someone is down there with him, doing something bad to him. The hallway is seemingly endless. She is walking in darkness, only a sliver of light at the end to guide her. This is not a dream. She is awake, eyes blinking fast. A hallucination, perhaps? She rises again, awash in shivers, envying Spider, who's found a resting place on the spare pillow and sleeps on with marathon stamina. Is Cooper sleeping now? Is Varney?

This is one of those nights whose ending you pray for even if you've never prayed before. She thinks of taking a Valium, or an Ativan, but then she notices the rising sun. She sits in a chair and watches the light, which is brown and stale, tarnished by the smoke of wildfires. She recognizes the look of a smoke-ruined sky. She saw it often as a child. The sky would darken ominously, turning the yellowish green color of an old bruise. If you didn't know otherwise, you might have thought apocalyptically. There was always a carping wind carrying tiny particles of ash that would stick in your nose and throat and make things taste funny. And the stench was awful—the reek of too much matter burning too fast. The sensation of the fire—its heat, its soot, its desperation—surrounded you, but you never knew exactly where the fire itself burned. Until you turned on the TV and saw the orange tongues leaping over roads and hillsides with the quick sinuousness of gymnasts.

During one of these fires, when Varney was nine or ten, they were sent home from school midday. No one could concentrate. Emergency clacked through the air. Even the teachers looked flushed and nervous as the sky darkened at noon. "We're dismissing you now. Go home quickly," the principal ordered over the intercom. At home Varney and Cady went to their rooms to pack their special things into a backpack, in case they needed to make a quick escape. She packed her collection of glass figurines. There was the kneeling fairy with the pale pink skirt and gilded wings. Hummer, the hummingbird with a ruby beak. The pair of dolphins arching out of a wavy turquoise sea. The Snow White grouping, with all seven dwarves. A glass-domed village, which when shaken stirred up eddies of snow. They were all tiny and perfect. Treasures she could fall into even at thirteen or fourteen or sixteen. She had to wrap each one in Kleenex first, then in many layers of newspaper and tape. She stashed them carefully in her towel-lined backpack. It kept her busy, away from the smells, the gruesome TV images. On top she put her tattered blanket from babyhood, along with Barkin, the rubbed-bare rabbit.

Her parents weren't home. "Sit tight," said their phone machine messages.

She went to check on Varney, but he wasn't in his room. His backpack lay unzipped, abandoned, filled with things swept randomly from a nearby shelf—action heroes, a cap gun, a slingshot, nothing treasured.

She called out but knew it was useless. She knew already he was gone—out to explore, to find the fire, to bask in the danger of its orange crackle. She thought she should follow, but follow where? She walked to where the streets ended at the barren hills. By now the sky was a dark gray in most places, a casing around the whole Earth, but inside the grayness, things were lit to a silvery blue. She felt squeezed. She could not bring herself to step beyond the pavement into the uninhabited dry hills. Only snakes and rodents lived out there, possibly mountain lions. There had been stories of attacks nearby.

She heard helicopters circling loudly overhead, but could not see them for the smoke. So back home she went. There, glued to the TV news, she cruised the channels, waiting for Varney to appear on the screen, at the door, anywhere. Or her parents, of course. She didn't cry. She simply waited, for hours, it seemed. It had always been this way—all the others were scattered, endangered, sinking, while she waited alone.

He staggered in after dark, when her parents were home and the fires had abated. He was flushed, splotchy, soot-smeared, breathless. In the kitchen, on tiptoe, he drank with his mouth cupped over the end of the faucet. He drank and drank, then looked at her with eyes lit.

"I saw it," he said. "I got *this close*." He measured a yard with his hands. "A humongous wall of fire. There were spirits in there, I swear. They were talking to me, Cady. I saw their eyes."

OUTSIDE, THE AIR feels dirty. The smell is foul. She circles the parking lot a few times. Was she ever as gentle as Cooper thought she had been? Or was it a pose? She tries to remember specific patients; if she were truly kind, wouldn't she remember their names? The girl with the ectopic pregnancy, the elderly man with the brain tumor—their names are gone now. She spoke nicely to them, but did those kind words mean anything beyond the duty of the moment? There's another memory lapse that bothers her—that she cannot remember her mother's face better. She remembers the things that Varney described in his letters—Beth's floating, bee's-breath quality; her distractedness; the sense that her attention was always else-where—but Jana does not have a clear imprint of her own mother's face. It was narrow, yes, and pale like Varney's, but what of its features? The eyes? The nose? The mouth? The eyes were squinty and blue, she thinks, but of even that she can't be sure. She thinks of Varney's letter doubting his love for his mother—was she deficient in this way, too? If only she had a picture, but all the family pictures they had—not very numer-ous—must still be somewhere in the California house.

Back inside the motel Jana takes three five-milligram Valium. It is midmorning. She takes off her clothes and thinks about bathing. On the way to the bathroom, she pauses on the bed to rest—it's not a good bed, with its scratchy polyester coverings, but better, surely, than Varney's—and the need to sleep comes over her, insurgent as a hurricane, oblivious to her nakedness, her rank odors, the Varney and Cooper trope of her thoughts.

In semiconsciousness she moles herself under the covers; she is carried by a molten wave of sleep to some distant island where nothing is as she knows it. It is the sleep of forgetfulness she has sought, but nevertheless her mind tromps on, offering up undulating colors, body parts with lives of their own, the microscopic image of a suppurating sore, and something she thinks is an inside view of Varney's hypothalamus.

The long slow drag back to consciousness. The phone a siren. The enlivening memory of imminent death. But a body that will barely cooperate, that has great difficulty command-ing the arm to stretch, to lift the receiver. *Speak, voice.*

"He wants to see you," says Chaplain Jack after she has ut-tered something. "How soon can you come? Now?"

She goes out to meet her voice, drag it back from the is-land. *Say yes, voice.*

"Good," he says. "We'll see you as soon as you can get here."

The motel's digital clock radio reads 11:15 A.M. She has slept a full twenty-four hours, or is it forty-eight? Her drugged body is a new acquaintance. Slack cheeks. Joints that wobble. Thoughts that arrive slowly at their destination. She showers carefully, aware of new possibilities—the soap she might slip on, the pummeling force of the water.

She dresses in her usual plain black pants, black sweater— the attire she wears under her white doctor's coat. She regrets the suggestion of mourning, wishes she had brought nicer, brighter, sexier clothes, things that would make Varney proud. She has even neglected to bring adornments—scarves, earrings, a necklace. She looks too stark and angular, frightening even to herself. But then she thinks of Varney, certainly unadorned also, and she decides it's better this way.

Spider prowls around her feet, rubbing her ankles. Jana lays out fresh food, but Spider forgoes eating and continues to rub until Jana kneels to stroke, offering what love she can, thinking of Varney, thinking how no one, even a cat, gets enough.

At the front desk of the correctional facility, she signs in, eyeing the guns on the hips of the uniformed guards, feeling an old paranoid anger rise. She hands over her purse, passes through a metal detector, is frisked by a guard, all the while talking herself out of an attitude and trying to ignore the harmonics of turbulence in her blood flow. Finally she is led into the inner sanctum and escorted to the hospice, where Chaplain Jack greets her at the door. He wears a shiny short-sleeved shirt covered with red chili peppers, and he grasps her hand with ministerial warmth. Her anger begins to seep away.

The hospice building is new, and on the inside, at least, it feels almost familiar to her, more like an intimate hospital than a prison (except, of course, for the security she must pass to get in here and the presence of subdued, but nevertheless armed, guards). The interior follows an oval design. A small central common area accommodates TV, vending machines, and a couch, where a few robed inmates sit playing cards. Circling the common area are the inmates' rooms and bathrooms, and at one end of the oval is the nurses' station.

Jana's ears are quiet today, her hearing acute, and she is struck by the susurrous murmuring from behind half-closed doors, where death, she knows, is bearing down fast. "Basta!" someone yells. Her nose fills with strong odors. Rubbing alcohol, floral-scented Lysol, new linoleum, all threaded with thin vapors of old vomit and laced with the cinnamony smell of something on the lunch tray. They do something odd to her, these familiar hospital smells.

"What?" says Chaplain Jack.

She has paused at the entrance to his office.

"The smell," she says.

He grins. "I'm afraid I'm immune. Hey, Ernie." He waves to an elderly man with a cane moving slowly to the common area. Jana tries not to gawk. She had, in her mind, filled this place with Varney-aged people.

"Leukemia," says Chaplain Jack as they settle into his office. "Ernie doesn't have too much longer. But then again, you never know. One good visit and they get new legs."

He leans back in his desk chair and watches her, his posture paternal and patient. She, fully awake now and far from patient, perches at the edge of her seat.

"We have a service this afternoon at one," he says. "Ruben passed away yesterday. A real character he was. Strange but deep. Not unlike Varney. Anyway, Varney may want to attend."

"Where will it be?"

"Right here in our chapel. You're welcome to come, too. A chime will indicate when it's beginning."

His gaze unnerves her. She can tell he's a man who is practiced at noticing and sees much more than he admits to. "But first—Varney, right?" he says. He winks and uncrosses his legs, suddenly businesslike. "A few ground rules. If he asks you to leave, you must leave. He is a dying man and his wishes must be respected. I insist on that. These men have a right to their dignity at the very least. Try not to get him upset. Try not to tire him out with too much talking. Limit your first visit, okay? There will be others."

Chaplain Jack has the good sense to walk slowly down the hallway to Varney's room; his bald pate glistens from the overhead lights. Jana hangs behind him. The door is open. In they step.

A spartan room. Dimly lit. Nothing on the walls. Two beds, one curtained. In the bed by the window is a man with tufted hair. He is skeletal as an Ethiopian baby.

"Varney, your sister," Chaplain Jack says, refraining, she notices, from using her name. And then Chaplain Jack is gone.

Jana and Varney—the man who is supposed to be Varney—stare at each other. She does not recognize anything about him. It surprises her to see he is no longer a boy (though, of course, she knew he wouldn't be). He's all grown-up, all tired out. The shape of his head looks different, the temporal muscles have atrophied, and his lips are covered with flaky white ulcers. On his neck is a small bandage covering a venous portal. Nearby stands a walker slung with an oxygen canister.

But the eyes. Yes, the eyes are Varney's, and the look he is giving her is Varney's look, too. Brother and sister begin to laugh, tentative, exploratory laughs, his high, hers lower. *Do you remember this about me, this laugh of mine?*

She goes to his bedside, takes his hand. It's a bundle of bones, hollow-seeming, matchstick light. She circles his shoulders with her arms, pulls him to her fiercely, so his sharp chin hits her chest hard, and he draws back coughing.

"Oh, Varney, I'm so sorry. Are you okay? I'm so sorry."

It takes several minutes for his coughing bout to subside. She stands, expecting someone to arrive, but no one does. Oh, the *littleness* of him. She could crush him so easily.

"Disgusting, aren't I?" he says. This voice—this high, squeaky ancient-child's voice—it can't be Varney's. It seems acted or borrowed. She has to work hard at remembering the old Varney.

His eyes, those are the clue. Look at the eyes. They still have their surprised look, which has fallen a few notches into wryness.

He's watching her, taking her in, waiting for her to say something.

She shakes her head. "No, I'm used to it."

He smiles. "Used to disgusting. That's nice." He looks down at his body as if it doesn't belong to him. His legs are covered, but she knows how they look—stringy, nearly useless.

"You just look different," she says. "You're still yourself," she says, remembering as she says this how clearly he reads the truth.

"You aren't Cady anymore. Chaplain says you have a different name."

She hesitates, then nods. He shudders involuntarily, jerks, winces, recovers.

"Don't worry about it," he says. "I would've done the same damn thing. Cut out. Cut off."

Shame gushes through her, then settles in her stomach as a hard ball of depression.

"You didn't get my letters?" he says.

"I got them."

"I guess you had your own reasons for not writing back." He looks out the window to a grassy area, where nothing is blooming. Shouldn't someone have planted colorful things out there?

"So who are you, anyway?" he asks without turning his head.

"Jana Thomas."

"I don't mean a *name*." His voice is scornful.

"I'm a doctor in Bellingham, Washington. I'm married and I've got a son. Is that what you mean?"

He's looking at her now. "A doctor, really? And a son? What's his name?"

"Evan. He's six."

A thought seethes under the splotchy skin of his face, and in that subtle fleeting movement something disturbs her; after a moment of looking, it comes to her—she sees shades of her parents. She remembers now the foreboding Beth used to carry in her clenched forehead, and the bluster Walter carried in his out-thrust chin; they are now married in this injured look of Varney's that comes across as a challenge.

"Your son doesn't know about me, does he?" Varney says.

She blinks, stalling, wanting desperately to lie. The slow shake of her head coincides with a chiming. Ruben's service, already. Varney strains to rise, leaning forward, grabbing with his clawlike hand a blue-striped cotton robe flung over the back of his raised hospital bed.

She starts to help but he waves her away. His breath hisses as he moves. He slides his legs to the far side of the bed, turning his back to her so she sees the swirled ink of a massive tattoo across his upper back. A dragon, she thinks, but he covers it with his robe before she can fully see. A prison tattoo—as possible a source of his AIDS as the sex. He grabs his walker with the oxygen and uses it to steady himself as he rises from the bed and proceeds laboriously to the door, wheeling his rig with him, his concentrated, slightly wry look bringing to her a sudden squadron of memories: Varney, fired up with an idea, heading out to the hills alone; Varney at her bedside, terrified by a dream, eyes feral.

At the door he stops. "A service," he says. "Guy named Ruben. Someday it'll be me."

She feels his impatience to move on. *Like Evan*, she thinks. "Can I come?"

He shrugs. "You don't know him."

"Can I come back to see you?"

"If you want."

He turns and makes his shaky way down the corridor. Of course he doesn't need her anymore. Long ago he passed beyond needing her. Before he turns out of sight, he is joined by a black man wearing navy blue sweats. He is straighter and huskier than Varney, healthier-looking. The man links his arm in Varney's. Varney does not resist, does not look back. The two vanish around the corner, and her gaze stays there where she last saw him, fixing her shame and loneliness into a piercing point.

Sound, real-world sound, rushes into her ears again—someone shouting, the summoning chimes. She moves back down the corridor toward the chaplain's office and sees, across the common room, the chapel, where inmates are passing through the double door. There are maybe ten or twelve men of all ages, black, Hispanic, white. They wear robes and slippers mostly, a few wear sweats. They all look battered.

Varney and his friend pass through the chapel doorway. An electric organ plays a melancholy piece she recognizes but cannot name. The chapel is simple, almost austere. Blond wood pews. White walls. It might be a lecture hall were it not for the small gold cross mounted on the wall alongside a Star of David. A vase of lilies sits on a table, and next to it Chaplain Jack stands at a podium, wearing a clerical collar.

"We have come to honor the memory of our friend, Ruben Francisco, a man who knew, despite his own pain and transgressions, how to lighten our hearts."

She stands at the back, hoping Varney won't turn. The doors have been closed, and the room, with its dim mauve light, its pews of reverent dying men, and the soothing presence of the chaplain, has transformed into a hushed and sacred place. A few men twine their arms around each other's backs. Some weep softly. What is it she hears beneath the quiet rustling? Their *breathing*? Their *heartbeats*?

"Ruben knew one of the most important things in life..."

"Amen," says one of the men in the front pew. Amens echo throughout the chapel. Varney sits near the front, upper back hunched, neck and chin falling forward in what she and Varney used to call the lizard look. His expression reveals nothing, neither agitation, nor engagement; her visit seems not to have marked him at all.

Chaplain Jack finishes his introduction and a hymn follows. "Let hope and sorrow now unite to consecrate life's ending..." Most of the men remain seated and utter speech more than song. Chaplain Jack leads them, his voice a lovely, articulate tenor. He looks from man to man, drawing each one in, nodding his encouragement. *I'll be here for you, too, when the time comes.*

BACK AT THE MOTEL she pulls the shades and lies on the bed in the swill of depression, yearning for Evan's silken skin, the reassurance of his hugs. It's Evan who needs her now, Evan she should return to.

She handles Spider roughly, cradling his small furred head, not shrinking from the strange soft wrinkly feel of his bare spots. The room's light is unnatural. Even with all the lights off, it won't go completely dark. The curtain is too sheer, so light presses nosily in from the courtyard. She closes her eyes. Spider's thin skin and crooked haunches feel so much like a rabbit's, without the benefit of sight. She has never felt as close to an animal as she has felt to Spider in the last few days. Marooned together they have formed affinities and rhythms. She can predict, it seems, when Spider will come seeking comfort.

She regards the phone with dread. She was supposed to call Cooper last night but didn't. If she calls, she will feel the truth of his accusations. She will have to admit to being unkind. He knows where she is now. He could call her. But he hasn't. He won't.

"I'm not Evan, I'm Boo-boo. And I have green feet." Evan aims his voice loosely so it drifts around the vicinity of the receiver, underscoring the distance in miles between them. Do all parents feel like this—that their children are moving too fast, talking too fast, growing too fast? Do they all feel as she does, that in all the dart and tangle, there's not enough dawdling?

"Well, hello there, Boo-boo," she says, buoyant with love. "If you have green feet, you must be an alien. How are things going? How's school?" Spider leaps from her grasp, ripping a small hole in the sheet with a rear claw.

"School's the rule. And you're a tool. And I'm a bool."

She laughs, though his rhymes push her away. "You're a poet, Evan."

"You're a doo-doo."

"A good doo-doo, I assume."

"No, baaaaaaad. When are you coming home, Mom? Gramma got me a Game Boy and I'm really good at it. Gramma says she doesn't get it at all. She won't even try. Daddy tried but he's really bad at it. Do you even know what a Game Boy is?"

It is an honest question and she wants to deliver an honest answer. Yes, she knows about Game Boy, but could she use one? Could she focus now on Evan's minutia?

"Oh yes, I know about Game Boy. You can teach me what I don't know."

"Okay. After school I will. You'll be home tomorrow?"

"Well, not tomorrow, but soon."

"Is that because you have a selfish streak?"

"What?"

"Daddy says you have a selfish streak."

"Really? Is Daddy there?"

"He told me to say he isn't here."

"But is he there?"

"I'm not allowed to tell you."

A scuffle ensues. "Tell her you love her and give me the phone," she hears Cooper telling him.

"I love you," Evan says. This distracted, commanded *I love you* is worse than nothing at all.

"Now go," Cooper instructs him, and she hears his skippering little tread fading. "I'm here," Cooper says, "but I'm not up for talking."

It is just as she imagined. First people will avoid conversations with her, then they will sever contact altogether until she is sealed into a life with only the most perfunctory of human interaction.

"Do you really think I'm so selfish. And unkind?"

"He wasn't supposed to say anything."

"Yes, but he did."

"You ask impossible questions, Jana."

"I know I might seem unkind sometimes. But I've been trying to protect Evan from so much."

"Evan told me you hit him."

"Only one time. It's not like I do it routinely. He was watching a news program about that murder, and there were bloody clothes. I couldn't stand it, you know, thinking of my brother and—"

"Jana, I don't know your brother and neither does Evan. As far as we know, he doesn't exist. Look, I didn't mean to get into this discussion, and I don't want to continue with it right now. I'm still thinking about everything."

"Come down here. Please, Cooper." She's pleading now like she didn't want to. "You and Evan. We need to talk in person. These things are so hard to discuss over the phone."

"What good would that do?"

"Maybe if you met Varney—?"

"I don't think so."

"He's Evan's flesh and blood."

"Aren't you the one that always wants to protect Evan? Now you want him to meet your criminal brother?"

Jana is quiet, stunned by the horrible reductiveness of words. "He's not just a criminal."

"What else is he?"

"I can't quite say. But I'm sure he's not violent anymore."

Cooper's breath heaves as if his lungs could fill endlessly. The phone seems to creak.

"Don't hang up yet," she implores.

"It's bedtime, Jana. I'm putting Evan to bed."

She hears movement she doesn't immediately understand. It makes her feel impotent as an insect in a jar.

"Hello there, hon." It's Seretha. "Cooper is putting Evan down."

"Yes," Jana says uselessly.

"Cooper told me about your brother, hon. And about your parents."

"Yes." Jana is adrift. Everything she has known until now has fallen away, as if a wax sheath has suddenly melted and revealed a vaporous, unanchorable core.

"It's a shame and I'm sorry about it." Seretha sighs heavily, not her usual martyr's sigh. "What your brother did is not your fault. I told that to Cooper." Her voice softens to a whisper.

"Between you and me—maybe I know a few things my Cooper doesn't know yet. You can't help what other people do. You can only do what you know is right for yourself. You hear?"

"Yes," Jana says. Why, when she feels so grateful to Seretha must she sound so witless? "Thanks. I'd better go now."

THE NEXT MORNING, Chaplain Jack's moon face greets her. He's impressively tall, she realizes—six foot four, perhaps— and he has an airiness that lightens and soothes whatever is around him. "He's doing good today," he says of Varney. And when she sees Varney in the common area regaling two men with a story, she sees he does look good. His eyes no longer seem to be sinking, and his thin body, rather than suggesting a cadaver, simmers with the sinewy fitness of a long-distance run- ner. He ejects words as if they are Morse code, without inflec- tion, but very fast. He turns, sees her, and freezes.

The other two men, one Hispanic and heavily tattooed, the other black, both almost as skinny as Varney, get up. "Hey man," they say. They nod to Jana but that's all. They're gone.

She sits on the couch vacated by the two men. It is covered with resilient brown polyester that scratches her thighs even through her pants. She hears someone retching down the hall. Varney stares at a quarter-inch scab on the back of his hand. He probes around its edges, then peels it off, watching blood trickle down his thumb. He doesn't wipe it, simply stares at the blood, breathing heavily. Does he mean this as a dare? *Here is my bad sick blood. Touch it if you dare. Touch me.*

"You looked so happy just now, talking to those men."

He shrugs. "I wasn't." He dabs his bleeding hand with the hem of his robe. "Why're you back? I thought you'd had it."

"I said I'd come back, didn't I?"

"People say anything."

A long silence passes.

"Cadence was such a beautiful name," he says.

"I'm still her. You can still call me Cady." But it's a lie, of course. Not much of her is Cady anymore. Maybe a tiny part, buried deep—the lover of glass figurines, the plain shy girl. She chose the name Jana for its hard sound. She thought she could follow its cue in making herself tough.

Panic streaks Varney's eyes. He rises quickly and heads down the hall in a lopsided trot, his walker scraping the floor loudly. She hears him close a bathroom door. He is gone for a long time. Twenty minutes. Half an hour. When he returns, he is panting.

"See what I mean? Disgusting. I've got to lie down."

Yearning to take his arm, but restraining herself, she walks him to his room. She is aware of the other man in the bed next to Varney's, breathing loudly behind the closed curtain.

"Shh," Varney says. "Doc's asleep." He lies on his partly raised bed by the window and closes his eyes.

"Can I get you anything?" she whispers.

He shakes his head.

"Should I stay?"

"If you want."

She has never seen him this still. Before, he always had a restless body, somewhat like hers, but now there is a soddenness in him, as if his body's molecules have been compacted to a new density. She wonders what his T-cell count is, but she doesn't want to pose the question. It doesn't matter, anyway. It's not predictive. She could know every medical fact about him and it would not be predictive. He could die tomorrow or he could live for months.

Something moves in her peripheral vision. A squirrel outside dashes across the prickly grass, nervous as an escapee. Just before it disappears, she spots its small black eye glinting perniciously.

"Wouldn't it be nice to have something growing out there?" she says quietly.

He appears not to have heard. Perhaps he has fallen asleep.

"Why?" he finally says, his scratchy soprano bringing to mind a character from the cartoons he used to watch. "What's the point?"

She knows what he's telling her, but it won't do. "Color would be nice," she insists. "Some bright color you could feast on. I could plant some flowers for you, if they'd let me. Or bring things for the walls. They'd allow that, wouldn't they? I've noticed posters and photographs in the other rooms."

He says nothing.

"Does your mind do colors like it used to? Remember when all your thoughts had colors?"

He opens his eyes and she greets them with relief. "I never saw colors," he says. He moves his eyes away again. "I just *felt* colors—red feelings, blue feelings, white ones. They got in my blood and swarmed around."

"Still?" she says.

"My body's checked out. Thoughts are all I've got. Most of them are sharp. They move around this shriveled body like razors. Every one of them hurts."

She wishes she'd said nothing. She wonders if her memories are all wrong. "I don't want you to die feeling terrible," she says.

He laughs without humor. "Nice of you to say so. But a little late. I've had a whole life in here, Cady. A lot of ugly stuff has happened, and a few good things. That's life, right? Since I got here in this hospice, I've known some good people. Chaplain Jack, he's a good man. But I'm done with living. Just like

Mom was. Flowers aren't going to help me, Cady. Ask Doc; he'll tell you." He nods at the curtained bed beside him.

"But when I arrived today, you looked so happy talking to those guys."

"You've never acted before?" He closes his eyes. Breath whirring, he falls asleep. Twitches travel from his feet to his eyelids. For a second he looks like a child, small and guileless. How fraudulent it feels to call herself a healer. She needs a different kit bag of techniques: the laying of hands, mantras, *something*.

Suddenly his voice rears up again. "I'm not asleep." He pauses, working his mouth to scare up saliva, keeping his eyes closed. "When I first got inside, I got hate mail, mail so ugly it could rot your brain just reading it. Andy Carnack's father wrote me. Letter after letter telling me I was scum. If I could've, I would've checked out back then. But I couldn't. You drag yourself through. You play the game." He pauses. "Every once in a while I still have flying dreams."

TWENTY-SIX

The chaplain invites her into his office. No, he *lures* her. Like a mother, he won't take no. She feels almost impounded in there and resistant as a truculent teenager. She doesn't mean to eat, either, but she finds herself holding half a buttered bagel.

"It's cruel," she says. "You can't abscond for sixteen years, abdicating responsibility entirely, and then breeze in at the end."

The chaplain draws two fingers slowly over his bald crown, elbow fanning over his ear. She imagines, for a minute, that he's spreading butter there.

"You can surrender to the need of the moment," he says.

"He's mad. He doesn't want me here."

"You can make yourself available. You hum loud against the darkness." His remarks come back at her with the steady reliability of bowling balls. She puts down the buttered bagel; she cannot eat and argue. "You don't know Varney. He's not going to change," she says. "I know Varney. I lived with him for years."

But her claim is without merit, and she knows it. If anyone knows Varney, she is not the one.

"Maybe," says Chaplain Jack, "but I do know people. Your brother goes to art class voluntarily. A man without hope does not attend art class."

His evenness infuriates her and she leaves. She doesn't need to justify herself to Chaplain Jack. A seagull is camped on her car, and he goes away only when she comes at him, yelling. He flies straight up, vanishing into whiteness.

Spider is gone from the room, and there is a message to check in at the motel's front office. She stands by the bed, the door to her room still open. She has no plan of action.

The clerk behind the desk admonishes her. "We have your cat in custody. The sign said very clearly that pets are not allowed. If you want to remain in your room with your cat, you're going to have to pay a pet deposit."

She hears Spider yowling behind a closed door in the inner recesses of the office. It sounds like the protest of a human being in deep despair. She realizes that she neglected to put out the DO NOT DISTURB sign when she left and that the maid must have found Spider. She pays the two-hundred-and-fifty-dollar deposit, which feels like extortion, but what choice does she have?

Spider is on the alert; his pupils have enlarged to fill his eye sockets. Though he has stopped howling, the sound remains lodged as a low din in Jana's ears. Back in the room Spider burrows in the bedclothes while Jana beeps into her machine for messages. There's another message from the attorney Frank Mordecai. A check-in call from Bill McElroy. A call from Rita Tencil. Life is piling up, moving on without her. She feels like a ditched caboose with no motor of her own to help her catch up.

Jana ignores the phone and lies on the bed, thinking how she is in a room that has been occupied by god knows how many people, and all of them have left traces of their skin, which has mingled with the dust and embedded itself in the carpets and crusted the blinds and windowsills. And in that skin reside traces of DNA, which Jana has no doubt inhaled by now, taken into her own person, possibly annexing traits from those other individuals, other families, other generations. Maybe this explains why people do such inexplicable things: Strange DNA moves in them, throwing everything up for grabs. When she was considering selling her parents' house, she couldn't let go of the thought of strangers living with her dead parents' skin. The thought subjugated her and she could not act.

She dozes briefly and awakens, thinking of Frank Mordecai, the man who will tell her that Cooper's love has run its course. She gets up and cleans out Spider's litter box, lays out fresh water and food. She's been so angry at Cooper recently, so hurt by him, it's hard to tell if there's still love to salvage. She remembers when Cooper seemed to adore her—he marveled at her medical know-how, at her long history of independence. She basked in his admiration and admired him back. A man who was calm and took his time and knew the myriad pleasures of day-to-day life. Like her, he was cautious, sensitive, slow to trust.

She watches Spider lunging at the food, crunching it noisily. Spider is the only one who seems to need her now. Maybe being needed is all that matters, anyway. Love is just a guise that dresses up the need, ennobles it somehow, or, at the very least, makes it less embarrassing.

She drinks part of a Coke. Half the day remains and she is rattling in it. She will call Frank Mordecai and get it over with, but she won't assent to anything (certainly not to giving up custody of Evan). She makes the call, standing; it's easier to feel strong when standing.

"Do you know a Mr. Anthony Cianetti?" Frank Mordecai asks her. "I believe he was a patient of yours."

She walks as far as the phone's receiver will allow, then back again, making a slow arc around the bedside table. "Yes."

"Mr. Cianetti has left you a sizable portion of his estate, almost a quarter of a million dollars. Some of his other heirs are set to challenge the will. Are you there?"

She is thinking of Mr. Cianetti's plaintive eyes, his eagerness to talk.

"Are you there?" Mr. Mordecai repeats.

"I don't want his money."

"Of course you do. He wanted you to have it. I spoke with him myself. You showed him kindness when no one else did. He said he loved you like a daughter."

Should she tell Frank Mordecai that until this phone call she had forgotten Mr. Cianetti, that she had only been behaving with Mr. Cianetti in a professional capacity, that she didn't even know his first name, and had he known who she was, he would certainly have despised her?

She gets off the phone, thinking of the old man. She remembers him clearly now. She remembers his composure, his acceptance of death. He was a sweet man, and she did, for the moment at least, care for him. She did not want to believe the granddaughter's charges of cruelty. Was that why he accepted death so readily—because he knew he'd inflicted pain? She strains to see a pattern in these things, but if there is one, it eludes her. What if she had stayed with Varney, set up a life nearby him, visited him regularly, bolstered his spirits, foregone motherhood. Was that the choice she should have made?

You move because you are built for movement, because your heartbeat and respiration are involuntary. Though you feel the part of you that is always dying, the rest moves forward, squeezed between destiny and choice.

SHE SITS IN SILENCE at Varney's bedside and sees a new world rising before her like a photographic image that has been there all along. It is a scene she can't be part of, the fraternity of twenty dying men. It takes silence to sense the filaments of connection between them: the croaked *hey*, nearly inaudible;

the bony hand laid on the equally bony shoulder; the crooked finger lifted an inch or two from the bedclothes to wave. Chaplain Jack travels from room to room like a town crier bearing the community's important news. He takes with him stories (Rico's mother had a heart attack; Alberto's brother got a job in computers); he hands cherished books from man to man. He repeats the men's names, reminding them of the unfinished business of living. And Raoul, too, Raoul the aide—the embodiment of willingness, unfazed by human waste, his good humor unassailable—he takes his broad white smile and cheerful disposition with him as he empties bedpans, changes sheets, wipes vomit and feces. The men ask after Raoul's one-year-old daughter, and he tells them she's walking. She takes three steps, gets scared, and falls. They laugh to hear this.

But it is more than Chaplain Jack or Raoul that binds the men; it is the men themselves: the elemental things they know; the things they regret; the darkness they've seen in themselves; the dignity they've salvaged. Their names are on each other's lips. *How's Jose doing? What's up with Travis?* Illness has pruned so much from their lives—the posturing and bargaining and haggling over power; appetite; musculature; even movement itself. With muted desires for food, sex, power, what is left?

There is, for some, family. But mostly—it seems to Jana as she sits quietly next to Varney or moves through the hallways as catlike as she can be—they're forging connections right here and now with one another. Not as a hedge against death, but as a hedge against meaningless death. She sits on the outside, but still she sees it. With Doc, for example, who's in bad shape. Usually he sleeps, and when he's awake, he rarely stops groaning. The other men bring him things, things he probably won't ever use—pudding or Jell-O cups saved from their trays, blank postcards, small books of prayer—but they bring them, anyway, like offerings, tokens, good-luck amulets, items placed on an altar as evidence of their devotion. They are, she thinks, like beings in some advanced stage of development—echoing the primitive stages of evolution when cells joined together and cooperated to keep an organism afloat, these men have rediscovered what it feels like to be part of something larger than themselves. They may be dying men, as Chaplain Jack says, but they're living men, too. And living men have futures. "When I get out, I'm gonna get me a motorcycle," Alberto says. He throws his head back against the common-room couch and laughs with near delirium, raking in smiles from the other men present.

These are men who will ride motorcycles over the deserts and jungles of their minds; they will see China; they will play major league baseball; they will make love to movie stars; they will taste hot dogs slathered in caviar. These are men who have learned, like superior intellectuals, to cull experience from their minds.

But what of Varney, silent smoldering Varney, who sits in bed like a curled wick with the TV on, knitting a scarf for Doc? Today he was chatting with Alberto until the minute she appeared, and then he closed up shop, returned to his bed, turned on the TV, and fell silent, knitting. He has only just learned to knit, and he works at it slowly, the unruly needles (conspicuously bendable and blunt at the tips as if made for young children) slipping often from his ungainly grasp. He has completed an inch now, maybe an inch and a half. Sitting in the cranked-up bed, legs out, his eyes skip from the monitor to his work and back. She sits in a beige plastic chair beside him, her gaze traipsing around the room—the bare, salmon-colored walls, the ailing coleus on the windowsill gathering dust, its leaves yellowing like the eyeballs of alcoholics.

Beside them Doc sleeps. Like Varney, Doc is thin, but he

still retains signs of his once-beefy weightlifter's physique. His face and neck bear the telltale purple splotches of Kaposi's sarcoma, but what strikes Jana most are the unusually flat planes of his head and his face, as if someone applied an iron to try to square off his skull and the resulting look is one of military preparedness. She does not understand Varney's devotion to Doc, who is so reticent and suspicious. Would Varney be equally devoted to anyone who was dying beside him?

Varney's art class drawing lies on the bedside table. It's a building of some kind, high and pointed like a cathedral or a turreted castle. Without turning to look at her, he reaches over and pulls the drawing out of her view.

"What is it?" she asks.

He crumples it. "Stupid."

"No," she says. "Don't." She tries to stop him but he leans out of reach. "What is it?" she says.

"She makes us do pictures of death." He shakes his head. "Stupid. Like we *know.* How can we *know?*"

But Chaplain Jack said he goes to art class voluntarily, implying that, by choosing to go, he has revealed a secret and elevated inner life.

Varney tosses the crumpled paper to the floor and seizes the remote control, surfing the channels so fast the passing images resist naming.

SHE PARADES BY the motel office on her way from her car to her room, and to create goodwill, she waves through the office window at the clerk. At this hour it is Byron in there (the same name as Varney's arresting officer, but this one short and overweight, with dark hair slicked with intentional oils). Both of the motel managers have begun to regard her strangely. She feels a punishing curiosity behind their attenuated glances, the same looks the 7-Eleven managers of her childhood gave to their Mexican patrons. She imagines them thinking: *Who is this woman who stays for more than a day or two at a place where itinerant businessmen are the norm? Who is this woman who speaks so little and smiles, but for whom smiling appears to be a conscious effort?*

Back at the room, Jana settles in with Spider, and a bean-and-cheese burrito from Taco Bell. She slathers the burrito with hot sauce to jump-start her taste buds, which have become so immune to desire they need hammering. She's been eating so badly of late, so erratically—long stretches with no food at all, then heavy doses of caffeine and starch. She would die if Evan had been eating as poorly as she has been. Surely these bad eating habits explain, in part, the feeling in her brain that the cells are agglutinated, stuck together like a clump of gelatinous frog's eggs. Hunger asserts itself without imparting pleasure, and she downs half the burrito in four scantily chewed bites. Spider watches her, responding to her small movements as if his head is a sensitive recording device. "You wouldn't like this," she tells him. "Believe me; it's beans!" But Spider continues watching, keeping close tabs; clearly he doesn't believe her.

Spider has moved in on her consciousness as if he is one of her patients. She thinks about his welfare more often than usual; she wonders how she comes across to him; she uses him for distraction. But his concerns can only distract her for so long. When she's finished with the burrito, she notices the message light flashing on her phone.

"We've got a big problem here," Cooper says on the voice mail. "Call me right away."

It is the only message, and it devours her entire being like a too-forceful shout. Her ears generate complex syncopated rhythms composed of Cooper's delivery of the two words *right* and *away*. Clutching Spider hard without realizing she's doing so, she makes the call. Seretha answers but hands the phone off quickly to Cooper, as if by prearrangement.

"Hold the line." She hears voices, doors closing. Then Cooper settles in, gusts of his breath scraping the receiver's mouthpiece.

"Okay," he says. "Here's the thing. Evan's been peeing on the playground. He whips it out and pees in front of the other kids. Day before yesterday he peed in someone's thermos top and pretended to drink it." He sighs, and with the return breath comes a sob, porous as honeycomb.

"He drank it?" she says stupidly.

"He *pretended* to drink it." He pauses, comes back evenly, quietly. "You see the point, don't you?"

She tries to picture this. Evan's innocent little penis, smooth and inexperienced, soft as a fetal pig. She imagines the other children standing around watching him, giggling, keeping a discrete distance lest he has other ideas in mind. His aim is perfect. He hits the tiny red cup with a satisfying plink. There is prowess there, pride. "You're really going to drink it?" says a pallid little girl in pigtails. "You could die." The urine in red plastic looks clean, but it still smells like urine. He touches the plastic rim to his lips, eyes squinting down at the image of his own eyes and nose reflected and magnified in the liquid.

"You see what I mean?" Cooper says.

"What?"

"I think it's anger, Jana." (Cooper says this in such an exquisitely unangry way.) "Anger at you."

She cannot speak. She lies there remembering. You could never tell how Varney meant things, whether he was serious or if everything he did was part of some obtuse practical joke with many stages of execution. But if the things he did were jokes, they often seemed to be missing a punch line. One morning

Cady awakened to a full-blown yell from Walter. "*What the fuck?!*" She'd never heard him use that word before, at least not so he meant it.

"Varney, get your ass in here."

Varney, thirteen or fourteen, the age of sleeping through anything, appeared at the bathroom door with uncharacteristic speed.

"Varney, what is in this cup?"

"How should I know?"

"It's urine, goddamn it. I almost drank it. Did you pee in this cup?"

"Why would I pee in a cup?"

"I don't care *why*, I asked you if you *did*."

"No, Dad; if it makes you happy, I didn't pee in your cup."

"Who did, then? Cady certainly didn't, and neither did your mother."

"Oh, probably a skunk. Or an intruder. Yeah, maybe a Mexican intruder that just came over the border and doesn't know you're not supposed to pee in cups in America."

That was the first day's battle of a war that went on for weeks. Varney ambling sleepily back to bed, pleased with his day's work; Walter heading off to work unhinged, knowing he'd come within a hair's width of drinking his son's pee.

Thereafter, every morning, the toothbrush cup held Varney's pee, sometimes only half full, sometimes all the way to the top; sometimes a deep citrine yellow, other times more dilute, but always there, acrid and defiant. Once, Walter rose at four-thirty in the morning to lie in wait for Varney, only to discover Varney had done his deed sometime in the middle of the night. After that it became a point of pride with Walter not to respond to it again. He simply emptied the urine and washed the cup. But of course they could all feel him fuming, a rage that suffused the entire house, dogging him at the breakfast table and scrambling with him into the car as he left for work. It went on like this for weeks: Varney presenting his nightly pee like some half-domesticated cat leaving its prey writhing on the living-room rug, Walter coming undone by it.

Once, Walter discarded the bathroom cup altogether, but Varney replaced it with a coffee cup from the kitchen—not just any cup, but Walter's favorite mug, imprinted with a salmon leaping above a bucolic river. Cady and Beth looked on, wondering how they could put an end to this contest of wills.

Then one day Varney simply lost interest. He stopped peeing in the cup, stopped relishing Walter's silent rages. He went on to other projects feeling he had somehow bested his father. Though perhaps Walter felt the same sense of victory. Cady never knew.

So what is she to make of Evan's behavior? It can't be hardwired. And Evan has never heard of Varney, let alone the details of Varney's ornate past, so it can't be consciously imitative. Is it simply a boy's way of expressing himself, using his penis to explore, exploit, and exalt himself?

"You're not saying *anything?*" Cooper says.

"It could be a phase?" she offers.

She recognizes the helplessness of his silence—the silence of the teacher who finds his student's dullness unfathomable.

"Yes, it could be a phase."

The impasse feels like a light implacable rain shower, so fine its source will never be used up, so unsoaking it can hardly even be called rain (maybe it's only mist or fog or something else altogether).

"Have you talked to Miss Tencil?" she says.

"Sure, I've talked to her a few times. I'm not the only one who thinks this is anger."

"He's dying, Cooper. How can I leave him when he's dying?"

"I know," Cooper says. "I wish—"

"Bring Evan down here. Please. We can talk about it down here."

Silence bellows again, and they give up at the same moment. Their lives seem so separate, their immediate concerns unbridgeable.

"Let me talk to Evan, okay?"

Cooper gets Evan, without protest.

"Mommy?" Evan says.

"I miss you, honey." The words call up the feeling even more strongly.

"When're you coming home?"

"Soon. But maybe Daddy will bring you down here."

"Gramma's making waffles for dinner. With strawberries and whipped cream."

"Yum. How's school going?"

"Good. Alex threw up on his desk today."

"That sounds unpleasant."

"We had to go to another room 'cause it smelled so bad."

She can't listen anymore. She feels run over by the details of his life—is anyone's life more than a patchwork of such details?—and it squashes her desire to question him further.

"I'm kissing you, honey. I'm kissing you through the phone." He smacks a return kiss, and when she signs off, he is still smacking.

She passes many hours of intermittent dozing and waking, unclear where thoughts leave off and dreams begin. Men traipse around her brain. She thinks of Walter and her own strange dance with him. He was afraid of her, she knew it. She sensed how her watchful silence made him feel judged. Once, the family went to an Italian restaurant overlooking the beach. They were waited on by an unabashedly gay waiter.

"There's a pansy if I've ever seen one," Walter said. Each time the waiter left the table, Walter launched into an exaggerated, clichéd gay act, flipping his eyelids, flicking his fingers, lisping, wiggling his torso suggestively. Beth and Varney felt called upon to smile, but Cady stayed stony.

"Stop, Walter," Beth begged. "He's going to see you." Cady wanted Walter to be seen. She wanted him humiliated. What he was doing was despicable.

"Cady isn't happy," Walter said after the waiter left the table for the third time. "Laugh, Cady. You're supposed to laugh."

"Ha, ha," she said.

On the way home, Walter made Cady sit in the front seat, next to him. She rolled down the side window and stared out over the night-slicked ocean.

"It was just a joke," Walter said. "Can't you take a joke?"

"It wasn't funny."

"Well, maybe you need to get yourself a funny bone." He stopped talking then, and everyone floated off into their separate capsules of privacy. In the back Beth and Varney seemed to be dozing.

"I was only calling a spade a spade," Walter said. His comment was sucked into the continuing silence. "I know you think I'm a pathetic man, Cady. But I have to be a loudmouth jokester—I don't have any other talents. Maybe if I had the energy of someone like Bill Hanneman, I could make something of myself. But, see, I'm lazy."

He had never said anything confessional like this—not to her, at least—and she had no idea what to say. She thought she should feel sorry for him, but right now she was still irked and caught off guard.

"Okay," he said after a while. "I know you don't want to hear any advice from me, but I'll say this one thing and then shut up. Take whatever you've got and run hard with it. That's the only way to get through life."

CHAPLAIN JACK ALWAYS has food. She is coming to count on it. Today he has Entenmann's blueberry muffins, foil-wrapped chunks of processed cheese, red grapes. "Eat as much as you want," he urges. She fills a small paper plate, trying not to look ravenous. He brings her peppermint tea he prepared on a hot plate. His smooth thick skin holds a sheen as if he is wearing the glitter young girls favor. She could sit here all day filling her belly, the sun warming her lap, listening to Chaplain Jack speak. The timbre of his voice makes her feel like a child again, without responsibility. Cooper used to make her feel this way when he urged her to move out of her head and into her body. "Be an animal," he used to urge her. She wants to be a hibernating animal now, one who sleeps out the dark days of winter until the world turns inside out with light. She doesn't tell Chaplain Jack she's a doctor.

"I used to believe that evil could ruin a person," he says. "But not anymore. Once you come to know these men, these *criminals*, you learn how good runs in their veins, too. Maybe you could say I believe in original saintliness the way others believe in original sin. We've all got the two streams in us—killer and saint, saint and killer."

On his desk a book entitled *Everyday Saints* lies open. He eats contemplatively, pausing between bites. She imagines the other book, the one entitled *Everyday Killers*.

DOC HAS STARTED having more frequent muscle spasms that warp and fold his planklike body. *Electrolyte imbalance*, she imagines, though she does not say this. Nurses come with pain med shots, which never seem to work well enough. She wants to ask what the medication is, what dose he's being given, but she holds her tongue, and Varney keeps knitting, no more willing than she to divulge her doctor identity.

"Can I help you?" she asks Doc when he shrieks from a spasm in his neck.

He glares at her, turns away.

Later she's in the common room with Varney. They're drinking Cokes from the vending machine and sitting on the couch. Nearby, Jesus—a short, dense, unsmiling man—visits with his mother. They whisper in Spanish, hold hands. The mother gazes at her son as if she's his lover. Jana knows well the feeling inside that expression.

"Why doesn't Doc like me?" she asks.

Varney stops knitting and regards her with surprise. He looks the way he looked as a much younger person, and it seems to her his wasting body is retracing its path back to childhood.

"He's *dying*, for Christ's sake."

Jesus and his mother look over, responding to the assaultive force of Varney's words. Jana doesn't react.

"I don't see the point of being a doctor," Varney says. "Look at me. Look at Doc." He tries to knit fast but the bending needles undermine his effort. Jana says nothing. What is the point? The doctor here is a brisk, heavyset woman whose only apparent tasks are the adjustment of pain meds and the pronouncement of death. A mere technician, not a lifesaver, a healer, a bearer of hope. Not like the chaplain, or Raoul. At first Jana had thought she would speak to Dr. Edna Johns and find out about Varney's protocol, but after hearing her conversing tersely with Doc behind the closed curtain, Jana thought better of it.

"How do I unravel?" Varney says.

Jana looks at him without comprehension.

"I dropped a stitch," he says.

"I'm no knitter," she says.

She tries to help him. They slide the inches of scarf off the needles, and one by one they undo the loops of yarn, all the way back to the dropped stitch in question. Then, supervising her closely, his breath a slow noisy rasp, Varney lets her slide the needle back on. She works slowly, clumsily, picking up the stitches one at a time, back to the beginning, until the scarf, or the few inches of scarf that remain, is anchored again.

SHE HAS BEEN here for ten days now. Thanksgiving has passed and she scarcely noticed, but for her call to Evan and Cooper. Christmas creeps up with characteristic steadiness. Muzak carols, stripped of lyrics, slide along the hallway ceilings. One of the social workers—a woman with frizzy hair, a toothy smile, and a penchant for bright, tropical colors—has decorated aggressively. She has put lights around the drinking fountain and the vending machines, hung ornaments in the doorways, sprayed Glasswax snowmen on the windows. Chaplain Jack has put chili pepper lights around his office entrance, and on his coffee table sits a plastic tree hung with colorful tin ornaments from Mexico.

Varney's scarf is eight inches long. He admires it every few minutes, stretching it out to its full length, wrapping it around his own neck. Jana and Varney sit quietly, breathing in sync; Varney's needles chatter; Doc sleeps; outside, a small brown bird pecks at the grass. She pours water from a plastic pitcher into two paper cups. She and Varney drink. He holds the cup to the side of his mouth to avoid touching his sores. He drinks one sip, two, wincing each time. He lets his eyes slide over her briefly before returning to his knitting. Are these moments the building blocks of intimacy?

She feels suddenly emboldened. She feels like talking. "In your letters you mentioned Piss Cat."

She searches Varney's face for some signal to continue, but, though his face certainly moves with twitches and frowns, none of its movements seems to communicate.

"Do you miss him?" she says.

Nothing. The knitting goes on. She tries not to notice Doc watching her. Varney may be hearing nothing, but Doc is taking in every word. She turns her chair so he's out of her sight lines.

"I bet you miss him," she says to Varney. "I would miss my husband, Cooper, if we didn't happen to be disagreeing right now. I miss Evan, my son."

Varney stops knitting, lays his head on the pillow, and closes his eyes. "What're you doing here, then?" he says. "Hobnobbing with the dying? Go back to your hoo-ha life."

"I didn't mean that," she says. "I'm glad to be here."

"Yeah, it's a laugh riot."

She remains silent for a long time, gazing outside at the coils of barbed wire, thinking about her *hoo-ha life*—a remote husband, a child who pees wantonly, anger rife. You can't be everywhere at once, but it does seem that you can always be in the wrong place. A great dust ball of depression is beginning to fuzz up around her, but then she sees Chaplain Jack in the hall. He limps by carrying a huge poinsettia plant and waves antically from behind it.

"Varney, why did you used to pee in Dad's cup?"

Varney turns his head, opens his eyes, and exchanges a look with Doc. For a brief intense moment she feels so excluded from everyone she wishes *she* were dying. *Bring another bed. Let me lie down, give in, give up.* The moment passes, but it has worked on her, robbing her pride, so she forges on shamelessly.

"Evan pees in cups, too. Just like you did, except he does it on the playground. The teacher thinks he's angry. My husband thinks he's angry. At me, of course. How should I know? He probably *is* angry. But what's a little pee? Everyone does it, that's for sure. And everyone's angry, right?"

She's talking louder and faster. Heat barrels through her face, and the noise rucks up. Varney has opened his eyes. He sits up. He isn't knitting. Doc watches, too.

"Hey, you know what—I think you'd like Bellingham. It's got a really great small-town feel. People there have minds of their own, but they're very friendly. Yeah, I really think you'd like it. Hell, Doc, you'd like it, too."

She stops to catch her breath. Her retinas swell. "Yeah, I'd say it's a good life—boats and sky and mountains. A real *hoo-ha* life."

And history means nothing, you want to say. Disease has taught you this. You only believe in the roll of the dice. The thing that doesn't happen is so often the very thing that was supposed to be likely to happen. The thing that does happen once seemed impossible.

Doc's MOTHER, Tricia, visits from Houston. She's taken a day off work, will stay for a day and a night before heading back. She wears a leather miniskirt, white mohair sweater, high heels, plenty of makeup. With her bleached and permed hair, she looks more like a girlfriend than a mother. She arrives at the door, escorted by Chaplain Jack.

"Doc?" the Chaplain says softly. "Doc? Your mom is here."

Doc opens his eyes and looks at the woman in front of him without reacting. His impassivity makes Jana wonder whether there has been a mistake. Maybe this isn't his mother after all.

"Baby?" she says with a heavy Texas drawl. "You okay, George?"

Jana is embarrassed for everyone. It's not right for a moment like this to unfold with so many onlookers.

"I'm going," Jana whispers to Varney, and her move seems to prompt Doc.

"This here is Varney and Varney's sister, Cady." It is the first time Doc has looked at her or indicated he knows her name. He introduced her using the name Varney uses, as if he knows her, likes her, as if she has a place here. But Tricia offers neither a hand nor a hello.

"Can't we get any privacy here?" she says to Doc.

Jana and Varney vacate the room. She steals glimpses of Varney manipulating his walker. Is he stronger now since her arrival as Chaplain Jack claims? Maybe. Is stronger desirable?

They take seats in the empty common room. Varney resumes his knitting while Jana sits with her eyes flickering open and closed, a gritty exhaustion quivering through her. She's sure there's no point to all this sitting, just sitting waiting for something worse to happen. If she were Varney's mother it would be easier. Her goal would be clearer, her need to protect him. Chaplain Jack says he sees mothers everywhere terrified for their sons. The ones who come here are still afraid for what might happen, though the worst has already happened.

Talk to me, she pleads silently of Varney. Out loud she says, "I think Evan is peeing because his imaginary friend died recently."

"She hasn't visited for eight years," says Varney. He doesn't look up from his knitting. "Doc is suddenly worth visiting because he's about to die."

Her anger soars again, hotter this time, more dangerous. She leaves without warning, without words. She gets up and walks away, past the open doors of the dying, past Chaplain Jack's empty office, her ears attuned for Varney's call. It wouldn't take much to summon her back—a mere whisper would do— but there is not a rustle or a peep from him. He doesn't care if she comes or goes. The years of her absence have steeled him against her. The old Varney is gone, the boy that saw colors everywhere, that told her what he felt, the wide-eyed boy who knew her breasts. If he were still alive, she could love him again, even with all that has happened.

Seagulls, seeming out of place so far inland, sail in high circles above her. She makes her way slowly to her car, forgetting at first where she has parked it. She feels the gaze of the tower sentries; they see a woman wandering, crazed perhaps. She pauses, scanning the cars—red, white, silver, black—all spanking clean. Sitting in a red Ford Fiesta is a blond woman bent over her steering wheel, ragged with despair. It's Doc's mom, Tricia. Jana watches the humped shoulders move up and down with her sobs. She pities Tricia. And envies her.

Two days after Tricia leaves, Doc takes a turn for the worse. His breathing is labored; he no longer speaks; his square pasty head never moves from the pillow; and all his shiftiness vanishes. The only muscular movement he still seems to make is the opening and closing of his eyes. Nurses come and go more frequently, taking vital signs, and Chaplain Jack checks in every hour or so to lay a hand on Doc's shoulder and offer a prayer.

Varney will not leave the room. When Jana arrives each morning, she finds him sitting by Doc's bed, his head down near Doc's ear. He is whispering things, singing in his eerie falsetto, keeping up a steady flow of words. An IV drip feeds the venous portal in Doc's neck with (she supposes) morphine or Demerol.

"He doesn't feel anything," Jana tries to tell Varney.

Varney shakes his head. "How would you know? You haven't died yet."

She sits with them because there is nothing else to do. A *practice round,* she thinks, as she listens to the hiss of Doc's breathing and watches Varney's spidery fingers tracing the deep furrows of Doc's forehead.

A sudden foul-smelling bulb of air wafts up from Doc.

"Shit," Varney says. They vacate the room while Raoul and a new aide named Pete negotiate the changing of the soiled sheets. Varney has his scarf with him. "It's long enough," he says. "Show me how to cast off."

"I have no idea how," she says.

He looks at her with flat eyes. His mouth hangs open slightly. His disease accuses her.

"I'll find someone who knows," she says.

At the nurses' station no one is a knitter. "Sorry," they say, offering her their professionally sorrowful looks. *Save it for death,* she thinks cynically. No one in the administration office can help her, either, but they give her scissors and she cuts the yarn and returns to Varney. Now he watches her as she weaves a length of yarn down the scarf's width, picking the stitches off the needle one at a time. They are both bent at the waist, quiet and focused collaborators. At the end of the row, she pulls the yarn tight, weaves it back into the body of the scarf, and ties a clumsy knot. It isn't perfect-looking, but it is a complete scarf. She hands it to Varney, who nods his thanks curtly, eyes pooling.

Back in the room Raoul awaits them. The bed has been changed, the air sprayed with a light citrus scent, which doesn't eliminate the smell of sickness but makes it tolerable.

"Bring blankets, Raoul," Varney says. "He's cold. Can't you see he's cold?" He lays the scarf on Doc's chest. "Look what I got for you," Varney whispers, shoving aside his walker and bending to Doc's ear. "It's a red scarf. It'll keep you warm. I knitted it myself."

The red of the scarf whitens Doc's already pasty complexion. Of course she has seen people die, often within a minute of their arrival in ER. She's seen deaths from heart attacks and seizures and car accidents and much more. You're not protected in ER; you see the worst of human fates. But when you diagnose fatal conditions, you usually send your patients off to die elsewhere—on hospital wards, or in the privacy of their homes.

She has never sat like this, keeping vigil, counting the hours, watching the minute changes in respiration, the graying of the skin, the gradually but visibly weakening pressure of the blood.

In her exhaustion she stares at Doc and the image of him blurs until he is indistinguishable from Varney. Then, unbidden, Evan fills her head. All her loves seem to invade and reconfigure her brain so easily, like viruses reprogramming the codes of cells. Seeing Evan so clearly, she has to move. She goes to the hallway, still picturing Evan; the look she imagines in his eye is giddy and indomitable as if, in her absence, he has truly crossed some line.

The lights on the plastic tree in the common room shoot bubbles down their shafts, oddly reminiscent of disease patterns. Christmas here is an uninvited holiday, inappropriate and insulting. She heads to the bathroom. Its stalls, with low walls, are built for crisis. They have no doors, only curtains as in some elementary schools. She sits long after she's done peeing, staring at the grouted tile work, hoping some of her anger will drain, but it doesn't. The sudden force of it scares her. It never comes in small manageable doses. Even the tiniest intimation of anger grows quickly into a full-tilt, fully armed rage, looking for its expression (it seems) in bullets, its satisfaction in blood. It's time to leave, go back to the motel to either sleep or run.

Back in the room, Varney lies on Doc's bed, humming tunelessly, their bodies both flat as graves. Doc's torso shudders hopelessly, his respiration has become agonal. He'll be gone, she guesses, within the hour. Varney looks up at her open-mouthed, saucer-eyed, disbelieving.

"Call his mom. Tell her to come fast." He hands her a slip of paper with a number on it.

"Won't Chaplain Jack do that?"

"You need to. She'll listen to a woman."

Doubtful, Jana thinks, but she takes the slip, anyway, to appease Varney, and what is the point of refusing?

TWENTY·SEVEN

Perched on the edge of her motel room bed, Jana makes the call to Tricia, wondering how it is that this duty has fallen to her, but resigned by now that it has. It is four-thirty and Jana hopes that Tricia won't be home so she can leave a message and be done with it, but Tricia *is* home.

"You met me—" Jana begins, trying to put out of her mind the diminishing look Tricia gave her.

Tricia remembers. "He's dead?" she says.

"Not yet, but soon."

There is a long silence, then Tricia's voice quivers through. Her Texas inflection, as if distilled by the phone, seems stronger. "I know. I know. You think you're okay with it but—" Sobs follow, a heavy avalanche of them. She drops the phone, fumbles for it, restores it to her ear. Jana pictures her buckled over a small kitchen table, dressed in white mohair and leather the way she was the day Jana met her, her tears so prolific they spill over the table's edge.

After some time Tricia says, "God won't forgive me, will He?"

"I'm sure He will," Jana says. It's not necessary to admit she knows nothing of God.

"I don't know what I did to make him go bad like he did."

It seems arrogant to provide answers (or just plain dumb), but after a while Jana can no longer preside over the despairing images Tricia's silence suggests. "I'm sure it's not your fault," she says. "You can't always account for what people do."

Tricia's tears cloud the connection again and Jana drifts, thinking how guilt is always the same, regardless of the magnitude of the transgression.

"Do you ever feel," Jana says when Tricia's weeping slackens, "that you could have done the bad thing instead of him?"

The silence thickens. Then: "My son raped a woman. I never feel that way."

CHAPLAIN JACK GREETS her with uncharacteristic somberness. "Doc is dead," he says. "He went a few hours after you left. Varney needs you." He squeezes his earlobe so a circle of white radiates out from his forefinger. His eyes hold steady, as if to sluice his sorrow. "We'll be having the service at eleven."

She lets herself be hugged, so she's engulfed by the chaplain's moist sweat and his faint herbal smell. It has been weeks since anyone but the chaplain has embraced her.

"You never get used to it," he says.

Minutes before her arrival in his room, Varney has ripped out his venous portal, swept everything off his table, smashed the failing coleus. When she enters his room, a female nurse and a male aide (neither does she recognize) are restraining him with a brusque wordlessness. Gloved and coolly insistent, they mop splattered blood and reintroduce his IV portal. After a minute or two, he gives up his resistance and goes limp. She stands in the corner, making herself scarce until the nurse and aide leave. "Call us if anything happens," the nurse says. "Make sure you leave the door open."

She moves the plastic chair next to his bed. He breathes heavily, still enervated by his outburst. She hands him his oxygen tube, but he waves it away.

"What happened?" she says.

"I'm trying to die, goddamn it, but they won't let me." His voice shocks her again. She cannot fix its timbre and pitch in her mind. Has it possibly gone higher since she left yesterday?

He runs out of steam again and lies still, staring bleakly out the window like a man already dead. Down the hall someone moans.

"Just let it happen," she says. "It will happen when it's supposed to."

"Not until they say so it won't. They want to control you to the fucking end. *Die with dignity*—forget it. That's bullshit." He turns away.

She strokes his arm. Its skin is rough as Spider's tongue and runneled with collapsed veins. She contemplates its riot of color for the first time—the purple and blue of the blood vessels, the yellow and white of weary epidermis, the brown of the scabs. There's even a pale spring green.

"Don't," he says. "Just go."

She withdraws her hand but remains sitting.

"What am I supposed to do?" he says. "Lie here and *cry*? Lie here and *hallucinate*? Every night I dream of Mr. Phillips. He's wearing pink stretch pants, and he's coming down a hallway to get me. He's yelling at me in a voice that sounds like Dad's. Then he begins laughing. Every goddamn night for the last month. Then there's the dream where Andy's body puts itself back together. He's lying in his casket putting his own body parts together, talking himself through it like he's reading an instruction manual."

She is paralyzed by the vigor of his feeling. She had no idea he was thinking these things. "Talk about it," she says. "You'll feel better."

"I don't *want* to talk. Talk doesn't do anything. You talk and you end up seeing how much stuff you wanted that you never got."

His words are projectiles, high and hostile as fighter jets. His eyes have grown terrible, too, dark and stygian. She would prefer not to look at them, but she can't look away, not now that she has finally gotten his attention.

"Chaplain Jack says you talk to people. You make them feel good."

"That's stories. That's different. And it's not what I want for myself. I don't need to make peace, either, with any god-damn thing. I just need to die and no one wants to let me." He coughs deeply and spits into a bowl beside his bed. "Fuck," he says apropos of nothing and everything.

A trolley squeaks by in the hallway outside his room. The TV from a room next door competes with Christmas Muzak.

"You'll die eventually," she says.

"Yeah, eventually. But while I'm waiting for *eventually*, I hurt everywhere, like a mother-fucking fire."

The chimes sound, summoning them to Doc's memorial. She waits for Varney to make a move. "Well?" she says. "Shall we go?"

"I'm not going."

"Really? Not going to Doc's service?"

"You go. I'll mourn him how I want. Did you call his mom?"

Jana nods. "She can't make it."

"That figures." He blinks. "Just go, okay. Pretend you never came here. Do the world a favor and forget I was ever born."

Outside in the hallway there is a slow caravan moving toward the chapel.

"I'm staying right here," she says.

"Don't expect me to talk."

He rolls away from her, vomits into a plastic bowl, his body convulsing to a fetal position each time he retches. When he's

done, she empties the bowl in the bathroom, rinses it, and resumes her seat. They remain in stillness and silence for a long
time. He lies on his side, facing the window, knees drawn up,
his body the picture of wretchedness. The smell of vomit
crowds in for a minute, then disperses like mist. A few live oak
leaves float across the window in a lazy diagonal path. She
stares at a point on the back of his head where his skull pro-
trudes. She feels a vicarious nausea, a vicarious wretchedness,
as if the blood they share has finally brought them to the same
point of feeling, an odd conjoinment and seesawing of wills.
She should let him alone. He has the right to be alone.

When she hears the chapel doors opening, people shuffling
back to their rooms, she says, "I'll leave if you want me to."

Silence.

"Do you?" she says.

Silence. Then, a sound emerges from him, and she has to
lower her ear to hear it. He turns his head and heaves his eyes
onto hers as if he is lifting something of inordinate weight. She
is jolted by their dark translucence; they appear backlit, as if
the light is radiating out from his brain, straight through his
eyes. She holds her breath, cherishing the kernel of the Varney
she remembers.

"If you want to do something for me, you'll find me some
way to get this over with fast," he whispers. "You're a doctor,
you know how."

She whispers back, touching his shoulder, trying to squeeze
understanding into him. "You know I can't do that, Varney.
Anything else."

He shrugs. "That's all I want." Sighing, he turns his head
away from her again, retracting his eyes.

She stays still so long her legs grow numb and her breath
runs shallow and the bones of her own body lighten and grow
brittle; her thoughts run thick with waking nightmares and

memories that are not originally hers. She remembers the plotting of their youth, the times they talked of running away, of skipping school, of torching the house. She fed him with her own wildness and battened herself down, freeing herself to laugh at his anger, his snake shooting, his peeing in cups. She was a rebel, too, but no one knew.

She stays in his room until dusk and the aide brings liquid dinner, which exudes an artificial strawberry smell. Varney doesn't acknowledge the drink and surely won't consume it. She walks slowly to the end of the hallway. A new patient is being installed in one of the rooms. She hears voices and sees a pair of feet, slippers hanging off them like curls of old skin. There's a waiting list for the twenty beds, Chaplain Jack says, a list of people who want to come in here to wait for death. People dying to die. She is not religious, has scarcely had a religious thought in her life, but it seems to her if Varney goes out as he is now, his soul will rattle uneasily around the universe forever, unsettling things, spreading grief. She thinks of the foment in his eyes, the pleading. She stands for a long time in front of the closed door of Chaplain Jack's office, staring at the strip of light at the bottom.

The door opens. Chaplain Jack pushes out with a golf jacket, a Giants baseball cap, a briefcase. "Hey there," he says.

Caught, she freezes. She accompanies Chaplain Jack to the exit, stuttering through hospice small talk, rehashing Doc's death and her brother's exacerbated state of grief.

"It's good he's got you to do what he has done for others," Chaplain Jack says. "We'll see you tomorrow."

Night spills over the two of them and splits them off to their cars.

Driving calms her. Her mind turns sane again. She thinks of the literature Chaplain Jack gave her the first day she came, filled with the rhetoric of acceptance and dignified peaceful dying, and she tries to imagine what she could do now that she sees Varney's position more clearly. Tomorrow she will meet with Chaplain Jack—he must have ideas about things she can do to help move Varney more quickly toward peace.

She crouches to Spider and strokes him hard as soon as she enters the room. The cat arches his back, purrs loudly, and Jana has the feeling she can almost read his thoughts, or at least she can feel the intensity of Spider's pleasure at her return. She strokes him for a long time before she looks up and notices the flashing red light on the phone. *Varney has died. He has willed himself to die.*

But it is Cooper's voice she listens to. "We're here," he says, his voice as calm as she's ever heard it. "In room one-oh-nine. Call us."

THEY WAIT FOR burritos in a dim, cavernous, neon-decorated Mexican restaurant. The clamor of a roving mariachi band, the squealing of birthday parties, the squeak and pop of balloon sculptures made by a woman who travels from table to table, all make it hard to hear. Oblivious, Evan slouches over the tiny screen of his Game Boy, his thumbs tapping quickly. Jana is riveted by him, by the steeliness of his attention, by the subtle weaving of his dimples in and out of fullness, pulsing almost like the opening and closing of heart valves. She can hardly keep her hands off him and periodically reaches across the space between them to pat his knee. She doesn't like his new toy; it sucks up his attention and draws him away from the world, but it's too soon to start in on this subject when there is so much else to be said. Evan has been so shy with her, scarcely speaking, clutching Cooper's hand (as if he's heard nasty things about her and is dubious about her as a mother). He hugged her fiercely when he first saw her, but then he let go quickly and begged to be allowed to go to the courtyard pool (which Cooper inexplicably refused). Jana would have let him but knew it was not her prerogative yet to give or withhold permission.

"Yes!" mutters Evan. "I beat the level."

"Do you think this toy is good for him?" Jana finally can't help asking, thinking of the stimulation bombarding his eyes, overloading his brain, possibly leading to seizures.

Cooper shrugs. "That, right now, is the least of my worries."

Cooper is growing his beard out again, but it is still in the scruffy stage. He looks weary and lost, and his vulnerability stirs in her steady waves of love. Now sucking his Dos Equis, he scans the restaurant with cool remove. He has not said much yet, and it feels to her as if he has come only to watch her, to evaluate the situation, to judge her fitness.

"How's the job?" she asks, trying to ease in.

"Is that really what you want to talk about now?" he says.

She lets it go and puts her lips to the salty rim of her margarita glass.

"Seretha wanted to come," he says. "But I told her no. She sends her love."

"She was very sweet to me on the phone."

Cooper nods, hands Evan his napkin, and moves the full milk glass back from the edge of the table. How can you love a man for simply thinking of a milk glass?

"You would have come down here, too, wouldn't you? If you'd had a sick brother?"

He holds up a hand, as if in a court of law. "Honest to god, I don't have a brother. Real or phantom."

She smiles faintly and glances at Evan, grateful for the role his presence is playing in maintaining their civility.

"Why did you think I couldn't handle it?" Cooper says. "Do you think of me as so bigoted?"

Evan raises his eyes to Cooper, then they skate quickly back down.

"Cooper—," Jana says.

"It's okay." And now he's soft again, gentle, parental. "I've told him. We've talked about it, haven't we, Ev?"

Evan doesn't look up.

"Evan?"

"Huh?"

"We've talked about your uncle, haven't we?"

"He's in prison and he's dying 'cause he likes men." Evan's thumbs don't stop moving.

"That's his version. It's not how I put it," says Cooper, shrugging apology.

Cooper picks at his Dos Equis label, tossing the torn bits onto the table. The waitress appears with their burritos, enforcing their silence, and moments later the roving songsters stop by, three of them with their sombreros and guitars and smiles, overwhelming them with a crooning love song. "'Besos,'" they sing, "'Yo amo sus besos...'" Jana smiles and tips the singers lavishly until they go away and the only sound remaining in her consciousness is the intrusively perky music from Evan's Game Boy.

"Did my uncle really *kill* his parents?" Evan says. "With a gun?"

"Shhh," Jana says, looking around. Cooper has emptied his beer, peeled off its label entirely, and is now beckoning the waitress for another.

"His mind wasn't right," Jana tells Evan. "He felt crazy."

Evan sits straight up, legs crossed in the posture of a grown-up. His pale, interested face seems to glow out of the restaurant's dimness like a neon coil. "Is he still crazy?"

"Just very sick."

"Is he really my uncle?"

"Yes."

"Then how come I never met him?"

She avoids Cooper's glance. She sees, in the depth of one of Evan's dimples, a freckle she has never noticed before.

"Can I see him?" Evan says.

"Tomorrow we might see him," she says quietly.

Cooper rises, setting his napkin down with more than the usual thrust.

"Where're you going?" she asks, afraid of his impetuousness.

"To the toilet, if you don't mind."

While Cooper is gone—for what seems like eons—the balloon lady comes to the table. She has a wasp-waisted Barbie-doll look, an overbite, and a high pandering voice. "What's your name?" she asks Evan.

"Evan."

"What would you like, Evan? I can do a doggie, a cat, a giraffe, a hat, a sword?"

"I want a sword."

The woman pulls three long balloons from her waist belt and inflates them with a noisy air gun. Then she begins twisting so they whine against each other.

Evan watches her work. "I've got a Game Boy," he tells her proudly.

"That's nice," she says. "I bet you play it all the time."

"You know what? My uncle shot someone dead with a gun."

"Evan." Jana frowns at him.

The balloon lady scowls, too, then smiles with her lips drawn forcefully over her teeth. Her blond hairdo fibrillates. "I don't think that's a nice story, do you? Tell me a pretty story."

Back from the bathroom, Cooper doesn't sit down. "I'm

tired. Evan is tired. You look pretty tired yourself. Enough until tomorrow. Okay?"

On the ride back to the motel, Cooper sits in the passenger's seat and Jana drives. The frisky Game Boy music fills the silence. At the motel they stand by the parked car, the orange lights gouging lines in all their faces, even Evan's. Evan pokes at the car's tire treads with his balloon sword.

"You could both come to my room," she says.

"Yeah," says Evan, "let's go to your room." He runs to her, drops his sword, and wraps his arms around her waist with the commitment of a mussel, lifting his feet from the pavement and imparting to her waist and pelvis the most delicious ache. She pats his back. Cooper's eyes skate quickly over her face with the unremembering expression of a stranger.

"You?" she says.

"I don't think so."

They do not touch.

"Say something," says Jana.

Cooper looks up to a sky busy with wisps of mist. "Tomorrow."

She and Evan climb into the same queen bed, leaving the second one empty. Evan, wearing pajama bottoms with tiny black Batmen leaping into a field of royal blue, snuggles up close to Jana, the skin of his chest against her bare upper arm. He wriggles and nests there, rooting into her shoulder, half on his side, one arm anchored on her belly, the other wrapped around a stuffed otter, adjusting and readjusting things, getting everything just right, as if he is preparing for a long season of hibernation during which he wants to be assured of her proximity. She stays still on her back and lets him dig around her however he wants. Finally he seems to rest. She smiles down at him. His eyes are fiery, far from sleep.

"Mom?"

"Yes."

"Why would someone kill someone else?"

His questions have so often been unanswerable. It has made her see how adults edit their questions, making sure they only pose the ones with accessible answers.

"Not everyone would kill," she says.

"But why did my uncle?"

"That's a hard question, Ev. That's a question I ask myself all the time. I guess maybe because he was really, really, really upset." No one knew—did they? Evil, the bifurcation of human nature, chemical imbalance, astrological plan, molecular movement. Cases could be made for all of these.

Evan rustles and folds one of his knees up to his belly. "Really, really, really, really, really, really, really, really upset?"

"Yes, yes," she says. "All those reallys."

"Gramma says sugar can make people kill. And drugs."

She strokes his hair. It hasn't been washed for a while and releases a slightly doggy smell. "Yes, sometimes. Drugs do make people do strange things."

Evan rolls over suddenly onto his back, skin still glued to hers. He holds his otter at arm's length and rattles him back and forth. "Mama?"

"Yes, honey?"

But his thought or question doesn't materialize into words. Spider leaps onto the bed and Evan makes a grotto among the bedclothes. "Spider's going to sleep right here." Evan tries to press Spider into a lying position.

"Don't do that, honey. He doesn't like it." Spider leaps from the bed and saunters into the bathroom.

"Do cats go to prison?"

"I don't think there's any prison for cats."

"But they kill mice and birds. Spider kills lots of mice."

"Yes, but that's just instinct. When they're living in the wild, they need mice and birds to survive."

"Leo's in prison."

"I thought Leo was dead."

"He's going to be dead. God will make him dead because he was bad."

He frowns, and she cannot restrain herself from suddenly gripping his whole small frame, wedging her arms beneath and around him, and squeezing him as hard as she ever has. He squeals—"Mama! Mo-om!" and hugs back with equal force. How has she survived this period without him? No wonder all her cells have been distraught.

"Mumma," he says, infantile, happy.

"It's time for us to go to sleep, okay?"

She turns out the light, and Evan resettles, giving himself over again to the simple somatic pleasure of preparing his palette for sleep. She feels his thoughts dimming to a low blue flame.

"Can I swim tomorrow?" he says out of the stillness.

"I don't see why not."

"Are we going to see my uncle?"

"I hope so, yes."

His breath is slow and regular, his voice lazy as syrup. "I'm going to tell him he shouldn't eat so much sugar."

TWENTY-EIGHT

Morning light moves like a stylus across the teal and orange coverlet of Cooper's motel room bed where Jana perches. Cooper is sitting at the small table, jotting notes in a tiny book. He has never been a note-taker, a man to keep track of things as they went along, so his attention to writing now surprises her (more, it disturbs her). She takes her plastic coffee cup from the bedside stand. The coffee, burned from sitting around too long in the automatic coffeemaker, is lukewarm, weak, and powder whitened. She drinks it like medicine, only for the caffeine, not the pleasure. But after a few sips, even the caffeine is not worth it, and she dumps it in the bathroom sink. When she comes out again, Cooper is standing and stowing the notebook in his back pocket. He looks startled to see her. It was his idea for her to come to his room. She wanted to go out to breakfast (and now after that bad coffee she definitely does), but he felt they needed privacy for their discussion. They have banished Evan to the courtyard, where she sees him through the sun-jeweled glass, happily pitching stones.

She sits on the bed again but feels pent up. Again the balance of light is not right. The side near the sliding glass door is blindingly bright, and the rest of the room is depressingly dim, a brownish light reminiscent of low-rent bars. The idea of hash-ing out domestic matters in this poorly lit space seems ill-fated. Cooper has brought the desk chair out from behind the table, and he sits in it backward. He is backlit, and to see his face, she must squint.

"I know we have to talk," she says. "But could you hug me first?"

They approach each other like novices. Their bellies and pelvises don't touch, and Cooper's head is turned sideways so his mouth and chin don't rest, as they usually do, in her hair.

"I can get clearance for you quickly, I think," she says. "For the families of the hospice patients it's pretty fast."

"Why are you pushing this? We've talked about it already. You don't think your brother and I are going to become friends, do you?" Cooper, hunched over his plastic cup of black coffee, speaks quietly. His hands look large and still.

"He's not a pariah," she says.

"I wouldn't know."

"I never thought you'd be friends. But you could just meet him—"

"Call me squeamish, call me scared, but I'd rather not go in there. I have no need to meet him."

Her eye is drawn behind Cooper's head to outside where Evan stands, not far from the sliding door, the trajectory of his pee heading straight ahead of him and landing in the foliage of a holly bush. A buzz goes through her; she loses the train of her thoughts. She closes her eyes, waits. *It's only a young boy peeing.*

"Then why did you come down here?" she finally says.

"Because you asked me to. You wanted to talk. And there's—" He pauses—"this stuff of Evan's to deal with. And you need to come back to Bellingham."

"You came to *get* me?"

"It's hardly a matter of *kidnapping.*"

"Evan wants to meet Varney."

"Evan's six years old—he doesn't know what he wants. You'll scare the lights out of him. Especially now, with all the changes he's been through recently."

"So you're worried about Evan, too?"

"No," he says loudly. "I'm not worried about him. But there's obviously a problem here."

The strands of their worry tornado together and take in the whole room.

"You're always saying I shelter him too much."

"Come on, Jana; taking him into a prison is different."

"You're right. Varney is family. He's my own brother and Evan's uncle. I admit that I should have told you about him sooner, but he exists now. He's back in our lives."

"Who are you doing this for? For Evan or for yourself? What's the point?"

"He's my brother. What more *point* do you need? If your mother were there, wouldn't you want us to see her?"

Cooper covers his eyes, a gesture that paints the room with his despair. She might as well cover her own eyes. Blind matching blind.

She goes to the sliding door and steps out. The sun forces her eyes closed and she has to work to reopen them. Evan is digging in some dirt where bright orange nasturtiums have been coaxed, at the wrong season, into growth. She walks up behind him.

"Hurry up," she says.

He comes without cajoling. "What?" he whispers.

"Just come."

She hurries him through the room, where he snatches his Game Boy from the dresser, peering questioningly at Cooper, who still sits in the chair where Jana left him.

"You're going?" Cooper says.

She shoulders her purse, all movement, all busy intent, the long-dormant rebel in her now the revenant and dizzy with un-rehearsed nerve. They walk out the door, unmoved by Cooper's expressive body parts—the set mouth, the narrow eyes, the hands fisted over one another—the assemblage of images saying no.

Cooper's unspoken objections gain credence in her own head as she and Evan drive away together, Evan's Game Boy chirping in the backseat. What *is* her point in bringing Evan here? To ease Varney's pain and anger; or as a cautionary tale for Evan? Whatever her original reasons were, she doubts them now.

"How was your drive down here, honey? Did it feel awfully long?"

She has to ask the question three times before she gets a terse *yeah* out of Evan. The conversationalist from last night is all sewn up. She hates being this kind of mother, nagging, false, asking questions she already knows the answers to only to promote conversation. A mother with no respect for privacy. Evan turns from his game to look out the window briefly. The sunlight reveals a tiny peninsula of blond hairs limning his temple. A Cooper inheritance, this remnant of extreme blondness, fine and pure and new as chick fuzz. All his facial muscles are at rest, and the resultant expression is one of deep balefulness. She sees, in this brief glance of his, a vast and unknown interior life.

"Honey, can I say something?" She waits for the talkative streak of last night to reassert itself. She hears nothing. She decides to forge on. "You can't just pee in public any old time, you know. Evan? Do you hear me?"

"Yeah, I know."

"You're too old for that. People won't understand. Right?"

"Yeah," he says wearily, her admonition tired and unwelcome.

The sight of a 7-Eleven reminds her that Evan has had no breakfast, not counting the leftover mints he saved from last night's Mexican restaurant. She pulls into the parking lot. When the car has come to a full stop, Evan looks up, dazed.

"What're we doing here?"

"Food?" she says.

He turns off his Game Boy and takes her hand willingly, and the familiar sight of the blocky green and orange 7-Eleven sign buoys her. Inside she watches him brighten at the sight of so much junk food. The place's familiarity works on her, relaxing her, so she does not say no to the Nestlé Crunch and the cherry Coke Evan selects. Back in the car he rips into the candy bar and guzzles his soda, gleeful, furtive, knowing he's gotten away with something without knowing why.

"Happy?" she says. The question stays with them, unanswered, unregistered, or answered already, and she is angry at herself for posing another one of those questions, for expecting talk for candy, for expecting Evan to be other than he is, and for being sad that he is not.

At the sight of the prison's massive white buildings, Evan stops playing again to stare, taking in every detail (she guesses) of the spirals of barbed wire lining the fence, the sentry towers at intervals along the walls. In the rearview mirror he looks unnaturally subdued.

"Let's go," she says when she has parked. He appears not to hear and slides off the seat reluctantly when she opens the back door.

"Is my uncle a really bad man?"

"He did a bad thing," she says. But if Varney is not bad, who is? She takes Evan's hand, and he squeezes hers hard. They move slowly toward the front entrance, everything striking her anew—the guns trembling on the hips of the guards, the airport-style metal detector they must pass through, the wands of the guards that frisk them, the signs that blare at them: NO WEAPONS. NO DRUGS. This is not child's fare. Remembering Varney's eyes—their absorbency, their tendency to forget nothing—she thinks of covering Evan's eyes, of turning back and speeding him away from this hotbed of criminality and death.

Inside the hospice Chaplain Jack welcomes them (so large, so genial, so present), shaking Evan's hand, man-to-man. "Varney's sleeping," he says. "I just came from his room."

He brings them to his office, where he settles into his chair and urges them to sit. He is focused entirely on Evan, admiring (Jana thinks) Evan's youth and his unexploded possibility. "What's your favorite sport?" Chaplain Jack asks of Evan.

It is a question that makes Jana feel deficient. What does Evan know of organized sports? He stares at the floor, then out the window, seemingly in a trance, ears (or at least social skills) out of commission, and Jana can't help wondering what Chaplain Jack sees at this moment, if he is doing what Jana herself so often does, examining this young, unresponsive, and wide-eyed boy for buried seeds of psychopathology and violence.

"You like baseball?" The question is benign, but Jana understands how Evan could feel otherwise; it comes from an insistent stranger with no hair.

She reaches out to pat Evan's knee. "He likes baseball," she says, though she's not sure he does. Chaplain Jack goes into a desk drawer and pulls out a small spongy ball designed like a baseball. He tosses it to Evan. Evan reacts just in time to catch it.

"Can he have candy?" the chaplain asks.

When Jana nods, he reaches into the drawer again and comes out with a cherry Tootsie Roll Pop, which he hands triumphantly to Evan. Evan holds the ball in one hand, the lollipop in the other, and continues to stare out the window as if fearful that something will be exacted from him in exchange. Jana watches—only a bad mother would produce such a withdrawn child.

"Say thank you," she says.

"Don't worry about it," says the chaplain, but she sees around his eyes a tinge of sadness.

"How *is* Varney today?" she says. Her question coincides with a sound from outside, a howl more large-cat–like than human. "*Dios!*"

Evan leaps into her lap. "What was that?" he says.

"Someone hurting," she says.

Chaplain Jack closes the door, but it only muffles the sound, which has metamorphosed into a low abject moaning. "Do you know why people are here?" he asks Evan.

Evan nods at Jana's lap. "They're bad so God is making them die."

Where did he get this idea? Is this what Cooper told him? *I never said that,* she starts to say, but falters after the *I.*

"Well, they are people who have done bad things, but God isn't making them die." The chaplain's voice is silky, unflappable. "It's just their time. And they're here to think about their lives and find peace before they die. You see?"

Evan's face seems like hard plastic in its refusal to move.

"Let me go check on Varney. He's been tired, but I'm sure he'll want to see you."

Chaplain Jack disappears. Evan squirms in her lap; his warmth and weight remind her of the good parts of their history. "You can eat your lollipop," she says. She wants to see him lose himself in the simple pleasure of sweet. She remembers the feeling so well, the feeling of turning away from the world, toggling off the worry and the shyness, so all that lay before her was the rapture of dissolving sugar and her own marauding tongue. "Go ahead," she says. He shakes his head, and she remembers the surfeit of candy he's already had.

Outside, the moan's pitch rises, becoming the kind of sound her brain will reproduce. She concentrates on the warm bodily goodness of Evan's frame, on the thought of Varney and Evan meeting, finally knowing each other and maybe mending some things.

"I want to go home," Evan says tremulously. "With you." The muscles of his legs turn wiry in her lap, making her own thighs tighten.

"We'll just stay for a little while," she says, her voice distorted by the singsong of forced cheerfulness. "You two can meet each other and then we'll go."

When Chaplain Jack returns, his face also carries fakery, belied by a smile that comes and goes, ramifying itself strangely across the glossy planes of his skin. "He's only good for a short visit," he says. "But go. He's expecting you."

They move down the hall slowly, Evan staring unabashedly at two black pajamaed inmates who hobble toward them. When they arrive at Varney's room, Evan resists Jana's tug. The room looks more barren and dismal than it has before, the walls still unadorned. Doc's bed, remade with fresh sheets, awaiting its new inhabitant, but meanwhile looking crisp, punitive, unwelcoming. It does not seem as if they are expected. Varney lies unmoving, his bed in its flattened position, his head turned toward the window, his body a tiny rise beneath the sheet.

"No," Evan says at the doorway, but she urges him inside (a hand at his back, a coaxing murmur), and almost simultaneous with the first slide of Evan's tears, Varney turns his head, looking pale, dark-eyed, so ravaged one might imagine he is risen from the dead but for the ferocity of his whisper.

"Damn him. I told him no."

"Varney, please," Jana says. "This is your nephew."

"Evan?" Varney says.

A current runs through Evan—disbelief, she thinks, at the high scratchy voice, the withered body, at hearing this cadaverous creature speak his name—but he does not cry out or flee; instead he seems to concentrate. Man and boy stare at each other with such intensity, Jana is locked out. It's an intensity that could turn to anything, she senses. It is not a standoff exactly, but the moment holds the charge of two individuals simultaneously arriving at the crossroads of choice. Evan breaks the stare first; his eyes case the room—Varney's bruised arm, the venous portal in his neck, the walker, the oxygen canister, the TV mounted on the wall, the view of barbed wire beyond the stretch of brown grass—and as they travel, his eyes rain tears.

"Fucking scary, isn't it," says Varney.

"Varney," Jana says.

"Don't Varney me. I'm just calling it like it is. Isn't that why you brought him here—so he won't end up like me?"

"That's not it."

Varney pants, reaching for words, for breath. "Come here, dude. You see that? You see this hand?" He reaches out to Evan, his spindly fingers wiggling in summons. "Come here and see this friggin' body of mine. Your mom is right—you don't want to end up like me. I'm a criminal; I'm a nutcase; I'm dying. What could be worse? Come here; touch me."

Transfixed, Evan no longer cries.

"I'm not going to hurt you; just touch me."

Evan's back remains pasted against Jana's legs. She pushes him forward. "Go. He won't hurt you."

Varney takes Evan's hand in his. Evan, tongue-tied, frozen, eyes imploding in disbelief, looks at his own small rounded hand as if it does not belong to him anymore, as if it has been

relinquished to the skeleton that Varney is, and will never return intact.

Varney expels a whir of laughter, creaky as a tired ceiling
fan. "Wouldn't you want to die if you were me? Wouldn't you?"
He demands an answer. Evan nods ever so slightly, and Varney
laughs again, obtusely, eerily, so Jana wonders for a moment if
dementia is setting in.

"I love death now. You tell that to your mother, okay," he
confides to Evan. Again Evan nods, almost imperceptibly.
"You're a good kid. I can tell you're a good kid. "

Varney releases Evan's hand and collapses back onto his pillows. Evan looks down at his hand as if it is surely different now,
as if he expects it to be mangled or discolored. Varney stares up
at the ceiling and takes a colossal breath that rallies everything.
The voice he emits is a falsetto roar. "Get out quick. Both of
you. I never said you could come in the first place."

His face has reddened with the effort of his shouting and
tears gutter in his eyes. Jana, flooded with remorse, puts a hand
on his shoulder.

"Get out!" he screeches.

Evan follows quickly in her wake. Behind them Varney
retches into his plastic receptacle. In the hallway they nearly
collide with a frail silver-haired black man using a walker. Jana
veers around him, walking quickly, Evan in tow. Chaplain
Jack is not in his office. She thinks of leaving Evan there, anyway, but instead she takes him with her, traveling the full
perimeter of the hallway as fast as she can, gripping Evan's
wrist. She finally finds Chaplain Jack leaning against the
nurses' station.

"Can you watch Evan for a moment?"

"Sure," the chaplain says. "We're buds, aren't we?"

Evan stares at the floor. She doesn't consult him, she simply turns him over to Chaplain Jack and says a firm no when he tries to follow her. "I'm coming back in a minute," she says, choosing not to monitor his eyes for fright, startling herself with this split-second assessment she's made about whose need is preeminent, whose distress must be addressed, whose pain must be stanched here and now.

The room smells of vomit, and Varney weeps without sound, eyes closed. She stands for a few minutes wondering— now that she's here—what to do, wondering how you can ever make amends for so many bad acts, so many misjudgments, so much negligence. Sorrow is not enough; guilt is not enough.

"I know you're in here," he says. "I hear you breathing." He opens his eyes but doesn't look at her. "Where's the kid?"

"With the chaplain. I shouldn't have brought him."

"You shouldn't have brought him."

"I know it sounds feeble, but I'm sorry."

"You want us to get close? You want his sweetness to rip me apart? You want him to know me just so he can mourn me? Jesus, Cady; you saw how scared he was. Who are you doing this for? Not him. Not me."

"I didn't think."

"All I want now is death. The rest is too much work."

"But do you have to die so *mad?*"

"I see; I'm supposed to have different feelings."

"That's not what I meant."

"You and Chaplain Jack. *Know your feelings. Change your feelings.* How many hurdles are you going to set for me? Just do this one thing and *then* we'll let you die."

"I'm sorry."

"After today, you owe me, Cady."

She nods.

He brings his eyes to hers. "You know what I want," he says. His eyeballs seem to be receding in their sockets so she can hardly make out the irises. Nothing about him can be easily read anymore, but his words and his gaze have earned new authority from the imminence of death. "If you can't do that for me, don't come back."

She finds Evan sitting in the common area, kneeling at a table where he builds a tower out of small colored blocks. Nearby Chaplain Jack speaks in a low voice to a crying, dreadlocked woman in red overalls. Evan steals occasional glances at the woman, but mostly he stays focused on the blocks, brutally intent, as if his life depends on the success of this endeavor. When Jana kneels beside him, he doesn't acknowledge her.

"He didn't mean to be so mean, honey. He was just upset." She pauses, trying to think what else could be said.

Evan turns, eyes swelling. "You mean really, really, really, really, really, really upset?"

"Oh no, honey, not like that." She ruffles his hair. "Are you okay?" She decides not to push when Evan doesn't answer.

Chaplain Jack hugs the woman, holding her for a long time before bidding her good-bye and coming over to Jana. "It'll get better," he says, standing over them, touching her shoulder, knowing, without knowing exactly, what has transpired. His directness demands that others look in his eyes, and when she does, she sees his optimism is real, though where he comes by it in Varney's case, she can't imagine. It *won't* get better. It will only get worse. Varney inching toward death, but not fast enough. Her own blunders compounding.

Evan's tower falls with an impressive clatter. He moans, rolls onto the carpet, and curls up on his side, flogging the table leg rhythmically with his foot. Desperate to leave before he escalates, she reaches down to lift him. His body falls against hers, but it squirms there uncomfortably, repelling her efforts at soothing. She notices his crotch is soaked with pee. Chaplain Jack's benign gaze crowds her.

"We shouldn't have come. He didn't want to see us. And Evan—" She stops herself. "We're going."

Chaplain Jack, hovering like a grandmother loathe to see them go, follows them to the door, where a guard will escort them to the front gate. "You'll be back," he says. It is not a question but a gentle command.

"What's the point?" she says.

"Don't ask for results. Just do the right thing, you know?"

Although she is carrying Evan, Chaplain Jack finds her forearms under Evan's bottom and grips them. His hands feel warm and mitt-like. His kindness permeates the air, bearing down on her, calling up a bite of annoyance. The same man who has called up in her an ancient longing.

Back at the motel they go to her room, she cleans up Evan, and phones Cooper. Evan, sunk into the Game Boy for the whole drive home, now pockets it, still beeping, opens the sliding door, and steps out into the courtyard, where the azure pool lures him.

"We're back," she tells Cooper.

"Can we go swimming?" Evan calls, advancing to the center of the courtyard without waiting for permission.

"It's too cold," she calls back.

"What?" Cooper says.

"He wants to go swimming."

"How did it go?"

She sighs.

"I knew it," he says. "What happened?"

"Nothing exactly. It's fine now. You were right, I guess."

He swallows loudly. She looks out at Evan, whose body will deliver the final report and tell her if it's fine. He crouches over a flower bed, spotting something beyond her view, then wanders over to the gated pool and gazes through the fencing. His face, from her angle, is crosshatched with metal, an image so strongly suggestive of incarceration, she has to look away. When she looks back, he is sitting to remove his socks and shoes. He does so neatly, balling his socks and stowing them inside his shoes, well-trained but not obsessional. He does not look like a damaged child, or a child recently terrorized. But a child's short-term memory is exceedingly short, and if there are dangerous memories to be rehashed, they have already been deeply stored and may not be retrieved until weeks, or months, or even years hence when some fresh but equally inscrutable experience brings new significance to this one. Her eyes are drawn to a room on the far side of the courtyard where a man half covered by the gauzy curtain looks out. It's Cooper, she's sure. He's also watching Evan. It stuns her how easily she recognizes Cooper, how familiar even a small slice of him is seen at great distance. She watches him push aside the curtain and hears the rustling of that action through the phone line.

"What now?" he says.

"I don't know."

"Well, you're calling the shots, aren't you? You got us down here."

She feels Cooper's question as a test: *Are we your family? Are you still a mother, still a wife?* She wishes she could revisit all the secrets she has kept over the years. She wants to peel back time and re-present the facts, directly this time, unvarnished. How much less dirty things would be now. She, herself—a concealing denying avoiding person, a lying person—is the one Evan must be warned not to emulate.

Her eyes flick from Cooper, who watches Evan, to Evan himself, a strange triangulation not quite completed by Cooper seeing her. "Can you see me?" she says.

"Of course I see you. You're right across the courtyard, almost directly opposite."

It startles her, her own assumption of his blindness. "I should stay until he dies."

"How long will that be?"

"I don't know exactly. But not long, I think." She steps out into the courtyard, taking the phone as far as its wall cord allows. The December sun fingers her face. "Are you coming home?" she asks.

"There's a lot to think about. A lot of decisions to be made."

"Yes," she says, though she does not feel the kind of control the word *decisions* implies. At her feet is a row of dark orange nasturtiums. They seem so bold, so promising. "I miss you," she says suddenly, wanting the past back so acutely. "How it used to be."

"Now is now," he says. He looks straight at her from behind the sliding glass door; above his scraggly incoming beard she sees, or thinks she sees, the slight curl of a smile, but at this distance of twenty yards or more, it is a smile that's impossible to read.

They let Evan swim (that much they agree on). He swims in his Batman underpants, the two of them standing at the edge of the pool, gazing at everything but each other as Evan splashes and yelps, wriggles and dives, reveling in the primitive visceral pleasure of water touching skin. The more waves he makes, the more the turquoise water fills with coins of light, which tumble against one another like silently accumulating riches.

To Evan it is a slumber party. They all three sleep in the same room—Evan in one of the double beds, Cooper and Jana in the other. Evan giggles; his dimples seem to emit tiny glints of light, or is it the spit on his teeth that sparkles? He can't rest for happiness, she thinks, for the sight of his parents in the same room, the thought of another swim tomorrow in the bright blue pool just outside. The visit to Varney is consequential as burnt toast. It takes many verses of Cooper's usual repertoire of songs—"This Land Is Your Land," "Dixie," "Take Me Out to the Ball Game"—before Evan's lashes begin to look as if they bear tiny weights and he blinks hard and fast against their force until his eyes shut with a plunk of finality. Cooper and Jana lie in silence while they wait for Evan's sleep to solidify.

Jana feels lonely without Evan's riveting energy. Cooper's body radiates surprising heat across the six inches of sheet that separate them. He seems like a different man than he used to be—different with her, at least. All the eye contact he used to exchange with her, the sudden smiles, the way his body would graze hers in passing—all of those things that singled her out as special have stopped. It's as if he's drawn a chalk circle around himself and said, "Come no closer." Or as if he has retreated inside some plastic chamber—she can see him in there, but all their transactions are muffled. He said yes to her spending the night here, but his reluctance was clear—he had sighed and raked his bushy curls so his yes seemed more like no.

"Are you still awake?" Jana whispers when the parabolas of Evan's breathing have regularized.

"Um." He lies on his back, lips and nose profiled by the courtyard's light coming through the sheer gauze curtain.

"Have you missed me?"

Without looking at her, Cooper nods, a slow repeated head movement that looks almost autistic.

"I have to tell you something," she says. The dark makes it easier, though the proximity of his body is both safe and dangerous. "I haven't always been Jana. I grew up with another name."

His nodding speaks of numbness now, of his being beyond the reach of shock.

"My first name was Cady." Her whisper is a mere filament. "Cadence Eloine Miller." She feels empty now, all her secrets told.

Would he rebuff her if she were to bridge the inches and place her hand on his forearm or upper arm or chest? The gesture of a friend. Not sexual. Not asking for anything in return. She adores their sex, but now it's not sex she wants, just common comfort. She blinks into the dim channel between them. The air seems to hold white granules, round as BBs, but she knows if she reached out, she would feel nothing. Evan snorts lightly, sits up and looks around the room in a vacant-eyed daze, then falls back down on the mattress and commits once more to the free fall of his sleep.

They do not speak for a while.

"Now that you know about my background, won't you worry about Evan?" she says, pushing past the veil of strange air, trying so hard to pinpoint his thoughts.

"Evan is Evan," Cooper whispers. "You're not Evan. I'm not. Your brother isn't. Give him a little credit for being himself. You know what I mean?"

"I guess so."

"You act sometimes—you've been acting recently—like *your* blood is so important. So much more influential than mine." He starts to say more, then stops himself. He adjusts his pillow, then continues. "I've always trusted what's in front of me. Things I can hold and see. We have to do that. That's all we can do."

"Varney used to pee," she says slowly, "in my father's bathroom cup. Doesn't that frighten you? That one fact?"

From the dark strip of Cooper's body comes a quick, loud bark. "Forget the past. Evan's a guy. He has a penis. He wants to use it. And he was angry."

"Shhh," she says, aware of Evan a few feet away, thinking of the fragility of this privacy.

There's a splash outside. The pool is closed, but someone is swimming. The thought frightens her. She closes her eyes, hating where they are, wondering if she should get up to make sure the sliding door to the courtyard is locked.

"There's stuff to deal with, of course," Cooper says more quietly. "But I don't worry about what's going to happen to Evan. Not in the long run." He pauses. "But you—" He sighs and falls silent, then sighs again, as if each exhalation is specific and meaningful. "How could you live all these years with such a big thing?"

The light flickers outside, plunging them in darkness for a few seconds before reestablishing itself. It reminds her of an approaching thunderstorm she and Cooper once watched. It was on a trip back east, the only time she has ever been there. She and Cooper went there early in her pregnancy, to see the sights. They spent the Fourth of July in a small town outside Boston. First they watched the local parade with its myriad decorated bicycles, its obscurely comedic floats, its fire engines. It seemed so different from western Fourth of Julys. She could not pinpoint the difference in words, but it had something to do with the feel of the humid air and a slight sharpness in the crowd around her. That evening they ate a picnic supper of crabmeat sandwiches and were waiting for the fireworks on the sloped emerald lawn of a public park when they heard rumbling in the distance. It was thunder. A low subterranean sound. It stopped, then came back louder, like a persistent interlocutor. Parts of the sky seemed to talk to one another, more and more voices joining. Then came the lightning. Not in daggerlike streaks, but in flashes, a startling white, strobing the field, illuminating the revelers' faces, slicking them to silver and mother-of-pearl. You couldn't ignore this storm—it stole attention like the unheralded arrival of a band of rowdy troubadors. It took over the warm twilight so thoroughly that people stopped eating, stopped talking, held their breath in unison, waiting for the rain (there *had* to be rain). She had never witnessed a thunderstorm like this, and she couldn't help feeling it was an event that had something to do with Cooper, with the way his presence in her life was changing everything. The air cooled noticeably. People gathered their picnics and fled for shelter. Jana was about to do the same, but Cooper laid a hand on the low soft rise of her newly pregnant belly. "Wait," he whispered. They stayed through the rainstorm, its luscious fat drops soaking them in seconds. They kissed with rainwater on their tongues. "It's good for the baby," Cooper said. "The baby will always love nature."

She can't think of this. Nostalgia spells the end of things and she can't give up. She stays awake most of the night, her eyes on Cooper as he sleeps. She envies him, his easy slide to sleep, the way he hands his tension off to the night. She wants so badly to touch his hair, his arm, any part of him. Once she drifts off briefly, then awakens, forgetting where and who she is.

In the morning, after Evan swims again, he and Cooper drive off in Cooper's truck, Evan in the passenger's seat, plugged into his Game Boy, cut off already. As soon as they vanish from sight, she yearns for their return, for another reassuring squeeze from Evan, for clarification from Cooper about what he meant as he kissed her cheek and said, "It's not a question of love." At the same time, she feels a wave of relief that she need no longer speculate about their silences (their thoughts, their feelings, their destinies).

The day is still developing; it is not yet noon. How long these hours must be for Varney, friendless now without Doc. He said not to come back, but won't he *want* her to visit, if only for the distraction? If only she could make a more accurate guess as to how long he really has to live. It matters, doesn't it? If he has only a few weeks isn't that easier to endure than months? But she pictures him nailing her with those receding, storm-racked eyes of his, saying: *Believe me. If you can't do that, don't come back.*

But maybe Chaplain Jack is right—maybe her visits under any circumstances make a difference. Maybe after a day or two he'll mellow. Maybe there are things he still can live for. But no, she knows Chaplain Jack is *not* right. Even after all these years, she knows some germ of Varney too well. His attitude *won't* change. He wants what he wants. And he has gotten so little.

She carries these thoughts out to the pool and takes a dip in her running shorts and sports bra, but the water is freezing, and unlike Evan, she can only stay in for a minute or so. She lies facedown on a towel on the deck, trying to will more strength from the sun. On the far side of the courtyard, some man in a white bathrobe is watching her. She closes her eyes again, deeply exhausted, reluctant to move. She realizes she must have slept a little last night, because she recalls a dream. Varney had climbed into a coffin and was waiting there until he died. Just waiting. *I have the wherewithal,* she thinks, still half claimed by her dream. The Valium and Ativan (almost a full bottle of each) could—given Varney's compromised state—easily "assist" him.

She wishes the pills weren't there—they're too accessible, too tempting. Varney wants out, and she wants to get back to Bellingham, to Evan, and to Cooper. She wants ER patients again. She wants normalcy, or some particle of normalcy. She has come to a place where every thought has been uncovered, every possible consequence explored. Still, she is stymied.

She rolls to her belly again. The man in the bathrobe is gone. Through the scrim of her eyelashes she sees a line of tiny ants traveling across the pool's concrete deck and disappearing into the grass. Each one supports a tiny crumb of something. The ants suggest the subterranean, which in turn suggests the dead, which in turn reminds her of something she occasionally feels guilty about: the whereabouts of her parents' remains. She told Bill Hanneman to have them cremated. She would take care of the ashes, she told him; sprinkle them in the ocean, perhaps. But in her haste to leave the state, she did not take the time to pick up the ashes. She thought she would retrieve them later, but later grew into *later still* and then into *much later*, and as of now the ashes have never been claimed. As far as she knows, Bill Hanneman must still have them, unless he decided to dispose of them himself. The ashes remind her of her glass collection that she also neglected to take with her.

In the sun's heat she dozes and pictures animated bits of glass moving in a line like diligent, spirited ants, each one holding aloft a glistening chip of memory.

TWENTY-NINE

Now, at the countdown to Christmas, they stonewall each other. Jana sits at Varney's bedside, hoping Chaplain Jack is right, hoping Varney's wasted body is grieving in the right way. He lies on his side, turned away from the door, ignoring her presence. Doc's empty bed stretches out in her peripheral vision like a large white flag. Everyone is begging for truce, but there is no truce in sight. A wordless day tumbles by like this, then two, then three. She stays all day, until the 8 P.M. close of visiting hours. When she goes out, it is night and the stars shimmer imperviously overhead. Back at the motel she talks to Spider as if he is human.

She remembers how sweet it used to feel to be revered by Varney. She used her extra four years to make herself queenly, and Varney was her willing subject, full of the unction and humility queens need. His reverence kept her high as a rickshaw rider. She made him fetch things: Cokes with straws, ropes of red licorice she stashed in her underwear drawer, ice to lay on her forehead as she lazed in the patio's sun. Sometimes she made him massage her feet. He took his servility sweetly, without expecting anything in return.

One time at the 7-Eleven, her ex-friend Brianna and a few of her other classmates made fun of her openly, mocking her for hanging out with her younger brother. "What a weirdo," Brianna sneered. Varney came to her defense, moving within inches of Brianna's face and rising on tiptoe. "Cady's too good for you," he said. The strangeness of him—his big eyes and tufted hair, his anomalous intensity, his unexpected force (for such a little guy), his breath hot as a dragon's on their faces— sent them away, and Cady had to restrain herself from covering him in kisses. How can she ever find a bridge between these memories and the Varney before her now?

IT IS ALMOST winter solstice. The day will be short. She smiles extra broadly at Tom, one of the front-gate security guards. He greets her by name, flirting with his expert sidelong glance, be- moaning the weather, which he thinks is too cold. She lingers, asking about his Christmas plans without revealing hers. "Bye, Tom," she says cheerfully as she passes through the metal detec- tor with a piece of his Dentyne gushing over her molars.

It's early. No music plays. The hospice still hums and sighs with the somnolent rhythms of sleep. Chaplain Jack wants to talk. He offers her coffee and Danish. She swallows the gum and accepts a cherry-cheese Danish. Her mouth fills with the unwanted flavors of cinnamon, cherry, sweet ricotta.

"I know," Chaplain Jack says. "His anger is hard to take, but don't let it scare you. It's part of his grief work and he'll move on from it. The main thing is he can't die alone. No one here dies alone."

Tired old news. She nods, her mouth full, her head full. The crown of Chaplain Jack's head bristles with sunlight. He says these things to all the family members, but it is his genius that he knows how to make everyone feel special. From down the hall comes a guttural roar from someone newly recognizing his waking state.

"Your boy," the Chaplain says.

She waits for him to say more about her boy, but he does-n't. He leans forward, a crumb of Danish stuck to the corner of his mouth. In her head she completes his sentence several ways . . . *seems lovely?* . . . *seems troubled?*

"You know what I say to the guys? You've got to live life like an alchemist—turn the shit to gold. Pardon my French. I tell them, all you ever have is the pieces in front of you, right? From these things you construct a life. Balancing the truths you know with the ones you're discovering. Balancing saint and killer, killer and saint."

He is trying to tell her something, but she is too preoccu-pied to find out what. She walks slowly to Varney's room, sens-ing how the air around her is freighted with the diaphanous consciousness of all the inmates, how all their thoughts are pooling into something that is almost a sound. She passes the common room, where the Christmas tree lights bubble silently. People are not sleeping. She peers into each room and sees the eyes of men gazing out like insomniac cats.

Varney is awake, too. His muted TV plays the *Today Show*, but he stares out the window, as usual. She closes the door as far as it's allowed. He turns to her in a noticing way. "What's it like out there?" he says.

The sound of his voice again—merciful, psychic. "Cool," she says. "Fifties maybe. Sunny. Why?"

"Aren't I allowed to be curious?"

"Have you had breakfast?"

"I guess."

She sees his untouched tray with the nutritive drink. "Have you had meds?"

He nods. The line where his lips come together seems dark and straight. "So?" A single syllable that slides over the possibilities.

You are trembling now, your blood a cadre of sirens, your hands clammy. The sweat-wettened pills stick to your breasts and belly, decomposing already. You can't remove them fast enough. Varney is sitting up, stowing what you give him, in the bedclothes. (White on white. Yellow on white.) You are like a scurrying rodent in your haste, in your feeling of furtive small-ness, but he acts with unruffled composure as if he knew this would happen, as if this was the day he had scheduled for you to come around.

"Shall I tell you what to expect?" you whisper.

"Later," he says.

He offers you his hand. It is cold and flaky. You hold it lightly to avoid the scabs. He traps your gaze in his. You want to revel in the sparkling of his eyes, the grateful clutch of his claw-like hand on your arm, but you are too skittish to linger. You need to walk a little. You touch his cheek lightly. "I'll be back in a sec." You step outside his room. You saunter down the hall, trying to don the guise of the woman who knows how to remain unperturbed in crisis, the professional calm of the doctor you may never be again. A few other people travel the hallway: a somber-looking inmate with a tattooed scalp, slower than slow; an orderly with a squeaky cart; a female nurse who looks like a man. You stride around them, past the empty common room, past Chaplain Jack's office (empty, door ajar). You gaze in at all the dying men, laid out on their beds like discarded slabs of old meat. The sight of them arrests you and you lean dizzily against a wall, closing your eyes. On your lids you see Varney decom-posing. First a kind of melting, his body losing its dimensional-ity until it is no more than a dark silhouette on the ground, like the figures drawn by police. Then, the silhouette fades to a gray that grows grainier and grainier until white takes over. You pic-ture yourself reaching down to see what remains and finding only a fine chalky dust, which smells like you.

The loss of your brother, who has been absent from your life for years, is suddenly beyond imagining. Intolerable. With Varney gone no one will know you, not the way you were as a girl, timid and alone, but queenly, too. With him gone, your past, until now only deactivated, will finally vanish.

Drowning in clamorous sound of your own ears firing, you hurry back. Back to Varney. His head is still plastered on the pillow and his body looks no different than usual, but he regards you like a young boy, coy and flirtatious and immeasurably appealing. His recessed eyes glow. He looks too happy to be a man on the edge of death.

"I don't think it's a good idea," you whisper. "I want you to give them back, okay?"

He shakes his head.

"Please, Varney—" You speak in a low, firm voice, knowing you mustn't show your desperation.

Keeping his eyes on you, he smiles his resistance. You think of the preceding days when he would not look at you at all, when his body's illness denounced you. You crouch so your face is near his. "Please. I don't want to lose you again."

He laughs. "You will—you'll lose me somehow or other. But right now I'm yours."

A mythic serenity surrounds him, a tranquility common to gods and generals, to people in charge. Beside him you are still a bee's hive of tics and fears.

"Don't worry," he says, following your roving eyes, keeping his voice a whisper. "It's going to be fine."

Who are you to dispute that?

He laughs again, not taunting or sarcastic, but happy, yes, genuinely happy. Losing and holding merge for you in a sudden bubble of exhilaration. In the hallway something metal clatters to the floor. "It's okay, I got it," someone yells.

You and Varney both laugh. "O Little Town of Bethlehem"

begins playing, bringing a rush of teary warmth to your chest. Chaplain Jack sticks his head in. "Hi, guys." He salutes and continues on his way.

"Your kid, Evan," Varney says. "He's a good kid."

You nod. "I worry too much."

"That he'll be like me, right? Rotting in some prison somewhere."

"No."

"Don't say no. All the moms that come here, they all say that. But if it's any comfort, Evan's not like me."

"How would you know?"

"Believe me, I just know." Neck palsied, he lifts his head slowly from the pillow, resisting your efforts to push him back down. "Okay, maybe he's wild sometimes. Maybe he's nervous. But the thing is you can't predict. You can't act as if. We're all messed up, we've all got crazy minds, we all want things we can't have, but it doesn't mean a damn thing."

He closes his eyes, smiling a little. "Right?" he says. His grip on her hand loosens. He moans a little, then quiets. She floats with his words.

"I have dreams," she says, "that it was me. I'm aiming and starting to shoot. Then I wake up."

"Yeah. Then you wake up. My problem is I never woke up." He laughs. She strokes his beleaguered arm. Like the bodies of her patients, it has so much to teach her.

"You remember that day we found the whale?" he says.

She wouldn't have remembered had he not mentioned it. It was a calm day in March after a big storm. They skipped school together and walked on the empty beach. The sky was glossed a lustrous platinum. The silvered water, far less boisterous than usual, nipped the sand. The birds had moved in—seagulls, pelicans, sandpipers—all combing the beach and plundering the water for treats the storm had uncovered. She and Varney kept stopping, picking up shells and driftwood and mica-studded rocks, sharing a bag of peanut M&M's.

A dark mound lay before them. It looked like a boulder, or an elephant seal, perhaps, something not usually present on this familiar strip of beach. Rocked by the water, it seemed to be alive. They approached with caution. It was as big as a small building. Up close they poked it with sticks; its leathery gray surface was grooved with lines like petroglyphs.

"It's a whale," Varney said with the cocky prescience of his nine or ten years.

And she saw he was right. A beached whale. It (*he? she?*) lay half in shallow water, half in dry sand. They searched for his eyes to see if he was dead or alive, but his eyes would not be found.

"Dare you to get on him," Varney said.

She did not dare, so Varney did himself, going down the beach a ways for a running start from which he could leap and scramble to the apex of the whale's solid back. He held out his arm, and doubtfully she clambered up the strange gray wall of whale until she stood beside Varney. The two of them looked out with new mastery on the world. They called out as if they were the discoverers of an island paradise. "Ahoy! Ahoy!" Their voices traveled the length of the empty beach.

"Yeah," she says. "I remember."

"I dreamed about it this morning. In my dream the whale was alive and nice to us."

The memory greases Varney; he wants to rise from bed and find adventure. Her admonitions won't stop him. He is hot to her touch, manic.

"Let's dance," he says. "Listen."

An embellished Muzak version of "I'm Dreaming of a White Christmas" plays softly outside.

"Dance," his high voice chants as he dangles his legs over

the side of the bed the way children do. "Dance." His robe and pajama bottoms hang limp on his wasted frame. She fears he may fall as he jumps to the floor. But he locates his balance and he finds her. He pulls her in a zany clubfooted cavorting around his room, singing tunelessly along—"'just like the ones I used to know...'"—in his permanent falsetto. It is like dancing with a broom. He is a mere spindle, a pole, a twig of a man. His mouth, with its sores, smells rancid.

Alberto appears at the door. "Crazy man," he says and wanders off.

Varney falters, almost falls, wants to keep going.

Here is Varney, barely whole, scarcely balanced, but burning with energy. His last dance. His last legs. She distills this moment for future mulling and telling, swaying along in high style and sudden good humor, wishing this were all—that this moment, with all its joy and dread, would be forever. And then the song ends and a small audience at the door, summoned by Alberto, claps (then scatters).

She steers Varney back to bed, where he collapses, panting, eyes closed. He smiles at the ceiling, still straining a little for breath, but not exhausted.

"Maybe I could have been a dancer." He laughs, rolls his head to her, and opens his eyes. "I'll never know what I could've been." He lies still for a minute. "After I'm gone, don't feel sorry, okay? I know no one owed me anything." His outgoing breath plucks at a wisp of dry skin hanging from one of his sores. "I'm glad you've been happy." He pauses and squints at her. "You have been happy, haven't you?"

Afraid to speak, she nods.

Suddenly he sits up. "Hey, let's go for a walk. Let's go find a whale or something." He moves to the edge of the bed again, unwilling to brook refusal. A slyness lights his face. "Wait. Close the door first."

Long past the point of being able to refuse him, she does as he says.

"Show me your breasts," he says as she returns to the bed.

"Varney," she says.

"Go on. I won't touch."

"Fucking shit," says a voice outside. Someone pounds a wall.

"Not here," she says.

"I need a pretty picture," he says. "You said so yourself."

Slowly, glancing at the door, she begins to unbutton. They're only breasts, for god's sake, nothing he hasn't seen before—though now she thinks back, she wonders when he last saw breasts. And whose?

Three buttons is all it takes. She parts the sides of her white shirt.

"Without the bra," he says.

"Varney," she says (with all the older-sister exasperation she can muster). But she does it, anyway. She untucks her shirt; she reaches back and unclasps the rear clasp of her bra and pulls her breasts free. Varney watches, blinking rapidly, but otherwise impassive. She looks down at her breasts, wondering what he sees. *They are good breasts*, she suddenly thinks. Neither too big nor too small, nicely spaced, not sagging, with protuberant nipples, and pale unmarred skin. *Underused*, she thinks. *Underappreciated*. But now she makes up for it. She and Varney admire together.

After a minute or so he nods. "Now we'll walk."

Of course, she thinks, accepting his commands with such receptivity that she wonders exactly how far she would go in granting his requests.

Arm in arm (leaving his walker behind), they take their whale walk, making their way jointly down the hallway like a couple, reaching for shells, pointing at the wheeling gulls, the curling waves. "A sand dollar," he says. "A jellyfish." She laughs at the pleasure of absurdity. She cannot believe she has lived so long without this, without him.

They pass the rooms of the other inmates. Most of the men are glued to their beds, listless; a few host visitors. She feels kinship with these men. She knows what Varney has always known—she is just like them. Varney waves and she waves, too. She suddenly wants them all to keep living so she can know them all as Varney does. She wants to learn everything about them—what they have done, the nature of their regrets. She wants to see the arcs of their lives—how they changed from lovable little boys into hell-popping criminals, and then into the chastened, gentle men they are today.

In Alberto's room they stop. "'O come all you faithful,'" Varney croaks.

Alberto turns from the TV. "Crazy," he says. He draws a lazy circle in the air. "It's *ye*, stupid—*ye* faithful."

Chaplain Jack stops them in the hallway. "Looks like you're feeling better."

"'Tis the season to be jolly," Varney sings.

She remains in his room all day, through the coming and going of meds and meals. They chat, at last, about trivia—the Simpsons (he loves them), cell phones (he hates them), the Internet (what's the big deal?). American culture leaks easily through the prison walls.

"Thank you for you-know-what," he says as she is leaving.

Doubt eats through her.

"I might not even use them," he says. "It's the trust."

"The trust," she echoes.

She is riveted by his hands, which move slowly over the sheets. She has always believed in the expressivity of hands. Hands have not been trained to lie like faces.

She drives away from Varney's slithery hands, hearing her mother's ethereal voice singing the pigeon song, the one that had no real meaning but still made young Cady cry. "'My pigeon house I open wide...'" Now the words bring with them intricate harmonics of longing. She thinks of the ebony porpoise she took from her mother's shop. She thinks of the smooth curve of its back. She thinks of the playfulness of porpoises.

BACK AT THE motel the message light blinks. Standing still, listening hard, Jana divines the message. In her listening, the whole motel comes alive, life thrusting forward. She hears water running in the room next door; a toddler laughing in the courtyard; Spider scratching in his kitty litter; in the corner of the sliding glass door, a fly buzzing to get out.

When she hears Chaplain Jack's voice—"Your brother has taken a turn for the worse"—she feels a calm come over her, a serenity that comes with knowing that inevitability has taken over, that there are certain things you cannot fight.

The first few times a patient died under her care—the very first was a horrible traffic accident that left an eighteen-year-old boy nearly faceless—she gave her whole body over to it. Steeped in adrenaline, her body fought for its own survival. She couldn't imagine declaring that boy dead. The cruelty of that. The self-importance. But she was the only doctor present; she had to do it. Then it fell to her to break the news to the boy's parents, who, thinking her too young, too inexperienced (or was it her femaleness?), did not believe her pronouncement and insisted on seeing "the person in charge." "I am the person in charge," she said softly, tears shuddering, barely containable just behind her lids.

Eventually her body, in the face of death, learned a new response. It entered a kind of remove, a trance, as if she, in declaring a patient's death, was only the acting vessel for a higher power. And now, with her own brother, she is composed, seeing so clearly the end, seeing so clearly her own culpability with or without the pills, seeing so clearly the liability of being human.

Perhaps she will be incarcerated; she can already feel the cool metal of the handcuffs pinching her wrists.

There is this: the cows along the hillsides, still, all of them, no longer eating; a cat in the road squashed to two dimensions; the sun trumpeting its final radiant colors; a man in the parking lot, wearing a business suit, picking his nose furtively ("Digging for gold," Varney used to say).

A guard she has never seen before checks her in. She sweats heavily. There are no squad cars, no handcuffs, no gun-toting sheriffs poised for anyone's arrest. Not yet. Chaplain Jack, pink-faced and available—always available, how can that be?—the complex folds of his face, capable of speaking in the dozens of nuances of grief. His pudgy hands in hers, warm as a womb. The smells of stewed meat, Lysol.

In Varney's room she sees but a husk of a brother, gaunt and unconscious, his breathing rickety as a spent battery. Alberto and Roy stand by the bed and so does one of the social workers, a short woman with a wide Slavic face and frizzy hair, a woman Jana has only seen in passing. It surprises her to see these others here—witnesses, helpers, friends, people who share none of Varney's blood. Standing, just standing, as if there is something to see. As if Varney's death is a public event.

She and Chaplain Jack take their places beside the other three.

"I'm his sister," she says quietly to the other woman. "Cady."

The woman nods. "Elaine. I saw your boy the other day."

They cannot leave, any of them, not for more than a quick trip to the bathroom. They are all self-appointed chaperones.

They must all be there to see the moment when life becomes not life, to see if they can discover, against all odds, where the spirit really goes.

Chaplain Jack brings chairs. Jana sits, she stands, she yawns; her mind drifts, then returns. She studies the black specks in the floor's charcoal linoleum. She studies the enlarged pores, each like a miniscule exploded volcano on Varney's forehead. She touches his hand lightly, imparting everything she can.

She's seen more than enough dead bodies; she should be immune. But she is not. It is as if all the bodies have accumulated somewhere in the back of her mind, beginning with the bodies of her parents before their cremation, repaired and beautified in the funeral home, the twenty or thirty patients she failed to save and then, beyond that, the bodies of people she's only read about, dying in famines and epidemics, in train wrecks and battles, in risky mountain ascents and overdoses. She has stored them all in her mind's slag heap as if, given time, she might get around to redressing their grievances (and her own). Varney sinks, and she holds his chilly hand and takes note of his fading color.

How different Varney is, shorn of his prickle, drifting in and out of consciousness. As she feels him leaving, she tries to sense where a person exists behind blood flow, behind the snap of muscle, behind blinking eyes. She drifts herself, centered one minute, vacant the next, as if Varney has tethered her and is dragging her little by little along with him. She wonders if it's true that the biggest changes, the ones that will truly make a difference, are the ones you never see (the shifting of tectonic plates, the imperceptible rising of temperatures).

And then, after all the puzzling, he is gone. She knows right away—how, she's not sure. (Describing it later, she will say it is a quenched glow—yes, she will say, the idea of the extinguished candle is exactly right). The other witnesses all see it, too. They sigh, rustle, murmur prayers, disperse. She says a prayer, too, though, knowing no real prayers, it is only Varney's name, repeated over and over. A bolt of cold passes up through her legs, a polar whiteness. She knows without checking how her feet look—desiccated and archless. She feels how the cold and the white have pithed her and robbed her face of all expression. She listens for something. For what? For anything death might have left behind. But there is only the striking silence. A silence unbearably precious, almost sacred, at least for a while. Next, a wall comes up, fast, offering no comebacks, no answers, no directions for going on. She and Varney will not speak again, and what of all the conversations left inside her?

SHE SITS IN Chaplain Jack's office. It is late and the window, which usually entertains sunshine, is now black with night, a long, impenetrable, two-dimensional sheet of it. Chaplain Jack, bespectacled, sits at his desk, jotting notes. Neither he nor Jana speaks. It is almost 11 P.M., and except for the night guards and the night nurse, everyone is asleep, or trying to sleep. The clock is an institutional one—black and white with prominent numbers and a loud tick, and it has a presence at this hour that it doesn't have at other hours of the day. Its ticking now makes Jana feel spent, useless.

I should leave, she thinks, but she does nothing about it.

Chaplain Jack removes his wire glasses, takes something that he fists from the slender top desk drawer, and swivels to her. "Some you take harder than others," he says. "Speaking for myself. You, being a doctor—yes, Varney told me—I'm sure you know that, too."

She nods. It doesn't matter anymore what he knows.

"I loved Varney," he says. He raises his eyebrows. It is just enough movement to jog free a tear from his right eye. He's a man for whom tears bring no shame, his own or anyone else's. "It's hard saying good-bye. To state the obvious."

She nods.

He leans forward, unfisting his hand, and lays a few white and yellow pills on the table between them. "We found these in the bedclothes. I'm assuming there were more."

Jana's eyes flick back and forth between the pills and Chaplain Jack's face, white and smooth and eerily riveting. His voice seems, in the ward's silence, unusually loud. She has never been in a confessional booth, but this is how it must feel, everything fallen away but the omniscient consciousness of that one other person and your own thoughts. All the focus on goodness and badness. Priest as detective.

"I know Varney loved you, and I think you loved him," the chaplain says.

"Of course," she says trying to slow the rapid movement of her eyes.

"Not *of course*," he says somewhat sharply. "There is no *of course*. This whole institution—the hospice, the prison— wouldn't exist if *of course* worked. *Of course* no one would ever kill his parents, you see? *Of course* no one would rape a child." He shakes his head hard. "You see?" He raises his voice, wanting her agreement. She's never heard him so insistent. "There are always millions of *ifs* and *buts*—you know?"

He stops himself, lifting his shoulders to ease his intensity as if removing an uncomfortable cassock. "You came here to see Varney. You listened to him. You forgave him, I think." He looks down at the pills, rolls them over with a single finger. "You wanted to help him, I believe. But it's hard to help when there's so little to do.

"I think you felt you owed your brother something. I don't think you harbored any ill will toward him. Otherwise you wouldn't have stayed." His hands rest quietly on his thighs. It is his eyes, with their slight slow lateral movements, that seem to ruminate, traveling the divergent paths of accusation and forgiveness. "Tell me that's true."

She has lost sight of the question. One truth is so easily canceled by another. There are too many truths out there jostling for preeminence. She would like to try to say this aloud, but she thinks Chaplain Jack knows—that there's no easy goodness, no easy truth, no answer that sums up adequately all the mind can hold. "True," she says slowly.

"It's not always a given," he says.

She won't let herself look away. She wants to say everything, to melt into the warm pool of Chaplain Jack's forgiveness.

Chaplain Jack rubs his eyes suddenly, breaking eye contact. She hates the feeling; she wanted to be carried by his singular attention a little bit longer. He grabs the rubbery flesh of his cheeks and pulls it away from the underlying bone. When released the skin falls lazily back into place. Then he picks up the pills and puts them back in his desk drawer. He closes the drawer and, back to her, busies himself straightening papers, putting pens and pencils in a jar.

"We won't be doing an autopsy," he says. "I don't think it's necessary. We all know he had AIDS." Each utterance of his makes her more and more passive, more and more a slave to his intent. "Hey, did you know in my other life I'm a fortune-teller?" He laughs, too raucously for a prelate and for the late hour. "Now," he says, standing. "*You* need to go home, and so do I. We'll talk about the arrangements tomorrow."

He embraces her hard, as if he is trying to press thought into her, press intention, press goodness. She steps into the cool California night without a brother.

———

ONLY AFTER SHE has roused Cooper from sleep does she realize it is too late to call, but by then it makes no sense to hang up.

"He's gone," she says. "He went tonight."

"Oh, Jana," he says softly.

Though there might be many readings of his words, she chooses the one she wants and forges on. "I know it's late but I had to tell you."

"Um. I'm glad you did." His voice drifts as if sleep still grips him. It suddenly occurs to her to wonder where he's sleeping. On the couch, probably, in Seretha's living room. Evan would be in the spare room, away from the noise.

"I still don't believe it," she says.

"You said it was close."

"Somehow, I still thought he'd live forever."

"What now?" he says. "What now—*Cady?*" His laugh is soft and filigreed with the uncensored giddiness of exhaustion. "I like that name. *Cady.*"

She nods, then realizes he can't see her. "So do I." She listens. "I'm coming home soon."

"Um." An even utterance, automatic as the lowing of cattle.

"I have to tie up a few things first. But tell Evan I'll be there in a couple of days. Tell him I love him."

"Uh-huh. Is there anything else I can do?"

Come to me, hug me, forget all that has happened, love me forever, be as you were. "Cook me something special when I get back."

He laughs. "You'll get through this."

You he says, not *we*, but even as she thinks this, she's aware of being overly interpretive. It's the middle of the night, after all, and he's trying to stay awake to comfort her. She herself is jazzed and would be capable of talking until dawn, asking every unposed question (*Do you wonder about me? Do you think I'm bad, too?*), but he is there on the lumpy couch with a job to go to in the morning, a kid to corral, a mother to please.

"All these conversations I never had—," she begins. "And now it's too late."

"Too late," he echoes softly.

"Go to sleep," she tells him.

THIRTY

Late the next day, after the cremation arrangements have been made, she checks out of the motel and drives south all night.

Parked in the driveway of her childhood home, she waits for dawn, the car windows open to the cool murmuring dark. A paper boy rides by, bike spokes whirring, his flung papers slapping the asphalt quietly. In the distance the freeway traffic is a steady basso profundo. Spider nestles more deeply into her lap. A slit of pink appears in the east and grows like a slow leak. Another day, irreversible, bringing what it will bring, this one arriving more purely than some, without smog or complication. Light-headed and clean, she will do what she has to do, task by task. Thoughts drift through her like soft wind—Varney laughing, Varney dancing, Varney dying.

At sunrise she stands in the small cement courtyard of her childhood home. Morning light slips around one corner of the house and floods the patio. A few bees forage in the hibiscus blossoms. Vinelike weeds have grown up from the cracks in the cement; spiderwebs, layered like thick gauze, striate the eaves; vigilant gray-green lizards, harboring neonlike secrets, stand at attention on the high stucco wall that separates this house from the next. Cracked brown palm fronds are strewn everywhere.

But it is the people-things that hold her eye. The public has invaded, leaving a sparkling confetti of broken glass chips—green, brown, clear—and fluttering piles of fast-food debris. Most prominent are the daggers of bold black graffiti that cover the walls of the house itself. Like optical art, it plays games with her mind, promising words while delivering none, thwarting her search for meaning.

Her gaze roves over the florid black scrolls, the rangy weeds, the chips of glass, the froth of layered spiderwebs, and she tries to make sense of the feeling they impart. It suggests so many people have been here in this courtyard—angry people, people having riotous fun. Her property manager has failed her, that much is clear, but she feels more odd than angry. She is a stranger here now. Despite her regular tax payments, despite the deed she holds somewhere in her files, this house is no longer hers.

With the tentative steps of an intruder, she wanders around, touching little, inspecting everything. She finds a crumpled black bra, a silver hoop earring, a dirt-stained beach towel, an empty CD case. Teenage things. A mourning dove coos from someplace nearby, but she can't see the bird itself. The haunting call swells through her chest, putting her glands on alert, ordering her to the front door.

She fumbles in her purse for the house key. It has always traveled with her—from California to Oregon to Washington—nestled beside the other keys for house, office, and car. She has not thought of this key regularly, but neither has she set it aside. Through all her moves, it has remained on her key ring, as if any minute she might head home. She presses the key into the slot and it stalls halfway in. It's likely that the property manager has changed the lock. Still, she fiddles, pressing, then releasing, then pressing again, frustration mounting as she reminds herself how keys have rules of their own. After a minute she stops pushing, breathes, imagines herself inside, and true to form, the key slides in and turns as it should.

She stands on the gray linoleum of the foyer, looking around. Inside there is none of the chaos she witnessed outside. Here there is reverberating emptiness and nothing for her eyes to fix on but whitewashed walls and packing boxes stacked in two columns to one side of the entrance. For all its emptiness, the house feels alive. She stares at the boxes, all labeled with black marker, and tries to remember packing them. She has no memory of that at all.

She begins to move from room to room, slowly, almost furtively; she does not belong here; she has been stripped of the proprietary confidence of ownership.

The house she remembers was darker, dingier, dirtier. Its corners harbored day-old food smells. Its carpets bore stains. This living room—bereft of furniture, its walls bright white— is not the same living room where her mother lay, drapes drawn, mired in dim, depression-stained light. The kitchen, its cabinet doors rehinged and painted white, cannot be the same place where her mother forced herself to cook. These rooms are the dried bones of an old life, remade into fresh casings ready for new life to begin in them. No one but Cady could construe a past from these colorless walls. She remembers the realtor sweeping through the house, announcing all the refur- bishing that would have to be done. *Who finally made these changes?* she wonders. The realtor hired someone, perhaps, or maybe Bill Hanneman took responsibility. It wasn't Cady. She would remember, she is sure. *And the boxes, who packed them?* Whoever is responsible for these things, it is clear that the Millers' family life, their stuff-of-headlines tragedy, has been nullified by someone who wanted to forget. And Cady?

She floats down the hallway, past the den and the bathroom, to the bedrooms at the end, hers and Varney's. She peers into her old room, trying to picture its once-pink walls, its little-girlness. She recalls the fierce superstition with which she guarded her collections. If her arrangements got altered, bad things would happen. When the tiny raised paw of her blue glass cat broke, she feigned illness, stayed home from school, and wept all day, and by night she really was sick. She wants to swaddle herself in childhood again, remember what it felt like, her own beginnings.

She moves to the center of the empty room and lies on the beige carpet in the space her bed once occupied. She closes her eyes, trying to summon memories, but nothing comes except perhaps the vague sensation that Varney might be next door perusing his own room, or sleeping. Then she remembers lying awake at night under her rose-patterned bedspread and dreaming of being a doctor. Back then, anything was possible.

She opens her eyes and gazes at the brown boxes, a dozen or more, filled with her past—her books and clothes, the glass figurines, the stuffed animals, Barbies, tea sets, school notebooks, old photographs. So many forgotten stories housed in those boxes. She thinks of unearthing pictures for Cooper to look at—the one of her parents at their high school prom, wearing chipmunk smiles, and the one of five-year-old Varney, startled, mouth smeared, looking up from an ice-cream cone. Maybe she'll be able to find the plastic army men Varney used to play with—intent green-and-brown men bearing rifles and pistols. Evan would love to play with those army men. She can already picture him arranging them in combat configurations at the base of the apple tree.

She closes her eyes again and her lids grow rich with pictures. The house may be empty, but her brain is certainly not—it is already salvaging things. She can almost feel her frontal lobe loosening, its synapses in rapid fire, releasing entombed long-forgotten stories.

An hour later, car crammed with boxes, she drives to Bill Hanneman's house and parks in his driveway, but she doesn't move right away—she stays fixed behind the wheel, contemplating everything. After almost fifteen minutes, the door opens. A man in charcoal sweats peers out, tall but crumpled-looking, with the unmistakable broad forehead of Bill Hanneman. She looks at him across the manicured square of lawn, the deeply imprinted geometry of his face and stature prodding recollections. History encroaches, as she knew it would, at the edges of this very new day. She cannot believe how old Bill Hanneman looks. Her memory has held him unchanged, but of course that is silly. The rules of physics, the precepts of biology, all posit that change, not stasis, is normative. Fields will give way to succeeding forests, dunes will shift, oceans will eat up shorelines, straight rivers will begin to meander. On the cellular and even the molecular level it is the same. Always changes. Always new cadences. How could she have thought it would be otherwise after so many years?

When he does not move, she gets out and goes to him, searching his bewildered face for recognition. A few threads of gray hair pirouette over his forehead against a backdrop of bald. He adjusts his glasses. Tottery, he holds the doorframe, the same Bill Hanneman, but now bereft of force. When recognition comes over him, he smiles with a sweetness she never noticed before.

"Cady Miller," he says. "Well, well."

She smiles and nods, and they embrace lightly and the feel of his dry bony body calls up a visceral memory of all the elderly patients she has served.

"I always wondered if you'd come back. I gave up trying to find you." He alternately shakes and nods his head, playing and replaying the marvel of it. "Come in."

He shuffles to the kitchen—slower, it seems, than a man in his seventies should be—and while he sits at the table and tells her where things are, she fixes them instant coffee and white toast with strawberry jam. Then they sit in the breakfast nook, sipping their coffee, absorbing each other silently, and watching the whitening day. A slight breeze coming through the open window toys with the gingham curtains. She feels no urgency to speak. She cuts her toast. She drinks. She gives herself over to the rising slur of traffic and the pigeons cooing under the eaves. One thing at a time.

Mr. Hanneman—Bill now, she supposes—holds his coffee cup with two hands. Thick strands of wiry white hair have sprouted over their freckled backs. "Well, well, well," he keeps muttering softly, still adjusting to her arrival. "You finally came. I knew you'd come. Your dad always said what a good girl you were."

"He admired you, too," she says. "He envied your energy."

"Energy." Bill laughs quietly. "Judy didn't think you'd come. But I always said yes."

"How is she?"

"Oh." His face goes blank and temporarily smoothed of wrinkles. "I thought you knew." He sighs, and she imagines she can see the swirl of his outgoing sadness being lifted by the breeze and taken outside to drift about the world at large. "She passed away."

"Oh, I'm so sorry to hear that. How long ago?"

Frowning, he looks around the room. "You know, I don't remember. Eva will tell you. Eva?" He pauses, listening for movement. "She's my girl. She comes in and looks after me. Eva!"

His call vanishes in the silence. "She's here somewhere," he says confidently.

He looks into his coffee, breathing heavily, air ticking noisily over saliva-furred teeth. She reaches out and covers his hand with hers, and the gesture makes her feel like his daughter. He looks up, smiling, and uses the back of his other hand to wipe a drop that was hovering at the tip of his nose.

"Dangerous business, getting old," he says. "Even for a vice president. Sometimes I envy your dad. You came to get your mum and dad?"

"Yes."

"So many years ago. I don't even know how many. Why are you coming now, after so many years?"

"My brother Varney died."

Bill blinks, as if absorbing her words through his eyes. The shelves of his lower lids are rimmed with red. "Is that so. That's too bad. I remember him. He was a good boy. A surfer, wasn't he?"

She nods.

"My wife, Judy, she died, too. A few days ago."

Later, when they've finished toast and coffee, she helps him fetch the urns from the mantelpiece where Bill has enshrined her parents with votive candles and two framed photographs. The urns are plain boxes, maybe eight inches by six inches by six inches, made of pine stained to the color of mahogany and sealed with brass latches. Such simple, compact receptacles to hold the complex stuff of personhood. She looks at the photographs, scarcely recognizing these smiling faces as her parents. There is no hint of impending tragedy about them. Both of them look youthful and happy. She will use these pictures to learn their faces again.

Bill pats one of the boxes. "She'll take good care of you, Walter."

She stares into Bill's watery eyes, thinking of what can and can't be recalled, wondering what will be hers to enshrine. She embraces him again and squeezes his still-substantial hand. He follows her outside and watches as she stows the urns carefully on the floor of the backseat.

"Walter's daughter," he says again, still scarcely believing.

They smile mute good-byes, and she drives off, the fluttering in her belly gaining force like a small proud voice, as if the cells of a new life already reside there.

ACKNOWLEDGMENTS

This novel owes its evolution to many beyond its author.

Invaluable factual and atmospheric information were supplied by Reverend Keith Knauf, director of Pastoral Care Service, CMF Hospice, Vacaville, California; Julian Bailey, J.D.; and Rick Caesar, M.D.

A number of people gave this text a close and insightful reading: Joy Pope-Alandete, Rick Caesar, Paul Calandrino, David Cole, Charlene Decker, Andrea Schwartz-Feit, Richard Howorth, David Lang, Ruth Knafo Setton, and Mary Wood.

Chang-rae Lee and Peter Ho Davies were both exceedingly generous with their wisdom. The Squaw Valley Community of Writers, the Sewanee Writers Conference, and my compadres at the University of Oregon provided a wonderful sense of community that sustained me in my solitude.

For encouragement along the path I will always be grateful to Stephan Vogel, Adrienne Kennedy, David Cole, Susan Cole, Ed Cohen, Julia Miles, Tom West, Susan Trott, Alice McDermott.

Debbie Reinisch played an important role in finding a home for this book.

This novel would have few readers were it not for the efforts of two tireless and passionate people: Deborah Schneider, my agent, and Ann Patty, my editor. Inexpressible thanks.

My mother, Judith Emmons, and my sisters, Patty Emmons and Ebe Emmons Apt—I thank you for believing in me and for not asking too many questions. Special thanks to Rich and Benny for the good stuff of life and for bearing with me.